HOARDING SECRETS

A DRAGON SPIRIT NOVEL: BOOK 3

C.I. BLACK

Gryphon's Gate Publishing

Gryphon's Gate Publishing

550 King St. N.

PO Box 42088 Conestoga

Waterloo, ON

N2L 6K5

Print ISBN: 978-1-988115-44-3

ebook ISBN: 978-1-988115-45-0

PROLOGUE

Her heart pounded in a thrumming tattoo that ratcheted her nerves and sent ice sweeping into her gut. She didn't recognize the simply adorned pink floral bedroom she'd just awakened in, didn't know where she was, had no idea how she'd gotten there, and all she wore was a tank top and underwear.

Her panic snapped stronger and her grip tightened on the blanket. Someone had undressed her. Someone had taken her and stripped off her clothes while she was unconscious. She—

Her pulse stuttered.

She. There wasn't anything after *she.* She knew she was a *she,* and knew within her fragile human flesh curled the spirit of a green dragon. Anything more clung to the back of her mind, murky, viscous, and out of reach. It spoke of power and strength and a soul-rending ache, an emptiness so consuming it threatened to steal all breath and thought.

No. She shoved the blanket back with a growl.

She was stronger than this. She couldn't explain how she knew, but she did, and she mentally clawed at the darkness within her. If she just concentrated, tore into the darkness, she'd remember. And when she did, whoever had taken her, stripped her of her clothes, her memories, even her name, would know the truth about abducting a dragon.

She jerked off the bed. Across from her sat an old-fashioned dresser — the only other piece of furniture in the room — complete with swirling scrollwork, stout legs ending in feet carved into the shape of dragon claws, and a tall mirror, captured on either side with wooden dragon tails. A hint of blue fire danced over its surface, flaring stronger when she thought about it, but it didn't burn her, nor did it help her figure anything out. Her reflection didn't help, either. Nothing jumped to mind, and she didn't recognize the woman staring back at her with large dark eyes. They should be green. That's what she was. Green, earth, life—

She blinked, but the woman didn't change into a dragon. She remained human, with straight dark hair cut an inch above her shoulders in a sharp, clean line. Her pale skin held a hint of a blush indicating good health — for whatever that was worth — but it wasn't green protective scales. She drew her hands up, examining her small, clawless digits in the reflection. Too small. Everything about her was too small, too delicate.

Her thoughts whirled. How could she be human? She was a dragon. That truth lay in the core of her being. Green drake.

And broken.

That darkness at the back of her mind shuddered, teasing her, reminding her she didn't know her name let alone who had done this to her, or how she'd gotten in this strange, pink floral bedroom with only a green tank top, a pair of black panties, and a gold locket hanging around her neck.

Her gaze dipped to the reflection of the locket. Lockets held things. Maybe there was a clue inside.

Yeah, and maybe she was grasping at straws. If the locket didn't hold answers, she needed to move on, find clothes, and get the hell out of wherever she was. She could find answers about who she was once she knew she was safe.

She grabbed the locket, an oval the size of her thumbnail and barely thick enough to hold anything inside. More of the strange blue fire burned around it, brighter than what enveloped the dresser. Only one word, only two letters long, was engraved on both sides.

"Si," she read out loud.

Lightning exploded in her head and a blinding blue flashed across her sight. Her knees buckled, and she grabbed the dresser to keep standing.

Ivy.

Her name was Ivy. And for hundreds of years she'd woken every morning not knowing who, only what, she was. Fleeting, hard to grasp images of her with a different human body — many different bodies — shot through her. But she couldn't hold onto them long enough to look at them, only to know that she'd been someone else before and that it didn't really matter. She was Ivy now, and she had the ability to read the memories of objects.

The thought came with a mix of relief and pain. Relief that now, in this body, she didn't have to start fresh every morning like she'd done for the hundreds of years since dragonkind had lost their dragon-forms in the Great Scourge. This body gave her a life, hope — albeit a small hope — for a future. The locket, along with her magic, was a lifeline, a way to keep herself sane, and not become soul sick every hundred years, needing to be reborn again and again.

But that hope was mixed with fear. A gut-churning knife of ice sliced into her soul. Her hope was her imprisonment. Regis, Prince of the Dragons, had discovered her power and claimed her as his own. She was too valuable for another coterie to have and she could never leave the Dragon Court. He'd capture and rebirth her before letting her go, and she'd be faced with the bleak emptiness of not knowing her friends or even herself until the insanity of soul sickness possessed her and her soul was stripped to its core and shoved into a new human body. Keeping her allegiance with Regis, a drake who'd rather see her dead than happy, was her only way to keep her tenuous grasp on that little bit more that kept her sane.

1

A woman screamed, and Grey's grip on the deck chair's arms tightened.

It wasn't real. It was a God damned memory. That was all.

Except that wasn't all. No matter how hard he tried, he couldn't control it. The memories — and he remembered everything — kept devouring reality and dragging him back into reliving every horror and regret in his over two thousand years of life.

The pressure in his chest squeezed tighter. A crowd of as-of-yet unseen people yelled and jeered. The woman — she'd been so kind to him — sobbed. Impossible sunlight, since it wasn't even dawn yet, flashed on water, blinding him.

He squeezed his eyes shut, determined to shove the memory back where it belonged.

In the here and now, he sat outside, in the dark, on Nero's patio on his estate on the outskirts of Newgate. It wasn't late afternoon. He wasn't in that Spanish village. And it wasn't 1527.

Heat swept through him, and sweat beaded on his face and along his neck as he fought to control himself.

It shouldn't be this bad. The Handmaiden had enspelled his seething memories to the back of his mind less than a month ago. Her magic lasted longer than that. Months. Sometimes close to a year.

The light flashed in his eyes again even though they were still closed, and the sobs grew stronger, the pitch deepening, growing masculine and multiplying.

Smoke swept around him and a cold blast of air hit him in the face, making his eyelids fly open. Ruined muddy ground pocked with the violence of warfare stretched before him, and broken and bloody bodies surrounded him, the horrific result of a massacre. Gunfire popped to his left and the *thwump* of cannons boomed farther away.

He clenched his jaw, clenched everything, desperate to push it all back and get in control. God, why couldn't he just remember the good times? There'd been lots of good times. He wouldn't mind succumbing to those memories.

As if summoned by the thought, the *thwomp* of cannons turned into the drums and the final chords of the movie *Dark Angel*. He'd loved that movie, loved all movies. He'd hoarded stories, scratched onto parchment or printed and bound into books, but he hadn't realized what really called to his soul until those tales were captured on film.

Yes. Remember those, all of those stories, all of his hoard back in his suite at Court. But his surroundings remained murky, revealing only a hint of the alley he'd stepped into to get from the theater to the all-night diner sliding into focus.

Shit.

His throat tightened even more, and sudden agony seared across his neck. He couldn't catch his breath, couldn't move beyond the pain. The reek of rotten food wafted around him and rain rattled against a windowpane.

"How fast can you heal?" a voice hissed and the alley fully solidified around him, dark and damp, a narrow space wide enough for a garbage truck to pick up the diner's refuse.

Not fast enough.

It was never fast enough. He was weak, crippled by memories that attacked his sense of reality at every moment. And a weak drake was a dead drake.

Except he wasn't dead. Hunter had saved him in that alley and then avenged the attack. And the Handmaiden continued to weave her magic into his mind and ease the agony his so-called earth magic inflicted on him.

But now both Hunter and the Handmaiden were gone.

He had no idea when either would be back and the reality of just how dependant he'd been on both of them hit with terrifying clarity. He shouldn't have been relying on them in the first place.

It was just so hard to focus, to stay in the here and now, without her. And so hard to hope for any kind of a future without friendship — and after that assassination attempt in the alley, Grey had withdrawn until Hunter had been his only remaining friend. He could trust Hunter. Grey didn't really know about anyone else.

"Come on, drake," the voice from that night in the alley hissed. "Show me what you've got."

But Grey didn't have anything. Blood pumped from his neck, hot between his fingers. Every breath was an agony. The moment he moved they'd take his head. Any attack would be useless. He was useless.

God damn it.

A roar bubbled in his throat. He wasn't useless. He held the memories of all of dragon history and was one of a few drakes remaining who could still recall the Great Scourge. Heck, he remembered times before the Scourge when drakes were predators hunting from the sky.

He wasn't weak. He was a dragon, and it was time he started acting like one.

He roared in full and wrenched from the chair, somehow finding the strength he hadn't had sixty-four years ago to punch at the drake who'd slit his throat.

The drake jerked back. "Jesus, Grey."

"Not this time." Grey swung again. He'd never been useless, and he was tired of hiding. If he'd learned anything in the last few weeks, it was a rediscovery of the drake who'd gone on five crusades with Hunter, lived as a mercenary for two centuries, roamed the world, and fought in numerous human wars. Yes, he yearned to forget, but he was still a dragon. And while a change of body would eliminate the magic that never let him forget, in dragon law that was illegal and it wouldn't be the clean slate he'd get from being reborn — also not an option, because the Handmaiden was missing. Which left him with fighting his magic and staying strong... no matter how exhausted he was.

The drake in front of him vanished with the whoosh of a gate. Another gate whooshed behind him, and Grey whipped around.

The world tilted. The nighttime alley vanished, turning into a starlit, partially snow-covered deck with a biting cold that stung his cheeks. The assailant materialized out of the darkness, with swarthy skin, dark eyes, and long black hair. Diablo. Friend, not a foe.

Shit. Grey bared his teeth, unable to fully rein in his aggression. Adrenaline still pounded through him, and his throat still burned with the memory of that vicious slice.

Diablo's eyes narrowed. "What the hell is wrong with you?"

"Nothing. I'm fine." But Grey's breath misted around his head with too-fast exhalations, belying any truth that he was fine. *Shit.*

Diablo cocked an eyebrow, accentuating the sculpted cheeks of his body's Native American heritage.

"Gee, I don't know," Grey said. "The Handmaiden is missing, Hunter has gone off to find her leaving his newly inamorated human sorcerer to figure out her wildly out-of-control powers by herself while dealing with the emotional strain of being separated, Regis has locked down Court, and it isn't safe for me to go home—"

A soft giggle carried through the darkness from the solarium.

"And the drake you've been pining over for... what? A good couple hundred years? Has found her inamorato and is still in the honeymoon stage." Diablo opened the patio door and stepped into one of the estate's many living rooms.

"Thanks for reminding me." Grey had carried a crush for Capri for longer than he'd wanted to admit, but the blue drake had never returned his feelings. Now he knew why. They weren't destined for each other. She'd found her inamorato and — with the destruction of her house — had temporarily moved, along with her lover, into Nero's mansion.

Diablo flicked on the light, shrugged out of his winter jacket, and headed to the bar. "Don't you have your own place?"

"Don't you? It's four in the morning. You're wearing the same clothes from yesterday. I wouldn't expect you to come here to do the walk of shame." Grey sagged into an armchair by the door. "There are children living here, for goodness' sake."

"It's five, and this isn't a walk of shame. I have a meeting with

Nero at six." Diablo poured three fingers worth of Nero's good scotch into a glass then reached for another glass.

"None for me."

"It's happy hour somewhere in the world. If you like, we could gate there and drink."

"You heal too fast for it to do anything."

"I like how it tastes." Diablo took a slow sip. His gaze settled on Grey, and he frowned. "Really. You look like shit. Yeah, you can't go back to Court, but why are you here? You're old enough to have more than a dozen places scattered over the planet."

Capri giggled again.

Jeez, Grey had never thought she was a giggler — and if he told her that to her face, he was sure she'd shoot him just to prove him wrong.

"Why are you here torturing yourself?" Diablo asked.

"Anaea's power is getting stronger, and her control isn't keeping up. She felt it was safer to stay here than be alone at her and Hunter's house."

"So you stay."

"I promised Hunter." At least this promise to Hunter gave him purpose. It might have dragged him out of Court's safe interdimensional sphere and into the human realm, not to mention endangered his life a number of times, but it gave him purpose. That and Court wasn't safe any more for any drake and certainly not for one who was clearly aligned with Hunter — Prince Regis's number one enemy.

"When this is done, Hunter is going to be in debt to you up to his eyeballs." Diablo dropped with predatory grace onto the sofa across from Grey. There was something dangerous about Diablo, more so than any other drake Grey knew, as if the dragon soul trapped within Diablo's fragile human body was bigger, meaner, than other drakes.

The light caught on something shiny smeared along the neck of his black T-shirt and a spray of drops down his chest. It hadn't been noticeable on Diablo from the other side of the room, but now, at the right angle—

"Is that blood?"

Diablo glanced down at his shirt and shrugged.

"I didn't think you had a line on any more human mages."

"I didn't. Walk of shame, remember."

"Jeez, tell me it's your blood and not some human woman's."

"What if it was consensual?" Diablo flashed a wicked grin.

"I don't want to know, and I'm pretty sure Nero doesn't, either. You might want to change before your meeting."

"That was my intention before I saw you needed a drink." Diablo downed his scotch in a swift gulp.

"I feel much better, thanks." The shadows at the edges of the room billowed. Grey tensed, concentrating on the blood splatter on Diablo's shirt. *Stay in the present. Just stay, at least until Diablo leaves.* He couldn't risk letting Diablo or anyone know how weak he really was.

Diablo stared into his empty glass then blew out a heavy breath. "Don't ask me, but I'm sure everyone else in this house would be happy to help you get your shit together."

"My shit is just fine." Grey flashed his teeth in a half-hearted show of aggression.

"So you say." Diablo stood and the reek of rotten food filled the room and far away, a telephone rang.

Grey's throat burned.

The ringing grew louder.

Diablo pursed his lips.

Just go already, so I can go crazy in private.

"How fast can you heal?"

Someone screamed... or was that the phone ringing again? The alley flickered over the living room then melted back into the shadows.

Another ring... scream?

Diablo's frown deepened. "Are you going to get that?"

No. It's just a memory. It wasn't real—

But if Diablo could hear it—

Crap. It was his phone.

The ring came again, and Grey pulled his phone from his pocket. *Please let it be Hunter and he's found the Handmaiden.* He looked at the call display and his chest tightened. The number listed was Tobias's, which meant no relief from the memories and more than likely some kind of mess with Court that could get him killed.

2

"Hello, Tobias," Grey said, fighting to push back the remembered alley where he'd been attacked. "What's wrong?"

Diablo raised his eyebrows but didn't say anything. No one at Court could know Grey was close with the Major Black Coterie. Association with Diablo alone could endanger Nero, and with the witch hunt Regis was currently on, it would mean Nero would more than just fall out of the Prince's favor.

"Why would you automatically think something is wrong?" Tobias growled.

"Because with Hunter and the Handmaiden gone and things still falling out from the assassination attempt on Barna, you've made it clear I'm *persona non grata* at Court."

"I was looking out for you."

"You were and I appreciate that." If Regis found out Tobias had warned Grey to leave Court, Tobias could take Grey's place in the Court's dungeons with the royal torturer. "So it means something is very wrong for you to be calling me. That and it's four in the morning."

"Five," Diablo mouthed.

"I thought it was five in Newgate. Have you moved?"

"Not what we were talking about," Grey said, trying to pull the conversation away from his location. He doubted Tobias would send men to arrest him, not after warning him to flee, but Regis could have increased any number of pressures on his chamberlain. Now was not a good time to be a drake in the royal coterie's employ.

"Right. I wish it wasn't so damned obvious something was wrong."

"Even if Regis wasn't after me, everything has still gone seriously sideways." The living room darkened for a moment, and a hint of reeking garbage tickled Grey's nose, but the alley didn't fully manifest. *Thank the Mother of All for that.* "I'd be an idiot to assume you were calling for social reasons."

"Yeah, because we're not social."

Definitely not with Grey, and he wasn't sure if Tobias was social with anyone. For a drake who had a hand in every aspect of dragon life and had all the contacts to go with that, he certainly kept to himself.

"Someone broke into the Handmaiden's chambers."

"Broke in?"

"As in forced open both her outer door and the door to her inner chambers and ransacked the place."

Shit. Things really had turned sideways if drakes were doing that. No one broke into the Handmaiden's chambers. Even if those rooms weren't officially sacred, everyone treated them like they were. Heck, very few drakes entered her inner chambers, let alone her outer one — Grey had only been past the outer chamber three times in the last nine hundred years. "How bad is it? Any idea what they were looking for?"

"It's bad, and I have no clue. I need you to come to Court."

Grey's heart skipped a beat. "You can't possibly think I did it."

Diablo jerked forward, even more alert.

"What?" Tobias asked, his tone surprised and confused. "No. I'd never think you'd ransack the Handmaiden's rooms."

"But Regis does. He wants to arrest me." Of course, Regis wouldn't have to make up something like breaking into the Handmaiden's chambers to issue an arrest warrant for Grey. He was sure the prince could issue one — if one hadn't already been issued — for associating with Hunter and Anaea.

"Regis doesn't know about this yet. You're the Handmaiden's man. Even if it isn't official, she's her own coterie."

Grey snorted. "That would make it, what? A coterie of one?"

"Two. You're her sworn servant. That makes you her Second. By law, you have the right to attend to her business when she's not in Court."

"That still doesn't ease my fear that Regis is going to arrest me the moment I step foot in Court."

Tobias's heavy breath *hissed* over the connection in an exasperated sigh. "Look. I have a bad feeling about this. I have no idea what magic and knowledge the Handmaiden is keeping secret to protect us. Do you?"

"No." Even as her servant, Grey only knew what she wanted him to. She'd revealed powerful magics before by surprising everyone and creating the Asar Nergal — the organization that hunted and killed human mages — shortly after the Great Scourge. She could have something else in her chambers that could tip the political balance. Except even the suggestion of another coup right now could throw Regis over the edge.

"If someone has their hands on something powerful that will set Regis off and threaten the lives of more drakes, I want to know. And if it's Regis, I want to know that, too, before he has a chance to cover it up. It's the Handmaiden's private chambers. That's sacred even to the Royal Coterie."

"Careful, words like that might make a drake think you weren't Regis's man."

"I'm the *Court's* man," he growled. "That makes me the Handmaiden's. She hasn't supported anyone else's claim to the throne, so I support Regis."

"I'm not sure she ever supported Regis's claim." But she never spoke against him, either. She'd kept more than an arm's length from dragon politics, something Grey had appreciated at the time. Swearing himself into her service might have alienated him from his coterie, but it also kept him out of most of the messes. Particularly the uprising in 1521 when Regis proclaimed his father, King Constantine, soul sick and took control of the throne. But now, with dragon politics pulling dragonkind apart, he wasn't sure how good it was for her to keep out of it. If she just took a stand, surely most drakes would abide by her decision.

"Supporting Regis has kept things stable, us hidden and alive."

"Until recently." And if Zenobia hadn't attempted her coup, things might have carried on as usual for another couple hundred years.

Darkness flickered across Grey's vision and cannon fire *thwumped* in the distance. He ground his teeth and willed himself to concentrate on Tobias's voice and the dangers at hand. If Regis really had commanded the Handmaiden's chambers be ransacked, who knew what the dragon prince would do next?

"That's why I need you. Regis will want me to assign my own man, but given how the prince is running things, that man will have to report to Regis as well. I won't be able to stall on revealing information or maybe even knowing the whole truth."

"You're afraid your man won't tell you everything?"

Diablo frowned. Yeah, it was never good if the chamberlain feared his own people were keeping things from him.

"My people are in a more precarious situation than I am. I at least know how to run Court, which makes Regis think twice about arresting me," Tobias said, his tone darkening. "And I *know* the head of my North American Clean Team thought it prudent less than a week ago to keep information from me."

"Capri had good reason." And the biggest reason was her human mage inamorato, who dragon law demanded Capri kill — something she'd never do.

"I'm only partially furious about that. What I'm really pissed about is this break-in. Too many drakes are making moves that permanently kill other drakes and that includes Regis. If pressed, I can argue that because you're her man, you noticed the break-in before I did."

"Way to cover your ass."

"Are you going to meet me at the Handmaiden's chambers or not?" Tobias asked, his tone suddenly exhausted.

"Your word this isn't a trap." It wasn't a guarantee, but Tobias was one of a few drakes whose word was still his bond.

"It's not a trap. I'm in the hall outside her chambers. Help me figure out what the hell is going on." He blew another sigh. "In the very least, you're sworn to her service. Help me put her room back so it isn't a disaster when she returns."

"I'll be there in five." Grey ended the call and shoved his phone into the back pocket of his slacks.

"Of course it's a trap," Diablo said. "I don't even know what it is, but I know if you return to Court, Regis will throw you in prison."

"Someone broke into the Handmaiden's chambers and ransacked them."

"So?"

"What do you think Regis would do right now if whoever it was used some kind of magic the Handmaiden had been protecting us from?"

Diablo's expression hardened. "If they already have it, there isn't anything we can do to stop Regis."

"I can at least figure out if anything was taken."

"And then what? Did the Handmaiden keep security cameras in her room?" Diablo snorted as if that was the most ridiculous thing in the world. "You have no way of knowing who to go after. You can't stop them."

"Won't know if I don't try." Grey stood and headed to the door leading onto the patio. God, this was a terrible idea, but doing nothing wasn't an option.

Diablo grabbed his glass and strode to the bar. "Won't be able to try from prison."

Grey pressed his hands to the misted glass door and drew in a steadying breath before summoning a gate to Court. If he didn't keep hold of his intended destination, his gate could move to his suite — on the opposite side of Court from the Handmaiden's chambers — or worse, latch onto the magical anchor for Court's official gate, depositing him at the feet of four of Regis's guards. "If I don't answer my phone in an hour, feel free to sneak into Court and break me out."

"You wish." Diablo poured himself another drink.

"Fine. Tell Anaea to tell Hunter to break me out." Grey hissed his power word and summoned the gate. A pinprick of black flared to life, grew into a devouring man-sized vortex, and he stepped through.

The world twisted. For a split second neither up nor down existed, then his foot hit something hard and the hall outside the Handmaiden's chamber door appeared. It was a plain granite passage — walls, floor, and ceiling — filled with a magical light from a source

Grey had never been able to pinpoint, just like all the other plain granite passages in Court.

A hint of fog, the threat that his memories were going to overwhelm him, danced over his sight. He clenched his jaw, straining to stay connected with the present. But the hall looked like all the other halls from the beginning of the creation of Court, and for a second he didn't know where or when he was.

Someone cleared his throat, drawing Grey's attention to a dragon at the end of the hall. Tobias. A drake in a muscular human body large enough to challenge Grey's northern Crusader. He had a wide, strong black aura, revealing he was old enough to remember the Great Scourge.

This had to be present time...?

"Glad you decided to risk it."

Yes, present time.

The chamberlain's steely gaze darted over Grey's, and his expression darkened even more.

"I know, I look like shit," Grey said. "Let's move on."

"Sure." Tobias stepped aside and pointed at the Handmaiden's door. It stood ajar and the lock had been broken as if it hadn't been magically enspelled shut.

"Null magic?" Grey asked. It was the only way to get around the protection spells the Handmaiden had cast on the door. Except the only drake who had possessed null magic had been Hunter before his encounter with Anaea had forced him to give up his Crusader's body.

"Or some kind of magic lockpick."

"That would take another sorcerer." A shiver swept over Grey. If there was another sorcerer around, Regis would completely lose his shit. Sorcerers had cast the Great Scourge, sentencing dragonkind into this parasitic spirit state. Sure, they lived an immortal life, but accidents — and even not-so-accidental *accidents* — happened. With no new dragons being born, since none could be born, dragonkind faced extinction.

Except it seemed some dragons didn't care. The Handmaiden, the dragons' only true sorcerer and the magical lifeline for all dragonkind, had been gone for only a few weeks — a mere blink of an eye in a dragon's reality — and yet that blink had resulted in the loss of over six dozen drakes. Dragonkind was ripping itself apart, and too many drakes didn't care that a death right now was a permanent death. Without the medallion present to capture a dragon's soul and the Handmaiden to cast the rebirth spell, which placed that dragon's soul into a new, unoccupied human vessel, the spirit of any drake killed in those few weeks was lost forever into the universal ether.

"Yeah, I don't like the idea of another sorcerer out there, either." Tobias pushed the door open, revealing the plain chamber inside. The Handmaiden's solitary chair and table sat, as usual, dead center, with nothing else in the room.

The image of her sitting there, a silver aura radiating around her, her eyes kind and sad, flashed over Grey's vision. Last time he'd been there, he'd begged her to rebirth him, to strip away everything that made him who he was — including the memories he couldn't forget and the magic that seared it with perfect clarity into his mind. She'd refused and instead sent another thread of power into him to ease his memories.

He'd known then she was going to leave. She'd been wearing shoes. She never wore shoes in Court, only when she was going to leave. And the last time she'd done that, the Dragon Court had been thrown into turmoil as well. Regis had imprisoned his soul sick father in his suite and taken the throne.

Grey stepped inside, barely feeling the tingling magic tickle over his skin from the gatelock which prevented anyone from free gating inside her chambers. He sucked in a quick breath and fought to shove the memory of the Handmaiden back into the recesses of his mind. The image grew transparent but didn't vanish. Just great. It looked like that was the best he was going to get, so he turned his focus to the door in the center of the back wall, leading to her inner chambers. It, too, stood ajar with the lock broken.

Inside, all the bookshelves were toppled over, her diaries, volumes upon volumes of leather-bound books, scattered across the floor, open, upside down, and with bent and torn pages. Her desk's top had been swept empty, everything shoved to the floor, and all the drawers were open — two had been pulled out and upended on the wicker couch a few feet away. The three dozen glass globes she'd hung on the stairwell that curled against the back wall, and the four dozen she'd hung along the balcony of the second level, had been smashed, and her two-story tapestry of a silver dragon in flight had been torn down.

An image of the Handmaiden standing on the staircase, her aura radiant, filled Grey's vision. She seemed otherwordly, more than just an ancient silver drake, but something else, something powerful. He tried to blink away the feeling and the vision. Now wasn't the time. She felt *different* — she always felt just a little bit different — because she kept to herself and didn't let anyone, not even Grey, get too close.

"We've got until lunch. That's when I... come to do my regular check. I'll have to report this then."

"You check on her regularly?" Grey asked, curious, but not wanting to ask the second-most powerful drake at Court what that pause had meant.

Tobias's expression hardened. "Every day."

Grey dragged his attention from the chamber and tried to focus on Tobias, but the room had darkened and filled with mist, a collision of too many memories all swirling together and all out of focus.

"The Handmaiden returning won't completely stabilize the political mess, but it'll help," Tobias said. "In the very least, the next time someone does something stupid, we can save more drake souls."

"Only if a medallion is present." And Hunter, the Prince's ex-assassin, held the only mobile one. The other medallion was embedded in the heart of the arena here at Court.

"Don't remind me." Tobias's phone rang. He checked the call display and swore. "I've got to go."

"Looks like *I* have until lunch to clean this up." Grey fought to see past the fog to the chaos he had to go through, but seeing didn't matter. He'd glimpsed it already and the mess was there, seared into his memory like everything else. He could only pray that going through her room might reveal where she'd gone, and then he could go and beg, once again, for her to end everything that made him *him*.

3

Ivy stood at the end of the hall leading to the Handmaiden's chambers and clutched her locket. There wasn't much stored there about the Handmaiden, only abstract knowledge from overheard conversations. Sure, the Handmaiden had been there when Ivy had been reborn. But that information came from a conversation with the only other drake Ivy could trust, Ophelia, shortly after they'd realized Ivy's newest body had the one type of earth magic that could save her from a life of constant confusion. Before her magic had manifested, she'd lived for almost sixty years as a recluse, with Ophelia telling her every morning who she was and who Ivy was and that it would be all right. According to Ophelia, that had been Ivy's life with all her other human vessels since the Great Scourge.

The bitter thought — that her earth magic ability to read the memories imprinted in objects was supposed to have freed her — kept whirling through her head.

She was supposed to be free. But she wasn't.

And that was just the way it was. She had to think past that, get through the day, and do whatever was asked of her.

She squared her shoulders and resisted the urge to tell herself that if she did this one job, she'd be done. The prince's chamberlain had told her that lie forty-five years ago when she'd offered to help him read the memories in a hall and identify all the conspirators plotting to overthrow the doyen of the Major Yellow Coterie.

That hadn't been the last time she'd used her magic at his command, and this wouldn't be the last time, either. At least this job didn't involve roaming the halls looking for possible traitors like she'd been doing for the last few weeks. Sure, reading the memories of the halls temporarily eased the constant ache in her soul, that missing piece that she couldn't permanently fill. But the fear of what might happen if she didn't find proof of deceit had replaced the ache. It was there, right at the forefront of the locket's memories. If she didn't give Regis what he wanted, terrible things would happen to her.

For days on end with long, exhausting hours, Ivy had been trying not to just absorb two thousand years of memories imprinted in the walls of Court, but to concentrate on memories that were new and relevant. She couldn't just revel in the memories like her soul and power wanted. She had to focus and find specific details. Regis wanted names, and if there weren't any to tell, he suspected her of holding back and keeping secrets.

It didn't matter that some of these halls hadn't seen a drake for hundreds of years — since Court's physical size hadn't shrunk with the dragons' diminishing numbers and chambers were just abandoned as the living population, for convenience, drew closer together. Regis wanted names.

And now—

She strode halfway down the hall to the Handmaiden's chambers, the fear in her gut churning.

Now Regis would want yet another name, and she feared if she couldn't give him someone, anyone, he'd send her to his torturer, Odyne.

A shiver rushed over Ivy. Ophelia had said the Handmaiden had banned King Constantine from using Odyne's earth magic once it became clear the agony she inflicted with her touch could continue for days, months, and even years. But Constantine was soul sick, and Regis had brought the royal torturer back.

Ivy reached the Handmaiden's door, but a rough, masculine voice saying something on the other side made her stop before pushing it open. Her pulse jumped and the ice in her gut surged into her chest.

Someone was inside. Probably two or more someones, since a single person didn't have reason to talk to himself... unless he was on the phone... or he'd succumbed to soul sickness and was crazy. Which could only make the encounter worse.

Mother of All, she didn't like people. They expected her to remember them, and there was always that lure, teasing and taunting her, to read the memories imprinted in their clothes, their jewelry, heck, whatever they had on their person. Except that didn't end well. It was an invasion of privacy, and every drake she'd read had reacted badly. Even her friend Ophelia — especially Ophelia — had responded with ferocious anger.

Frankly, it was safest — and easiest — to avoid everyone.

Ivy glanced back down the hall, every instinct screaming to return to her room and wait.

Except Tobias had made it clear that Regis had no patience. He wanted to know what had happened in the Handmaiden's chambers, and he wanted to know now.

The door opened, revealing Tobias, with his wild black hair and dark searing eyes, standing in a stark chamber with a chair and table dead center — the only furniture and both lit with wild blue memory fire. He wore his usual heavy engraved cross from a human time period hundreds of years ago. And as always, the cross pulsed with blue flames only she could see, promising deep, strong memories. Something she'd never have for herself.

Her power word jumped into her mind, and she clenched her jaw against saying it or even subvocalizing it. The word squirmed within her, desperate to be said. More flames surged around the cross, and she wrenched her gaze to the room behind Tobias, determined to stay in control.

At the back of the chamber was another open door with another man standing in the entrance. Massive, even for human standards, his broad shoulders filled the doorway and his blond locks almost brushed the top of the frame. His pale blue gaze seized hers, as if he could see into her soul, and froze her in place. Except it wasn't just her who was frozen. It was him, both of them, along with the air in the room. Even time itself. There was no present, no future, and no longed-for past. It was just them, only them, always them. Apart from everything and everyone.

Tobias cleared his throat and the drake across the room blinked, releasing her from his gaze. But that only made her attention jump to the writhing blue blaze swirling impossibly all around him, not just from pieces of jewelry or clothes. Even from this far away the pull of old, powerful memories clawed at her, sucking her toward him. Her knees trembled, and she gripped the doorframe to keep standing. A massive silver aura flickered through the blue, white lightning cutting through the blue fire, but even without that, she'd have known he was an ancient drake. As old as, even older than, the Great Scourge. Two thousand years of memories in his jewelry, his trophies—

Mother of All, she'd give anything to read his hoard. A collection that old would satisfy the ever-consuming ache in her soul for years.

Her pulse picked up. But at the thought of spending time with his hoard or spending time with him? She didn't know.

"The Handmaiden's man was just leaving," Tobias growled.

"Yeah," the silver drake said, but he didn't move from the doorway.

A phone rang. Tobias drew his from his pocket and glanced at the screen. His expression darkened — Ivy hadn't thought it could get any darker — and he ran a hand through his hair. "I've got to go."

"Is it this?" the silver drake asked.

"No."

The silver drake shifted. "Is that good or bad?"

"Is anything good right now?" Tobias's glare jumped to Ivy. "Do your job. Grey isn't staying." He stormed from the room, taking the seductive blue flames of his memories with him. A part of her wanted to chase after him and ask what was going on.

Except a bigger part didn't want to ask. What she really wanted was to see the truth, the whole truth, for herself. Dragons lied. That knowledge was imprinted clear and strong in her locket. And Tobias had lied to her once before — probably more than once, if she wanted to go searching for the weaker memories in her locket. Dragons looked out for themselves and maybe their coterie members, but that was it. Ivy wasn't a member of a coterie — no matter how much Tobias had insisted she was a part of the Royal Coterie. She *belonged to*, she wasn't *a part of*, the Royal Coterie. She was an object to be used as it suited Regis. If she wanted to keep her locket, not to mention the body that allowed her to have any memory longer than a day, she had to obey.

The silver drake — Tobias had called him Grey — cleared his throat and drew her attention from the now empty hall back to him and the door to the inner chamber. The weight of time blazed around him, seductive and captivating. She'd never seen a drake with so much memory clinging to him, as if his remembrances were more than just him, a living entity unto itself.

She inched closer, unable to help herself. Maybe she could read just one. Something small so he wouldn't notice. Except she'd never been able to get away with that before. She didn't know what the other drake felt, but the memories in her locket made it clear they always felt something, always knew she was using her magic on them.

There was also no way she'd be able to stop with just one.

Mother of All. Just looking at him made her power word fill her mind and bubble at the back of her throat, as if it possessed a mind of its own.

She forced her attention to his eyes, unable to look away and desperate to see past the flames. But a great weight filled his gaze as if the flames of his memories were transformed there into an enormous pressure, the pull and weight of a dying sun collapsing into itself. It drew at her with a soul-deep ache similar to her own. She didn't know why or how he suffered, but soul to soul, without a doubt he was a kindred spirit, the other side of her coin. She ached with a loss she couldn't explain, an emptiness, a knowing she was missing pieces of herself, and he seemed too full, straining, almost bursting, and unable to release the pressure.

Against all common sense, she took another step closer and bumped the arm of the chair in the room's center. Her attention jumped to the furniture, and the pressure of his memories vanished, but her heart pounded too fast. She stood more than just two steps from the door and hadn't noticed moving.

The perpetual ice in her gut, that fear that she was always in danger, always at a disadvantage, churned faster. Even now, with her attention locked on the floor between her foot and the chair leg, she could feel his pull. It curled inside her, a craving she didn't know how long she could refuse and one she wasn't sure she wanted to.

A growl bubbled in her throat. Mother of All, she was a dragon, too. She lived her life in fear. One more terror — even if it was terror at her inability to control herself — shouldn't stop her.

No. It *wasn't* going to stop her.

"The chamberlain said you were leaving," she said — still staring at the floor, but at least she'd managed to say something.

"Yes."

It didn't sound as if he was moving.

"I have a job to do." The urge to look up, to say her power word, to satisfy the ache within her, made her muscles twitch. She fought to keep still and not hug herself to do so. That was a sign of weakness, and it was bad enough she was refusing to make eye contact. Anything else and she'd look like prey.

"What is your job?"

"I work for the chamberlain."

"I know that. But he didn't say what you do."

"And neither will I." Her power, her secret. Too many drakes knew about her earth magic already, and she was trapped in a coterie controlled by a madman. She wasn't going to tell anyone else. "Please. I can't keep the chamberlain waiting."

"We've met, you know."

What? Her gaze jumped up and the flames surged around him until he was lit with a blazing blue halo. Surely, she'd remember him. Surely, she'd have imprinted all that memory into her locket.

"It was brief. A few days ago. In the gateroom."

She didn't know why he was telling her this. Had she been rude to him? Had she stared at him like she was staring at him now, dumb, without any thought but the urge to feel the strength of his memories surging through her? The urge to feel other strong things—

Her heart skipped a beat, and she shoved that thought away before she could examine it. Focus on the job. Focus on surviving.

Except surviving wasn't enough any more. That knowledge, like the truth that all drakes lied, was stored clear and sad in her locket as well.

She mentally grasped at her ache, her desire, and the yearning to succumb to his memories, and shoved it as deep inside her as she could, then she forced herself to march the remaining distance to the inner door. Now she stood on the edge of his flames, their essence licking over her skin, straining her willpower.

She gritted her teeth. "Do I need to call the chamberlain back?"

"No. I'll go." But he didn't move from the doorway and his gaze stayed locked on hers, as if he was trapped in the same vortex, whirling, throbbing, captured.

He leaned closer, forcing her to tip her head back to maintain eye contact. And yet she couldn't look away. His flames slid across her cheeks and down her neck, drawing a shiver. His gaze dipped to her lips, and the shiver grew stronger, filled with a new desire.

Her pulse pounded, thrumming to every cell of her body, as if somehow being this close to him changed the primal resonance in the core of her being.

He dipped closer, his lips brushing hers and skimming across her cheek to her ear. His jaw, rough with stubble, slid against her skin, jaw to jaw, in a whisper of dragon courtship.

The thrum exploded with desire and fiery memory, and shock snapped through her. She yanked back and hit the back of her head on the doorframe. The world tilted and froze. The fire of his memories seared her. No clear images arose, but the power swept into her, and for a moment, no longer than one quick pound of her heart, the ache in her soul was gone. Glorious strength filled her. She was complete, whole, powerful, on the verge of bursting from the memory filling her.

She drew breath and his fire within her vanished. The world wrenched again, the loss of everything, of self, of a complete essence, it all crushed her, and she pressed her back against the doorframe to keep standing.

He reached for her arm — likely to steady her — but she jerked away. She couldn't let him touch her again. She'd succumb and let her earth magic read everything he remembered, whether he wanted her to or not. She'd see everything, good and bad. But it was the bad no one wanted her to see. She'd see it all. Every deep dark secret, every hurt, every mistake he was trying to forget and even those he might think he'd forgotten.

God. It had just been one touch, and she hadn't even used her power word. She hadn't even experienced his memories in full, just skimmed the outside edge.

She slipped past him into the Handmaiden's inner chamber, somehow fighting the urge to brush against him and experience that surge of memory again, while clinging to the door to keep standing.

"Get out." She clutched the door handle, certain if she let go the world would topple and toss her to the ground.

His eyes were too wide, filled with shock. He knew she'd done something, knew she'd violated him and had no way of knowing that she hadn't done it on purpose. It hurt to see him look at her like that, and yet it was for the best. The temptation was too much. She could never, never see him again.

4

She shut the door in Grey's face. He could have stopped her by shoving his foot in the jamb, but the idea didn't hit him until the door was closed. That, and she looked just as stunned as he felt. More so, since she'd almost fallen over. He'd just brushed his jaw against hers. He hadn't been able to do anything else. The stillness she'd radiated made it impossible to focus on anything else. He'd needed to get close, closer, have her pressed against him, anything to ease the memories raging through him. Before he'd realized what he was doing, he'd kissed her.

He pressed his forehead to the door but didn't open it. With the barrier between them, it was easier to focus. And jeez, kissing Tobias's agent had been stupid. Beyond stupid. It was bad enough she'd seen him here — Tobias had warned him to leave, he'd just been five minutes too late for Grey to get out of the Handmaiden's gatelocked chambers and gate out of Court — but if there was even a suggestion that Tobias's agent was aligned with Grey, both her and Tobias could face Regis's wrath. Anything could set the prince off, and Tobias's position was tenuous at best.

The urge to open the door and brush his jaw against hers again — not just a whisper of a caress but with the dragon ferocity curled tight within him — surged through him. He ground his teeth and clenched his hands behind his back. She was trouble with a capital T. One he couldn't afford to have. He had more than enough on his plate. He'd managed to get most of the Handmaiden's room back to the way he remembered — Tobias had assured him cleaning up wouldn't affect his agent's ability to do her job.

His heart skipped a beat. Just a touch. That was all he needed from her.

Her.

He didn't even know her name. All he knew was that she didn't make hundreds of memories flare within him. Only one, from a few days ago, when Capri and her human had been caught up in the mess around the attempted assassination of the doyen of the Major Brown Coterie. Grey had been in the human world again, his life in danger, again. His gate had jumped to the anchor at Court and she'd been standing there, shocked, a beacon of calm in the sea of memories raging through him.

His hands slipped to the door handle, but he yanked back before he could open the door and forced himself to move to the other side of the Handmaiden's chair and table.

Keep going. Out the door. Into the hall. Leave her.

But he couldn't make his legs take him any farther.

Mother, please. For all he knew, as soon as she'd closed the door, she'd called Court security and Regis's men were on the way to arrest him. He couldn't stay and he couldn't summon a gate until he'd left the Handmaiden's chambers.

He forced himself to face the way out.

Now go into the hall. Just. Do. It. He'd done harder things before. Hell, he'd battled his fear of the human realm to summon a gate when he'd thought Hunter's life was in jeopardy, and then gated there numerous times in the last few weeks. Taking six steps out of a room was easy.

Really.

He started to turn back to the inner chamber.

No. With a roar, he wrenched himself into the hall and slammed the door shut.

Something snapped, as if the distance of the Handmaiden's chamber and two closed doors was what he'd needed to break whatever spell Tobias's agent had cast on him. Except he knew she hadn't cast anything. She just *was*. Calm. Young. A drake with a fraction of the history of any other drake. When he looked at her, memories didn't flood him. Even the memories of the Handmaiden's chambers had eased — probably due to his fascination with *her*.

His phone rang and he drew it from his pocket. No number. That meant it was Anaea, Diablo, or Nero. It could also be Hunter.

Please let it be Hunter and he's found the Handmaiden.

"Hello?"

"I thought we agreed it wasn't safe for you to return to Court," Nero growled over the line, no doubt his concern more for the safety of his *puzur*, his unusual, secret coterie of natural human mages than for Grey's well-being.

"Tobias assured me it was safe."

"That's not what Diablo said."

Which was true. Tobias hadn't said it was safe, only that it wasn't a trap. "I'm leaving now. We need to talk."

"Yes," Nero said, his tone dark. "We do."

A masculine voice from down the hall said something, and two Court guards — both broad-shouldered, muscular men, a foot shorter than Grey — sauntered around the corner.

Shit.

Grey ended the call and pocketed his phone as he headed in the opposite direction, praying the guards wouldn't notice him.

"Hey," one of them called in a reedy tenor.

So much for that.

Grey rushed around the closest corner and bolted down the hall, trying to get to the next turn before the guards could see him. If he fought, even if he won, the guards would get a good look at him and report back to Regis. That would only make things worse. If there wasn't already an official warrant for Grey's arrest, one would certainly be issued. If he lost, it would be worse than worse. Buying enough time to make a gate and hope the guards didn't recognize him was his best bet.

"Stop." This voice was deeper, a rich baritone.

Grey picked up speed and hurried around the corner. The two chambers in this hall had been sealed five hundred years ago. At the very least, he had to get to the next hall over, and at best, without them seeing which room he'd then enter.

"I said stop," Baritone yelled.

A blast of wind pounded into Grey's back and slammed him into the wall beside the first branch in the passage. His forehead cracked against the granite and pain snapped through his skull.

He staggered, fighting to keep his balance. The hall twisted and the reek of rotting garbage rushed around him.

Not now.

Wind billowed again, this time slicing across his back.

"How fast can you heal, drake?" the memory hissed.

Not fast enough. It was never fast enough. He couldn't even stand and fight. He didn't have a weapon and he had no offensive earth magic.

The hall darkened and cold bit his face and fingers, except for a searing heat oozing from his temple down his cheek.

Blood. But the drakes in the alley had slashed his throat, not his face.

His thoughts stuttered.

The heat slipped under his jaw and slid down his neck.

He wasn't in the alley or anywhere on earth. He was in Court and in danger.

Another slice of wind cut into his shoulder and the guards' footsteps pounded closer.

He blinked, trying to clear his vision, but the darkness remained, blinding him to his reality and yet not manifesting into a memory.

"Hold him," Tenor said.

A hand shoved against Grey's back.

God damn it. Out of options.

Grey wrenched his elbow up and slammed it into the face of the drake holding him. The pressure on his back vanished and a foggy hall materialized around him. Yes, there were two drakes. This was the present.

He grabbed the wrist of the drake he'd just stunned, thrust him against the granite wall, and dislocated his shoulder in one quick, violent twist.

The other drake grabbed the hilt of the machete sheathed at his hip and opened his mouth. To say his power word? Call for help? Grey didn't know and didn't want to find out. He rammed his fist into the drake's neck before he could speak then yanked the machete free and slashed the guard's throat. Blood sprayed the front of Grey's dress shirt and splattered over his hands and arms. The guard clamped his hands over the wound, blood bubbling between his fingers, and staggered back.

The other drake behind Grey roared, and he spun to face him, slashing at neck height. The tip of the blade caught flesh, but the cut wasn't deep enough to stop the guard.

Grey swung again. The only way to win this fight was to be faster, more aggressive, pray they didn't have rapid healing and that he'd incapacitate them long enough to get away and make a gate.

The drake jerked back, and Grey's second swing missed. Light flashed in Grey's eyes and someone screamed. He gritted his teeth and swung again. A hand grabbed his wrist and biceps. The guard. It had to be the guard in front of him, the one still standing. Grey twisted before the drake could snap his elbow and rammed his heel into the drake's knee.

Crack. The drake screamed, his face materializing through the light. Grey sliced the machete across the guard's neck and shoved him back. More blood sprayed Grey. The guard collapsed beside the other one, who still gurgled but was climbing to his feet. Grey kicked him in the head, sending him tumbling over. The guard's eyes rolled back and he stopped moving. But that wouldn't last for long. While most drakes didn't have rapid healing, they healed fast enough — and always faster than Grey.

He bolted around the corner, only half able to see through the haze of memories crowding his vision, dropped the machete then took off down another hall. Light flickered, blinding him, and the woman howled.

His breath hitched in his throat. His only saving grace in that fight had been almost two thousand years of fighting experience in his current human body, and he'd learned being vicious and fast was often the edge that won a fight.

The first of a dozen doors leading to abandoned chambers came into sight… or was that memory? He didn't know if he saw reality or not. Did it matter? He wiped the blood off his hand on the clean underside of his shirt and grabbed a very real door handle. The room's magic light flared to life, revealing an empty living room with kitchenette at the back, very much like the living quarters in his suite or Hunter's here at Court.

Hunter's Court furniture popped into sight, every available space on the wall covered with a painting or drawing or photograph of the sky. A part of him understood Hunter's obsession with the sky. He could still remember flying, feeling the wind in his face and the strength in his wings. But he remembered it with perfect clarity as if he'd just been flying moments ago.

Hunter's suite vanished, turning into a clear cloudless sky.

No.

Grey squeezed his eyes shut, but the sky was still there, the earth a patchwork of fields and forests and lakes far below.

No no no.

Concentrate, damn it. He wasn't flying, he was in Court, and he couldn't stay. The guards had healed by now, and it wouldn't take them long to find him standing, stunned, in this chamber.

A pinprick of darkness bled into the remembered cloudless blue, and he grasped at it. Gates were a black vortex leading through interdimensional space from one spot to another. A sci-fi movie would call it a wormhole or some such thing. He needed that. Now.

He hissed his power word, summoning the magic to open a gate. The power swept down his arm and burst from his hand. The darkness in his sky grew, devouring the blue, sucking at his soul, urging him to step through.

For a second, his vision cleared, revealing the empty chamber. The door to the hall opened, and the guards rushed inside, their uniforms stained with blood. The one in front yelled and raised his machete.

Grey wrenched forward into the gate, and the vortex sucked him in and spat him out into Nero's living room, right where he'd left six hours ago. The lights were no longer on, but it was noon and brilliant sunlight shone through the massive bank of windows behind him. Diablo was gone, but Nero and Ryan sat in the armchairs across from the couch.

Ryan jerked to his feet and rushed to Grey. "Is that blood?"

"Not mine," Grey gasped. Darkness from too many memories flooded around him, and he fought to stay in the living room with wide-eyed Ryan and glaring Nero.

"What the hell is wrong with you?" Nero asked from his seat on the couch, his expression pinched as if he were in pain. If Grey hadn't known that dragons never aged, he would have sworn the silver patches of hair at Nero's temples had gotten bigger. "Regis has every Court guard on the lookout for you, and I just heard he's placed a gate-trap on your suite."

"Gate-trap?" Ryan asked. A handsome, muscular man with a square jaw and bright green eyes, he had a blue aura that made him look like a young blue drake — while Grey knew the man was human. The only way a dragon would be able to know Ryan was a mage was if that dragon possessed the rare ability to tell the difference in auras. Something Grey didn't have.

"It lets someone gate in but not gate out." Nero rubbed his temples. "The radius isn't big, it might not even cover the entirety of a drake's suite at Court, but—"

"Then it's a good thing I'm not going back," Grey said. Any chance of safely returning was ruined forever by the fight with the Court guards. Not even Tobias would be able to protect him if he set foot in Court again.

Grey's pulse jumped, sudden and furious. He was stuck in the human world. The world where drakes ambushed him, where he'd nearly died for good.

"How fast can you heal?" the voice hissed.

Sweat burst across Grey's forehead and his throat ached.

"Shit." Ryan's eyes widened even more and his attention leapt over Grey's shoulder to the bank of floor-to-ceiling windows overlooking the back of Nero's massive estate. His aura flared, a sign his earth magic ability to see impending deaths had activated.

"Nero. Kid on the right. Grey. Get the one on the left."

Ryan bolted past Grey and a blast of cold air — the now open patio door — slammed into Grey's back. Nero leapt to his feet and raced past Grey.

He turned. Anaea, Raven, and six teens stood in knee-high snow. An earth magic training session to help those kids, natural human mages, control their newly awakened power — although Grey had no idea what was being taught. Everyone was screaming and scrambling away from Anaea, whose aura had grown to blindingly bright and was surrounded in a raging wind storm.

The wind slammed into Ryan and knocked him back. He rolled, scrambled to his feet, and dove for one of the kids. Nero raced toward the one on the right, while Raven — her waist-length ponytail whipping around her — grabbed the closest kid. That left two kids unprotected, Jeff — a bulky seventeen-year-old — and Mia — Nero's fourteen-year-old auger.

They were too far apart. Grey couldn't protect them both, but Ryan had said to grab the kid on the left. Jeff. He was just going to have to trust Ryan's mystic sight.

5

Anaea's aura contracted for a split second then exploded with more force and light. The wave slammed into Grey, knocking him over, and the living room windows shattered. Massive shards of glass swept into the whirlwind. Pulse pounding, Grey scrambled to his feet, lunged for Jeff, and shoved him out of the way as shards slammed into the snow beside them.

Mia screamed. A piece the size and length of Grey's arm hurtled toward her. Raven yelled her power word, and a blast of her wind slammed the glass into the trunk of the oak tree on the patio's far side.

Anaea sobbed and her power wrenched her off her feet.

"Where's Capri?" Grey yelled over the howl of the wind.

Nero jerked his kid out of the way of another flying shard. "On a call."

Shit. Capri's earth magic to manipulate the minds of humans was the only sure-fire way to stop Anaea — and even then, there wasn't a guarantee it would work.

"Take a breath, Anaea," Raven yelled.

"I'm trying," Anaea said between clenched teeth. The whirlwind roared stronger and branches ripped free from the oak.

Grey yanked Jeff to his feet. "Help the others get clear."

Jeff gave a tight nod, his expression filled with fear and determination, and he rushed to Mia, getting knocked off his feet by a blast of wind as he reached her.

"Anaea." Grey shoved against the vortex, trying to reach her. "Anaea, look at me."

"I don't want to." Tears leaked from her eyes but were caught up in her wind before dripping from her cheeks. "I'll hurt you. I thought I was getting control. I thought—"

"I need you to look at me." He had to get to her and calm her power before she tore the house apart.

Snow whipped around him. Jeff, Mia, Ryan, and two of the other kids were scrambling around the side of the house. They were almost clear. Raven and the two remaining kids weren't far behind them.

"Look at me," Grey yelled.

Anaea's gaze jumped to him, and a blast of wind slammed into his chest.

She gasped and the whirlwind surged, ripping up chunks of hardened snow and the ornamental garden stones underneath.

"You can control this. Raven said to take a breath. Just take a breath."

"I'm trying," she sobbed.

"Take one with me." Grey drew in a slow breath.

Her panicked sobbing turned into agonizing grief. "Oh, Grey. How can you just breathe? How can you stand? All that pain? It's so strong. I feel it all." Light blazed from her eyes and bored into him as if she could see his bleeding — always bleeding — soul. "Grey, I didn't know."

"I just breathe. All I can do is breathe." He didn't want to get into it. He never wanted to get into it, and if he ever did, now wouldn't be the time. "Take a breath with me."

He drew in another slow breath.

Anaea matched him.

The whirlwind trembled.

Something — ice or glass, he didn't know — sliced his cheek, a quick bite of pain. He drew another breath.

A rock thudded into the ground beside his foot. Snow showered him, bright flecks reflecting the noon sunlight.

Anaea trembled. Her wind slashed around her, one last violent blow, then dumped her to the ground. Grey scrambled to her, pulled her into his arms, and held her close.

"How can I feel your pain? Or the kids' fear." A sob shook her. "All that fear."

Grey tightened his grip. "You're a sorcerer. You can call on every kind of earth magic, and it looks like your ability to sense emotions has just awakened."

"Wonderful," she said, her voice thick with disgust. She turned to him, her eyes filled with a soul-deep ache he recognized within himself. "How—?"

"I just do." He yanked his attention away, unable to continue seeing his inner turmoil reflected in Anaea's eyes. "Let's get you home."

"No," Raven said from the patio.

Anaea tensed. "It's safer for everyone if I'm not here."

"Not for you. Not if you lose control and incapacitate Grey before he can stop you." The young black drake, Nero's third in command, crossed her arms as if expecting Anaea to argue. "All the kids go through it. They all understand."

"They're all terrified." Anaea's gaze dipped to her hands as if her power lay there and not in every cell of her body. "I'm terrified."

"All the more reason to stay with people who can help," Nero said through the shattered living room window. He stood inside with snow and glass shards around his feet. Ryan stood a few feet behind him with a broom and bucket, already preparing to start the cleanup as if broken windows happened all the time. If the situation hadn't been so serious, Grey might have laughed. Ryan had only been living in Nero's house for a few days, and already it seemed he fit in as if he'd been there for years.

"Isolation isn't the answer," Raven said. "We all knew the risk when we invited you in. You're staying."

Anaea pulled out of Grey's grip and staggered to her feet. She looked exhausted, which she probably was. Channeling that much magic so quickly could tire even a drake with rapid healing. She opened her mouth, probably to disagree, but Raven stormed across the snow to her.

"You're too tired to argue with me, and I suspect you're unable to stop reading my emotions, so you can sense how I feel about this."

Anaea frowned then rolled her eyes. "Fine. I'll argue with you about this once I've had a good sleep."

"I have no doubt." Raven grabbed Anaea's arm, and a tendril of Raven's wind took Anaea's weight and carried her inside.

Nero watched them go then turned his attention to Grey. "Don't think this incident has made me forget that you were stupid enough to return to Court. Or that you gated here already covered in blood. Whatever Tobias called you for wasn't worth the risk."

"Unfortunately this was." Murky fog flickered around Grey, and someone screamed. No one reacted. He clenched his jaw and focused on the cold seeping into him as his adrenaline drained away. "Someone ransacked the Handmaiden's inner chamber."

"Tobias gave me the heads-up," Nero said, leading Grey and Ryan out of the living room with its shattered windows, down the hall, and into one of his classrooms — windows intact. "It's still not worth risking my *puzur* if you're captured and tortured."

Nero stood at the front of the room by the giant whiteboard in the teacher's position and glared at Grey until he sat in the closest chair.

"No one might have a coterie, let alone a secret one, if someone makes another move against Regis." Grey sat but shifted, unable to get comfortable under Nero's glare. "If someone makes a move with magic stolen from the Handmaiden, no one is safe." The remembered scream came again then turned into a howling wind. Ice bit Grey's cheeks and turned his fingers numb as if he hadn't gone inside and now stood in the middle of a storm.

"Do you know what they took?" Ryan asked, his voice a whisper against the remembered howling. "What were they looking for?"

A hint of green light bled through the fog. Not Nero's or Ryan's aura, but that of Tobias's agent, that woman who radiated stillness in the middle of the whirlwind that raged in his head. He grasped for it, desperate to keep himself in the room in any way possible. "I don't know, but they took the scroll with the power words to control the lock on the Handmaiden's private residence." A locking magic more powerful than the locks on her chamber doors at Court.

"I thought her chambers at Court was her residence," Nero said.

"Another reason this is a problem." Grey tightened his grasp around the remembered calm and the classroom jumped into focus, revealing Ryan in the chair beside him and Nero still standing by the whiteboard. "I don't know if that was what they were specifically looking for and ransacking the rest of the room was just a cover, or if getting the power words to the Handmaiden's magical lock was a last resort. Either way, whoever broke in knew about her private residence and knew he needed to get the lock's power words to get in."

"And if *you* didn't know she had another residence—" Ryan said with a glance at Nero.

"—that makes it a short list of people looking for something in the Handmaiden's possession," Grey finished.

"But how short?" Nero asked.

"I wish I knew. For certain Tobias, Regis, and Constantine knew about her residence. She's had two servants before me, Bahiti and Servius, who are both still alive and they'd know, but they've known about it for centuries. Why make a move now? I also told Anaea to tell Hunter about the residence a few days ago so he could look for her there. So he knows." But if Nero, Regis's favorite doyen, didn't know about the Handmaiden's private residence, Grey could only guess at who else might be on the list. And it gave more weight to Tobias's fear that somehow Regis was behind this and acting in secret so drakes didn't riot when they learned he was stealing from the Handmaiden. Of course, it didn't prove anything, either.

"Tobias wouldn't have called you in if he was behind it," Nero said.

Ryan frowned. "Unless he's trying to hide the fact that he's responsible."

"No, this isn't Tobias's style," Nero said.

"And all of this is well and good, but I've already wasted six hours learning that they have the power words." Not to mention he'd ruined any chance of ever returning to Court. "If I want to stop them from getting whatever they're looking for, I have to leave now."

"You shouldn't go alone," Ryan said.

"Except there isn't anyone who can join me," Grey said. "No one can be associated with me without risking Regis's ire." Which was the hard truth. If Hunter was around, he'd have Grey's back without a second thought, but Hunter's mission to find the Handmaiden and get her to help Anaea was more important than ever.

Ryan shifted.

"No," Nero said before he could volunteer. "I need you helping Diablo. We still have those last few unnatural human mages from Zenobia's coup running around endangering all of us and—"

"You still haven't found the leak in your team?" Grey asked.

"No. And until I do, I can only trust Diablo and Ryan," Nero said. "Everything is stretched thin. Now is a terrible time for someone to steal something from the Handmaiden."

"No kidding." The room darkened for a second but thankfully it didn't stay, only causing a writhing, semi-translucent fog. "If things get really bad, I've got Diablo on speed dial as a last resort."

"I hate this," Ryan said.

Nero flashed his teeth, revealing his frustration. "So do I."

"Hey." Grey shoved up to his feet. "Hunter's probably already looked for her at her private residence, but you never know. Maybe she'll be there and that will solve everything." It was a next-to-nothing chance, but he had to hope. If they didn't find her soon, Anaea could accidentally kill everyone around and all of drake society would tear itself apart.

6

The room's memories blazed around Ivy and everything was tinged blue with the fire of her power. The soothing comfort of reading new memories seeped, a gentle warmth after a long deep chill, through her veins, and the tension across her neck and shoulders eased. It had been prevalent since waking. For a second, she was complete, but the feeling didn't last. It wasn't nearly as strong as when Grey had brushed his jaw against hers and his memory fire had shivered over her cheeks and down her neck, igniting a toe-curling need within her, but it wasn't nearly as dangerous, either.

Succumbing to her desires could only make her situation worse, and she could only pray Grey wasn't still standing in the Handmaiden's outer chamber when she was finished... even if a part of her really wanted him to.

She shoved that thought back. *Concentrate on what Tobias wanted. Find out what happened here. Nothing more.*

Her power — thankfully — surged, and a memory of the Handmaiden appeared, gliding down the stairs. Her image shifted and she sat behind the desk. It shifted again and now she stood beneath the glass globes hanging from the stairs and second-story balcony — those broken and in the wastebasket by the door. The woman's aura glowed with both strength and softness at the same time. She was comfort and peace, creativity and play, and a ferocious dragon trapped in a human vessel, like Ivy.

With all the time the Handmaiden had spent in this chamber, a sense of her self had been imbued into the walls, into the core of each atom they were made of. She was a drake to be feared and worshiped. She was a drake to be cherished and loved—

The room's memories jumped to one of Tobias standing in the doorway, unwilling to step deeper into the room, and the Handmaiden sitting in one of two wicker chairs by the desk, shaking her head with a rueful smile.

"I said join me." She pointed to the chair across from her.

Tobias's gaze jumped to it, but Ivy couldn't tell if he wanted to join her or not.

"Tell me what Constantine is doing now."

Tobias pursed his lips.

"I could cast an auger spell, but they give me a headache, and it's easier if you just share how the King is doing."

The memory wavered. It felt as if the room had jumped to another memory, but the Handmaiden still sat in her wicker chair and Tobias still stood in the doorway.

"Ophelia is almost positive he's soul sick." His words snapped inside Ivy, and icy panic clutched her chest. *Soul sick. Crazy.* That was her fate.

But it wasn't. Not with this body. Except how long would she be allowed to keep it?

Forever.

But only if she did what they said. Always what they said.

Her pulse roared, a frantic pounding that surged with her fear, freezing down her arms and legs.

Do what they say. Obey.

Her throat tightened. What was the point of having salvation from insanity if she wasn't free? And how long could she carry on like this?

She needed a plan.

The memories of the room snapped away, leaving her surrounded by ghostly blue flames promising soothing relief but also the aching reminder of her servitude.

Mother of All, no more. She gripped her locket. *Come up with a plan to free yourself. Ophelia might help, or she might not.* Ivy wasn't entirely certain how loyal her friend was to Tobias. Without a doubt, Tobias would try to keep her. *Possible options: run away—*

No, she didn't have the skills to hide. They'd be able to find her.

Fake her death?

Same problem. She didn't know enough about anything to make any good decisions.

Learn and figure something out.

Tears burned her eyes, and a growl bubbled in her throat. Mother of All, she was *not* going to cry. She'd read this room, give Tobias what he wanted, and bide her time. It was the only thing she could do.

She subvocalized her power word and concentrated on the room's most recent memories. They weren't necessarily the strongest — those were usually events tied with strong emotions — but they were still easier to draw into her mind than those ancient memories without emotions that blended into all the other old, emotionless memories.

The Handmaiden's man, Grey, jumped into focus, along with a deep craving to find him, bathe in his memory fire, and feel powerful again.

No. Focus on the room's memories. The. Room.

She dragged her attention back to the chamber. It lay in shambles, half the bookshelves toppled over with books scattered everywhere, the desk swiped clean, and shattered glass globes littering the floor. Grey righted two shelves and started sorting through the books, carefully — reverently — smoothing bent pages and covers. Sweat glistened at his temples, and tight lines crinkled at his eyes and around his mouth. His complexion was gray. It had been pale before. It was only now, with the absence of his fiery memories roaring around him, that she could really see him.

She yearned to stay there and watch him for as long as it had taken him to tidy the room to the way it was now. If she couldn't have the real him, somehow the remembered him would do. Which didn't make any sense. The promise of his memories wasn't in this memory — since the room couldn't sense memories like she could. But she didn't want to look away, wanted him to look up and see her, meet her gaze again… kiss her again.

Which was impossible. This was just a memory.

And watching Grey wasn't the assignment. Find out who'd done it and see what they'd taken. After that, figure out how to get free of Tobias and the Royal Coterie.

She released the memory and slipped backward in time, moving the memory as fast as she could to get through it in the shortest time possible without missing an important detail. Grey left. Tobias opened the door. The room was in shambles. He pulled out his phone — or rather put it away — then left. Then a while of nothing, and then a woman was leaving.

Ivy slowed the memory to normal time and watched the woman, a black drake — from her midnight aura — move backwards to the desk. Not surprising, Ivy didn't recognize the drake, but that didn't matter. If Ivy concentrated on remembering the drake's image, Ophelia could pull it from her mind. Maybe she'd recognize this black drake and the culprit could be brought to swift justice.

The items on the desk jumped up from the floor onto the desk and the woman swept backwards and straightened. She pulled a small scroll, about the length and width of her thumb, from her pocket, looked at it, then put it in a small box that sat on the corner of the desk.

What is it? Ivy asked the room.

The memory jerked away from the black drake, and Grey materialized again, righting the first of the two wicker chairs.

No, the scroll.

Another jerk. Tobias sat in the closest chair. Somehow, he'd worked up the nerve to go past the threshold and join the Handmaiden.

The scroll.

The room's memory dimmed. Blue flames swept around her, and the Handmaiden's form materialized by the globes and on the stairs at the same time. If the room knew what was on the scroll, it wasn't going to tell her. Ivy could only pray that knowing this scroll had been taken would be enough to please Tobias.

She rushed the memory back a little farther, watched the black drake search the Handmaiden's desk, topple furniture, and flip through dozens of books from the farthest shelf as if looking for something but not finding it.

With nothing else that was helpful, Ivy released her earth magic and stepped into the small, barren outer chamber. If she told Tobias now, that would give her the rest of the day to figure out a way to escape before she had to start — more or less — at the beginning again tomorrow.

The door to the hall flew open and two guards strode in. They peeled away, one to each side, and revealed Prince Regis, his expression dark, the look heightened by his black and gold doublet, breeches, and hose from a human era long past. Blue flames danced on the many gold chains around his neck and the rings on every finger, but only a hint came from his clothes — they might be an old style, but they weren't old and didn't hold much of a history. His gold aura shimmered bright and strong, like Tobias's and Grey's, indicating he, too, was an ancient drake and old enough to remember the Great Scourge.

Ivy dropped to her knees. "Your Highness."

Regis shifted his massive weight but didn't move from the doorway. Even if she could leave without drawing offense, he'd blocked her only escape.

"It's time we had a chat," he said.

Ice snapped through Ivy and flash-froze solid in her gut. That was a sentence she'd never wanted to hear from the prince. Every instinct screamed. *Get out. Flee. Regis is dangerous.* Those thoughts had been clear, strongly imprinted in her locket when she'd read it that morning. But there was nowhere to go, and even if she could get past him, the two guards already in the room would stop her before she even got that far.

"Of course, your Highness," she said, her voice shaking along with her body. If she said the wrong thing, looked at him the wrong way, he could have her reborn—

Except with the Handmaiden gone, no one could be reborn. She was the only drake with the magic ability to cast the rebirth spell. Which didn't mean Regis wouldn't think of something just as horrible for Ivy.

"I'm sure you've noticed with your last assignments that things have been dangerous at Court." Regis sauntered to the chair at the center of the room, drawing closer to Ivy, and sat.

Her insides squirmed with the need to inch away.

He slid his hands down the worn wooden arms and surveyed the barren walls as if seeing the room in a new light. "Don't tell me you haven't noticed. Don't tell me you haven't heard them whispering lies about me."

"Only if the halls remember."

He squinted, his gaze unfocused, seeing her but not really seeing her.

"She's the drake who doesn't leave her quarters," a man with a gravelly voice said from the doorway. A new drake now stood framed by the guards, young and orange — according to the strength and color of his aura. He wore a tailored black suit that matched his black hair and trimmed beard and accentuated his pale skin and sharp facial features. He wasn't particularly big, not like Regis's girth or Grey's height, but he exuded a darker sense of danger than either drake.

He brushed his suit jacket back, rested his hands on the hilts of a matching katana and wakizashi, and flashed his perfect teeth at her. Heat radiated from his eyes, and she wasn't sure if the teeth flash was a sexual invitation or aggression. It felt like both.

"No drake just stays in her suite, Bolo," Regis said.

She wrenched her attention back to Regis. This new drake, Bolo, might be physically dangerous, but Regis was the real threat. "I read the halls and report to the chamberlain."

"And now you report directly to me." Regis leaned back in the chair, getting more comfortable, and slapped the arms. "Here."

"Here?" The word slipped out before she could stop it.

"What? You have a problem with that?" Regis barked a harsh laugh, drawing a shiver through Ivy that ran bone deep. His gaze jumped to Bolo. "She has a problem with that, assassin."

"No, I don't." The shiver tightened in her chest.

Bolo leaned against the doorframe, his hands still on his weapons. "How useful is she?"

"Very," Tobias growled from behind him.

Bolo jerked forward, revealing Tobias standing in the doorway. For a second Bolo's menace vanished, exposing a young, cocky drake playing a part. Compared to Tobias and Regis, every other drake in the room was a hatchling, and Tobias right now was the top predator. If she could see power and danger as a physical force, it would have been radiating off Tobias in giant, ferocious waves.

He shouldered past Bolo, dropped into a formal bow at Regis's feet then stood — not waiting for permission to stand. "Consider the change in reporting done." Tobias glanced at Ivy. "What did the room tell you?"

She swallowed, trying to get her throat — let alone the rest of her muscles — to loosen enough to speak. "It was a single female black drake, not ancient, but not too young, who ransacked the room."

Tobias nodded as if he was satisfied with her single-sentence answer — which, according to the memories in the locket, wasn't like him at all. He wanted details, every little one she had. Reports lasted an hour with him pressing, asking and re-asking, to squeeze out everything she saw even if she didn't fully understand it.

"A black drake? That's it?" Regis huffed. He leaned over the chair's arm toward her, his face ugly with fury. "You need to be more specific than that."

Ivy shrank back, fear and disgust at herself churning within her. She was a drake. She was stronger than this. And yet he held her life in his hands. He could do whatever he wanted to her, and she wouldn't be able to stop him. "I don't know her name."

Bolo snorted. "You'd be better at your job if you left your suite."

"Her position in the chamberlain's office is only one part of our investigative services," Tobias said.

Bolo huffed.

"She never knows the drakes and yet my agents find them." Tobias glared at the orange drake, and he shifted back. "Every time."

"Yes, yes." Regis brushed nonexistent lint from his doublet, feigning boredom, but his rage still boiled in his eyes. "You can't name the drake. What was she after? What did she take?"

Ivy glanced at Tobias, unable to stop herself. Her locket told her Regis might be the prince, but Tobias was her boss.

Regis growled.

Her heart skipped a beat. "I don't know what she was after. She pulled every book off the shelf and looked in many of them. Then she searched the Handmaiden's desk and took a small scroll."

"What was on the scroll?"

"I don't know."

Regis jerked to his feet and hissed at her.

She wrenched back, lost her balance, and tumbled onto her butt.

Her pulse roared and every muscle tensed, the need to flee — as well as the need to fight even though she didn't know how — screaming through her.

"What's on the scroll?"

"The room only tells me what it remembers. The scroll had been in a box. If the scroll had been put in the box then brought into the room, it wouldn't know what was on it."

Regis glared at Tobias. "What's on the scroll?"

"I don't know."

"Well, find out." Regis stormed from the room, with Bolo and the guards following.

Tobias growled, and Ivy's pulse jumped again. His attention flew to her, and rage at her situation, at being trapped, and at Tobias for tricking her all those years ago, flashed through her. Followed by frozen panic.

With Regis wanting direct reports, and creepy Bolo knowing she never left her suite except for an assignment, escaping now seemed even harder than before.

7

"The black drake took a scroll," Tobias said, his voice harsh, tightening Ivy's nerves until she was sure she'd shatter.

"Yes." Her voice came out a whisper.

Tobias blinked as if he hadn't really seen her then ran his hands through his wild locks and rolled his shoulders back.

"I really don't know what's on the scroll," she said.

"Neither do I. And with the Handmaiden gone, the only other drake who would most likely know just had a fight with some Court guards and now I have to issue an official warrant for his arrest."

"Grey?" Something within Ivy stuttered, but she wasn't sure what, only that she'd mentally or emotionally gasped and couldn't explain why. "Is he all right?"

"He gated out of Court before anyone could ask any questions." Tobias frowned. "Why so curious? You've never been curious about anyone else before."

"All that memory clinging to him," Ophelia said from the doorway.

Ivy's pulse picked up. *Think about Grey and— and his memories— Don't think about—*

She stopped herself before she could think about her yearning to escape and have Ophelia's magic to read minds pick up on anything.

"He's an ancient drake," Ophelia said. "I'm sure to Ivy his stuff is as bright as the sun at high noon on a cloudless day."

Tobias cocked an eyebrow. "I'm almost as old as he is. So is Regis."

Ophelia matched Tobias's brow. "So imagine how hard it is for Ivy to hold her earth magic back when you're around."

Tobias pursed his lips, his gaze locked with Ophelia's. Something passed between them, but Ivy wasn't sure what. An unsaid understanding, maybe? Shared secrets that one of them held over the other?

Ophelia's lip curled back, revealing a hint of teeth. Those and the whites of her eyes were the only things on her — among her dark hair, eyes, skin, and pantsuit — that were pale. Then her gaze dipped, giving Tobias dominance between them — although Ivy wasn't certain any more if he was the dominant drake.

"Ivy has an identity on the culprit." Tobias reached for his hair again, but stopped and crossed his arms tight against his broad chest instead. "Let's get that. Then, Ivy, I need you to remember how to make a gate."

"Make a gate?" Those words didn't make sense. Gates were used to travel. They implied she was leaving Court, but she'd never left Court before. She barely left her suite.

"I have to assume the scroll isn't the only thing the drake was after. I need you to go to the Handmaiden's private residence and check for evidence our culprit was there." Tobias glanced past Ophelia into the hall. "That, and it would be best if you were out of Regis's sight for a while."

Those words made even less sense. She belonged to Regis. Tobias had made that clear—

Except Ivy didn't know if that was what he'd said or not, only that it was imprinted in her locket.

"You're too valuable to lose on an accidental slip of his temper," Tobias said. "Ophelia?"

"I'll get her situated, get the culprit's I.D., and update you in twenty." Ophelia grabbed Ivy's arm and tugged her to her feet. "Come on."

Tobias tapped his temple, indicating Ophelia's ability to read minds. "You got the gate location to the Handmaiden's residence?"

"I'm insulted you feel you have to ask." Ophelia guided Ivy into the hall.

Tobias sighed. "It's been a tough day."

"On top of a lot of other tough days, I know." Ophelia said her power word, summoned a gate against the wall opposite the door, and pulled Ivy through.

The world went black, the familiar dark woolly air of Ophelia's gate muffling Ivy's senses, then her foot hit solid floor and they stepped into their living room.

Ophelia headed to the bookcase behind the beige overstuffed couch and shoved the large piece of furniture aside, revealing a safe hidden on the bottom shelf. Ivy couldn't stop staring at her, her thoughts whirling. Was Tobias actually trying to protect her from Regis? Did the Handmaiden actually have a second, private residence?

"Yes, he is. You're a valuable member of his team."

And by *member* she meant tool.

"Don't you forget that," Ophelia said without looking up from entering the code for the safe. "And yes, according to Tobias, the Handmaiden does have a private residence outside of Court. We've been prepared for the chance you'll have to leave Court on assignment for years now. We know you can create a gate at a gate anchor, which is good because there's too much happening here for me to go with you."

"I can create a gate?" She brushed her locket. Sure enough, imprinted there was the memory of being with Ophelia and learning a second power word to create a gate at Court's anchor gate, which connected to another gate anchor somewhere in the human world. So, too, was the feeling that if she ever did that without permission, she'd be hunted down and brought back to Court... or worse.

Ophelia opened the heavy safe door and drew out a small blue booklet, a beige leather wallet, and a black purse big enough to hold the wallet and other necessities and with a strap long enough to sling across her chest. "This is your passport and credit card. You're an American citizen and you live in Newgate."

Only half of Ophelia's words made sense. She didn't know what a passport was or an American citizen. She'd never come across any of that while living in Court. Newgate, however, was the human city most drakes, particularly the younger and weaker ones, talked about.

"I should have told Tobias an hour instead of twenty minutes."

Ophelia pinched the bridge of her nose. "Grab your locket and don't forget this. Don't ever forget this." She glared at Ivy. "For you, leaving Court *is* dangerous. If you lose that locket, you lose everything. Even if I'm around, the memories of you on my ring and watch can restore some of your memories but they won't be able to restore everything. Only our moments together. You'll lose all memories of Tobias and of your time in Court." The muscles in her jaw tightened. "You'll lose all memories of Regis, and that could get you killed. He doesn't know you can't remember, only that you can read memories from rooms."

Ivy shivered. Mother of All, she felt she was always going to be afraid.

A new, horrible thought flashed into her mind. If she lost her locket, did she also lose her power word?

"I hope not," Ophelia said. "For years we worked on finding your earth magic and the power words to activate it. There are times when I sense the power word is instinctual, but I'm not sure. No one else is in your... situation. I don't know what will happen if you forget it. I might have been able to convince Tobias it's safer for you to work outside of Court for the next while, but he's still sworn to the prince's service and there's more than just someone ransacking the Handmaiden's chambers going on. Now, pay attention."

Ivy focused on Ophelia past her whirling thoughts and fought not to think about how terrifying — or how hopeful — leaving Court made her feel. This was a chance to escape. It was also a chance that could kill her.

TOBIAS LEANED AGAINST THE FRACTURED ALTAR IN THE REBIRTH chamber. The cleanup of the debris and ash from the attack a few weeks ago had finally been finished. All that remained was the fissure slicing through the massive granite slab in the center of the room and the chips and cracks in the dragons sculpted around the pillars ringing the chamber and along the ceiling. Even without a century's worth of dust, the place felt more like an abandoned temple than the living — albeit struggling — heart of dragon society.

And while the metaphorical heart of his people was struggling, his burned with rage. He didn't know if Regis was responsible for ransacking the Handmaiden's private chambers but because of his rule, he'd set up the environment where some drake thought it was a good idea.

Her private quarters!

He couldn't get the thought out of his head. Their goddess was dead. The Handmaiden was the closest drake they had to a sacred presence. Just because she was gone didn't mean anyone had permission to desecrate her things. Even if she wasn't next-to-sacred, it didn't give them permission.

"But drakes are desperate," Ophelia said from the shadows beyond the pillars in front of him.

Tobias straightened, reached to run his hands through his hair, but managed to stop before completing the move. He'd already God damn broken himself of that habit. "You're late."

"Ivy had questions." Ophelia eased from the shadows.

"I bet." When Regis had learned of Ivy's magical ability, he'd made it clear to Tobias she was to remain in the Royal Coterie's employ — and Tobias still had no idea how the prince had known about her.

"Someone told him," Ophelia said — as she'd said before when the conversation had come up. "No, I don't know who, and we've got bigger problems than how we have to keep lying to Ivy to ensure her safety."

"Yeah, like a drake ransacking the Handmaiden's private chambers. Any whispers about what they might have been looking for?"

"No, but given the state of things, I doubt it's good." She pinched the bridge of her nose — a sign she was struggling to concentrate past the constant noise of other peoples' thoughts in her head. "So far no one's figured out Regis is succumbing to soul sickness. He has more sane moments than not. But that's not going to last."

"Have you confirmed Constantine is missing? Did Regis kill him?" If Regis had killed his father, that could be grounds to dethrone him. Of course, there still weren't any good options to replace him. With Regis and Constantine the only gold drakes who'd survived the Great Scourge, there weren't any other direct descendents of the royal line.

"Unless you look past Constantine's line. He defeated the Zhongguo dragon empress before the Scourge, joining the two great dragon clans." Ophelia brushed a hand over the foot of the dragon carved into the pillar beside her. "The other option is to go with a new Royal Coterie. Hunter hasn't even raised a banner and drakes are talking about flocking to it."

"You know better than I that Hunter will never take the throne."

"He'd never take it willingly."

"You'd honestly force the throne on someone who doesn't want it?"

"Better than those who do," Ophelia said.

"Do you have any names? Who'd follow Hunter's banner?" Although if Ophelia told him, he'd be obligated to issue a warrant for those drakes' arrests and report his information to Regis. Sometimes Tobias had mixed feelings about that. On one hand, he'd been the Royal Coterie's chamberlain for hundreds of years. On the other hand, with the Handmaiden gone, rebirth as a method of punishment was off the table, and the alternatives made his stomach churn.

"I have nothing certain. Everyone has unsettled thoughts about Regis. You included. I can confirm that Constantine is gone. I slipped into his suite during the last guard change. It's empty." Ophelia pursed her lips. "I can only offer an educated guess that Regis didn't dispose of him. In what I think are his sane moments, he's worried about where Constantine is."

"Which would imply Regis didn't kill his father and had nothing to do with his disappearance."

"I've also gotten nothing about what happened to Constantine from anyone on the Counseling Coteries."

"So they weren't involved." A growl curled in Tobias's throat. "So what the hell happened to him?"

"And is that the question we want to be worrying about? Regis's sane moments are getting fewer and farther between and someone going through the Handmaiden's chambers has made him more paranoid."

Tobias snorted. "Is it paranoia if someone really is after you?"

Ophelia rolled her eyes. "If Ivy doesn't come up with something, he'll have her arrested."

"Only if he can get his hands on her."

"We both know that's a terrible plan. If you keep her out of Court for too long, he'll arrest you."

"I'm hoping it won't come to that." Except he didn't know how to avoid any of that. If Ivy did come through, someone else would jeopardize Tobias's safety. Every day, more of him wondered if Hunter had had the right idea by leaving, but then Regis would have Tobias's hoard — all his glorious piles of paper — and there wouldn't be anyone to protect those special drakes employed by the Royal Coterie, like Ivy or Capri or Ophelia.

"I'm perfectly capable of taking care of myself."

The growl broke free. None of this would be an issue if the Handmaiden hadn't left.

Except that wasn't what made him so frustrated.

She hadn't told him she was going. But that wasn't it, either. It hurt to think she hadn't trusted him, or that she hadn't cared to mention she was leaving, or both. He'd thought — imagined? wanted? — that there was something between them, that all the time they'd spent together had meant something.

"I'm sure it did," Ophelia said.

"But you don't know, because she's the only drake whose thoughts you can't read."

"Yes. But she didn't tell Grey, either. He only figured it out a few hours beforehand because he noticed she was wearing shoes."

"She never wears shoes." Unless she was leaving Court. The vise grip in his chest tightened even more.

Shit. Pull it together. There were more important things to worry about than hurt feelings.

"Okay." He ran his hands through his hair, too tired to fight the bad habit. "Ivy has her assignment. We've got until tonight to meet her at the rendezvous spot, so the mess with the Handmaiden's chambers is as taken care of as it can be until we have more information."

"I'm still working on finding the leak in the Asar Nergal," Ophelia said. "I'm off to talk with Nero once we're done."

"If you so happen to see Grey, find out what he knows about this scroll. I don't want to be caught unaware if whatever is on it is powerful enough to make another drake think a coup is a good idea."

"If Regis keeps up with what he's doing, there will be another regardless."

"I'm trying not to think about that." *Keep Court together and keep as many drakes as possible alive until the Handmaiden returns... if she returns.*

The vise in his chest tightened even more. Mother of All, that couldn't happen. Too many drakes depended on her. And maybe she'd just gotten fed up with all of them. Including him.

8

Thick darkness surrounded Constantine. An inky suffocating miasma, it pressed around him, binding him tight in an eternal nothingness without beginning or end. He didn't know how long he'd been there. A part of him thought he'd been asleep for a long time before the darkness. Another part didn't think that was right but wasn't sure how or why, while a bigger part screamed with desperate angry howling.

The screaming grew louder, and his pulse pounded faster. Agonizing flashes of searing lightning, cutting through his soul, exploded within him, consuming the miasma. Between one rapid thud of his heart and the next, the darkness vanished. All thought vanished.

He roared and wrenched against invisible bonds. His breath came in desperate pants, and he writhed against slices into his flesh that he couldn't defend against. He couldn't see the attacker, couldn't tell when the next strike would come. There was only screaming and pain and a small whisper deep within his soul, crying for sleep, for the darkness, for anything to stop it.

Just end it. End him.

No.

Please. But he knew his pleas wouldn't be answered. They never had before. He was agony and energy, trapped in a never-ending cycle. There always would be pain, as there always had been. And he deserved it. He didn't know how or why, but core-deep he knew he did.

"I failed," he gasped, the thought jumping to the forefront of his mind. Yes, that was what had happened. He'd failed those closest to him, those dearest. He'd let selfishness... or ambition... Mother of All! He had to remember, had to know why he deserved this.

You don't, the agony whispered. *You didn't know. No one knew, and you paid the price.*

"I don't understand."

Darkness shuddered around the edges of the lightning, promising relief, blissful nothingness. He mentally grabbed for it, but the lightning flashed. Panic shot through him, and he yanked himself back, drawing into a tight ball in a desperate, ineffective attempt to ward off another strike. It sliced into him, tearing his soul, blinding him with searing white and devouring the promise of cool darkness. Just as he deserved.

No. A face materialized from the light, with a long black snout and piercing black eyes. Everything about the drake was darkness, except it — *She* — wasn't darkness. She was salvation and kindness, ferocity and power. She was the Mother of All Dragonkind, the goddess who'd sacrificed Her essence to power the spell that had saved Her dragons' spirits.

Her darkness billowed, sweeping out from Her eyes, devouring the blazing lightning and muffling it again with the soothing miasma.

You fell, She said.

"From the heavens. We all fell."

No, your soul fell, and I didn't have the courage to save you.

The Mother of All had more courage than any drake imaginable. She'd made the greatest sacrifice of all.

A pinprick of white light bled through the darkness, and Constantine shrank back, but instead of searing agony, a human woman with the aura of an ancient silver drake appeared.

"I feared if I rebirthed your soul, elder drakes would take advantage of you and convince you to avenge Regis's usurpation of your throne."

"I was soul sick. Regis had an obligation to take it." The truth flashed into his thoughts. No one had known how dangerous it was for drakes to change vessels, until it was too late. It had been too late for him. Regis had been his heir. He'd been well trained. Constantine hadn't been in a position to abdicate and Regis had made the right call.

"But now his fear of the Great Scourge, of human mages, is consuming him," the woman— the Handmaiden said.

"We must protect ourselves."

"Only from evil." The Handmaiden cupped his cheeks and her pale gaze locked onto his soul, freezing it in place. "We were predators but we were never evil. We kill to survive. Never without cause."

"But those humans who cast the Scourge—"

"—were a small few among many human mages and sorcerers. Humans, just like drakes, are good and bad." The Handmaiden's eyes filled with fear. "And the bad is coming."

———

THE GATE CLOSEST TO THE HANDMAIDEN'S PRIVATE RESIDENCE — opened by Ophelia because she had a sense for the location — dumped Ivy on a dark cliff's edge with snow halfway up her calves. Freezing wind howled, biting her face and hands, slicing through her too-thin shirt and jeans.

If she'd known she was going to end up on a mountainside, she would have worn warmer clothes. Not that the cold would kill her, but it was still uncomfortable. Although not nearly as uncomfortable as the ache in her soul. Reading the memories of the Handmaiden's chambers at Court had eased it, but that use of her power had been short, not long enough for any kind of enduring relief, and now the ache had returned, a reminder that she was missing key elements of herself. That she was irrevocably broken.

She fought to control those thoughts and concentrate on the job at hand — and no way was she going to think about how even just a brush of Grey's memory fire had made her feel.

Above her only pinpricks of stars and a sliver of moon lit up the night sky, while a few feet away, the cliff's edge ended in a sheer drop into nothing. Not a trip she'd like to take. The fall, like the cold, also wouldn't kill her — the only way to kill a drake was decapitation —

but she still didn't want the agony of experiencing and then healing from that kind of drop.

Her phone rang. It had to be decked out with satellite capabilities which meant there was nowhere Tobias couldn't reach her.

She pulled it from her purse. "Hello?"

"Don't step too far forward," Tobias growled. "You're in the heart of the Himalayas and without the ability to free gate, it'll take you days to hike back to civilization."

"Oh, I'll just climb back up the rock face."

Tobias snorted. "Are you seeing that same fall I did? Or has something changed in five hundred years since I was last there?"

"I'm sure something has changed. And no, I'm not seeing anything. It's the middle of the night." Not to mention freezing, and while she was wearing winter boots, they weren't sturdy enough to be hiking in a mountain range.

"Right. Time difference. Well, trust me. It's not a fall you want to make or a climb you'd be able to do. Not without the magic ability to control stone."

"Got it. And I got clear instructions from Ophelia back at Court." Which made her wonder why he was calling. Had Ophelia told him about her wanting to escape? She'd tried to keep that thought from her mind while the other drake had been giving her instructions, but something might have slipped out. Definitely the shock of being shoved out of Court had shaken her mental resolve.

She still couldn't quite get her mind around it. There wasn't a memory in the locket indicating this had ever happened before — and she was certain this was something she'd make sure she never forgot. And did it mean she could trust Ophelia or Tobias? She wasn't sure she fully believed the explanation about why they let her continue thinking she was trapped at Court. Yes, the human world wasn't safe for her. There was more risk of losing her locket here than the relative safety at Court. But to make her think she belonged to Regis—

Except going into the human world didn't make her any less Regis's servant.

"If you can't get to a gate to be at the office tower in Newgate by ten tonight, I expect you to call in."

She pressed her palm against the front of her jacket, capturing her locket between her clothes and her chest.

If she lost it, she'd be lost. Everything she knew about herself, about her experiences, would be gone. She'd have to start all over again.

"You got that?" Tobias asked.

Of course, if she forgot, she wouldn't know she was trapped. Maybe that would be a good thing. "I got that."

But in fifty years or so — more if she was really lucky — she'd be in the same spot: knowing she was a prisoner, too useful to be free.

No, she needed to figure out how to escape. She'd have to cut ties with Ophelia, but the black drake had admitted lying to her. No doubt she was telling Tobias all of Ivy's private thoughts, even though Ivy wasn't allowed to read Ophelia's memories to remind her of their friendship.

The ever-present knot in Ivy's gut snapped tight. What if they didn't have a friendship? Yes, they shared a suite — because Ivy had read the memories of the room — and yes, from that it looked like they had a friendship. But what if it was one big lie?

"You've imprinted into your locket that the gate for the office tower smells like lilacs and sounds like wind chimes," Tobias said, his voice gravel across the connection.

Ivy wrenched her attention back to him. "Ophelia played a recording of the chimes and made me smell fresh lilacs." Except she had no idea if she could gate to Tobias's office tower anchor. Save for knowing she'd made a gate before, there was nothing in her locket about how she'd actually done it.

"Good. Confirm the culprit was or wasn't there. Nothing else."

"Yes." The knot in Ivy's gut tightened even more. "Confirmation only."

"You have nine hours, but I expect you at the office tower a lot sooner."

So she really didn't have nine hours. Escape was her only option. She was out of Court now, with permission — something she'd never thought would ever happen. There was no way in hell she was going back.

Which meant the sooner she read the Handmaiden's front room, the more time she'd have to figure something out — since she wasn't going to risk having to return to Tobias without an escape plan or with an incomplete assignment.

She turned away from the cliff's edge to a passage in the sheer rock wall behind her, a wide black slash in the dark gray and shimmering ice. Ophelia had said the door to the Handmaiden's private residence lay in a clearing on the other side. She'd also said there was a gatelock spell in the area, so even if Ivy could gate without an anchor, this was as close as she'd be able to get.

Ophelia hadn't said much else about the residence and Ivy got the sense — she wasn't quite sure how — that her friend hadn't actually been there and her information came from someone else — probably Tobias.

Ivy turned on her phone's flashlight app to better see around her. She'd been told not many drakes knew about this private residence, so she doubted anyone visited. Which meant footprints would be a good first indication that someone else had been there.

She shone the light on the snow around her legs. Nothing.

The knot in her gut eased.

This was good. She'd get inside, out of the biting wind, confirm no one had been there, and then she had hours to figure out her next move. She could do this. She didn't know how or where to get information or learn anything about Regis and Court, but that was the first step. She could lie and say the reading took longer than she'd expected and not go to the office tower in time. Maybe the Handmaiden would have something in her residence that could help. In the very least, a map of anchors so she could gate someplace warmer.

She hugged herself, but that did little to stop her shivering. Moving was the only way to get warm. Teeth chattering, she trudged through the calf-deep snow into the passage. Sheltered from the wind, it was only marginally warmer, and with a sliver of paler darkness ahead, it wouldn't last long. The walls and floor were smooth like the halls at Court, the stone carved by powerful magic, and only wisps of snow gathered at the edges as if when the wind blew in the right direction to fill the passage with snow, it blew with too much force. There was only a hint of memory licking over its surface, as if not much — and no strong emotions — had ever been there.

Beyond stood a thigh-high snowdrift and a clearing... more like a courtyard. The cliffs towering all around were magically smooth, and snow and ice had been shaped into a frozen garden with trees and bushes, flowers and benches. All without color, all meticulously carved with fine details, as if a real garden had been flash-frozen into ice and transported into this mountainous middle-of-nowhere.

Ivy shoved through the snowdrift into calf-high snow, pressed her locket to her chest, and concentrated. No way was she forgetting something like this. It stole her breath and made her ache. She was missing so much trapped at Court: real gardens, vast landscapes, places filled with years and years of memories. Certainly more memories than this place. The weakness of the fire around her suggested no one had been this way for years, maybe even centuries.

At the back of the garden stood a gray door, only a few shades paler than the rock around it. It was the only door. There weren't any signs of any other places to go, so Ivy trudged to it and grasped the latch.

Lightning shot into her hand with a painful snap and she dropped her phone. It, with its light, disappeared into the snow, and pain radiated from her palm up her arm and into her chest.

Crap. Stupid drake.

She shoved her hand into the snow and grabbed the phone, hoping the cold would numb the pain. She should have known the Handmaiden would have a lock on her door. Doors at Court had locks. It made sense doors out of Court would have them, too.

Which decreased the odds of that black drake coming here and ransacking the place. To do due diligence, though, she should still read the memories on the door, although the memory fire on the handle had been pretty weak before she'd touched it. Now the fire flared a little stronger, indicating her shock had been imprinted onto it.

And really, she didn't have to read anything. She could just leave and get on with figuring out her escape plan.

No, if she had to face Tobias and Ophelia again, she wanted it clear in her thoughts that she had done her job.

She turned off her flashlight app and shoved her phone into her purse. Her power word flashed into her mind, and she drew breath to say it when something *shushed* behind her. The sound wasn't loud, but every instinct she had said it was more than just the wind.

Her gaze jumped to the passage, but without night sight, all she could make out was its dark slash in the slightly paler gray cliffs.

The *shush* came again. No, more than one *shush*, the rhythm steady and drawing closer.

Someone was coming. It had to be the black drake.

Maybe Ivy could buy her freedom by apprehending that drake. Except she didn't know if she had any combat skills. There weren't any memories of that in her locket, so she had to assume no. Her best bet was to hide and follow. If she could tell Tobias where the black drake was, maybe she could use that as a bargaining chip.

She scrambled to a large ice-bush near the gray door and held her breath. Then realized her footprints led straight to her hiding spot.

9

G rey tightened his grip on the hilt of his short sword and wished he'd brought his broadsword instead. But the larger weapon was harder to hide, even with a winter coat that came down to mid-thigh, and he didn't want to risk needing to gate back to Nero's to switch weapons if he had to go some place populated. With the world writhing around him, murky with memories that were getting harder and harder to shake, he couldn't afford for his gate to slip and send him to the gateroom in Court. Not after his run-in with those Court guards. Whether Tobias wanted to or not, he'd have to issue a writ for Grey's arrest or risk Regis's ire. And Grey doubted he'd risk Regis's ire. Not for Grey.

He reached the opening to the Handmaiden's ice garden and felt the tingling magic of her gatelock as the hair on his arms prickled. Still powerful, just like the locks around her chambers at Court. No one was getting out of here without getting at least halfway into this tunnel first.

Beyond, in the ice garden, the footsteps of whoever had arrived before him plowed through the snowbank and left a path straight to the gray door on the far side.

Impossible sunlight sparkled off the frozen topiaries, and the Handmaiden stood in front of the door, holding it open, a brilliant white aura blazing around her.

Grey's heart skipped a beat. She was here. She was waiting for him—

But that didn't make sense. It was night right now. Not noon.

He blinked. The sunlight vanished, and the wind gusted, biting his cheeks and slipping down the neck of his coat. A shiver swept through him and the dark memory fog billowed, consuming the edges of his vision. He blinked again, fighting to keep in the present, and focused on the footprints in the snow. Those were new, not part of a memory. Those meant danger. Whoever had ransacked the Handmaiden's chambers at Court was already there and had the power words to get past the magical lock on the door.

Grey's only advantage was the element of surprise. The culprit didn't know he'd been followed, and Grey could catch him unaware.

He shoved through the snowbank and kept to the path already created. The strides weren't as far apart as Grey would have taken, and the footprints were smaller than his, which told him the culprit was shorter.

Good. That gave him the advantage of reach. There also weren't many drakes left alive who had his combat experience.

That didn't mean they couldn't be better than him in a fight, but he had over two thousand years of dirty tricks to draw on, which gave him another advantage. Hopefully, that would be enough to subdue someone long enough for him to restrain whoever it was, since killing was a last resort. Too many dragon souls had been lost to the universal ether already. He might not be a fast healer, but with his experience, he didn't necessarily have to be.

Sunlight flickered again. He ground his teeth, forcing all his attention to the path. It led right to the door, and there wasn't the telltale swoosh through the snow indicating the door had been opened. In fact, there were three footsteps to the side—

He jerked toward the frozen shrub, and the drake from the Handmaiden's chamber, Tobias's agent, roared and lunged at him.

She swiped at him with hands held like claws. He shifted, letting her rush by, rammed his free hand into her back, and slammed her against the rock face beside the door. Before she could regain her balance, he pinned her in place and pressed the edge of his sword against her neck.

A shiver raced up his arm. The billowing darkness, the constant threat against the here-and-now, vanished and calm flooded in. Everything stood in crisp detail, the bite of cold on his cheeks and hands and his breath puffing around his head.

Her breath, frozen wisps — as if she were a real drake with a fiery breath — curled along her jaw, over her ear, and slipped past her dark hair. It framed her delicate face, caught in profile as she struggled to glare at him while pinned front-first to the rock. Beneath his arm and her clothes — too thin this high up in the mountains without giving her away as a drake — he could feel her body, taut and ready to strike again at her first opportunity.

She blinked, drawing his attention to her large dark eye, filled with rage and determination, and the all-consuming stillness from before. His heart thudded, slow, strong, sure as if just being close to her centered his soul back within his stolen human vessel. This was right, a completion to something he hadn't known was incomplete. He could stay this way forever with no past, no future, just pure, clean present.

The urge to draw closer, be fully within her aura of calm, clawed in his chest. She was his salvation, his way free of his two-thousand-year nightmare. With her, he wouldn't need the Handmaiden to keep sending soothing magic into his mind. If the Handmaiden didn't return, he wouldn't have to beg Anaea for help and reveal just how pathetic a drake he was.

The woman blinked again, making the calm within Grey shudder as if her gaze was the link, the anchor, to his inner stillness.

His focus sharpened even more. The cold bit his hands and cheeks with a gloriously crisp sting, the ice sculpture reflected the night sky, pinpricks of stars captured in a crystalline moment, and the drake under his arm trembled.

Another blink, a mere few quick pounds of his heart between first capturing her and now, and the ferocity in her gaze bled into fear.

His heart skipped a beat, and the clarity froze in horrific reality. She feared him.

He jerked back. What the hell was he thinking? It didn't matter that she could somehow strip his consuming memories with just her presence. He couldn't keep her like the movies in his hoard. She was a drake. A living, breathing person. And one who belonged to the Royal Coterie. She was Tobias's agent.

Shit.

Shit shit shit.

"What are you doing here?" he growled, even though the logical explanation was that Tobias had sent her.

"The chamberlain told me to follow up." She wrenched around and faced him. A shiver shuddered through her, and she wrapped her arms tight across her chest. "But the door is locked so I'll be on my way."

"Fine." Common sense told him to step back, let her leave, but he couldn't turn the thought into action and stayed, as frozen as the garden around them, too close, trapping her against the rock wall.

Another shiver slid over her and the muscles in her jaw clenched. She didn't want to be near him. She feared him. Why couldn't he just step away?

But he knew why. If she left, if she just stepped out of range, the gloom of too many memories would come flooding back. This calm, this crystalline clarity, would vanish, and the resonance of his soul, the core part of himself that he hadn't realized had been off kilter, would return to its trembling uncertainty.

"Tobias needs a report," she said, her voice wavering and her breath trembling between them—

With fear. Of him. Not anything else.

"Right." He wrenched back. Murky memory crackled at the edge of his vision, filled with ghostly screams and sobs. He forced himself still, fighting the urge to return to her aura of calm. She was Tobias's agent. A member of the Royal Coterie.

Jeez. For a drake who couldn't forget, he was having a hard time keeping those details in mind.

Something clicked.

He ground his teeth, determined to stay in the present. She might be afraid of him, but that didn't mean she wouldn't try to attack him again.

Except another click came. She jumped and her attention jerked to the door as it opened. In present time.

Someone was leaving the Handmaiden's private residence, and

while Grey could hope it was Hunter or the Handmaiden, he had a terrible suspicion it was whoever had ransacked the Handmaiden's chamber at Court.

Grey swept his sword toward the door and shifted his stance as Jet emerged, stepping into the entrance. A black drake in a lithe East Indian body dressed head to toe in black, she was the last person he would have expected to see caught up in dragon politics. She was young by Grey's standards, only 450 years old — although much older than Tobias's agent — and last time he'd checked, Jet had disavowed all things dragon. Of course, that had been before 1946 and Grey's self-imposed exile from the human realm. A lot could have changed in those few years... a lot *had* changed within the last month.

Jet's large dark eyes widened for a heartbeat, the mere second it took for her to process that Grey had found her and was armed, then her hand on the door tightened and the other dropped to the hilt of the curved saber at her hip.

Ivy squeaked, her reaction a split-second behind Jet's, and Grey lunged forward, jabbing at the black drake's chest.

Jet yanked the door against Grey's sword, parrying the strike, and he wedged his shoulder against the gray wood and stone frame before she could lock him out. Not that there was anywhere for Jet to go. There was only one entrance to the Handmaiden's private residence, and with the magical gatelock on the area, Jet wouldn't be able to free gate and escape. Except losing her now would make finding her in the maze inside the mountain that much more difficult. Not to mention, if he lost sight of her, she could use her earth magic to camouflage herself and be even harder to find.

He shoved the door aside, keeping his gaze locked on her. Fog billowed at the edge of his vision, and he fought to stay in the present. She could still use her magic to hide, but if he could stay focused on her when it took effect, it would make it easier to see the telltale shimmer of her power enveloping her when she moved.

With a growl, Jet drew her saber and slashed at Grey, the movement fluid from centuries of experience. About three hundred years ago, Jet had become a mercenary. Last he'd heard, she'd become a bounty hunter working solely in the human world.

Grey parried her attack and sidestepped, sliding past the doorframe and fully entering the Handmaiden's small fifteen-by-fifteen antechamber with its rack for coats, mat for boots, and eleventh-century settee for sitting.

Jet swept forward with a wide strike to Grey's ribs, an obvious attempt to force him another step from the door so she could make her escape. He stepped into the attack, catching her wrist- to-wrist, and shoved her to the settee. She leapt onto it then flipped sideways over the edge. She was fast and skilled, but he had size and strength on his side. If he was going to win, though, he had to use that. Now. Anything prolonged increased the risk she'd get in a lucky blow, and with his slow healing, he'd be dead. He had to finish her first.

Except if he killed her, he wouldn't know who had hired her or what she was trying to steal. And without a doubt, Jet wasn't acting alone. There was no way she just happened to know about the Hand-maiden's private residence.

He surged forward. If he wanted to subdue her, he needed to get hands on her and not let go.

How the hell had he managed to get into this mess again?

Jet swept her saber up. Grey slid his blade around and under her guard — a move better suited for a narrower sword, but he managed to make it work.

She twisted, and his blade slid against her ribs. With a hiss, she jerked around him and lunged for the door, where Tobias's agent stood. The young drake gasped and leapt back but wasn't going to be fast enough to get out of Jet's way.

Jet's saber slashed in a wicked arc toward Tobias's agent.

Grey's heart skipped a beat, and he dove at them. His shoulder slammed into Jet's back and he shoved her into the wall beside the door. She rammed her elbow into his ribs and knocked him back before he could gain his balance. Memory fog flooded his vision and he blinked, fighting to clear it.

He jabbed where he'd last seen her, but her saber materialized out of the gloom, batted his sword to the side, and her foot slammed into his chest, knocking him into Tobias's agent and in front of the exit. The fog vanished and the room snapped into crystal clarity. He could see every vein in the rock, the whorls of grain in the wooden coat rack, and the pills in the settee's fabric, indicating use.

Jet's gaze jumped over his shoulder to Tobias's agent. She flashed her teeth — a clear sign of aggression — and bolted across the antechamber. With a growl, she opened the ornamented glass and wrought iron door on the other side and raced into the maze of the Handmaiden's residence.

10

"Shit." Grey raced after Jet, but the sudden distance from Tobias's agent made memories shudder around him and blur his vision. He grabbed the knob of the ornamented glass door leading into the Handmaiden's residence. Maybe Jet hadn't had enough time to activate her earth magic and disappear.

And maybe he was a crazy drake too deep into this mess.

He wrenched the door open but didn't rush through.

The landing inside was empty. As expected. But no saber came slashing toward his head — which suggested the fight hadn't been the complete disaster he'd thought it had been and Jet was now wary of him.

Beyond lay a great hall, the main floor one story down and filled with a twisting maze of eight-foot tall bookcases, creating passages, nooks, and dead ends. A few feet away on either side stood wide spiral wrought iron staircases, leading down to the hall and up to the third- and fourth-story balconies. Lined with shelves packed with more books and knickknacks, the balconies curled along the edge of the great hall on both sides and disappeared into the darkness at the back.

"We have to catch up to her," Tobias's agent said.

"She could be anywhere. She can camouflage herself." Which meant all she had to do was wait for them to rush into the maze beyond then escape out the door. "We have to wait her out."

"You mean sit here and wait for her to try to get past us?" Her voice jumped in pitch.

Guess she didn't like the thought of waiting. Yeah, well, neither did he.

"That could take forever," she said.

"Yep." Grey studied shelves beside her, hoping for the telltale shimmer to give Jet away. If he trusted his memories not to overwhelm him, he'd summon his most recent memory of the Handmaiden's residence and look for anything that wasn't the same. His past experience with another drake who'd had camouflaging earth magic meant he knew it wasn't exact. There'd be discrepancies that, if he had time to concentrate, he could pick out. And if he were Jet, he'd stick close to the door. Of course, not close enough to be accidentally spotted by a cursory glance, but, hey, he could hope.

"I don't have forever," Tobias's agent said.

"No one says you have to stay." Even though everything within him screamed she should. If she left, there was a risk his memories would overwhelm him and Jet would get by or kill him.

And that was the only reason he wanted her to stay. Really.

Her attention jumped to the door behind her.

His heart skipped a beat.

Because her leaving meant memory problems for him.

Except that wasn't the entire truth. Yes, her presence righted his equilibrium and swept away the fog, but there was something else about her, something he couldn't explain but wanted to.

He ground his teeth and wrenched his thoughts to the mess at hand. Find Jet. Capture her and figure out who the hell was making a play for the dragon throne this time — because without a doubt ransacking the Handmaiden's chambers and invading her private residence was part of another drake's ambition to endanger the lives of more dragons.

Tobias's agent swore and her gaze jumped back to the great hall. "If I leave, I have no idea how I'm going to explain this to Tobias."

"Say you lost her."

"He'd never believe me."

"He's seen the great hall. He'd believe you."

Her expression darkened. "No, because I can tell you where she went." She hissed a word, too quiet for Grey to make it out, and her aura flared, a brilliant green.

The fog undulating at the edge of his vision vanished and the great hall snapped into sharp clarity, with no memories overlying his vision as if he were seeing the swirling wrought iron railing and the leather-bound books and everything else for the first time.

Tobias's agent's gaze jerked up and she gasped. "Halfway up the steps."

The crystal-clear railing shimmered — light reflecting in water — and Jet materialized. She swung over the railing and hurtled toward him, her saber raised to take his head—

No, the angle was wrong. She was after Tobias's agent.

Grey shoved Tobias's agent aside and swept his short sword up to block Jet's strike. The black drake's blade slid off his, and she twisted, bringing her saber around with a quick counter. Grey yanked his blade down but knew if he didn't jump out of the way, he wouldn't be fast enough to avoid getting cut.

He leapt back and Jet's blade sliced a mere breath past him. She was quick with her agile and powerful body. And Grey wasn't. He had strength and reach on her, but he couldn't risk her getting in a strike he couldn't quickly heal from. An aggressive, strong blitz attack was his best bet, except that technique was meant to kill, not capture. Shit.

She lunged in again. Grey sidestepped, letting her blade skim his coat — thankfully not slicing skin — and captured her sword arm and sword against his body. She wrenched against his grip, but he held tight and snapped her elbow. She'd heal soon enough but hopefully the pain would be sufficient distraction for him to gain full control of the fight.

With a howl, she reached into her black leather jacket, pulled out a modern handgun, like the ones carried by cops in the movies he had in his hoard, and shot him in the chest. Agony exploded through him, and fog flooded his vision. The bang roared around him, over and over again, caught in a sudden memory loop, and he fought to stay in the present. The next shot could be at his head, which would completely incapacitate him. He had to hold on, just a little bit longer.

He tightened his grip on her broken arm and slammed his fist into her face. She jerked back, but couldn't break free, and yanked the gun up to his face. He grabbed it. She heaved against his grip, but he twisted her hand and gun back, drawing another scream.

The gun clattered to the floor, and Jet rammed her fist into the wound in his chest. Lightning shot through him and his knees buckled. His grip on her arm loosened and she broke free. With a roar, she swept around with a wicked kick toward his head. He fought to bring his short sword up, but he couldn't concentrate past the agony and the inability to catch his breath.

Another gunshot roared around him and Jet staggered, her foot sweeping an inch from his face. Another bang, and Jet jerked, blood spurting from her neck.

Tobias's agent stood by the steps, the gun gripped in shaking hands. "I don't know if a bullet to the brain will kill a drake, but I'm willing to find out."

Jet growled and flashed her teeth.

Tobias's agent tensed and her hands stopped trembling, as if concentrating on the shot somehow gave her confidence. "I've shot twice and hit twice. Heart and neck. Wanna bet I won't make the headshot?"

Grey grabbed at the wall behind him to keep standing. He still held his sword, but all he could manage was to gasp for air. "We need her alive. Need—" Blood bubbled in his throat and he coughed.

Tobias's agent's gaze jumped to him, and Jet lunged toward her. She leapt out of the way, hit the railing behind her, and fired again. The shot slammed into Jet's shoulder. The black drake rammed into Tobias's agent and shoved her over the railing. Tobias's agent screamed and grabbed for the railing, dropping the gun to the great hall below.

Grey jerked toward them, but Jet kicked him in the head, knocked him to the ground, then bolted out the door. The great hall spun around him and darkness swept over and through him. The Handmaiden's musical laughter rang through the hall, followed by the roar of gunfire. All the while everything within him screamed to get up and help Tobias's agent. Mother of All, he didn't even know her name, but he couldn't let her fall. He had no idea if she was a slow healer like he was, but the fall would likely break something and then they'd be stuck there until at least one of them was healed enough to drag the other back to the gate anchor outside.

He fought to see past the darkness and the pain. Tobias's agent clutched the railing, her eyes wide and locked on him. No, on the floor beside him and the growing pool of his blood.

11

I vy clutched the railing, her heart pounding. He wasn't healing. Mother of All, he wasn't healing! Except he was a drake. The magic in his soul had to be healing his human body. But the blood staining the front of his light gray coat and pooling around him just kept growing, oozing from the wound in his chest, while his back heaved with desperate gurgling gasps. The memory fire around him — still impossibly engulfing him and not just radiating from a few items on his person — flared, consuming his dragon aura, and if he didn't impossibly glow like a miniature sun with at least centuries worth of memories, she would have thought him human.

He lifted his gaze to hers, his sharp blue eyes capturing her, and the fire around him snapped with a sudden, vicious flare, then dimmed.

Her pulse stuttered. She hadn't even read his memories — God, to read those memories, or even just feel the kiss of that fire again! But his fire shouldn't have dimmed, not without activating her magic. It shouldn't have—

Her grip slipped. Icy panic swept through her and she scrambled to regain her hold on the railing, the instinct to avoid falling stronger than her faith in her soul's magic to heal her.

Grey lunged for her, reached through the wrought iron railing, and seized her wrist in a crushing grip. Memory fire licked over her skin and down her arm, drawing a shiver. His expression twisted with pain, but he hauled her up until her fingers were tight around the top bar and her feet were on the edge of the balcony.

Panting, he released her, leaving her wrist cold, and clutched the railing as if that was the only thing holding him up. Blood shimmered over the entire front of his coat and oozed down his pant leg. Sweat beaded at his temples and his complexion was too pale, verging on an unhealthy gray. The fire of his memories shuddered around him but didn't fully manifest as it had before, and his piercing gaze never left hers.

Her pulse fluttered, but she couldn't tell if it was from adrenaline from the fight, the almost-fall, or something else, something to do with this man who, even in agony, had saved her.

"The fall wouldn't have killed me," she said, unable to tear her gaze from his, yearning for him to come closer and just let his fire brush against her.

"Neither will the gunshot." He frowned. "Unless you also plan on taking my head."

"Why would I do that?" Mother, why couldn't she look away?

"You work for Regis and I think I just made it onto his most wanted list."

"I work for Tobias." But Regis had made it clear that he owned her and now wanted face-to-face reports. Would he ask her to kill the Handmaiden's man? She doubted she'd be able to take Grey's head unless he was as injured as he was now, and after her pathetic attack on him in the ice garden, she knew she didn't have any fighting skills—

Although maybe that wasn't true. She'd shot that black drake, Jet, exactly where she'd intended, both times, and she hadn't had to think twice about grabbing the gun and firing as if she'd known how to use the weapon all along.

He gasped, his breath wet and painful. "Tobias works for the prince—"

"I'm not anyone's assassin." But would Regis change the nature of her assignments? A shudder swept through her. Nothing was safe. That was clearly imprinted in her locket. She fought to drag her attention away from Grey, to the wall beside his head, the blood — his blood — slicking the floor, anywhere but his eyes. "Killing you isn't my assignment, and if I don't go back until this is done, Tobias can't change it."

"So what *is* your assignment?" His eyes narrowed and his gaze intensified, as if he could see into her dragon soul through her human eyes.

"Find out if that black drake—"

"Jet. That's her name."

"Okay. Find out if Jet had been here and if she took anything."

"Yeah, because you're going to know what's missing." His attention jumped to the massive hall behind her, releasing her from his gaze. "I know you haven't been here before, so it's ridiculous to think you'd possibly know."

"Maybe I *was* here before." She shifted away from him and climbed over the railing onto the balcony, but couldn't bring herself to move farther than just out of reach. "Does the Handmaiden tell you everything?"

"No." The fire of his memories flared again. The flames pulled at her, tempting her to move closer, release her earth magic, and ease the ache in her soul. "But I have very little memory of you, and the Handmaiden has never mentioned you."

"And you remember everything," she said, unable to hide the sarcasm from her tone. "Now who's being ridiculous?"

He cocked an eyebrow and sudden realization snapped through her.

"Oh, my God, you *do* remember everything." That explained why the fire around him was so strong. It wasn't just that he was old — he might not even be as old as she first thought — but being able to remember everything meant all of his memories were fresh, strong, and ready to be recalled with a thought. She ached just thinking about how that would feel, how she could wake knowing who she was, what she'd done yesterday, and who her friends were. Mother, what she wouldn't give to have a fraction of that.

"So I know you've never been here. Wanna try your explanation again?"

Her power word started to unfurl within her throat, and she fought to keep it back.

"You also knew where Jet was hiding. So I'm going to bet it's connected to your earth magic and that magic isn't the ability to see the invisible." He staggered back to the ornamented glass and wrought iron door leading out of the Handmaiden's residence, dropped to one knee, and pressed a hand against the still-bleeding gunshot wound. His sword lay within reach but he didn't grab it, just kept staring at her as if waiting for her to talk or attack.

"I never really gave you an explanation in the first place," she said, trying to buy herself time to find any other option than fighting or talking. With his sword close by, even injured, she'd never win, but if she told him the truth, he could use her like Tobias did.

Except Tobias had said Grey was the Handmaiden's man. Everything about the Handmaiden in Ivy's locket said that while she was a mysterious sorcerer, she was kind and honorable. Would she accept someone's oath into her service if he wasn't the same? If Ivy asked, would Grey help her escape Court?

He had just said Regis wanted him dead. Clearly, he didn't have any love for the dragon prince.

Mother! She couldn't believe she was even considering it, and she had no idea what his answer would be.

"I'm not obligated to give you an explanation." But she *was* going to have to make a decision about him.

"You're not." He coughed, the sound still ragged and wet.

Everything within her stuttered again. "Why aren't you healing?" It hurt just looking at him, and she had no idea why. She'd just met this man. He'd said he didn't have a lot of memories of her, so there'd never been anything between them... unless he didn't recognize her aura and he'd meant something to her before she'd been reborn into this body. But even then, she wouldn't remember him. This feeling... this connection was impossible.

He coughed again, and every muscle clenched in agony. Even the fire of his memories flared, rigid and sharp, biting her senses.

She jerked a step toward him, unable to help herself, but froze when she realized what she was doing. "You should put more pressure on that. At least until it stops bleeding."

"I still need to know what your deal is."

But the more she thought about it, the more fearing she'd attack him didn't make sense. "If you're so worried about me trying to kill you, then why save me from falling off the balcony?"

"Because if your goal isn't to kill me when I'm down, then I'd appreciate help back to the gate so I can get back up and return to figure out what Jet was after. She has a head start and whatever her plan, it risks destabilizing Court more than it already is," he said. "If you broke your leg, we'd have to wait for one of us to heal enough to help the other. I don't know how fast you heal."

"Faster than that." At least, she thought she was. If she thought about it, she wasn't really sure.

He snorted. "Yeah, everyone is faster than this."

Which might explain why he'd sworn himself into the Handmaiden's service. If he was really as old as she thought, he should be holding a high rank in his coterie, possibly even be the doyen, but with that came challenges — usually deadly ones. As the Handmaiden's man, he didn't hold an envious position and was never in anyone's political way.

"So, what's it going to be? Tell me what your deal is and help me back to the gate?" He shrugged then gasped, and a tight moan escaped. "Or what?"

If she walked away, she'd have more time to come up with a plan to escape Court, but if she couldn't figure out something, she'd still have to report to Tobias. And just telling him Jet had been here but not knowing what she'd done would make him suspicious. If Ophelia was around, with her ability to read thoughts, she'd know Ivy had abandoned the assignment.

Crap.

She bit back a growl. The fastest way to do this was to tell Grey the truth. She might not be able to ask Grey for help, but not revealing her earth magic to him only wasted time she didn't have. It would be easier to hide her interaction with Grey from Ophelia if there wasn't any doubt about her fulfilling the assignment.

"I can tell what Jet took and what she did here because my earth magic reads the memories of things, like the room."

He frowned but she couldn't tell if that was because he didn't understand or if he was trying to figure out how to use her. "So you knew where she was hiding because—?"

"The room told me."

"Well, that's more useful than remembering every God damned little thing."

"Yeah," she said, her throat tightening. What she wouldn't give to remember *any* God damned little thing without needing to use her earth magic every morning.

"I know you have to report what you learn to Tobias, but would you be willing to share it with me?"

She stared at him, his words rushing through her. Did he just ask if she was willing to share? As if she had a choice in the matter?

"I don't think it'll create problems for you with Tobias. He asked me to look into this. But it could be an issue if Regis finds out."

No one had asked her if she was willing to help before. Not that she could remember.

His frown deepened. "You keep staring at me. I can't tell if that's a yes or a no."

Neither could she.

"So?"

"Yes, on one condition." The words leapt out before she realized what she was saying.

"I wouldn't expect anything less of a drake." A hint of a smile pulled at his lips. "What are your terms?"

Her brain froze. What were her terms? Was she really going to use him to help her leave Court? From his own confession, it didn't sound as if she'd be putting him in any more danger with Regis than he already was.

Mother of All, she was going to use him.

She gripped her locket, letting her desperation and hope fill her and willing this moment into it. She couldn't risk falling asleep and forgetting this... forgetting him. "A favor for a favor."

"Are you going to tell me what this favor is?"

"Not yet." She couldn't just ask him to help her escape. Even she knew enough about the dragon Court that what she wanted wasn't a fair trade and he'd figure that out the moment she asked for it. No, information about what Jet had done didn't equal all the work she was sure would be necessary to make her disappear. But if she could stick around him, learn more about the human world by surreptitiously reading his memories — something she wasn't sure she'd be able to do, but God, it was her only hope — then she'd be able to figure out what would be fair.

His gaze searched hers, sending shivers racing through her, and for a moment she wondered if he'd lied about his earth magic and if he really possessed the power to tell if she was lying.

Which she wasn't. *It would be fine.* She would find a way to use him instead of being the one who was used.

"Do we have a deal or not?" She couldn't believe she was being so forthright. She might be a drake, but she'd always been at a disadvantage before.

"I have one other condition."

The ice in her gut — the fear that constantly lived with her that she'd somehow forgotten while staring at this man — tightened. Hard. It reminded her of who and what she really was. A drake without a memory and helpless.

"What?" she asked, her voice small and her unable to make it stronger.

"You tell me your name." He held out a bloody hand, looked at it, then pulled it back. "I'm Grey."

The ice softened and the ache in her chest — she wasn't sure if it was for the yearning to read his memories or something else — throbbed. "I'm Ivy."

His gaze held hers for a heartbeat more, his eyes filled with a longing and pain. The same pain she'd seen in him before. The memory fire flared around him, and his attention slid past her to the massive hall behind her.

More fire danced around him as his memory gained strength. Every fiber of her being screamed to move closer, read whatever he was remembering. Perhaps if he was already thinking about it, he wouldn't notice if she read it. She'd just be an invisible hitch-hiker—

But if he noticed, he'd break their deal and she'd have no way to escape Court.

The fire burned brighter, drawing a groan from deep within her.

She hugged herself, trembling with the urge to inch forward.

His expression hardened. With a hiss, he jerked back and the memory fire vanished. His gaze sharpened again and snapped to hers.

"We're wasting time," he said, his tone sharp as he picked up his sword and wiped it clean on the edge of his coat. "What was Jet doing here?"

Right. The deal... and her assignment. She yanked her attention away from him, but the need to say her power word and read his memories didn't fade.

She drew in a breath. *Focus on the room. Concentrate.* She was going to use her magic. This residence was old. Surely, it had hundreds of memories and could ease her inner ache for a while. Except she didn't know how often the Handmaiden came here. Centuries of being empty wouldn't provide a satisfying read. Although it would make it easier to find the memory of Jet.

But she didn't want to read the room. She wanted to read Grey. Even with his memory fire somehow muted, the urge to pry, to be enveloped in his strong, vibrant memories, was all she could think about.

"Do you need me out of the room?" He shifted closer to the wall and used it to help him stand. "Tobias told me earlier to leave the Handmaiden's chambers so you could work."

"No." Mother, she could barely think straight with him standing beside her, but Ophelia wasn't there and wouldn't be able to pull the memory of the room reading from her head. "I'll probably need you to explain things. Can you walk?"

"Walk, yes. Run, probably not." He slid the blade into the sheath at his hip.

"I don't think I'll run." A hint of fire danced in the center of the hall below her. *Yes. Concentrate on that.*

"You don't think—?"

"Sometimes I'm not completely conscious of my surroundings when I use my magic."

"I can relate," he said, so softly she wasn't sure if she'd heard him correctly.

The fire in the hall below flickered, and she hissed her power word before she could second guess herself... or turn her attention back to him.

Her power roared to life and leapt toward Grey. Even clinging to the railing, keeping her back to him, she could feel the heat of his memories. Power surged through her, the ache in her soul vanished, and she was complete, whole, and powerful.

The great hall darkened, shrouded in an unnatural twilight, and the reek of garbage engulfed her.

"How fast can you heal, drake?" a voice rasped.

Panic snapped through her, but she didn't know if it was hers or his.

And not the point. She didn't have permission, and he wouldn't understand that this was an accident. It would look like she was purposefully prying into his secrets.

She mentally wrenched at her magic, but it clung to him and the darkness completely devoured the room, revealing an alley. A chill slithered through her, making her teeth chatter, and rain rattled against glass. A knife leapt into view with blood slicking its edge and dripping from its point, plopping into a puddle by her foot— *his* foot. Grey's foot.

Her pulse pounded faster. Pain seared across her neck and she gasped for air. She couldn't catch her breath, couldn't think past the agony—

No, *he* couldn't. And *he* wasn't going to heal fast enough to fight back.

Someone roared, but she couldn't focus enough to see what was happening.

Breathe. You're not the one hurt. But a memory had never seized her like this before. She'd certainly never *felt* one. And God, why did it have to be such a painful one?

Another roar. Screaming. Then a blinding flare of magic. The medallion capturing a dragon's soul — something she only knew because this was Grey's memory.

Not anyone she was supposed to be reading.

Jet. Tell me about Jet. She clawed at her magic, trying to stop it. If it was no longer activated, the memory would stop and she could try again.

Light from the medallion seared her mental eyes.

No. Show me Jet. She fought to just turn her magic off. *In the Handmaiden's secret residence.*

Another scream. The form of an enormous man towering above her appeared in the darkness, shadow himself but edged with a brilliant red aura, revealing an ancient drake. Just like Grey.

Her power flared at the thought, a sudden strong burst, and the twilight alley flickered, with the Handmaiden's hall visible underneath.

The red drake knelt, no longer towering, but still a match physically to Grey, and a deep familiar love filled her.

Her power flickered, weakened, and the twilight alley regained strength—

No, became something else... a hall...? a foyer...? The damp and reek were gone, but fear still clutched her chest. The red drake now stood before her, same brilliant aura, but his human body had narrower shoulders—

Please. Grey's thoughts? Hers? She couldn't tell where she ended and he began.

Please. She fought harder to turn her magic off. Her mind stuttered. The Handmaiden's massive hall had reappeared when her magic had been stronger.

Maybe the way out wasn't back, but through. Seizing that thought, she screamed her power word, using the burst of energy from the yell to deepen her focus on her power. The red drake vanished and the gloom of Grey's memories exploded, revealing the hall engulfed in the familiar blue haze of memory fire when her power was activated. The image of Jet rushed down the stairs and Ivy followed, refusing to check if Grey was behind her for fear her magic would latch onto him again.

G rey gasped, his body weightless and the pressure of his unwanted memories gone. Then the fog flooded around his vision as Ivy bolted down the stairs. She'd done something, but he had no idea what. All he knew was, for that moment, she had burned away the fog of too many memories. And whatever she'd just done, it had been stronger than when they'd run into each other in Court, like standing in the heart of a sun and letting it sear away the miasma in his soul.

And then it was gone.

Her eyes had widened, as if she'd seen something horrible, something—

Ah, shit. Her earth magic was the ability to read memories, and she was a young drake. She might not have complete control of it. If she didn't, then she might have seen one of the terrors haunting him.

Except she'd specifically said "things." She hadn't said memories in general.

He wasn't sure he really knew what that meant. Could she read his shirt and know he'd had a conversation with Nero less than an hour ago? Maybe that was what she'd seen. Maybe she'd seen Anaea with her suddenly awakened empathy losing control of her wind power. What else had he done wearing this shirt? … These pants? … God, his boots! He'd been wearing these boots since Anaea had called almost a month ago from the human world and said something was wrong with Hunter, when his best friend's soul had been trapped inside her.

He forced himself after Ivy, his body screaming with pain.

"Ivy." He didn't know what he was going to say or do, but he had to do something. If she did know Grey was in contact with Nero, he couldn't let her tell Regis or even Tobias.

She slowed by a narrow passage that branched off the main hall, but she didn't look back at him.

"Ivy." He staggered closer. Mother, his chest hurt. The gunshot wound might have stopped bleeding by now, but the internal injuries were still healing and could take a few days, depending on how serious they were. "Ivy."

She glanced back, but her gaze was unfocused as if she couldn't see him or was looking at something else. Her aura pulsed, not as brilliant as when she'd first activated her magic, but still stronger than before. A dimness he hadn't realized had been there melted in the center of his vision, the Handmaiden's hall billowed back into clarity, and the few memories he had of being there didn't flood in. Just like when he'd been near Ivy before.

He inched a step away. The hall dimmed, like a movie mostly drained of color.

A step forward. Technicolor returned.

He bit back a growl. Yeah, he'd known she righted his unbalanced soul. If he was being honest with himself, he'd known the moment he'd met her. But now it was clear it wasn't just *her* — her calm, her newness, his lack of memories of her — that burned away the fog threatening to consume him. It was something about her magic — especially when she was using it — that swept it all away and righted whatever that something was that lay unstable within him.

Except she was Tobias's agent, she still had an obligation to her prince, and Grey had no idea if she was considered as valuable as Capri. Only a few other drakes could do what Capri did and those drakes were on the other Clean Teams protecting dragonkind. Was Ivy's magic just as valuable? He had to assume yes. It was dangerous to assume no.

Which still didn't deal with the issue of what memories she'd seen from his clothes.

He couldn't let her return to Court, and he sure as hell couldn't keep her to solve his memory problem. She wasn't some pet he could keep locked up, and if Nero learned she endangered his unsanctioned coterie, he'd kill her and to hell with trying to save her soul from the universal ether.

And if Nero didn't kill her, Diablo would. That drake had no qualms with killing, especially to protect dragonkind, and Grey didn't doubt he wouldn't have a second thought about killing to protect his coterie.

Shit.

God damned fucking shit.

In the blink of an eye, the day had gone from bad to terrible, and he had no idea what he was going to do with Ivy. He couldn't tell her the truth. Not until he had a plan. And he couldn't let her return to Court.

Ivy frowned, her gaze still unfocused. She brushed two fingers over a sigil carved into the side of a nearby bookshelf, then headed down the narrow aisle, deeper into the Handmaiden's maze.

He followed her around a corner to a nook crowded with leather-bound books.

His first priority was to get his hands on her cell phone and disable it without her knowing, then keep her focused on this mess with Jet. With luck, that would buy him time to figure out what the hell he was going to do with her.

Her attention jumped to an empty podium. She gasped then turned back to the shelves.

"She ripped out a page," she said as she drew out one of the books.

"She what?" Who what? His mind stuttered, still caught on the problem of Ivy and what she now knew, then jumped to Jet. Then the book.

Hot rage snapped through him. "She ripped out a page!"

Ivy's frown deepened. Her aura flared and a tremble swept through her. "I'm trying to see if the room knows what's in the book—"

Her aura exploded in a sudden blinding flare. She gasped and jerked away from the shelf, bumping into Grey. The room burst into focus and the weight of his memories — a weight he hadn't fully realized had returned — vanished.

His arm snaked around her waist, drawing her against his chest, before he realized what he was doing. Heat and calm flooded him. The fog was gone, and the urge to hold her tighter and never let go filled him. He needed her, wanted her, craved her soul-deep with a desire that went beyond soothing his memories. It went straight to the core of his being.

A shiver curled up his spine, a low tremble that rumbled through him. The urge to brush his lips against her jaw, to kiss her — fully kiss her, not the whisper of lips from before — clawed inside him.

But that would only make the rest of the day harder. Whatever he was going to do with her, however he was going to protect Nero and Anaea and all the other members of his new, unexpected coterie, would be God-damned harder if he kissed her.

He shoved away from her, dragging the fog of his memories around him, desperate to forget how much he wanted to embrace her again.

"Did I hurt you?" she asked, her arms wrapped tight around her. "Sometimes my magic is hard to control. The memories fight back or—" She pursed her lips, her wide-eyed gaze locked on his. "Or in this case, they try to show me everything at once. It can be... difficult."

"Yeah." *Don't reach for her. Don't reach.*

Her eyes flashed wide. "I hurt you?"

"No." He was going to end up hurting himself when all was said and done. There was no good way to deal with her. "I meant, I get it. Memories can be difficult."

She shifted, and everything within him begged for her to draw closer. Just one more step. That would bring her within reach and burn away all of his darkness, all those difficult memories. Just once more. Just—

Jeez. No. Don't even get started.

He drew back and leaned against the shelf behind him, hoping the move looked nonchalant and not desperate. "Did you see what was on the page?"

"Sure." She grabbed the book, set it on the podium, and opened it. "Except I can't read whatever this is."

He had to move to see the page. For a split second, he contemplated staying where he was — as far away from her as possible, given the circumstances — but that wouldn't deal with the problem of Jet and whatever she was after, and if he was being honest with himself, it wouldn't help him deal with Ivy.

Maybe if he glanced at the page he'd recognize the book and be able to remember it. Knowing what page Jet had taken would be a fantastic break.

Ivy flipped to the middle of the book and brushed her fingers along the ragged remains of the torn page. "I can't believe she'd just rip out a page. Out of one of the Handmaiden's books."

Neither could Grey. "But if she didn't want anyone else to have access to whatever was on it, the only way to guarantee no one else got it was to take it." Except Grey might remember it.

He drew in a breath to steel himself, but that only stabbed pain through him and made his two steps closer more a stagger than a walk. Ancient Cantonese covered the top half of the page, while the bottom half had numbers that didn't appear to be in any order except that they were at least a hundred numbers apart and always increased. Beside them were notes, either "not ready" or "changing" jotted beside them.

He didn't recognize the visible page, which meant the Handmaiden had never asked him to read this book. Wonderful. "How are your art skills? Can you reproduce the missing page?"

"Could I—?" Ivy frowned. Her aura flared, revealing a hint of the power he knew lay within her, then returned to normal. "It's hard to focus on just it. There's some emotion attached to Jet ripping it out, but there are other, stronger emotions in this nook that are tied to other memories that keep pulling me away."

"So that's a no." Which meant he had to hope what was left would give some clue about what Jet — or rather her employer — was after.

Ivy growled and jerked away from the book. "I have to report this." She pulled a cell phone from the front pocket of her purse and turned it on.

"Wait." He couldn't let her call Tobias. "Wouldn't it be better to tell Tobias exactly what Jet was after?"

"You know someone who can translate that?" She sounded too happy about the idea of avoiding her boss. Of course, maybe it wasn't Tobias she wanted to avoid.

"I'm older than I look." And after a couple hundred years, he'd discovered that learning things was a clear advantage for him among other dragons — and it was easy, with his earth magic that he couldn't turn off and made him remember everything. He could read, write, and speak every major language on the planet, along with a few obscure and now dead ones.

"I didn't want to say," Ivy said. "You know… about your age."

"It's only human women who worry about their age." Although he'd give up everything to be new and young like Ivy, without the press of thousands of bad memories threatening to consume him.

He shoved that thought back. There wasn't anything he could do about it right now. Maybe this search for something in the Handmaiden's possession would help him find her. Maybe the Mother would be kind and Anaea would gain some control over her sorcerer's magic.

And maybe he could convince Ivy to stay with him.

Nope. Bad dragon. Not an option.

"The Handmaiden's books are written in a mix of Sumerian, Cantonese, Latin, Hebrew, and Greek. She sometimes asks me to read them."

"Why would she do that?"

He'd been asking himself that question for centuries now. "In case of a fire. I don't know."

"Did she ask you to read this book?" She frowned. "Except you wouldn't have asked if I could reproduce the page if you had."

And she was smart, too.

Keeping her from Tobias just became more difficult. If he wasn't careful, she'd figure out what he was doing before he'd figured out what to do with her.

"So what does it say?"

The page started halfway through a sentence. "—this key to find the pieces. Place the pieces of the glyph on the podium, and after the spell's six-quarter day duration is complete, they and the spell will be joined."

Ivy leaned closer, drawing a heated shiver through Grey. "Pieces to what?"

"I fear dragonkind isn't ready," Grey read, "for the power adding the two coin pieces to the medallion would bring." A chill replaced the heat. "They are infants again, reborn in these human bodies. The power to control the whole rebirth spell is too dangerous for one dragon to have."

"Holy Mother! Did that say what I think it said?" Ivy asked.

"That there's a way for someone other than the Handmaiden to cast the rebirth spell?" The chill sank into his bones. Controlling the rebirth spell opened the doors to a coup where dragons died but no souls were lost.

His dread deepened, churning into a hard stone. It meant Regis could punish with impunity. It didn't matter that this could be another way for Grey to find peace. He was the only dragon who wanted his soul stripped back to its essential core. For everyone else, rebirth was a death sentence, one Regis had liberally used before the Handmaiden had left.

13

Servius sat on a long stone bench at the back of a deserted temple to the Mother in one of the abandoned levels of Court. The magic that illuminated all of Court's rooms and halls also ensured they were dust- and cobweb-free, which made this out-of-the-way space a perfect place to meet Jet. No one came here any more, and even if someone did walk down these empty halls, there wouldn't be any footprints. As well, this was still a temple to the dragon goddess, the Mother of All, and while most drakes worshiped at their coterie's temple, it wasn't unheard of for drakes to find solace in some of the small public groves and nooks scattered throughout Court.

He snorted and glared at the statue of the Mother dragon at the front of the room. There were statues like it or little carvings of Her scattered throughout Court. They weren't in-your-face obvious and out in the open, but they were there, always ready to be noticed in the most unexpected places. It was as if the Handmaiden hadn't wanted dragonkind to forget Her or what She'd sacrificed.

As if any drake *could* forget. Certainly not any drake old enough to remember the Great Scourge could forget that horrible fall from the sky and the death of so many of them in the blink of an eye.

The Mother statue sat back on Her haunches with Her wings outstretched. When the Handmaiden had found and built Court with her magic, creating a safe haven for all of dragonkind, Servius had thought these statues — the ones with the Mother with Her wings outstretched — meant She was going to wrap them around Her children and protect them like She'd protected them by sacrificing Herself to save their souls.

But now it looked more like She was trying to get the hell out of there and was trapped, frozen in stone, unable to flee.

Just like so many drakes, particularly the young ones, the ones reborn without a memory of the Scourge. They didn't have the weight of that terrible time clinging to their spirits and many didn't understand why the dragon laws were as restrictive as they were.

They certainly didn't understand why Regis was tightening an already iron grasp on dragon society. So they escaped to the human world, pretending it didn't affect them and hoping Regis wouldn't notice.

A part of Servius yearned to join them. Hell, even the Handmaiden had left, which indicated just how bad things had become. But fleeing wasn't the right choice. Standing up, taking control, and fixing the problem. That was the only way.

Except without the medallion to save dragon souls from dissolving into the universal ether and without the Handmaiden to rebirth those souls into new vessels, no dragon could wrest control from Regis. Not without diminishing their already diminished numbers.

Air whooshed at the front of the room, and Jet stepped through a gate to stand between the first row of benches and the dragon statue. Blood stained her neck and she held her arm close to her side as if it hurt.

"I got the page, but the Handmaiden's man and a green drake were there." Jet pulled a folded piece of paper from the inside of her jacket and handed it to Servius.

"We knew Tobias or Grey would discover the Handmaiden's chambers." Although it surprised Servius that the discovery had been made so quickly. He'd been counting on at least a day before anyone found the mess Jet had been told to leave and at least half a day — better a whole day — more for them to think about going to the Handmaiden's private residence. A part of Servius had been hoping the Handmaiden hadn't told either drake about her private abode in the Himalayas, but given how long Grey had served her, that hope was unlikely. What he'd really hoped was that the mess would have been blamed on the fractious sect of the Divine Mother who protested the Handmaiden's presence, claiming she was trying to get dragonkind to worship her instead of the Mother of All.

That had been the real hope. Dragon society wasn't going to hold together much longer and someone needed to take Regis's throne, forcing Servius to rush the creation of the magic lockpicking spell. But that meant the spell broke the Handmaiden's doors and the break-in became obvious. Redirection to the sect was the best plan. Or at least it had been. "The green drake had to be one of Tobias's agents."

"Yeah, well, she could see through my illusions, and she shot me."

"You're lucky Grey didn't take your head." Grey's overdeveloped sense of duty was probably the only thing that had saved Jet. For over a thousand years, Grey and Hunter had fought side by side in every human conflict they could find, as if their beasts couldn't be contained within their frail human vessels. Even if Grey wasn't the fastest-healing drake around, all those years of combat experience counted for a lot. If he'd actually gotten a vessel with more earth magic than just free gating, he could have seriously challenged Hunter for the position of royal assassin — not that the silver drake would have ever challenged Hunter. He had stood by, and was still standing by, the red drake, even now that Hunter had become the prince's number one enemy.

"He's lucky *I* didn't take *his* head." Jet shrugged and winced.

Servius cocked an eyebrow. Grey hadn't been alive for as long as he had because he was easily defeated.

"Next time I'm taking out that green drake first. That'll solve my problem with Grey."

"If you did your job right, there won't be a next time." Servius opened the page Jet had handed him and read it.

God damn it. He bit back a growl and Jet inched back a step. The coin was in two pieces and the key to finding both of them was in the *ekas* in Seville.

He'd wanted the location of the coin, not some treasure hunt, but that wasn't how the Handmaiden worked. He'd spent enough time in her employ, stealing her spells and useful tidbits of information, like the coin, before he'd resigned and Grey had taken his place, to know there wasn't anything straightforward about the Handmaiden.

He jerked his attention to Jet. "There won't be a next time, correct? You didn't let them see this page and they don't know what I'm after."

"They didn't and they don't. As instructed, I didn't disturb anything in her secret residence, and I returned the book to where I found it. With a place that big, it would take years—" Jet huffed. "It would take hundreds of years for them to find the book with the missing page. And even then, they'd have no way of knowing what was on that page."

"Good. Did you read it?"

"My ancient Cantonese is a little rusty, but it looks like the coin is in pieces and those pieces are hidden. Step one to finding them is to go to the *ekas* in Seville."

"Are you healed enough to go?" When he'd looked into Jet before hiring her, he'd discovered she was efficiently deadly at her job, and even though she wasn't a rapid healer, she wasn't detrimentally slow, either. And while she might still underestimate Grey in the future, if she didn't encounter him again, Servius's plans would proceed without issue.

Jet rolled her shoulders back and straightened her arm. "Yep, the break is all fixed, but I'll have to use the gate anchor to get there." She shrugged and stepped back, making space to form her free gate and leave Court. "I've never been to Seville before."

Servius fought the urge to roll his eyes. Had he ever been that young? If she'd never been to Seville before, then she'd never been to the *ekas*. "Hand me your phone."

Jet's eyes narrowed.

"You need an address to the *ekas*. The gate goes to the courtyard of a dragon-kept public house across the river, not directly there."

Jet huffed again. "That wasn't well thought out."

"Sure it was. When the *ekas* was built, there were still some human sorcerers who could make gates. No one wanted them to be able to lock onto an anchor and step into the middle of a safe haven." And while some drakes now had gate anchors created as part of their establishments as a courtesy for younger, less powerful drakes, none of the *ekases* had been given anchors.

Jet handed over her phone and Servius entered the address. "Call when you have the key."

"I know how to do my job." She took her phone back and hissed her power word. A gate formed under her feet and she disappeared.

It was a risk, sending her after the key. There was a chance that, when she found both pieces of the coin, she'd betray him and sell it to the highest bidder, but the risk of being exposed was greater — especially now that Servius knew Grey and one of Tobias's agents were on the case.

He couldn't afford to have Regis know he was after the coin until the last possible minute. Too much could go wrong, and if Servius didn't have the coin in a medallion first, everything would fall apart.

It was bad enough he hadn't been able to hide breaking into the Handmaiden's chambers at Court and the plan to ransack them hadn't worked. Tobias and all his agents were supposed to be busy looking for a perpetrator in Court. Their first suspects should have been a member of the sect of the Divine Mother.

But the bad luck kept coming. The Handmaiden's man was also involved and he shouldn't have been anywhere near the Handmaiden's chambers. Since he'd stuck by his red drake friend who'd disavowed the prince, Grey had been moved into the top two of Regis's most wanted list. Did that drake have no sense of self-preservation?

Servius headed out of the temple and into the plain granite hall. He needed more information about Tobias's agent and anything Regis was planning, and to do that, he needed to spend time with the monster calling himself Prince of the Dragons.

It was the only way to gather as much information as possible. Nothing could be overlooked in the next couple of days. Not with things already having gone wrong, and not if he wanted to survive his coup—

No, not a coup. That had been Zenobia's problem. She'd wanted to grab the throne without having any right to it. This was Servius's rightful ascension. The prince might be one of the two remaining gold drakes and the son of Constantine, the Sumerian dragon king who'd defeated the Zhongguo dragon empress before the Scourge, but that didn't mean there weren't other options for royal succession. Like himself.

He was a direct descendant of the empress, one of two grandsons. Neither his father nor his uncle had survived the Scourge, but their offspring had, and while his cousin Nero might be in Regis's pocket, Servius wasn't, and he had every intention of saving dragonkind from Regis's insanity. Even if it meant he had to rebirth everyone who stood in his way.

He reached a narrow, curling staircase, leading down to the heart of the dragon Court. It was early afternoon, but Regis didn't have a schedule any more, and Servius wouldn't know where the prince was unless he talked with Tobias. It was a safe bet with Tobias — who didn't have much of a schedule, either — to guess he was in his chamberlain's office. Recently the black dragon was spending more and more time there, and rumor had it he now slept there instead of returning to his suite.

Five flights down, Servius reached the greater promenade and headed toward the chamberlain's office, but Regis's booming voice in the opposite direction made him stop.

The prince was yelling about something, and without a doubt, another drake was about to be sent to his torturer.

Servius squared his shoulders and forced himself to turn around and head toward Regis. Save that it was obvious Regis was becoming soul sick and mentally unstable, there was no reason to be afraid. Servius had taken every precaution to avoid discovery. He and Jet were using an app that erased their texts the moment they were read, thereby eliminating any evidence she was working for him. Everything else, like creating the magical two-shot lockpick spell and a spell to pull the medallion from the heart of the arena — since regular earth manipulation magic didn't work on it — had been done in private. And while he'd worked the spells as fast as he could, it had still taken him over a hundred years to weave the two of them.

As well, no one, not even the Handmaiden, knew Servius's earth magic was a medium degree of sorcerer's ability. Everyone thought he was an ancient drake with no earth magic at all. No one knew he'd spent the last two thousand years weaving three difficult permanent spells into his human body, tattoos carefully drawn into his flesh giving him the power to mimic the earth magic abilities to control earth and wind, and to free gate.

It had taken him centuries just to cast each spell — and he wouldn't have even been able to do that if he hadn't stolen the glyphs he'd used for the tattoos from the Handmaiden's grimoire. Only one drake had ever learned about his magic and he was now dead. No one else was going to learn the truth until he had control of the complete rebirth spell and had dealt with Regis, the prince's favorite drakes — his cousin Nero included — and anyone else who threatened his claim to the throne.

"Aren't you supposed to be able to find him?" Regis growled.

Five sycophants, dressed to match Regis's Henry the VIII hideousness, stood a good four feet behind him, staring at a young orange drake in a tailored black suit that accentuated his sharp facial features and his black hair and beard. The drake radiated a deadly intensity, clearly unable to hide his dangerous intent, which only made him look more inexperienced. Even Jet was old enough to disguise how dangerous she actually was.

"Only if he's within a hundred mile radius," the young drake said, either too naive or stupid to know he shouldn't piss off Regis. "And it doesn't work across dimensions."

"Well, I *know* you can't free gate, so you better start hopping from gate to gate and pray he steps within a hundred mile radius of you."

The young drake's expression darkened, and one of the sycophants — a yellow drake in a willowy female body, wearing a full-skirted gown in deep gold and orange — gasped.

Regis bared his teeth. Not just a quick flash, but outright bared, and growled.

The orange drake's eyes widened, and if the situation wasn't so dangerous, Servius would have laughed at how realization swept across the orange drake's features and then turned to horror at what he'd said.

For a moment, Servius considered stepping back and letting the matter play out. He'd yet to be seen, and interrupting Regis when he wanted to turn a drake into an object lesson about obedience could be dangerous for the drake doing the interrupting. But if this orange drake did have the earth magic ability to find Grey — even if it was a limited radius — that could be useful.

Servius shoved his hand into his pocket and gripped the coin-sized copper disc with the spell on it to pull the medallion from the heart of the arena. The disc was a one-shot deal. He'd only get one chance, and there was no point in risking capture without the coin.

"You're looking for the Handmaiden's man?" Servius asked, pleased his voice didn't crack.

"I am," Regis hissed as he jerked to face Servius, his teeth exposed and his wide face red with rage. "What do you want, Servius?"

"I couldn't help overhearing." Servius fought to keep still, his chest tight and his pulse pounding in his ears. Disgust curled in his gut, and he mentally clutched at that. He shouldn't fear Regis. He was almost as old as Regis, with as much right to the throne, and was more magically powerful. Regis thrived on fear, consumed it as if it sustained him and not the magic within his dragon soul. Servius would be damned if he became the prince's next victim.

"The drake attacked two royal guards and I don't care that he's the Handmaiden's servant. Enough is enough. He *will* pay for his crimes." Regis's gaze shot to the orange drake. "If Bolo can't find him, I'll give his job to someone who can."

"I'd heard something happened with the Handmaiden's chambers."

"How did you hear that?" the orange drake, Bolo, asked.

Servius shrugged — the action taking more effort to keep smooth than he liked. "Court is small and I'm the Third for the Minor Black Coterie. You don't think I would have risen to that position without having connections here at Court?"

"Your connections have gossiped about private Court business," Regis said, his voice a low growl again.

Servius's pulse sped up, racing in a wild tattoo. This was his opening. "Those connections also thought Grey was going to the *ekas* in Seville."

If he was fortunate, Grey wouldn't go to Seville, because he knew nothing about the key to finding the pieces of the rebirth coin. But on the slim chance he figured it out, adding another drake, especially one out to apprehend or kill Grey, could only help keep Grey out of Jet's way. The black drake might be confident in her abilities, but Servius wasn't willing to take any chances. Failure wasn't an option.

Regis's eyes narrowed. "How would your connections know that?"

"They told me Grey and the Handmaiden used to spend time there, in the temple, during the..." Damn, he needed a reason.

"They'd spent time there... during... the Inquisition." It was the only thing he could think of.

Bolo frowned, but Regis's expression grew darker. The Inquisition had been a bad time for many drakes, and some of Constantine's most aggressive restrictions on what dragons could and couldn't do — the same ones Regis now fully supported — had been brought into law then. Without a doubt, Grey and the Handmaiden had been to the *ekas* — a safe haven for dragonkind during their worst moments in history — in Seville during that time.

"Go," Regis barked, making Bolo and the sycophants jump. "And don't come back without the silver drake." Regis bared his teeth again. "Or word that he's dead."

———

DIABLO SHIFTED, UNABLE TO GET COMFORTABLE ON THE CAFE'S HARD wooden chair, and checked his phone for the third time in ten minutes. No message from Grey. Not that he'd expected the silver drake to call, but he hadn't looked good before he'd gone to Court to meet with Tobias, and he'd looked worse when he'd returned. Now he was at one of the Handmaiden's residences — one so private not even Nero knew about it — alone, possibly confronting whoever had ransacked the Handmaiden's chambers.

A hint of a growl bubbled in Diablo's throat and he swallowed it back. His beast, curled too-tight within him, wanted to join Grey for the confrontation. Heck, it didn't care if it was Grey he confronted. He just God damned needed to fight something.

"Hey," a feminine voice said.

He jerked his attention up, not realizing it was still stuck on his phone's blank display. Eva stood across from him, gripping the back of a chair now half pulled out from the table.

"Everything okay?"

"Yeah," he said, with more growl than he'd like.

She raised a delicate eyebrow and finished pulling out the chair, her doubt radiating through him. "You sure? There's this churning thundercloud above your head giving you away."

He fought the urge to glance up. There wasn't a cloud. His earth magic was rapid free gating, night sight, enhanced physical abilities, and his Mother-cursed empathy — not that anyone else knew about the empathy. He couldn't control the weather, and what his empathy was picking up from her emotions — besides concern and — as always — her attraction to him, was that she was just doing that human thing where they exaggerated obvious emotions.

Which in itself wasn't great, since he was supposed to be happy to be there to have a late lunch with her. And he was. He just also had other, pressing problems on his mind. Like Grey—

Not that he cared about the drake. Really. Grey wasn't a part of his public coterie, or even his hidden *puzur,* but right now if he got caught, both of Diablo's coteries were in danger.

Honestly. That was the worry.

Not to mention Diablo was also worried about Nero. He was struggling with his magic as dugga of the Asar Nergal and having trouble pinpointing the few remaining human mages from Zenobia's coup. To add to that, they still had the problem of a leak within their organization tipping off those human mages when someone was sent to apprehend them.

"Earth to D," Eva said, a hint of a smile pulling at her lush lips. He'd met this striking woman — his new neighbor, actually — only a week ago when Court's politics had wrenched him into its shit. Which wasn't true, either. A crazy human with the ability to see auras had thought dragons and human mages were demons and had killed Andy Reynolds, a human mage and Diablo's closest friend. That was more than just Court shit.

His chest tightened and his beast twisted tighter, hot with rage and grief. He needed to break something, someone, *feel* less, anything.

Except that was the thing Andy had managed to help him with. Not releasing his beast and not destroying everything around him, accepting that feeling everyone else's emotions was just a part of who he was.

"Hey." Eva snaked a hand across the table and brushed her fingers against his, a soft, subtle move, merely a hint of a caress of flesh against flesh, but somehow it eased the seething monster within him. "Remember the good times with him."

"I'm that easy to read?" He focused on her heart-shaped face and hazel eyes. Her honey-blond hair hung past her shoulders, tussled carefree locks — a style all the rage right now with humans — but he couldn't shake the feeling that she really belonged in a different era. Perhaps it was because it had been a long time since things had been right with him, and he didn't want her to belong to his messy here and now. He wanted her to be from his less messy past.

Of course, who was he kidding? While the here and now had taken Andy, it had also given him Andy, the only one — drake and human alike — who'd been able to teach him to control his beast since he woke in the rebirth chamber in 1632.

Still, the sense that she didn't belong, just like him, was one of the things that intrigued him. That, and her aura, or rather the fact that as a human she had an aura, something only drakes and human mages had. Hers wasn't as strong as the full mages who had lived in and been trained at Nero's special program, which meant she probably didn't even know she had earth magic. Maybe her soul was just so strong that he was seeing her soul magic. Rare, but not unheard of. If he asked her, would she say she'd never been seriously sick? That could be a result of strong soul magic.

Except he couldn't shake the nagging feeling that there was more to this captivating woman that just a human on the verge — but with never fully realized — earth magic.

And maybe that was just his beast making trouble, because just being with her calmed him down in ways he'd never been calm with anyone, even Andy.

"I've seen that look before." She offered a sad smile. "On friends who've lost loved ones. You told me your friend just passed. It takes time."

Time he didn't have, not with the leak in the Asar Nergal or the growing problems at Court.

He glanced at his phone. Still no message from Grey.

"Would it help to talk about it?"

"My friend?" Not that he could talk about Andy's death.

"Or whatever has you staring at your phone."

"No, sorry." He shoved his phone into his pants pocket. "Work is blowing up."

"Then let's reschedule. It's not like we haven't had lunch or coffee almost every day since we met." A hint of mischief crept into her smile and her attraction to him slid across his senses. "Maybe we could upgrade to dinner."

"Dinner, huh?" The idea had occurred to him after their first date, but he wasn't the kind of drake to just jump into a relationship, particularly with a human. Humans didn't heal like drakes and if his beast got out, the best outcome was that she'd be terrified of him. The worse was seriously maimed or dead.

"I might even be interested in breakfast." Her emotions flared and her desire seared through him.

"After dinner, of course," he said, playing along.

Her smile turned wicked and blossomed, lighting her face and sparkling in her eyes. "Of course."

And, Mother help him, the beast within agreed.

14

G rey reread the page. "Control the whole rebirth spell." He didn't want to accept that anyone, especially Regis, could get his hands on the rebirth spell. God, Tobias had been right about the Handmaiden hiding powerful magic. These coin pieces were something no drake should have.

"I don't like the idea of someone other than the Handmaiden having that spell," Ivy said, her voice small. "The page Jet took has to have the key to finding the pieces of this coin."

That much was clear. But there wasn't anything else on the page indicating what the key might be. There was only the list of numbers with the notes, "not ready" and "changing" and really only four of those notes were "changing": 124, 1049, 1497, and 2012. There was also a small mark — for all he knew her pen might have slipped — beside the 1201 listing.

They reminded Grey of dates. If the Handmaiden was straining herself by casting the complicated auger spell every hundred or so years, to determine if dragonkind was ready to have control of the powerful rebirth spell, then the list made a certain amount of sense.

It hadn't been until the mid-100s that the fallout of body sharing — dragon souls in occupied human vessels, which created human mages — had finally been dealt with.

The Asar Nergal had been formed and Constantine had managed

to bring all the coteries' doyens back together, and hosted the first *pahar* since the Great Scourge.

Grey wasn't sure what happened between 1049 and 1109, since he'd spent all of that time avoiding Court and working as a mercenary with Hunter. But the 1497 listing could refer to Regis taking the throne from his soul sick father in 1521, and this century certainly was seeing a lot of upheaval.

Even the mark beside the 1201 listing could mean something, since he'd sworn himself into the Handmaiden's service in 1295. Of course, that was probably him seeing meaning where there wasn't any. She'd never asked him to do anything while in her service except read her journals, and even then it was clear he hadn't been asked to read her most important ones.

"I can't go back to Tobias without knowing where Jet went." Ivy hissed something too quietly for Grey to make it out. It was probably her power word, and her aura flared, confirming the guess. The room snapped into crystal clarity, and a shudder swept through Grey. "If I can copy the page, we'll have the information Jet has."

The urge to grab Ivy, establish physical contact — deep physical contact — clawed through him. He needed to hold her, have her close, have *her*. Except that was just his *condition* speaking, his inability to control his unwanted earth magic and his desperate need for the relief her power offered.

But he'd already decided if he gave in to this obsession, even just once, it would only make everything else more difficult. Why couldn't he just keep that in mind?

She squeezed her eyes shut and her aura flared. Her head jerked toward the entrance of the nook, and she gripped the podium as if it took everything she had to stay where she was. Her chest heaved with fast gasps, and the muscles in her neck tightened with strain.

"Show me the page," she growled.

Another burst of her aura. Grey's sight sharpened even more, the edges of reality too crisp and clear and painful to look at. Grey hugged himself. *Don't move. Don't touch her.* But Mother, it was all he could think of.

She wrenched away from the podium, her eyes still closed, and stumbled. He lurched forward to grab her before he realized what he was doing, but she took another quick staggering step, closing the distance between them too fast. Her body bumped his before he could correct his mistake and his arms started to sweep around her again, like they had the last time she'd bumped into him when she'd had her earth magic activated.

Everything within him screamed yes and no in a clamor that roared through him. It tore at him, his soul cried for what he craved, and his mind cried for what he knew he should really do.

He leapt back and hit a shelf. A heavy leather-bound tome toppled over. He grabbed it before it fell, but knocked a vase and three other books to the floor.

Ivy gasped. Her aura snapped to its dimmer setting, and her arms wrapped across her chest as if she were trying to protect herself, but Grey couldn't figure out from what. Probably him. Good male drakes didn't touch a female without her consent. You'd lose a claw — and if you were lucky, only a claw and nothing else. Not to mention a smart drake didn't get close with someone who endangered everything you held dear. No matter how much his insides screamed he had to stay near her.

"I can't keep my focus," she said, her gaze holding his soul captive for a heartbeat.

"Tobias will understand." He wrenched his attention from her and dropped to the floor to put the books back on the shelf — the vase, now in dozens of pieces, he couldn't do much about.

"It's not Tobias I'm worried about. It's—"

"You need to be careful about saying things like that." It didn't matter that he knew who she was talking about and agreed with her. She was a member of the Royal Coterie. Regis would take talk like that as treason. Grey piled the books in the crook of his arm and straightened, drawing a spike of pain through his still-healing chest. "Tell Tobias that I got involved and impeded your investigation."

"Except you've helped. Besides, I'm pretty sure Tobias won't believe me if I said you got in the way." The worry in her eyes twisted the mix of need and fear — along with the physical throb of his injuries — in Grey's chest.

Mother, he was looking at her again. He hadn't realized he'd turned back to her. He forced his attention away again and shoved the books back onto the shelf. "Regis will believe it. That's all you really need."

A hint of gold numbering caught his eye from beside the heavy tome that had toppled over and created the mess on the floor.

"I just— I don't want to go back with nothing," she said, her voice mixed with…? He wasn't sure. Determination? Fear? Something else. She was hiding something — of course, so was he, so he couldn't really judge — but he couldn't help wondering if she was staying because she needed more information about the memory she'd gotten from his clothes. Without a doubt she'd become one of Regis's favorites if she revealed the truth about Nero harboring human mages. It was a good plan. Show a hint of fear about Regis to a known enemy to the crown, win Grey's sympathy, then learn one of his many secrets, and cash in.

Except he wasn't sure that was what she was hiding and he couldn't focus on the problem, in part because of her but also because the gold numbering staring back at him was the number 1477. That was the number of the journal the Handmaiden had asked him to read before she'd left Court.

"What are you looking at?" She brushed his sleeve, making him jump. He hadn't noticed her stepping so close, and now all he could think about was holding her again.

Jeez. Focus. The journal's spine popped into sharp detail, every scuff on the leather and the cracks in the gold leaf numbers crisp. "It's one of the Handmaiden's journals."

"We're surrounded by her books. Some of them are probably journals."

He scanned the shelf. No other spines with gold numbers. "But there aren't any other journals here."

"Maybe it's been misplaced?"

"No. It's still in my suite at Court."

"A copy, then?"

"It has to be a copy." He tried to draw into his mind the image of the spine of the journal hidden in the safe in his wardrobe at Court, but couldn't. The spine in front of him shuddered, as if he was looking at it through water, then jerked rigid, too bright and too crisp. Shit. When his inability to forget was actually useful, he found himself standing beside the one drake whose magic made him forget. "I'm sure it can't be the original."

But without being able to compare the spines, he wouldn't know for sure, and he wasn't going to reveal to Ivy how she affected him. She could use that against him. And really, for all he knew, the Handmaiden had put a spell on the book and it had materialized here for him to notice. Original or copy, that wasn't what mattered.

"So why would this be shelved here?"

"Because she needs me to see it." He glanced at the podium and the dates on the page of the open book. The Handmaiden had to have been casting an auger spell and she had to have known that a possible future would put the secret of the coin pieces and the rebirth spell in jeopardy.

With the auger spell, she wouldn't know for sure that Jet would tear out that page, but she would have known it was a possibility. Putting this journal here and asking Grey to reread it had to have been in anticipation of this possibility. "There was always a rumor that she cast an auger spell."

"I'm guessing we've just proved it isn't a rumor?"

"And she set this journal here to protect against a possible future." The Handmaiden had also said, the last time he'd seen her and she'd asked him to reread the book, that it would be important. Thankfully, that had happened only a few weeks ago and he didn't need his magic to remember it.

"Which means you know what's on the page Jet has."

Except he didn't. There wasn't anything in that book that mentioned pieces of a coin that, once placed inside the medallion, gave someone full control of the rebirth spell. Even without his earth magic memory, he was pretty sure he wouldn't forget a detail like that. "I'm not sure it's that simple. These journals were kept in her inner chamber at Court, and today has already proven that chamber wasn't safe."

"But if she's been regularly casting an auger spell, she'd have known that." Ivy frowned. "If I'd known that, I would have put whatever I needed you to know in some kind of code."

That was his guess, as well.

"If the book was intended for you, she would have given you the key to the code." Ivy pursed her lips. "Is the number on the spine, 1477, significant?"

"It's the year the journal deals with." Except that wasn't the whole truth. All throughout her journals, there were additions peppered through the pages from times before and times after the year indicated on the spines.

"Your eyes just widened." Ivy straightened and leaned closer. "What?"

"There's an entry at the back of this book." He opened the journal and flipped to the last page. The entry wasn't very long, but he remembered thinking every time he read it — all four times — that it was odd.

Ivy sighed and pointed to the open page. "I can't read that, either."

"It's written in old Greek. This is an entry about seeing the opening night of a play written by William Shakespeare, *Much Ado About Nothing*. She said she really enjoys how he plays with words, particularly the joke said by Isabella about one of the characters being 'civil as an orange.'"

Her frown deepened. "I'm not familiar with that play."

Thankfully he was, and thank the Mother he'd reread this journal entry only a few weeks ago and didn't need his earth magic to remember why it was so strange. "The play on words is that Isabella is saying the character is bitter. 'Civil' is pronounced with the emphasis on the 'vil', so ci-VIL, like the city, Seville in Spain, a place where you get bitter oranges."

"That's an awfully vague clue. Does that mean we're going to Seville? Where?"

"Actually it's not so vague. This journal is for the year 1477 but *Much Ado About Nothing* was written in late 1598 or so. As well, that line wasn't said by Isabella. It was said by Beatrix." He shifted a step back from Ivy. The room's clarity faded a bit and a hint of his memory tickled at the back of his mind, offering him certainty with his details. "Queen Isabella of Spain was in Seville in 1477 when she was convinced to create the Spanish Inquisition." A hint of fog curled at the edge of his vision and even this close to Ivy, a flicker of sunlight on water flashed in his eyes.

Ivy brushed her locket and frowned. "I've heard that wasn't a great time for dragons."

"It wasn't." He fought to keep back a shudder. "But if that's the clue, then I know where Jet is going. She's going to the *ekas* in the old Jewish quarter. That underground dragon meeting place became a safe haven for us during the Inquisition."

She sighed and squared her shoulders. "I should tell Tobias."

She should, but he couldn't let her and risk her revealing Nero's coterie. "Or you could come with me."

"We've already learned I'm pretty useless in a fight. I won't be able to help if we run into Jet." But she didn't sound as if she wanted to report in.

Maybe he wouldn't have to disable her phone after all. If she'd discovered her phone was broken, she'd be on to him, and the longer he kept his intentions secret, the better. "But if we don't find Jet at the *ekas*, you're our best bet at figuring out what she did."

"She does have a head start on us." Ivy flashed a hint of teeth, and the churning need within Grey warmed.

Oh, this was bad. "So what are we waiting for?" Very, very bad.

15

I vy followed Grey — who still moved as if in agony — back to the stairs leading up to the second-floor balcony. Her mind whirled, and the knot in her gut clenched tight and radiated from her stomach across her chest. Someone was after a magic coin that could give a dragon other than the Handmaiden the power to rebirth any drake they wanted.

No. Not just give *any dragon* the power. Regis.

Shivers raced over her. If she told Tobias what Jet was after, he'd tell Regis, and Regis would stop at nothing to get it.

Mother, she was supposed to report to Regis in person. If she lied to him and got caught, she had no idea what he'd do.

Her teeth chattered, and she clenched her jaw.

She couldn't trust Regis, but she also didn't know if she could trust Tobias or Ophelia. She didn't even know if she could trust Grey — no matter how much she yearned to have his memories fill her again, even just have his memory fire brushing her skin.

With a grunt, he bent and grabbed Jet's gun from where Ivy had dropped it when she'd been about to fall off the balcony. He handed it to her then climbed the stairs — his pace steady but his movements tight — and strode past the pool of his blood, a flicker in the memory fire around him the only indication of an emotion at seeing it. "We're going to need to replace my bloody coat when we get to Seville. It might be—" He frowned and headed into the antechamber. "I think it's close to nine at night there, but if it's like other modern human cities, most streets are pretty well lit. We can't afford to get stopped before reaching the *ekas*."

"Why not just gate to the *ekas*?" She looked for a place to put the gun that would be easier to get to than inside her purse, but the weapon didn't fit in her jeans pockets and she wasn't going to cram it in the waistband of her pants. That seemed dangerous.

"All *ekases*, like all temples to the Mother and all places important to the Handmaiden, have a gatelock on them." He opened the outside door and a blast of cold air slammed into Ivy.

Grey gasped and tugged his coat tighter around him. His gaze dropped to the snowy ground just beyond the door. Three sets of footprints headed to the door and one headed away.

"Those weren't there before," Ivy said. "I mean the third set heading in." The set heading out was obviously made by Jet when she'd fled.

"Looks like Jet's camouflage magic now extends to covering up her tracks." Grey started to crouch, gasped, and straightened instead of finishing the move down. "There are a few other drakes who can use their personal camouflage earth magic to effect their environment, as well."

"That explains why it didn't look like the door had been opened when I got here."

The fire around Grey — a fire that still should have only been radiating from things he wore, like a chain or a watch, but which somehow completely covered him — flickered again, drawing Ivy closer, taunting her to hiss her power word and read whatever he was remembering. The memory from before, the one she'd accidently latched onto, swept into her mind's eye. Pain and horror surged through her, but she didn't force it away. Somehow, even this remembered terror soothed the constant ache within her and made her feel complete.

She'd never experienced anything like it before. He had to be wearing something from the time of that memory. It was the only way to explain how she could be seeing it. And yet a part of her knew he wasn't. His clothes, his shoes, his watch, all had other memories imprinted in them. But this memory — and the promising flicker of others — were all him. Maybe because his magic made every memory sharp as if it had just happened. Maybe because there was something about this drake that drew her, something more than just the seductive strength of his memory fire.

The urge to activate her magic grew stronger.

Just say it. Just one little word.

But he'd know and would refuse to honor their agreement. She couldn't afford to lose the favor he owed her. That was more valuable than easing the ache within her or feeling powerful. Freedom was more important. If she was free, safe from Regis, she could rebuild her hoard of items imprinted with loving, joyous memories. She might still wake not knowing who she was, but that initial fear would disappear when she said her power word. It wouldn't magnify.

She forced herself back a step, praying even a few feet more between them would help her stay in control. But the fire around him danced, cajoling her, making her insides squirm.

Think about something else. Anything else.

The muscles in his jaw clenched and he strode across the ice garden toward the passage leading to the gate anchor on the other side. The wind whipped the strands of shoulder-length blond hair that had broken free of the ponytail at the nape of his neck, and with the scruff of an almost-beard and his broad muscular shoulders straining the fabric of his coat, he looked fierce, like a drake coiled tight within his human warrior.

The urge within her warmed to a desire. It had to be her craving to be as strong and ferocious as him. Not the weak hatchling that she was. Certainly not trapped and broken.

But in the heart of her soul, she knew that wasn't the full truth. There was something about Grey that called to something within her. Perhaps it was that they were opposite sides of the same coin. He remembered everything and she remembered nothing. Perhaps it was something more feral than that, something locked deep within her dragon spirit.

The heat sank lower, sliding past the knot in her gut, and realization flashed hot through her, burning over her cheeks and down her neck.

She was attracted to him. And not just to his memory fire.

That had never happened before. At least there wasn't anything in her locket about taking a lover. She met very few drakes while hiding in her suite at Court, and being intimate with anyone — even if it was just a deep friendship — was problematic. Her uncertain relationship with Ophelia was proof of that. Sleeping with someone was... was...

She couldn't even wrap her mind around how difficult it would be.

Her pulse pounded faster. Mother of All, he was... was—

"So the gate," she said, jumping to the first thing she could think of that didn't involve fantasizing about something she couldn't—*shouldn't* have, and certainly not with one of Regis's enemies. Not to mention, what if she really was confusing attraction with her desire to read his memories? She'd never encountered anyone like him before. She could easily be mistaking the need to ease the ache in her soul with attraction. And yet—

"What about the gate?" He marched into the shadows of the passage.

Yes, what about the gate? She pulled her phone from her purse, turned on her flashlight app, and followed him inside. "You said we can't go directly to the *ekas* because of a gatelock. How close can we get?"

He glanced back at her, his pale gaze making her pulse jump. "If I'd been to Seville within the last fifty years, I'd know what was around the *ekas* and free gate us, but it's been—" He jerked his attention away from her and strode out of the passage to the cliff's edge. "Let's just say it's been a while. It's safest to gate to the Seville anchor and walk the twenty minutes to the *ekas*."

"Because you're afraid the gate will dump us in a wall or something?"

"You can gate, right?" Grey's frown deepened. "You know gates don't work that way. They always form in a location where you can step out."

"Right." Except she didn't know. She knew nothing about gates, only that she could make one if she had an anchor.

"I'm afraid of the gate dumping us into a busy public square." He hissed his power word and a black vortex formed beside his feet. "I'm already on the prince's bad side. I'd hate to piss off the head of the European Clean Team, too."

What the heck was a European Clean Team? She brushed her locket. Nothing there. "Yeah."

"You don't think Viridian wouldn't lose his shit?" His vortex whipped up the snow, whirling it around them, and he held out his hand to her.

She stared at it, everything within telling her to take hold and not let go, and all logic and self-preservation telling her not to. They didn't need to hold hands to use the same gate, and yet it was all she wanted.

"I know he doesn't go to Court often, but I'd guess that you're at least fifty. You must have run into him in Tobias's office." His gaze dipped to his still-empty hand and uncertainty flickered across his expression.

With a blink, determination replaced the uncertainty, and he started to withdraw his hand. Her heart skipped a beat and she grabbed it before the offer was gone. Heat swept through her chest, and she fought the urge to flash her teeth at him in a sexual challenge. A growl rumbled in her throat, the reminder that, weak and young as she was, she was still a dragon.

And she was God damned going to remember that.

She tightened her grip on Grey's hand, his memory fire licking her skin and making her shiver, and stepped into the gate. The woolly blackness clogged her senses, up and down vanished, and for a heartbeat she was suspended in the black nothing that lay between interdimensional spaces.

Then her foot hit something hard. The impact jarred up her leg and swept through her body, wrenching her back to earth. She stood in a small courtyard, surrounded by three-story buildings, all flickering with moderate memory fire promising centuries of memories. A single tree stood in the center — likely the only place the poor plant could get sunlight — and a heavy wrought iron gate stood to her left. Compared to the frozen cliffside in the Himalayas, the air was mild, although she suspected that humans — and slow healers like Grey, whose soul magic didn't protect them as much against feeling the effects of the climate — would still wear a coat to keep warm.

"First order of business, a new coat." He released her hand and strode to a worn wooden door opposite the gate.

A chill raced over her at the loss of contact, and a mix of emotions — none of which she wanted to deal with — flooded her.

He eased the door open a crack and peered in. "Stay here."

"Sure." Except stepping through that door could teach her about the human world, and if she was never going back to Court, she needed all the information she could get, and fast.

The memory fire around Grey flared. He gasped and seized the doorframe with his free hand. The muscles in his neck strained for a moment, then he drew in a ragged breath. "Better yet, join me and watch my back."

He stepped inside without waiting for an answer and she followed. If she asked, would he tell her why he'd changed his mind? And did it really matter?

Inside lay a narrow hall made more narrow by wire racks and metal barrels stacked along the right side. At the end stood an unob- structed arched entrance where the roar of many voices, talking and laughing, mixed with music. Between them and the entrance were doorways on the left. A woman in a black T-shirt and jeans, carrying a tray laden with plates of food, stepped out of the farthest doorway.

Grey grabbed Ivy's hand and jerked her into the nearest doorway. She stumbled against him, pressing her hands against his thick biceps to catch her balance. More heat swelled within her and more of his memory fire tickled over her hands.

He grabbed her shoulders and steadied her then turned to the room, a messy office / lounge / storage area with more metal racks filled with boxes and bags. A desk piled with papers sat in the back corner, reminding her of Tobias's office, and in the middle was a sagging leather couch and coffee table. Just inside the door on both sides were hooks filled with coats, purses, and bags.

Grey turned to the hooks. "Here's hoping this works for me."

"What works for you?"

"Finding a coat that will fit. Hunter says he always could and his human was almost as big as mine." He grabbed the closest black coat and held it up. Too small. "You might have noticed most humans aren't my size."

"I haven't met many humans." She hadn't met any, actually, but given that all dragons now inhabited human vessels, she could figure out that Grey was taller and broader than normal.

"Does this fit?" He grabbed a navy raincoat and handed it to her. "It doesn't have to be perfect."

She put it on. It was a little big, but it wouldn't hamper her movements. Grey sorted through a dozen more coats that were too small before finding a black thigh-length coat. He shrugged out of his bloody heavy winter coat and put on the light one. It strained across his shoulders and he wouldn't be able to button up the front — so no hiding his blood-soaked dress shirt — but it was long enough to hide the sword sheathed at his hip.

"Watch the door." He slipped out of the coat, tossed it on the back of the couch, and headed to a stack of T-shirts on the wire rack. "This is going to take a minute."

With a quick search that started at the bottom of the pile, he pulled out a shirt and tossed it on the coat, then unbuttoned his ruined dress shirt, revealing a broad muscular chest. Even sticky with blood, she couldn't help but wonder how it would feel to draw her hands across all that muscle, to have it pressed against her body, to dig her nails into his flesh.

A red welt near his heart indicated where he'd been shot, as well as proved just how slow a healer he was. Maybe just some gentle nail digging. He shouldn't have even had a scar by now and yet his flesh was still marked, which meant any organs damaged were still knitting back together.

His gaze lifted to hers and captured her soul again. Time stopped, every breath, every heartbeat, every thought. It all froze, suspended on her desire and need for his memories, for him. The blue memory flames flickered around him, but they were at the edge of her vision. All she could see was the crystal clarity in his eyes and the weight and darkness of the memories trapped within him.

What she wouldn't give to take those memories from him. Not because it would ease the constant ache within her, but it would ease the pain lying within him clearly etched on his face. But her magic didn't work that way. She didn't take memories. She only experienced them.

Except that didn't ease the craving clawing within her, to say her power word and take that experience without his permission.

She raised her hand, unable to stop herself, and cupped his cheek. Memory fire brushed over her skin, shivering across her wrist and down her arm. Strength swept into her soul and the ache vanished. For a second the weight trapped in his gaze vanished, too, then he closed his eyes and leaned into her touch, rubbing his jaw against her palm, his stubble rasping against her skin.

Her pulse pounded. Need burned tight in her chest, through her whole body. He drew closer, his breath mingling with the sweep of memory fire against her cheeks, his lips close, taunting her, tempting her. She needed to feel them pressed against her in full, not just a whisper like before. She craved the feel of him, of his body and his fire, outside and in. If she didn't pull herself together, she was going to whisper her power word and kiss him, diving into his soul while connecting their bodies.

A metallic clang clattered behind her, and someone yelled. Grey's gaze jerked to the doorway, freeing her. She wrenched her attention to the hall and turned her back on him, her pulse roaring, while praying she could hold back her power word and resist activating her magic.

This was a mistake. A big mistake. She didn't have permission. He'd know and she'd have ruined her chance of escape, all because she couldn't hold herself together.

Fabric rustled behind her and Grey drew close. His powerful aura, with a heavy mix of memory fire, slid against her aura, drawing a shiver and low rumble deep in her throat.

Mother, please!

"You just about done?" she forced out, flashing her teeth at him, unable to help herself and struggling to make the expression fierce, not seductive. God, she'd bring him all the meat and shinies he wanted in exchange for an hour with his memories... and him. But she doubted he'd think that was a fair deal.

He dropped his ruined dress shirt into the metal wastebasket beside the door. It hit with a wet *thunk*, and the image of all that blood pooled in the Handmaiden's secret residence flashed through her mind's eye.

"Yeah." He glanced into the hall then slipped past her, his body brushing against her, making her heart pound ever faster.

Holy Mother! She needed more than just a brushing. That was all this drake did. A brush of bodies. A brush of lips. A brush of memory fire. That wasn't what her dragon spirit wanted at all.

But what she really wanted was to figure out how to escape Court and how best to use the favor Grey owed her to do that. Jeez. Nothing else was important—

Which wasn't true. Making sure Regis didn't get the coin and control the full rebirth spell was also important. "What are the odds that we got here before Jet?"

She followed Grey out the door and back into the small court-yard, as a black vortex whooshed into existence against the wall of the building beside them.

Jet jumped out and her gaze snapped to Grey and Ivy.

"Ah, shit," Grey growled, and he drew his sword.

16

G rey lunged at Jet, praying she still wasn't fully aware of her surroundings after gating and that this was his chance to subdue her, but she jerked out of the way and drew her saber.

Shit. That had been his best bet. His chest still burned from the gunshot wound, and his movements weren't anywhere as fluid and strong as they should be to take on someone as skilled as Jet without killing her. As well, gloomy fog flickered at the edge of his vision, threatening to envelop him in memories even though he only stood six feet away from Ivy.

He lunged in again, forcing his body to move faster than it wanted. Pain screamed through his torso, but if catching Jet unaware wasn't an option, fast and furious was his only other choice. Finish the fight before it could get started.

Jet leapt to the side. His blade caught her jacket, and she stumbled off balance for a second.

With a growl, he grabbed for her sword arm, hoping to capture it in a joint lock like before. They still didn't know who she worked for, and while Grey had a short list of suspects, there wasn't any evidence pointing to any of them. As well, losing another dragon soul, Jet's included, to the universal ether had to be a last resort.

She swept her saber up toward his wrist and twisted out of the way. Her blade sliced up his forearm, drawing a fiery line from his elbow to his palm, but thankfully didn't sever the nerves to his hand.

She sneered, her weapon raised above her head, and swung at his neck, her blade a blur.

Hazy fog flooded his vision and he leapt forward, blindly grabbing for her sword arm. He seized her bicep and plunged his sword into her gut. She screamed, but fire sliced into his side. She'd countered with the same attack, a dagger in her off hand.

Darkness devoured his vision, and his muscles trembled, threatening his grip on her sword arm. She twisted to the side and rammed her foot into his hip, shoving him back.

He staggered, his heel catching on an uneven cobblestone.

Impossible sunlight flickered in water and a crowd roared. The reek of rotting food engulfed him, choking him. Water rattled against a window and someone laughed with malicious mirth. A bang exploded, and a woman howled.

Another staggering step back, and the courtyard wrenched into crystalline focus. He'd stumbled close enough to Ivy for her presence to clear his vision. Jet grasped her chest with one hand, blood oozing between her fingers, her expression wild.

Ivy held the gun in her hands, still pointed at Jet. "Shit, I thought that would at least drop her for a second."

And that was the problem. How the hell were they going to capture Jet if she healed too fast for even a gunshot to incapacitate her?

No, their only solution was to get to the *ekas* before her and destroy the key to finding the coin pieces so no one could have them.

Jet raised her saber and lunged at Grey as a black vortex whooshed over the wall behind her and a young orange dragon in a black suit stepped through.

"Oh, Mother," Ivy hissed. "It's Bolo, the prince's assassin."

"That's not—" He was going to say that wasn't the prince's assassin, but Hunter no longer held that job and without a doubt, Regis was interviewing drakes to take the position.

Grey side-stepped Jet's attack, fighting the pain consuming him, slammed his foot into the side of her knee, and swung his sword toward her chest. She staggered but didn't fall, and swept her saber up to block Grey's swing. Over her shoulder, the orange drake, Bolo, glanced across the courtyard and his eyes widened when he saw Ivy.

His surprise turned into a sneer and all the color drained from her face. Behind her, the door to the restaurant flew open and two men, one on a cell phone, rushed out. Sirens wailed in the distance, without a doubt heading to the courtyard because someone had heard that gunshot, and now the guy on the phone was telling the police there were three maniacs fighting it out with swords and a woman with a gun.

So much for not pissing off Viridian, and there wasn't much hope of containing any of this. Not with someone having already called the police.

Jet shifted, releasing her saber from his and letting Grey's blade slice the bicep of her sword arm in order to free her weapon. With a hiss, she jabbed the weapon at his inner thigh. He leapt to the side, but she countered with another fast slice.

More fog billowed over his vision. Three feet and he was out of range of Ivy's aura.

Another slice—

Or was that a flicker of sunlight on water—

No. It was metal reflecting streetlight. At gut height.

He blocked. Steel clanged against steel, and he strained to stay focused on the courtyard and Jet. He had to figure out how to get out of there before the police arrived.

The bigger of the two men who'd been in the doorway had stepped closer to Ivy and was yelling at them. Ivy had the gun hidden, and Bolo—

Jet released her pressure against his sword. He shifted, using the sudden forward movement to lunge in. She sidestepped and kicked him in the ribs. He stumbled back. Metal flashed against streetlight again, but from behind.

He wrenched around, bringing his sword up to block a swing at his neck from Bolo. Jet bared her teeth and bolted from the courtyard.

Shit. God damn fucking shit.

"The writ is to bring you in alive," Bolo said, jerking Grey's attention from Jet. The orange drake leaned closer, his sneer deepening. "But I'm pretty sure my prince won't really care."

"And I'm pretty sure you leaning in just put you off balance." Grey grabbed the orange drake's wrist and yanked him forward. Bolo stumbled, and Grey swept his blade through his abdomen. The drake howled. The human who'd been yelling at them from the doorway screamed, and the guy on the phone gasped.

Bolo dropped his sword and fell to his knees, clutching his stomach.

Ivy rushed to them and kicked Bolo's katana out of his reach. "She's getting away."

The orange drake struggled to draw the matching wakizashi at his hip, but Grey ran his sword through the drake's chest, drawing another scream.

"And that's not going to keep him down. As much as I'd like to take his head, I don't want to join the others responsible for our extinction." Grey jerked his chin to the wrought iron gate. "Let's go."

Ivy rushed out of the courtyard, and Grey followed, his body burning with fiery agony. Blood still trickled down his arm from the long slice and oozed from the hole in his gut.

They ran into a narrow one-way street, with a dozen mopeds and scooters parked tight against the right-hand wall between garbage and recycling bins. Ahead lay a wider, brighter crossroad, but there was no way he was going to be able to run the mile to the *ekas* as injured as he was and certainly not fast enough to get there before Jet.

"We need to gate," he said, gasping to catch his breath.

"But you said—" Her hands clenched and she stopped running. "Right. We won't catch up to Jet in time."

Thankfully, she didn't mention that he could barely run. A few feet away stood the entrance to a parking garage. A single orange light shone inside and he didn't see any security cameras — not that there weren't any inside, but he could hope. Gating from the garage was at least better than the street, where those guys from the restaurant, or worse the police, could see them.

"In here." He staggered inside — still no sight of cameras — hissed his power word and summoned a gate. Trying to ignore the agony within him or the annoying trickle of blood oozing down his leg, he concentrated on the courtyard around the corner from the *ekas*. It had been pretty much unkempt and abandoned five hundred and fifty years ago. Here was hoping it still was.

17

G rey grabbed Ivy's hand, reveling in the sudden clarity of the black vortex in front of him, the damp cool of the parking garage, and the smell of vehicle exhaust and oil. They stepped into the gate and his magic powering the vortex stuttered, drawing back to the anchor behind him.

Shit. They couldn't afford to step back into that courtyard. If the police weren't there already, they would be soon.

With a growl, he forced more magic and concentration into the gate. It spat them out into a silent, dark courtyard. It was similar to the one where Seville's gate anchor sat, small with two- and three-story buildings blocking in three sides, but this courtyard was even smaller. There wasn't room for a tree, only a bush that took up half the yard and looked like it had never been trimmed.

Thank the Mother of All the courtyard was still as abandoned as he remembered. He gritted his teeth and forced his body to move to the gate and into the street beyond the courtyard. He didn't know what he was going to do if Jet was already there. As injured as he was, there was no way he'd win a fight.

"Do you still have that gun?" he asked.

Ivy held out the weapon.

"Check how much ammo you have left." A part of him wanted to take the weapon from her, and while he had experience with various sidearms — from before the 1946 attack — his instincts said she was a better shot. Not to mention it was better if they were both armed.

"I've four bullets left."

Here was hoping they wouldn't need more.

There were two doors to the *ekas*, a front door a block down and around the corner on a narrow street, and a side door which exited into an even narrower alley on the far side of the building from them. And while some *ekases* had remained popular establishments for dragons to visit, this one in Seville was close to being abandoned. A dragon could still visit and worship in the temple to the Mother in the basement, but there wasn't a proprietor on site and it wasn't regularly stocked with supplies.

Grey strode to the heavy wood and iron front door — like all the doors to the neighboring buildings — and grabbed the latch. Magic shivered over his hand and up his arm, sending spikes of pain through the still-healing slice. The spell recognized his dragon spirit, released the lock, and he eased the door open.

The tingling magic of a gatelock whispered over his skin as he crossed the threshold. It was a fraction of the strength it should be. A drake with a powerful gating ability, like Diablo, who could rapid free gate in the middle of a fight, could probably break through the spell. Grey had no idea if he could or not, and given his injuries and tenuous clutch on reality, didn't want to try. Jet, while not a hatchling but still not an ancient drake, hopefully didn't know she could even try.

Inside, the common room lay wreathed in shadows, with only a hint of light coming through the single grimy barred front window. His night sight — not strong enough to have perfect vision in the dark like other drakes, but good enough that he wasn't going to blindly stumble into something — kicked in. A dozen wooden tables and four dozen matching chairs filled the room. Half the chairs and tables stood as if they'd been trapped in time, with their stubby candles in red glass jars on the tabletops, while the other half had been tipped over and broken, as if a tornado had swept through, selecting furniture at random, two here, three there, and one in the middle of others that were completely untouched.

He stepped inside so Ivy could join him, and closed the door. Everything was covered in a thick layer of dust with garlands of cobwebs. It didn't look like anyone had been here in at least a century, but—

Ivy hissed her power word. Her aura flared, and Grey shifted closer to her before he could stop himself.

She clenched her jaw, took a step away, and her aura returned to normal. "Jet's already here. She used her earth magic to hide her footsteps and went through that back door."

"Well, shit." Grey tightened his grip on his sword and forced himself to move away from Ivy. Even without her magic activated, he was still drawn to her on a subconscious level that worried him. If every time she used her magic he needed to get closer, what else would she see about those he was trying to protect?

A soft clatter beyond the door yanked him from his thoughts. One problem at a time, and Jet was at the top of his list of problems.

"Get your flashlight app out, but keep the light low," he said.

Ivy drew her phone from her purse and they crossed the common room to the door. If memory served him correctly — and since he was still within range of Ivy's memory dampening aura, he was forced to guess at what his actual memory of this place was — beyond this door lay a kitchen and the stairwell down to the temple of the Mother. The clatter hadn't been loud, so he was guessing — and hoping he was wrong — that the sound had come from the basement.

He glanced at Ivy, and she turned off the light app and put her phone away. While in the dim light she appeared calm, her breath was a little too fast for a dragon who had much experience with combat.

"Take a breath. If Jet is here, keep back and have that gun ready," he said, then cracked open the door to the kitchen.

No one in sight.

No sound, either.

He opened the door farther, revealing that, if the tornado of destruction had swept through here, it had done so after the kitchen had been gutted. Where the ovens should have been was an empty space with blackened stone walls. Ash was still heaped in the fireplace — that had been the main source of cooking once upon a time — and more dust and cobwebs and debris from broken cupboards and countertops littered the area, but there were no signs of pots or pans or any other cooking implements.

With both the common room and kitchen in disarray, Regis had clearly not made maintaining this *ekas* a priority. Of course, with his desire for all drakes to move back to the safety of Court and never return to the human world, it made sense he'd abandon all the ancient meeting houses, which had been formed just after the Scourge and before the Handmaiden had discovered the interdimensional sphere that had become Court.

The clatter came again. Louder this time and without a doubt from behind the door near the fireplace — the one leading downstairs, not the one on the other side of the room leading to the alley.

A quick check behind the closer door confirmed the stone stairwell leading down was empty — at least as far as he could see, until the stairs curved around before reaching the basement floor. With a breath that made his chest and gut hurt more than it steadied him, he crept down the stairs. If luck was on his side, Jet would be too busy with whatever she was doing to notice him and he'd be able to get the jump on her. This time. Because surely one of these times that plan would actually work.

He reached the curve in the stairs and crouched. Yellow light flickered through the partially opened door leading to the temple of the Mother, the kind of light that trembled, reminding him of candlelight. But that was ridiculous. Even if Jet didn't have night sight, she was a modern drake. Even Grey had a phone with a flashlight app on it.

"Can you see her?" Ivy whispered.

"No. I need to get closer." As much as he wanted to just barrel in and attack, given his injuries, that wasn't the best plan. "Remember, keep—"

"Keep back and shoot the bitch." She flashed him a hint of teeth. "I'm not going to forget after our last couple of fights." Between one second and the next, her ferocity vanished. "Not, at least, between now and stopping her."

"Good." He wanted to say something more, yearning to help her with her confidence. She might be young, but he would have thought being in Tobias's employ would have helped her with that. Of course, being a member of Regis's coterie might not have helped anything, particularly given Regis's recent fury over Zenobia's coup, Hunter quitting, and Barna's refusal to stop his activities in the human realm. "You've got this."

Grey eased the rest of the way down the stairs to the partially opened doorway. Inside, Jet had lit candles. The small temple, while in the same kind of disarray as upstairs, was illuminated with the glow of dozens of candles and two oil lamps. She'd gathered them to the right, setting them beside broken and upended chairs, creating a semi-circle to provide enough light to examine a tapestry.

She took a step back and held up her phone. Not to examine or add more light, but to take a picture.

The tapestry was the one that had been there in the 1400s, when he'd visited last, depicting the two great temples to the Mother in Arrapha and Chang'an. It was ridiculous to think this enormous woven cloth that had been on display for centuries held the key to finding the two coin pieces. There wasn't enough detail to indicate where in either of the massive temples the pieces of a coin — that couldn't be larger than a quarter — were hidden. But maybe there was a small detail he hadn't considered. If he left now, told Ivy to stand a good ten feet away, he'd be able to remember every stitch.

But that wouldn't deal with the problem that Jet had pictures and would be able to crack the code as well.

Jet pocketed her phone in her jeans back pocket, and Grey tensed. She just needed to step closer and he'd have the advantage. But instead, she grabbed the tapestry and flipped it over, revealing the image of a gold dragon with wings spread, about to take flight. She pulled out her phone and took more pictures.

He blinked and a second image, this one of the tapestry's back, overlaid the first, with slightly different shadows. Ivy's power might make it more difficult to draw on his memories, but his earth magic to remember everything still worked. Without a doubt, *this* had to be the key. Perhaps the front and back images joined together some-how. Perhaps—

Jet ripped the tapestry from the wall and kicked an oil lamp onto it. Oil spilled, soaking into the fabric, and flames swept along its path. Ivy gasped and Jet's attention jumped to the doorway.

"I see you finally made it." She drew her saber. "A little too late, I'd say."

Not really. He'd seen the back. Even if he wanted to, he wouldn't be able to forget it. But very few people knew he had that ability and he wasn't about to let someone like Jet know. Besides, he couldn't let Jet leave and figure anything out. "It's only too late if I can't get your phone."

"What makes you think from our last encounters that you're capable of taking my phone?" She flashed her teeth at him, all aggression.

"You still have a red slash in your gut where I stabbed you."

"Yours is still bleeding." Her sneer deepened, and the fire behind her blazed hotter, the flames devouring the tapestry and jumping to the pieces of wooden chairs. "I bet the smoke inhalation incapacitates you first, and I just waltz out of here."

With how fast he healed? Yeah, he'd bet that, too. Jeez, he was going to have to make a move, but he had no advantage. He was really starting to regret the need to keep her alive to answer questions, not to mention the voice of reason at the back of his head that said not another dragon soul could be lost.

Ivy shifted, her foot softly scuffing against the stone floor. She was still out of sight behind him.

Well, he had one advantage.

"Even if you have to hit me, shoot her," he said under his breath, and he rushed into the room, swinging for Jet's head.

The attack was obvious, and Jet swept her saber up to block his strike, but he twisted at the last minute and grabbed for her sword arm. If he could wrap her up in a grappling hold, Ivy could shoot her.

But Jet wrenched back and swiped her saber at him in a wild swing designed to force him away. He leapt back on instinct. Her blade sliced through the front of his coat but thankfully didn't cut skin.

Ivy stepped into the doorway, the gun raised. Jet grabbed a shireken from her hip and threw it at Ivy. The blade hit her shoulder with a wet *thunk*, drawing a scream. Jet launched herself at Ivy, and Grey lunged for Jet. He grabbed the edge of her jacket and wrenched, but she grabbed the gun. Ivy held tight. Jet twisted, using Grey's pull to jerk Ivy off balance and crash her into him.

Dropping his sword, he half-caught, half-deflected her to the floor beside him and tightened his grip on Jet's jacket. With a growl, he yanked her toward him. She stumbled, turned, and wrenched the tip of her blade toward his gut. He heaved to the side, but this time the blade caught skin, slicing into his side and drawing more biting fire.

God fucking damn it. He was getting tired of being stabbed. He twisted more of her jacket around his hand, limiting her distance and therefore her mobility with the saber, and punched her in the face.

She staggered back but he held tight and hit her again. Her nose crunched. Blood gushed out of it.

"I'm taking that phone," he growled.

"You keep telling yourself that." She dropped her saber and, using his grip on her jacket, shrugged out of it.

Grey staggered forward, off balance, and she snapped her foot out and slammed it into his chest, knocking him back.

"Better luck next time." She bolted out of the temple, tossing a grenade into the doorway as she hit the stairs. "If there is a next time."

Grey's heart skipped a beat and panic crushed his chest. The room wasn't big enough. There wasn't enough cover.

Protect Ivy.

Everything within him screamed that he had to protect her.

He grabbed her, wrenched her away from the grenade, and held her in front of him. With a roar, he yelled his power word, willing everything he had, every ounce of strength and will and life into his magic.

Please break the lock. Please open faster than the grenade. Please. He had to protect her. Every cell in his being howled. *Protect her.*

The grenade erupted behind him as they tumbled into the gate.

Fiery agony raced over his back, stealing all breath, all thought, and his ears rang, even with the muffling sensation of the gate. His magic holding the gate open wavered, straining against the magic of the weakened gatelock, and jumping to the anchor where they'd first arrived.

He mentally seized his power, forcing every last ounce of strength he had into keeping it open, and locked on the courtyard just outside the *ekas*. If Jet hadn't gated away, she couldn't have gotten far. He had to find her, catch her—

His foot hit hard ground and his legs gave way. He shoved Ivy out of the way, the best he could do to avoid falling on her, and slammed into the ground. The ringing in his ears made it hard to concentrate, and every breath burned through him. Everything hurt. *Mother, it hurt!*

But there wasn't any time. If Jet was still there, he had to grab her. *Get up. Move.*

He shoved up to his hands and knees and glanced at Ivy. "Are you all right?"

Her eyes were too wide, her face too pale.

"Tell me you're all right." The panic that had seized his chest in the *ekas* tightened. She had to be all right. He couldn't explain why or how. He'd just met this drake and he still had no idea what to do with her and what she might have seen from his clothes.

It was the shock of the moment. That was all. An instinct from all his years fighting and protecting dragon and human comrades.

He tried to shake the feeling away, to focus on the job, but the sudden movement ignited a burst of agony that raced through him.

God damn it. Get up and finish the job.

"Are. You. All right?" he asked through gritted teeth, his head swimming and the cobblestones under his hands blurring.

"Your back," she said, her voice somehow centering him and cutting through the ringing and shuddering.

"It will heal." If he really thought about it, it should have been worse. They should have been dead. He could only guess he'd entered the gate before the worst of the shrapnel had struck. "Can you stand? We can't let Jet get away." He fought to straighten and stand.

Ivy scrambled to his side and helped him, one handed, the gun still held in her other hand. Thank the Mother they still had a weapon. Her help answered one of his questions — could she stand? — while her movements also suggested her injuries weren't so bad that it would take long for her soul magic to heal them.

The vise around his chest eased, but that only returned all his focus to the pain consuming him.

18

I vy helped Grey stand, her ears ringing and her head spinning as if she were still within the gate. Her pulse pounded and the frozen knot in her gut had swept through her limbs, making them tremble.

"We have to catch her." He staggered, unbalanced, and she tightened her grip on his arm, trying to steady him.

He was crazy. Even with only the dim illumination coming from the streetlight ten feet away, she could tell his back was a bloody, shredded mess. He shouldn't be standing and he certainly shouldn't be going after Jet. The woman had seriously injured him twice and while both their swords had been abandoned in the temple, that didn't mean she was without a weapon. This injured, it would be easy for someone to decapitate Grey and separate his soul from his human body.

Her heart raced faster. She couldn't let that happen. Bolo had seen her with him. He would tell Regis, and she didn't know if Tobias would be able to protect her from him... or if he even wanted to. She wasn't even sure what about Regis terrified her, only that the knowledge imprinted in her locket and her encounter with him earlier that day screamed he was dangerous, that he would hurt her and take joy from it.

Grey was her only hope at freedom. Even if that meant searching his memories to find some secret she could use to force him to help her.

"Come on." He staggered to the wrought iron gate leading to the street. "We can't let Jet examine those photos. She can't get that coin."

God, she really hoped she wouldn't have to steal his memories to use against him. Even if Ivy didn't know much about dragons, she knew, on a soul-deep level, Grey was a dragon who cared. He valued the difference between right and wrong. He'd protected her with his body. She only had a few cuts from the grenade's shrapnel and those were already healing. She didn't know if Ophelia or Tobias would have done that for her. Surely that had to mean something… she just didn't know what.

He pulled the wrought iron gate open and stumbled onto the street.

"She has to be gone by now." Ivy rushed to his side but didn't know how to help him walk without wrapping an arm across his back. "She would have gated out of the building before she even reached the top of the stairs."

"I'm hoping not. The only reason I broke through the gatelock was sheer desperation." He slid his gaze to hers, capturing her dragon soul like he had back at the Handmaiden's residence. "And I'm not so proud that I can't admit it. I thought you were going to die." His eyes widened a fraction, as if his admission had surprised him, then he yanked his attention back to the street. "I thought we were both going to die."

The warmth in her chest billowed. More proof of her silly attraction to him, nothing more. But that only increased her trembling. She'd almost died. She'd been useless in that fight and *he'd* almost died.

She shoved that thought aside. Don't think about the danger and *don't* think about the attraction. He was her ticket out of Court and she was damned well going to keep him alive long enough to be free.

They reached the *ekas's* front door. "I'm guessing she exited out the kitchen door into the alley, but—"

"I can check." She drew back from him, hissed her power word, and prayed her magic wouldn't latch onto him again. It almost had when they'd first entered the *ekas* and she'd checked for Jet. It had taken everything she had to force her power into the room and not let it revel in the strength of his memories, like it had when she'd read that horrible one in the Handmaiden's residence.

Her magic seized a weak recent memory from the street and Ivy mentally pushed more power into it. Jet appeared, standing before the *ekas's* front door, but instead of leaving, she was entering. Well, hey. Finally, a little bit of luck, with landing one of the street's memories that was close to the time she wanted. She was only five to fifteen minutes off and didn't need to try jumping a large amount of time to see what she wanted.

Out of the corner of Ivy's eye, Grey's ever-present memory fire danced around him. Muted, as if his injuries were somehow keeping it suppressed, but still tempting her, luring her, he the only flame around and she a helpless moth.

Except she wasn't helpless, and if she remembered only one thing, it had to be that. It all came down to what she was willing to do to be free. And she was willing to do almost anything.

Even if a tiny voice within her begged that it wouldn't have to come to that.

Ivy yanked the street's memory forward. She and Grey reached the door and entered. A bang erupted, but Jet didn't exit.

"She wasn't here," Ivy said, easing back on the power she was pouring into her magic so she could pay attention to him but not fully release her hold on the memory. Perhaps the other side of the street could help. Perhaps she could take just a peek at one of Grey's memories again. Use it to steady herself.

Jeez, no.

"We should try the alley," Grey said.

Her gaze jumped to him, drawn of its own volition. No matter how much she wanted to avoid the temptation of his memory fire, she just couldn't help herself.

His gaze was locked on the street, as if looking for signs of Jet. Fire danced over his skin and wisps of blue smoke curled around him, teasing her to draw it into her and watch it. Just a peek. Just—

No. She wrenched her focus from him, forcing it down the street.

"If she wasn't in the alley, then—" He released a shuddering, agony-filled groan. "Then I don't know what."

Movement at the edge of the alley caught her attention. She rolled the memory back twenty seconds. A piece of newspaper and a crushed soda can tumbled out onto the street, blown by a sudden, powerful wind. She'd felt a gust like that many times that day, every time someone made a gate.

"She gated from the alley." Which meant maybe there was a clue or something that would help them stop her.

Ivy rushed down the street, rolling the memory back to thirty seconds before the gust, and watched Jet pull her phone from her ear, shove it into the back pocket of her jeans, and summon a gate.

Grey grabbed Ivy's arm and jerked her back. "Jeez, Ivy. She could have still been there."

Her power surged, sucking in a hint of Grey's memory. The reek of rotten food filled her nostrils—

Not now. She tugged free from Grey's grip and hurried to where Jet had been standing. "She was talking with someone."

Her magic leapt back to Grey and the alley dimmed, overlaid with another wet, gloomy alley. Malicious laughter, just a whisper, sent shivers down her spine. She— no, *he* couldn't heal that fast. Not fast enough to survive—

No. She tore her magic free and slapped her palm against the wall where Jet had been standing. *Jet. I need to see her. I need to see the alley's memory from a few minutes ago.*

The memory stuttered— but it wasn't the memory. It was her power heaving between the street and Grey.

Ivy clenched her jaw and squeezed her eyes shut.

Come on. Roll back. Just a few minutes.

An explosion roared around her. She jumped and opened her eyes, her heart pounding and fear freezing her gut. But it was just a memory.

A narrow wooden door banged open a few feet away, and Jet leapt out on a whoosh of smoke and dust.

"Good fucking riddance to the two of them," Jet said with a dark chuckle and pulled out her phone.

"What do you see?" Grey asked, his voice distant even though she could feel his memory fire sliding against her skin, threatening her hold on her magic.

Jet pulled her phone from her back pocket, hit a button, and placed it against her ear.

"What do you see?" Grey asked again, his tone more insistent.

"Let me concentrate."

His memory fire drew closer — he had to be only a foot away. "Ivy—"

Her magic leapt onto him. The alley outside the *ekas* vanished and returned to his alley.

"Make it fast," he said. Not from the memory but in real time.

"It'll go faster if you take four steps back," she growled.

His presence jerked away and dimmed.

She heaved her power back to the alley, refocused on Jet, and rolled the memory back to the moment the black drake had placed the phone against her ear.

"I thought you said the Handmaiden was tricky," Jet said. "No. Knowing the tapestry is the key and seeing both sides… it's kind of obvious." She rolled her eyes at whatever the other person said. "Yes, you don't want to know the details. Deniability and all that. Well, just know I'm going for the easy one first. It'll take about seven hours, but I'll still be ahead of schedule. You're going to pay me double for that, by the way." Jet flashed her teeth even though she was alone. "No, I said double." Her teeth-flash turned into fully bared. "Because I'm throwing in getting rid of Grey and Tobias's agent for free." She glanced down the alley toward Ivy.

On instinct, Ivy shrank back, even though she knew Jet couldn't see her.

"Consider them a casualty of war. Not every soul can be saved." Jet pocketed her phone.

Ivy released the memory and turned to Grey. He leaned against the wall, his breath short sharp gasps and his expression tight.

"She's figured out the key to finding the coin pieces for the rebirth coin, and she thinks we're dead."

"You got one thing right," a gravelly voice said from the mouth of the alley. Bolo.

Grey wrenched around and faced him. Ivy's heart skipped a beat. Grey was too injured to face the prince's assassin. He would die, and she couldn't let that happen.

Bolo sneered, a wicked gleam lighting his eyes. He raised both katana and wakizashi and growled low in his throat. "You will be dead."

19

Grey straightened, every inch of his body burning with agony. He had to finish this fight before it started because he wouldn't be able to create a gate with Bolo attacking him.

Bolo bared his teeth, making him look even more like a petulant hatchling.

Except being this injured, even a petulant hatchling could take Grey's head.

This was turning into a really shitty day to top the last few weeks of shitty days.

Fine. Whatever. Just do it. A quick pounce, get past the blades, and incapacitate him. It was his only way to win.

Mother, he was going to need a whole lot of luck.

Bolo hissed, Grey tensed, ready to pounce, but Ivy jerked forward and roared. A full, ferocious dragon battle cry.

Bolo's attention leapt to her as she yanked the gun up and fired. The bullet slammed into his chest. His eyes widened, his surprise at being shot clear. He staggered back, and Grey leapt at him, grabbed his head, and smashed it against the side of the *ekas*.

Bolo sagged to the ground, stunned. Ivy stared at them, the gun trained on Bolo, but her eyes were as wide as his had been, as if she couldn't believe what she'd done.

Yeah, well. That made two of them. She'd just shot the prince's new assassin. It didn't matter what Tobias would want. Regis would arrest Ivy and send her to Odyne for centuries of torture.

"That's not going to keep him down for long." Grey took a step toward her, but his knees buckled. He grabbed the wall to keep standing. "Let's get the hell out of here."

She gave a tight nod, her eyes still too wide, but her gun remained trained on Bolo.

Grey said his power word and a gate's black vortex swept over the wall in front of him. He concentrated on his studio in Newgate, the old boxing gym where he'd let Capri and Ryan hide when her house had been destroyed. Grey needed a safe place to go where no drake could find him and Ivy, and where he couldn't endanger Nero and his coteries.

Bolo groaned. Ivy sidestepped into the gate, keeping her focus on Bolo until the last minute. Grey followed, throwing himself through, unable to take a real step. Just get to his studio. That was all he needed.

Except a small voice, deep in the back of his mind, said he needed more than a safe place to heal his body. He needed to heal his mind and soul. He needed Ivy.

No, he needed the Handmaiden to use her magic, or Anaea to figure out how the Handmaiden eased his memories.

He needed to be reborn so he could finally forget. Wasn't that what he really wanted?

But he wasn't so certain any more. If he forgot everything, he wouldn't be able to protect Anaea, or help Capri or Nero or those teens living in his house, those just trying to make sense of a crazy world. He wouldn't be able to protect Ivy.

His heart skipped a beat, and panic seized him, sending white-hot agony screaming through his chest. He had to protect her. If he did nothing else, he had to make sure Regis didn't get his hands on her. And he wasn't sure it still mattered that he was trying to keep her from Court because she'd seen one of his memories that endangered Nero or not.

The gate's magic stuttered, and the exit jerked away from his studio and latched onto the anchor at Court. He scrambled to yank it back, but the fear gripping him squeezed tighter and his power wrenched against his control. The pain roared into a searing inferno and his hold on his studio vanished. He hadn't been there enough times recently. He couldn't keep it in his mind. Mother, he could barely keep anything in mind.

But he couldn't go to Court. Everyone he wanted to protect would be hurt. Ivy would be arrested. Nero would be in danger—

His thoughts locked on Nero's house. He'd spent more time there and gated there more in the last two weeks than anywhere. It was safe and familiar. And yes, Ivy's presence endangered them all, but it would be worse if she was back at Court.

He clutched onto the mental image of Nero's living room, praying, begging, fighting through the agony, for his gate to send them there and not to Court.

His foot hit solid ground... floor... it didn't matter which. The muscles in his legs gave out and he collapsed to his hands and knees. Frozen air swept around him, biting his cheeks and making him shiver, which sent more pain lancing through him.

"Mother of All," someone said. It sounded like Raven.

He forced his head up. They'd arrived in the living room in Nero's house with all the busted windows. Raven, Diablo, Ryan, Anaea, and half a dozen of the older kids were hanging bright blue tarps.

"Grey—" Anaea dropped her edge of tarp and rushed toward him.

Ivy jerked the gun up and pointed it at Anaea, making her stop.

"You don't honestly think that's going to stop us?" Diablo said, his tone dark.

Ivy hissed, her teeth fully bared, and yanked the gun toward him.

"They're friends," Grey gasped.

The muscles in Ivy's legs tightened. Her gaze swept over the group, and Grey could only pray she wasn't one of the few dragons who could tell the difference between a drake's aura and that of a human mage. Although with the teens in the room, things already looked suspicious, since the Handmaiden didn't rebirth dragon souls into human bodies that weren't adult.

"Come on," Diablo growled. "Shoot me."

"I'm not sure he's a friend," Ivy said.

"I'll give you that. But everyone else is." Grey sagged forward and pressed his forehead to the cold carpet. He just needed a minute—

Okay, maybe more than a minute. It was just so hard to concentrate. But he didn't have a minute. Nothing had changed. Jet had a head start on them and he still couldn't let anyone get their hands on the full rebirth spell.

"I need to talk with the doyen," Grey said.

Anaea huffed — at least it sounded like Anaea. "You need a doctor." Yep, it had to have been Anaea who'd huffed. She was still getting used to the fact that dragons didn't have doctors.

Diablo growled and Ivy's feet shifted closer to Grey.

"Diablo." Grey tipped his head enough to see the black drake. "Please." It was the best he could get out, even though everything within him howled to get up and attack Diablo, be the bigger, stronger drake.

Jeez, that reaction had to be from too much adrenaline from the fight and the pain, since even on a good day, Diablo could probably kick his ass and Grey knew better.

"You—" Raven glared at Diablo. "Promise to play nice."

Diablo rolled his eyes. "Fine."

"And I'll take our guest to the kitchen." Raven handed her tarp to Jeff and brushed her hands on her thighs.

Grey's chest tightened. If Ivy left, he'd be in pain *and* unable to control his memories. He'd be useless when he really couldn't afford to be. "No. Ivy needs to talk with the doyen, as well."

"I'm not sure the doyen wants to talk with her," Diablo said.

"She shot the prince's new assassin to save me." Grey forced himself up and sat back on his heels. *Mother, that hurt!* "She can't go back to Court."

Diablo cocked an eyebrow, his expression clear. She couldn't go back without leverage and learning about Nero's unsanctioned coterie would give her all the leverage she needed.

Grey matched Diablo's stare, willing him to understand that Ivy might already know and it didn't matter what she wanted. She was never going back to Court.

Anaea gasped and understanding flashed across her face. "Raven, call Nero."

Diablo glared at her. Yeah, she'd used Nero's name and now Ivy knew who the doyen was. Anaea met Diablo's stare and the muscle in his jaw tightened as he, too, had a flash of realization.

Good. Everyone was on the same horrible page.

"Can I please get out of the cold?" Grey asked. "I'd rather just be in agony than in agony and freezing."

"Diablo, Ryan, help Grey." Anaea headed to the door and gestured to Ivy to follow.

Ivy glanced at Grey. With the crystal clarity of her aura brushing against his, her eyes were still too big — even if there was a ferocious dragon simmering in those dark depths — and the pulse at her neck was too fast. He could only hope she hadn't figured out that knowing Nero was the doyen Grey was working with meant they'd never allow her to leave.

But a bigger part of him begged that she wouldn't *want* to leave.

Diablo grabbed Grey under the right armpit and helped him stand. "What the hell have you gotten into?" he hissed.

Ryan grabbed under the other arm and steadied Grey. "I want to know why you aren't healing?"

"I am healing. Just really, really slowly." So God-damned slowly. He took a staggering step forward, gritted his teeth, and took a few more. He didn't want Ivy to get too far ahead of him and force him to reveal to Diablo and Ryan that he was having trouble with reality, too.

"And what about the green drake?" Diablo asked. "I don't know if Anaea can cast a rebirth spell again."

Ryan's eyes flashed wide. Guess he hadn't figured out that Ivy wasn't leaving this house, at least not as Ivy.

"I don't know." But he did know. Diablo was right. Rebirthing Ivy or keeping her a prisoner was the only answer, the one Grey hadn't wanted to admit to himself back in the Handmaiden's residence when he'd realized she'd read a memory from his clothes.

And yet he couldn't accept that. Locking her up or resetting her soul to its base condition wasn't protecting her, and the voice in the back of his head, the one that had started screaming in the *ekas* and was growing stronger by the minute, said he had to protect her.

"If you can't do it, I will," Diablo said. "It's my job. It's not yours."

But this was Grey's mess and he was already indebted to Diablo and Nero and this secret coterie. He'd never shirked his responsibility before and he wasn't about to now.

"I can convince her to stay." He had to, and not just because it protected her life.

20

I vy followed the silver drake with the brilliant white aura out of the room with the broken windows and down a hall, to an office with floor-to-ceiling bookshelves covering every space of wall that wasn't window. A heavy wooden desk and leather office chair sat at the back, facing two low-backed brown leather chairs. Folders and papers were stacked neatly in a tray beside a cup with pens and a closed laptop computer. If the shelves hadn't been so neat — and the desk so big — the room would have reminded her of Tobias's office.

But that hint of a similarity just made her heart pound faster.

She'd shot the prince's assassin.

If she hadn't wanted to go back before, now she had no choice. It didn't matter if she could trust Tobias and Ophelia or not. She couldn't go back. She *wouldn't* go back.

The silver drake pointed to one of the chairs. Her expression was soft, her eyes sad, but she also held herself with the ferocity of a mature dragon, not a hatchling like some of the other dragons back in that living room. Except Ivy couldn't figure out how old this silver drake was. Her aura said ancient and powerful, but she only had a hint of memory fire dancing around her. The halls and room around them had more memory fire than her. If she was as old as Grey, she should have had a similar degree of memory fire as Grey, certainly at least as much as Tobias or Regis, on something she was wearing... unless, of course, this drake liked to wear new things—although Ivy had yet to run into someone who didn't have something, a necklace, ring, or watch, they'd been holding onto for a while.

"Can I get you anything?" the silver drake asked.

The black drake who radiated waves of predatory danger snorted. Grey had called him Diablo. "She's meeting the doyen, not here for tea."

The silver drake's aura flared and a hint of magic wind gusted through the room.

"Anaea is just being polite," Grey said as Diablo and another man moved to help him to the other low-backed chair. Grey's expression tightened and he didn't sit. "I'd rather not bleed all over the upholstery."

The other drake who'd been helping him, a young blue drake according to his aura who Anaea had called Ryan, grabbed a plain wooden chair by the door and set it beside Ivy.

The black drake, Diablo, sagged into the low-backed chair instead, one leg hanging over the arm until the silver drake, Anaea, glared at him. Then he got up and sauntered to the back of the room.

Ivy tightened her grip on the gun. Yes, Diablo was right. It wouldn't stop them, but it made her feel safer, made her feel like she could protect Grey in his injured state. It didn't matter that he'd said these dragons were friends. She needed him. He was her ticket out of Court… although it had sounded like these dragons didn't want her to return, either.

Air whooshed in the hall and an ancient black drake with memory fire blazing from the rings on his hands and cufflinks on his shirt — like the flames Anaea should have had — strode into the room. His gaze landed on Ivy and his eyes narrowed.

A growl bubbled in the back of her throat, and she fought the urge to bare her teeth. If this was doyen Nero, submission was better than aggression. He ruled his coterie because he was stronger and more powerful than any other member.

She brushed her locket, drawing out what she knew about doyens and coteries. Only bits and pieces. Dragon political life was compli-cated and she hadn't wanted to bog herself down with too much information that changed too quickly.

Nero's attention jumped to Grey, and a dangerous fury boiled in his eyes and tightened his jaw.

Her pulse picked up. Grey had disobeyed his doyen by bringing her here — that much was clear in that black drake's initial reaction to their arrival — Grey was in danger and too injured to defend himself, and God-damn it, she wasn't going to let some selfish doyen take his displeasure out on Grey, not when Grey was trying to stop whoever Jet worked for — most likely Regis — from getting control of the rebirth spell.

The growl she'd been holding back broke through her restraint, and she straightened in the chair, ready to fight. To hell with the fact that she couldn't fight. She was tired of being weak and helpless, and she'd God damned shot the prince's assassin. She couldn't afford to be anything but a confident dragon.

Nero cocked a dark eyebrow and Anaea shifted, her aura fluttering, but Ivy couldn't tell with what magic. Diablo crossed his arms, leaned against the bookshelf beside Anaea, and snorted.

"It's been a shitty day," Grey said, his tone exhausted and tight with pain. "This is the agent Tobias assigned to the ransacking of the Handmaiden's chambers. Ivy."

"One of Tobias's agents shot Regis's new assassin?" Diablo's eyebrows raised, looking, for a second, as if he was impressed.

"He was endangering the mission," Ivy said, with more growl than she'd intended.

"Which would suggest Regis doesn't know anything about Jet." Grey shifted but didn't look more comfortable.

The ice knotted in Ivy's gut tightened. "Unless Bolo was sent to stop you so Jet could get the key." That would confirm Regis was Jet's employer.

Nero cleared his throat. "I think you need to catch me up."

"To make a long story short, someone hired Jet to go after a coin that, once it's inserted into the hole in the medallion, completes the rebirth spell." Grey met Nero's gaze head on which, according to everything Ivy knew, should have enraged the doyen, but didn't. "It takes the Handmaiden out of the equation. Whoever controls this completed medallion controls Court."

"They'd have to get their hands on the medallion first," Diablo said.

"I know most of them are lost." The blue drake, Ryan, frowned. "But isn't there one in the arena at Court?"

"It would take some serious magic to get to it," Grey said, "but I wouldn't put it past whoever is after it. They had a lockpicking spell to break the magical locks on the doors to the Handmaiden's chambers at Court—"

"And they knew about the Handmaiden's secret residence." Nero sat on the edge of his desk.

"It sounds like you also might have proof that Regis is involved," Anaea said.

"Or not proof," Grey said. "Bolo didn't seem to know anything about Jet."

"Jeez, Grey. Are you telling me a hatchling like Bolo is responsible for your back?" Diablo asked.

"No, that was a grenade," Grey said. "From Jet, after she stabbed me a couple of times."

"And shot you in the chest." The knot in Ivy's gut tightened even more.

"She shot you?" Anaea's aura flared again, her fury manifesting in a burst of wind.

Another growl rumbled in Ivy's throat, and she fought the urge to tell this strange drake to back the hell off. Grey was hers—

Hers!

Her heart stuttered.

Hers to *use.*

That was what she'd meant. She needed him. He'd promised her a favor and she was going to cash in. She was going to use him to get away from Regis and Court and everything dragon that wanted to keep her a prisoner and use her.

That was all.

"The gunshot is almost fully healed." A piece of shrapnel oozed out of Grey's back, clattered against the chair, and plopped onto the rug beneath him. "And my body is close to expelling all the shrapnel. I'll heal."

"Really fucking slowly," Diablo said.

"Still healing." Grey glared at Diablo.

"You want me to set up a fan to help your soul magic along?"

"Ha ha. My healing isn't the problem."

Diablo snorted. "I would beg to differ on that one."

"This coin is," Nero said.

"The good thing is that the Handmaiden broke it into two pieces and hid them." Another piece of shrapnel plopped onto the floor. "The bad—"

"Let me guess." Diablo jerked away from the wall. "Jet knows where those pieces are."

"And the prize goes to the brooding drake in the corner," Grey said.

Diablo flashed his teeth at him. "Fuck you."

"Get in line."

"Back on topic," Nero growled.

"Well, I... overheard her—" Ivy glanced at Grey, but he didn't open his mouth to correct her and reveal her earth magic. "It was before she gated away. She was talking on the phone with someone, saying she was going after the easy one first and would have it in seven hours."

Nero drummed his fingers on his desktop. "Any idea what that means?"

Grey pursed his lips and his gaze locked on Ivy's, his expression sad and pained and... and she didn't know what. She'd never seen emotion like that on anyone before — at least not that she could, in her limited memory, remember.

"If Ivy steps into the hall, I'll be able to tell you."

The knot in her gut snapped, freezing into her chest. "If I what?"

Diablo snorted and Anaea frowned.

"You want me to leave?" She couldn't wrap her mind around that. Sure, he hadn't explicitly said they were in this together, but she'd thought she'd proven herself useful. Certainly useful enough to be kept around. If he thought she couldn't help any more, he'd send her back to Court and that couldn't happen.

"Remember my earth magic?" he asked.

Diablo's eyes narrowed. "You have an earth magic other than free gating?"

"Yes," Ivy said. "You remember everything."

Grey's gaze locked on his hands. He squeezed them and another piece of shrapnel oozed out of his back. "You seem to be the antithesis to my ability."

That shrapnel hit the chair, the sound somehow too loud in the sudden stillness. No one moved. It felt as if time stood still.

He had confessed his magic in front of these drakes. He was either desperate or he trusted them. He—

"Wait, I affect your magic?"

Ryan shot Anaea a strange look. Ivy had no idea what it meant, and Anaea gave a tight nod.

"Yeah. I'd rather you not share that with anyone. Not even Tobias."

"You have my word." Since she wasn't going to see Tobias again. Yes, she'd call in and report when it was getting close to ten that evening, but she wasn't going anywhere near him where he could apprehend her, and she certainly wasn't going anywhere near Ophelia who could read her thoughts. "The priority is this coin. Tobias will understand that." At least she hoped so.

"Tobias will," Nero said, but his expression darkened as if there was more to the situation and it didn't make him happy.

And he was going to be even more unhappy when he learned the truth about what she planned.

"I can't believe you've had an earth magic all this time and no one knew about it," Diablo said.

"It's not really useful in a fight." Grey shrugged and winced. "Ivy, if you could step out the door, I'll remember what was on that tapestry and figure out what Jet knows."

"Sure." She glanced at the door, but didn't want to leave. It was ridiculous. There wasn't anything they could say or do while she was out of the room that she couldn't learn about. All she had to do was peek at the most recent memories in the room or on Grey's clothes. He knew that, so he couldn't be trying to exclude her. There wouldn't be any point.

Anaea stepped toward the door. "How far do we need to go?"

"The next door down will do." Grey's pale gaze, filled with apology and that strange emotion Ivy didn't recognize, locked onto her. "I just need a couple of minutes."

"Sure." She followed Anaea into the hall and down to the next doorway, and the silver drake pounced.

Anaea seized Ivy's arm, jerked her to face her, and shoved her against the wall while a magical wind swept around Ivy and pinned her in place. "I want to make this clear in terms you understand."

Ivy wrenched against the wind and hissed back, baring her teeth.

"Grey is family," Anaea growled, "and I will do whatever it takes to protect my family."

Lucky Grey. That thought hurt. Ivy wished she had someone who'd fight for her like this, someone who cared half as much. If she was smart, she'd back off. Leave him to Anaea and his coterie and walk away, but she couldn't. Mother of All, she just couldn't and she feared it had nothing to do with needing him to help her escape Court.

"I've met scarier drakes than you," Ivy said. Regis without a doubt, even Bolo, had more menace, but not nearly a fraction of the magical strength. She yanked herself away from the wall and Anaea's wind slammed her back.

"You haven't met anyone like me." Anaea's aura flared, a brilliant glow that burned Ivy's eyes with a power that had been hidden before. This drake was more dangerous than Bolo or Regis. She was the embodiment of pure, raw power. "You endanger him and I promise there won't be enough of your soul left to dissolve into the universal ether."

Holy Mother! This drake really could destroy every last fiber of her being.

The knot in Ivy's gut snapped, too cold, sending shivers through her, and a small voice in the back of her head screamed, *Don't show fear. Never show fear.* Something she was sure she was failing at.

"I'll leave when he tells me to," she forced out. She didn't want to leave at all, but knew, soul-deep, if he told her to go, she would.

That thought brought sudden, overwhelming grief. It swept over her chest and up her neck, choking her. Tears welled in her eyes and a new horrible thought filled her. Anaea had wanted to help him the moment they'd gated there, and she was threatening Ivy, demonstrating she was a more powerful drake and she would do anything to protect Grey.

"I won't endanger your mate. I promise." They were both ancient silver drakes. If she'd been thinking straight, she would have figured it out the moment she'd arrived. She fought to breathe, but the constriction in her throat and chest ached with a new crushing weight. What the hell was wrong with her?

"You think Grey is my mate?" Anaea asked.

"Isn't he?"

"Grey is family." The wind vanished, but Anaea's aura still radiated enormous power. "You don't want to know what I'd do to protect my inamorato."

"I won't endanger him, either." She didn't want to endanger anyone. She just wanted to be free... except a part of her also wanted to know what it felt like to have someone so ferociously dedicated to her.

She brushed her locket, but there was nothing there to indicate she'd ever had a friend like Anaea. All she had were Ophelia and Tobias and they'd proven they couldn't be trusted. When she left Court — and she *was* leaving Court! — there wouldn't even be them.

21

F og swept around Grey a few seconds after Ivy left the room, and the smell of reeking garbage clogged his nose.

Mother, he was getting tired of that memory and its constant reminder that his inability to heal quickly was a liability, not only to him but to others around him.

Metal clattered against a stone floor, and Jet's grenade popped into sight.

His heart skipped a beat, and every muscle tensed.

Protect Ivy.

He jerked around to find her, but the memory shuddered and a hint of a green light sliced through it at the edge of his vision.

Right. A memory. Ivy was safe. She stood just down the hall.

The image of her, roaring and shooting Bolo, swept into sight. Her aura radiated strength, revealing a hint of just how powerful her soul would become when she got older. She'd been ferocious, and he'd been unable to take his eyes from her.

"Hey," a masculine voice said.

Another flash of green, and the *ekas's* wall vanished. Diablo grabbed Grey's shoulder, wrenching him farther away from the memory of Ivy and back into Nero's office.

Right. Remember the tapestry. The sooner he did, the sooner Ivy could return and keep his magic at bay.

The gloom shuddered around him, and for a second he contemplated calling her back. It had been less than an hour since he'd seen the tapestry, and even in the middle of a fight, his memory was pretty good without his magic. But he couldn't risk missing something. He needed to remember it exactly. Any small detail could be the answer.

He drew in a breath to steady himself, but it lanced pain through his back and chest. The darkness in his sight billowed and the grenade clattered over the stone floor again.

Not what he wanted to see.

Jeez, why was it so hard to concentrate? He hadn't had this much problem in the Handmaiden's chambers earlier that day, and the memory fog that threatened to consume him was now stronger than before.

Just see the tapestry. He'd seen it before. It had been hanging in the *ekas* for centuries before the Spanish Inquisition.

Right. It was a depiction of the two great temples of the Mother.

Jet had taken a picture of that—

The image of Jet in the *ekas* taking a picture of the tapestry filled Grey's vision. The light from the candles and oil lamps flickered and a smoky haze drifted in the dim illumination to the ceiling. Every chip in the floor and walls, every whorl in the wooden chairs, and every stitch in the tapestry jumped into focus. A bead of sweat trickled down Jet's neck. She flipped the tapestry and took another picture.

A gold dragon with wings spread, about to take flight, filled the entire back. It was reminiscent of the many dragon images in the sacred rooms at Court, and at the temples to the Mother scattered throughout the human realm. There was one in each great temple, as well.

This had to be the key. The coins had to be hidden in the statues at the great temples. Both images were innocuous. Even with a sunburst flaring from the heart of the dragon on the back of the tapestry, no one would know these were clues to a hidden treasure because no one — save for apparently a very select few — knew the treasure existed.

The image of the tapestry shuddered, and the grenade clattered against stone.

It wasn't the alley where he'd had his throat slit, but this wasn't a better memory to keep jumping back to.

"I know where the coins are." He drew in a sharp breath, spiking more pain and using that to yank himself back into the present. "Let's get Ivy in here and figure out what we're doing."

"Let's not and say we did," Diablo said. "We both know she's never leaving this house again. She's seen the kids."

"She's not reacting as if she knows what they are." Except Grey knew that was a weak excuse. The fact that Grey was here with Nero endangered the coterie. Knowing Nero was hiding human mages was only an added bonus.

"If she goes missing, Tobias will ask questions," Nero said.

Diablo shrugged. "As far as anyone knows, she was last seen with Grey."

"And what do you propose? Locking her up in the basement for the rest of her life?" Grey glared at Diablo. Grey was the older, bigger drake. He might be hurt and wouldn't be able to win the fight even on a good day, but he sure as hell could make the black drake hurt.

Diablo met Grey's stare and flashed a hint of teeth, excitement and danger lighting his eyes. "At least until Anaea figures out how to wipe her memory." He blinked, a lazy movement as if he didn't care that Grey was about to throttle him. "Sorcerers can do that, right?"

"You're not erasing her memories." Grey wrenched forward.

Diablo vanished, and the *whoosh* of a rapid free gate gusted behind Grey. He jerked around, his body screaming in pain, and blocked Diablo's punch to his head.

"Enough," Nero growled. "I'll take care of it. We're not wiping Ivy's memories, and we're not imprisoning her. Regis's new assassin has the ability to sense a dragon's essence. All he has to do is summon his power in Newgate, and he'll find her here."

"We can't just do nothing," Diablo said, his voice dark. "She endangers the children."

"Well, we're not killing her, either." Grey's heart thudded, hard. Nero hadn't become doyen of the Major Black Coterie or the dugga of the Asar Nergal because he was soft. "We're not losing any more souls to the ether."

"You're not a hatchling, so stop acting like one." Nero's aura flared and a hint of his magical wind hissed through the room. "I'm doyen, and I protect mine."

Something Grey was acutely aware of. That, and the fact that he wasn't a member of Nero's official or unofficial coterie. He was an outsider, as he'd always been. His own coterie hadn't understood his friendship with Hunter, one of the few remaining red drakes, and when Grey had realized he wouldn't find a home with his own kind — along with the fact that his memories were starting to overwhelm him — he'd sworn himself into the service of the Handmaiden. Better an outcast with her than tying his fate to King Constantine and getting caught up in Court politics.

"Tobias is smart. If Ivy doesn't report in, he'll get suspicious." Nero's glare shifted to Diablo who met his stare head on. "And don't discount— *never* discount the chamberlain's resourcefulness. He manages all aspects of Court, including the Asar Nergal and Internal Inspection. He gathers agents who can reveal hidden secrets, and I have no doubt that's Ivy's earth magic."

"So we're screwed." A shudder swept through Diablo, and the wild danger, the one that seemed to scream for a fight, flickered across his expression. His attention jumped to Grey, and the danger burned into hot fury. "You screwed us."

He roared and half-lunged, half-rapid free gated with a *whoosh* and *pop*. He was five feet away, then he was up close and seizing the front of Grey's borrowed coat.

Grey jerked back, but Diablo wrenched around with a hip throw and tossed Grey with his enhanced strength. He crashed into the bookshelf. White hot pain exploded through him.

A magical wind burst into the room and slammed Diablo against its far side. Nero rose from his desk, radiating waves of menace, his aura pulsing with ancient power. He wasn't in as big of a human body as Grey, and his body wasn't as young as Diablo's, but without a doubt, he was the more powerful, more ruthless drake.

"I. Am. Doyen," he said, his voice low and soft and filled with danger. "You don't question me. You obey."

Diablo hissed and bared his teeth.

"You obey." Nero's wind slammed him to the floor and pinned him there.

Ivy and Anaea rushed through the doorway. The room snapped

into sharp focus, every book, speck of fluff caught on the rug, and chip in the old wooden floor becoming crystal clear. Anaea's aura flared with a brilliant white that made Grey's eyes water. Ivy's breath came fast, her complexion pale, her eyes wide.

Nero knelt and hissed, his voice so low Grey could barely hear it. "Tobias and Ivy are my problems. Yours are the human mages." He straightened and his gaze swept over everyone in the room. "Never forget who's doyen."

"Yes, doyen," Ivy said, her gaze dropping to the floor. The submissive action made Grey's chest ache. To react so quickly to a complete stranger indicated it had been made clear to her she was young and weak. The question was, who had made it clear? Regis? Or had Tobias been involved in that?

Grey wouldn't have thought Tobias was that kind of drake, but if it kept his people in line — particularly with a prince who jumped at every slight — Grey wouldn't put it past the chamberlain.

Nero's wind vanished and he eased onto the edge of his desk again. "Grey. You know where the coins are?"

Grey grabbed the edge of the bookshelf and stood. "They're in the dragon statues in the two great temples."

"Jet said she was going for the easy one," Ivy said from the doorway, her gaze still lowered.

"Which one would be easy?" Ryan asked from the back of the room, his tense body belying his relaxed lean against the shelves. "The one in Chang'an or the one in the mountains near Arrapha?"

"Ivy said she overheard Jet saying it would take seven hours," Grey said. "It has to be the temple in Iraq. That temple's gatelock has an enormous radius and even if she gated as close as possible, she'd still have to hike it in."

"I agree." Diablo sat in one of the low-backed chairs and slouched as if he hadn't just been bashed against the floor. "It wouldn't take her that long to get to the temple in Chang'an, even if she used the nearby gate anchor and didn't know her way."

"Not to mention the dragon statue from the Chang'an great temple isn't in the temple," Nero said. "The humans found it in 1923 and moved it into a museum. Last week it was shipped to The Royal Vancouver Museum in Canada on loan for restoration and a special exhibit next month." He opened his laptop.

"And you just so happen to know this?" Anaea asked.

"I make a pilgrimage to the Chang'an dragon every year." Nero glared at Diablo. "I have the reputation of a Traditionalist for a reason."

Grey squared his shoulders. He just had to hold it together for a little bit longer. Except he wasn't sure he was going to be able to do that. "If we want to stop Jet, we need at least one of the coin halves. I guess we're going to Canada."

Ivy gave a tight nod, her expression darkened as if she was coming to a realization she didn't like. "I should report to Tobias, and you should go with someone with more fighting experience. I can buy you a few hours, let you stop Jet first and get the coin piece so they can never be joined, but—"

"No," Grey said, the word rushing out before he could stop it.

Nero and Diablo stared at him, while Anaea and Ryan shared a concerned glance.

Shit. "I mean, if we don't want to raise any suspicions, we need to keep things as they are and not get anyone else involved."

"Tobias can still tell the prince that you're staying on mission," Nero said. "If Grey goes after the coin piece alone, you lose that story."

"I shot the prince's new assassin," Ivy said, her voice soft but edged with steely resignation. Yeah, she knew her options were limited, too.

"Tobias will believe that was to protect the mission. If Grey is the only drake who knows where these coin pieces are and the goal is to prevent Jet from getting the complete coin, then Grey can't be assassinated, no matter what the prince wants." Nero pursed his lips and frowned. "Yes, that's what you'll tell Tobias. When are you required to report in?"

"Ten tonight."

"Good. It will still take Jet seven hours to get the coin piece in Arrapha—"

"So we need to get to Vancouver." Grey squared his shoulders, snapping pain through him.

"You need to take a few hours and heal," Anaea said.

Diablo huffed and rolled his eyes. "I'd also suggest a plan."

22

An hour later, Ivy's head was stuffed with so much information she feared accidentally brushing her locket and imprinting any of it there. Especially the bits she didn't quite understand, like the details about electronic security systems and guard rotations. The only thing she had fully understood was that they were going to sneak in as guests of a museum's opening reception for an exhibition of northern Canadian art.

And while Nero had come up with a logical argument as to why she needed to accompany Grey to get the coin piece, she was certain it was a terrible idea. She couldn't fight and wouldn't be able to help him if he got into trouble. She was barely a second set of eyes because she didn't have a clue about half the things she should probably be looking for. In less than four hours, she'd experienced more than she had in her entire life. She was sure of that. There wasn't even a hint of anything like this in the locket and without a doubt, something like this would have been imprinted there.

She also wasn't sure why any of his friends weren't going with him instead. Although if he was Regis's enemy, anyone seen with him was in danger—

Which meant she could use that knowledge of who these drakes were as leverage to get her freedom. She could threaten them with revealing to the prince that they were helping Grey. A doyen like

Nero and a drake as ancient as Anaea surely had standing in Court that they wouldn't want to lose.

Except a part of her wasn't sure giving these people up was worth her freedom. She could do it then forget about it, but she couldn't help but wonder if something that cruel would permanently stain her soul.

"So we have a plan," Nero said.

"You mean Ivy and I do." Grey stood. After everyone had decided they needed a plan, he'd returned to the wooden chair and more pieces of shrapnel, covered in thick blood, had oozed out of his back as they'd talked.

"You have a couple more hours before you need to head out," Anaea said. "You should get cleaned up and grab a nap."

"The room across from yours is empty." Ryan stood and headed to the door. "I'll tell Raven Ivy is taking it for the night... early evening?"

Diablo snorted. "She's going to love that, having to do extra sheets because of a few hours."

"Actually, I think you're on laundry duty this week," Ryan said.

"Like hell I am," Diablo growled.

Ryan bared his teeth and flipped Diablo his middle finger.

"It's too dangerous." Nero typed something on his laptop. "Ivy's been here for too long already. If Bolo gets too close, he'll be able to track you here. You'll need to recoup someplace else."

"I'll book you a couple of rooms in a hotel in Vancouver. Hun—" Anaea glanced at Ivy. "H has a few aliases Court doesn't know about."

"Book an executive suite at the Sutton Court Hotel. It's close to the museum, but outside of the range of the gatelock enspelled into the dragon statue." Nero typed something into the laptop. "Ryan—"

"Yep, I'll get on finding museum reception appropriate clothing for them." Ryan strode from the room.

"I know a safe place to gate into in Vancouver." Grey drew in a breath, his expression still pained but not nearly as much as it had been a hour ago. "I'll gate us there."

"And risk your gate jumping to Court," Diablo said, "Don't be an idiot."

Nero turned his laptop, revealing a split screen with the picture of a luxury hotel lobby and one of a loading bay.

"Got it." Diablo grabbed Ivy's wrist and placed a hand on Grey's shoulder, and a vortex whooshed around them.

Ivy's foot hit solid ground. She stumbled, and Diablo shifted his grip to her upper arm and steadied her. She opened her mouth to thank him, but he glared at her and she snapped it closed.

They stood in a dark parking lot outside a loading bay. Above towered a ten-story high rise with large floor-to-ceiling windows, most of them fully covered with heavy drapes. Diablo pulled his phone from his pocket and glanced at the display.

"Anaea says the suite is booked. It's on the sixth floor. Room 603. Stick to the stairwell to limit the chance that you accidentally show your messed up back to any security cameras." He handed his phone to Grey. "Use the app on the phone to pick the electronic lock. I'll officially check you in when I come back with the clothes."

Grey took the phone. "Thanks."

Diablo flashed his teeth, the smile wicked with a little aggression. "Do you need me to carry your sorry ass up?"

"I'm fine."

"Well, don't call me when you get stuck on the fourth-floor landing."

"Can't." Grey held up Diablo's phone. "I've got your phone."

"Whatever." Diablo vanished with a whoosh.

"Come on." Grey squared his shoulders and winced. "I could really use a shower."

Ivy followed him through a side security door and up a back concrete stairwell. Despite his gruff exterior, it was clear Diablo cared. All the others who'd been in Nero's office had cared, too. Even the doyen lashing out at Diablo to prove his dominance hadn't lessened the feeling that they were all a family. And Grey was a part of that.

She risked brushing her locket and searched for anything in her history like what Grey had, even though she knew it wasn't there. Surely if she had people who cared for her like they cared for Grey, that would have been the first thing the locket showed her every morning. Instead, she was filled with fear. No one close to her could be trusted and everyone was dangerous.

No one in Doyen Nero's house could be trusted, either.

Grey was still a stranger, no matter what her attraction to him said. Attraction was only attraction. It didn't mean anything. Her need to keep him close was only because she wasn't going to ever step foot in Court again. Nothing more.

They reached the sixth floor and stepped into a cream and tan hall with warm lighting. Room 603 was only a few doors down, and Grey held Diablo's phone in front of the door's electronic lock until it beeped. They entered a spacious hotel suite with a moderate level of memory fire, decorated in the same colors as the hall. There were two open bedroom doors — one bedroom on either side of the suite — with a kitchenette and a living room between them.

"Do you want the room on the left or the right?' Grey asked.

"It doesn't matter." She couldn't afford to fall asleep and forget everything. Not until she'd imprinted a plan to escape Court into her locket.

"Right." He pursed his lips, and his gaze slid to hers and locked there. "Okay."

The knot in her gut tightened with a flickering of heated desire, mixed with the yearning to bathe in the memory fire dancing over him, along with her ever-present frozen fear.

"If you want to back out of this, I'll understand."

She should say yes. She didn't have the skills to break into a museum or — if they showed up — to fight Jet or Bolo. But agreeing that she should back out meant abandoning her chance at freedom.

It meant abandoning him.

Now her chest as well as her gut ached.

"So…" he said.

She didn't know if he'd taken her lack of response as agreement or disagreement. A smart drake would recognize her weaknesses and set her desire to the side for the safety of everyone involved. "I don't know how useful I'll be."

"More useful than you think." He released her from his gaze and turned to the closest bedroom, but didn't move. "Ivy—"

"Don't think I'm not in." The words spilled out. She also couldn't let Regis get his hands on the rebirth spell, giving him free rein to essentially kill without killing any drake he wanted to. No one could get control of the full spell. "I'm in. I just don't want to be a liability."

"You're not the liability." The muscles in his jaw clenched. "I am. I can't control my magic," he said, his voice a low harsh growl. "But you can."

"I don't understand."

"My magic is always on. It's not that I can recall everything whenever I want. It's that I recall everything all the time whether I want to or not."

"That's got to be—" She couldn't think of words to describe that. Terrible? Wonderful? It explained why his memory fire was so strong. It probably explained why it looked like the memory encompassed all of him and not just his clothes or treasured items. It certainly explained why it was so hard not to say her power word and let his memories wash over her. It might even explain why she sensed she could read *his* memories and not just the memories in his clothes. "You said back in the doyen's office that I affect your magic, and asked me to leave when you were trying to remember the tapestry."

"Yeah." A piece of shrapnel oozed out of his back and plopped onto the floor. "Son of a—"

Realization hit her, and she bit back a gasp. It was always on. *Mother, was he always seeing that horrible memory? How old was it? How long had he lived with that?* "You see *that* all the time?"

"Not when you're near." He grabbed the piece of shrapnel and tried to wipe the blood off the carpet with a clean edge of his stolen coat, but only managed to smear it in. "Can I tell you while I clean up in the bathroom?"

"You shouldn't be telling me any of this." Even if she didn't want to, Regis could force her to tell him whatever she knew as well as everything about his friends—

The cold in her gut flared. Just a meeting with Ophelia endangered him. She'd read Ivy's thoughts and know everything.

"You have to know," Grey said. "We can't afford to be separated when we break into the museum." He kicked off his boots and headed through the bedroom and into the bathroom. "Here's the truth. My magic is stronger than my will and I struggle to stay in the present. I swore myself into the Handmaiden's service because she promised to help me."

Ivy followed but stopped at the bathroom's doorway, even though the room was large enough for two. More than large enough, with pale marble countertops and gleaming white tiles on the floor, around the multi-person tub, and in the massive glassed-in shower — so big it didn't have a door, just an opening between the tiled walls and the glass panels. If she drew closer, she risked saying her power word and succumbing to the need clawing through her. "So the Handmaiden—?"

He shrugged out of his coat and pulled off his ruined T-shirt, revealing a sculpted muscular chest and abs. Memory fire danced over his skin, mesmerizing, calling her, and the memory of how it had felt whispering over her skin back in the Handmaiden's chambers at Court rushed through her.

A shiver trembled down her spine and the heat in her chest melted the renewed ice churning within her. Even without all that memory fire and with blood crusted on his skin and two angry half-healed slashes along his right side, Grey was breathtaking. There was more than just her craving for his memories attracting her, and without his shirt, she was even more aware of just how powerful he was. If a drake was forced to take human form, this is what he would look like — broad shoulders, massive chest, and thick, muscular arms. Beyond all that, his strength of spirit radiated a blazing ancient aura, crackling with more memory fire.

With all those memories he couldn't forget.

"The Handmaiden used her magic to help me control my... condition." He dropped his coat and shirt onto the floor beside the too-small wastebasket.

The need to draw closer, let him wrap his body, aura, and memories around her, strained her control and made the ache within her swell—

Except Tobias had said, when he'd told her to read the Handmaiden's chambers that morning, that the Handmaiden had left Court. If she was helping Grey— "The Handmaiden is gone."

"You see my problem." He flashed her a hint of teeth. She was pretty sure it wasn't meant as a sexual invitation, but another shiver slid through her anyway.

She clenched her jaw against the reaction and tried to focus on what he was saying — which was getting harder by the second and he was just standing there... shirtless, ablaze in magical flame. "So the Handmaiden uses her magic to stop yours—"

"More like she turns it to a dimmer setting." He took a cloth from a shelf beside the sink and held it out to her. "Could you check my back to see if I've expelled all the shrapnel?"

She stared at the cloth with its invitation to cross the threshold and step into the bathroom.

Her pulse pounded faster, rushing in her ears. She doubted he meant the invitation — just like his flash of teeth — as a sexual one, but her mind was stuck there, stuttering on how just looking at him made her feel.

Jeez. Just concentrate. He was injured and it was easier for her to check his back instead of him straining to see it in the mirror.

Really.

But his pale gaze slid from the cloth in his hand and up her body with a fire that melted the rest of the frozen knot in her gut. With one look, he captured her soul again and the warmth within her burst into an inferno.

"I'll still need a shower to get properly cleaned up, but there's no point in that if more shrapnel is going to come out." He shifted closer, and the fire in his eyes said there was more to this shower than just washing away the gore.

She tried to swallow, but her mouth was dry. Everything within her thrummed, vibrating on a level she'd never experienced before. Was this what desire felt like? Had anyone ever looked at her like this? There wasn't an experience in her locket that even came close to this.

23

Ivy's heart pounded harder and Grey's gaze dipped to the cloth in his extended hand.

"Would you?" he asked.

Would she? Her brain stuttered.

His back.

Right. His back. She took the cloth and her index finger brushed his. A snap of electric attraction shot up her arm, and her breath hitched.

His eyes widened. He'd felt it, too. Surely he'd felt it, too. But he turned his back to her, pressed his hands against the glass shower stall, and exposed the wide expanse of his muscled back. "With the Hand—" he said, his voice gruff, thick with...

Mother, she wanted it to be the same searing desire she felt coursing through her.

She turned to the sink and ran the hot water, waiting for it to warm up before dampening the cloth, praying that looking away from him would help her concentrate. Except this close, she was hyper-aware of him and could feel the heat of his memory fire, teasing her to activate her magic and take relief from her desire.

He cleared his throat. "I've been struggling since the Handmaiden left, but you... I can't explain it. You don't just dim my magic. You turn it off. Everything becomes clear, as if I didn't realize the world was so off kilter, like—"

"Like you were missing something." Just like she was. "And now you've found it."

"Yes." His memory fire crackled stronger against her skin, and her power word strained in her throat. "My memories have gotten stronger since this morning. Probably because my soul magic is working overtime trying to keep me together. If we get separated during the museum break-in, I don't know if I'll be able to keep it together long enough to get the coin piece to safety. Your first priority has to be keeping it from Jet. Even if that means leaving me behind."

"I can't win a fight against Jet."

"It's not very dragonly, but run away. Protect the coin piece at all costs."

"I understand." Except she didn't know if she could leave him. Even if they got separated, she didn't think her conscience— her *soul* could abandon him.

Her throat tightened and the heat in her heart burned stronger. He was willing to sacrifice everything to keep their people safe. He'd shared his darkest secret with her, not knowing she'd forget it in the morning. She didn't doubt he'd kept this secret from his friends. With the little she knew about dragon politics, she knew a dragon didn't reveal a weakness like this. Which meant he felt keeping the coin piece out of the wrong hands was more important than his safety.

She ran the cloth under the water, wrung it out, and forced herself to turn to him and clean his injured back. Those broad shoulders, thick with powerful muscle, carried the weight of dragonkind and she suspected his friends only knew a fraction of his burden.

"If we're talking liabilities, then you should know—" She brushed the cloth against his back, savoring the feeling of his memory fire tickling her hands and making all his glorious muscles tense. "—I have no memory. If I fall asleep or am knocked out, when I wake I won't remember everything... I probably won't remember anything."

"Amnesia? I don't know if I've ever heard of a drake with amnesia."

"I thought every drake has amnesia after the rebirth spell?"

"I suppose you're right." He glanced at her, his pale gaze filled with concern, something he had every right to feel. It was bad enough she was incompetent in a fight. Her lack of memory could endanger him.

"I've always thought of my memory problem like the rebirth spell. Every morning I wake not knowing who or where I am, only that I'm a young green drake." She wiped away a patch of crusted blood and exposed an angry red welt, where his body had expelled shrapnel and was now knitting itself back together. "Except I'm not completely reset. I understand language and can read. I know what things are, like a refrigerator, and I know that's where I keep food cold. I just don't know anything about dragon politics and history, who's who, and I know nothing about me."

"We say the rebirth process resets a dragon's soul, but it's more complicated than that. It strips away everything personal but leaves enough information to survive, like languages, reading and writing, and basic fighting abilities — if you ever learned any."

She snorted. "Guess I never did."

"Your aim with a firearm is pretty impressive." The cloth caught the edge of a still-open wound in the middle of his back and drew a hiss.

"Sorry."

"Does it look like there's still shrapnel in there?"

She dabbed at the gash. The edges were starting to seal shut and turn into a welt, like the few she'd already cleaned up. "I think you're good."

There were only a few more then...

Her gaze dipped to the crusted blood patch below the waistband of his pants, and her heart sped even faster. *Oh, Mother.*

"It must be scary."

"Scary?" Yes... No... Her pulse roared. Surely he could hear it.

"Waking every morning not knowing who you are."

Her brain stuttered over his words. "Waking— Yes. But I—" She brushed a hand over her locket. "I read the memories in my locket. I know I only know a fraction of what I've experienced. I can feel, soul deep, that I'm missing things. It aches—" Her throat tightened. "It aches all the time. The only time it doesn't is when I'm filling myself with memories from the rooms and objects around me, but that doesn't last."

"Ivy—"

"I just need to make do. It's all I've got." Tears burned her eyes and she fought to keep them back. God damn it. She had to pull herself together. She was a dragon. Dragons were stronger than this. But she'd never said this out loud before, never told anyone this secret, and with the ever-present ache that consumed her, speaking her truth was too much to bear.

"Hey." He turned and cupped her hand between his.

His memory fire crackled against her skin, no longer a gentle caress but an insistent flame. Her power word clogged her throat, making it ache as much as the emptiness in her soul.

"You have to know—" God, she shouldn't confess it, but it was wrong lying to him. Every drake had secrets and with a hiss of her power word, she could see his. He wouldn't want anything to do with her once he knew. Revealing a secret was different from having someone who could pry.

That thought hurt the most, but she still had to tell him. It was the right thing to do. If he was willing to endanger himself for the good of their people — and for a prince who wanted to kill him — she could tell him the truth. Even if that meant him wanting nothing to do with her.

A tear broke free, leaving a traitorous trail across her cheek, exposing how weak a dragon she really was.

"Hey," he said again, his tender tone making her ache even more. "Once the Handmaiden returns, we'll figure out if something can help you."

"You would do that for me?"

"I'm the drake dragons go to when they're in trouble." He shrugged and winced. "I'm due to cash in on some favors, and I'll cash a few in for you."

The ache swelled, filling her chest and making it hard to breathe. "You have to know the truth." *Say it. Just say.* "I can read your memories. Not just what's in your clothes, but you. I don't know how or why. I can't with any other drake. I—"

His eyes narrowed. "So when you used your magic in the Handmaiden's secret residence…?"

"I saw a wet alley reeking with garbage. I didn't mean to, it just happened. It was so terrible." Another tear broke free and heat flooded her face. This was the worst part, the part that made her insides churn with shame. "And it still stopped the ache."

His grip on her hand tightened. "I wish you'd seen something else."

"I won't let it happen again." She sniffed and fought back another tear. Shame or not, she was still a dragon and if Grey could live with his overwhelming memories, she could live with her emptiness. "I'm sorry."

"I'm just sorry it was such a horrible memory." His gaze softened. "I have over two thousand years of memories and the one that keeps coming back is that Godforsaken alley."

"It wasn't all bad. There was a red drake there, a friend... a brother? Your love for him is so strong."

"Hunter." Warmth and a hint of sadness crept into his eyes. "Anaea's inamorato."

The ache grew stronger. Even without a memory, she was pretty sure no one thought of her with the affection Grey had for Hunter. The cold hard truth was that she was alone and she didn't want to be, but she had no idea who she could trust.

Another tear escaped. God damn it. Why couldn't she just stop crying? "Some dragon I am."

He brushed his thumb across her damp cheeks, wiping away the tears, and his memory fire tickled across her skin. Her power word pressed against her throat, straining to break free.

"Please, you have to stop touching me." Her magic flickered, drawing his fire under her flesh — she hadn't even activated it — and a hint of dark alley billowed around her. She shoved it back and fought to concentrate on holding her power in.

His expression changed, not with worry or fear... but... she had no idea with what. "If I give you a memory, how long will it ease your ache?"

"What?" She couldn't have heard that right.

"If I give you a memory, how long will it stay with you?"

"I don't know. The memories from things around us last anywhere from a few minutes to a few hours."

"What about when you read my memory back in the Handmaiden's residence?"

She thought back to the accident, but couldn't remember if the ache had gone and if so, for how long. "Too much was happening. I'm not sure."

"Okay." He sat on the edge of the tub and pulled her down to sit across from him. "We have a few hours. I'll share a memory and we'll see how long it lasts."

She jerked her hands from his, afraid she wouldn't be able to stay in control if he kept touching her. "Why would you do that?"

"To minimize our liabilities." He said it so matter-of-factly, as if sharing his memories to ensure she was at her best was a common thing, but no one had ever suggested it before. Without a doubt, she would have permanently imprinted that in her locket if someone had.

He held out his hand, palm up, in a gesture for her to take it. "Just by standing next to me, you solve my problem. Let me see if sharing a few memories can help you."

"Sharing too much will endanger you and your friends." But every part of her screamed to take his hand and accept his offer. "How do you even know I won't take what you share and use it against you?"

"Will you?"

"You're going to just take my word for it?" She gripped the washcloth with both hands, as if that could ground her and help her understand how a stranger would be willing to do this for her.

"Promise you won't report to Tobias until after you've gone to sleep." His gaze dipped to his hand, still open in invitation.

She stared at it. A simple gesture, to just hold it and see his secrets. Except it was anything but simple. If she didn't imprint whatever memory he gave her into her locket, she wouldn't remember it the next time she woke, so she wouldn't. It wasn't right to keep his memory.

"Deal." She shifted closer but couldn't make herself take his hand.

He pursed his lips, his hand still extended.

"It's really hard not to say my power word. If I take your hand, I might not be able to control myself." She tightened her grip on the cloth. "I want you to be ready."

"Do you know how it works? Do I think of something or do you?"

"I don't know. When I read objects and rooms, I usually see the most recent memory or the one with the strongest emotions first. You—" Her pulse pounded faster. "I've never experienced anything like you before."

A hint of a mocking smile darkened his eyes. "Very few drakes have, baby."

"Oh, you think you're so special?" She slapped her hands over her mouth. "Oh, my goodness, I'm so sorry. I didn't mean—"

He burst out laughing, the sound low and rich and sending warmth swelling through her. "Let's see if we can give you a little peace. I'll concentrate on a positive memory, but—"

"With me here, you won't be able to control your magic. Wait, if I shut your magic off, how will you be able to give me a memory?"

"I do remember things without my magic." His smile turned wry and a hint of sensual heat filled his gaze. "It's been a busy couple of weeks. I'm sure I can think of something worth sharing."

The heat within her shivered back in response. Oh, Mother, she wanted more from him than just a few shared memories.

24

"Take my hand," Grey said.

Ivy swallowed, her mouth still too dry and the ice in her gut exploding into butterflies. Her power word bubbled past her throat, into her mouth, and she seized his hand, squishing the damp bloody washcloth between their fingers.

"Si," she hissed. Her power flooded into him and he gasped.

Blinding blue flames flooded the bathroom, consuming Ivy's vision until it was all she could see. No memory. Nothing. She strained to grasp onto something, anything, but there was just fire, blazing, searing, consuming fire.

Her pulse pounded and the heat from before flash-froze into the knot in her gut. This wasn't going to work. It had been foolish to think it would. She couldn't read his memories. Never had. The alley must have been stuck on his clothes or shoes or something.

Her power faltered. The glassed-in shower stall behind Grey flickered into sight, then vanished again in the blue blaze. Pressure seared her chest as if the fire was pouring into her, filling her up until she thought she'd burst, but she wasn't seeing anything, and she had no idea if her constant ache would be eased if she didn't experience a memory.

A gruff voice growled something, but she couldn't make out the words. He sounded angry... and so very familiar. It wasn't Grey, but she couldn't explain how she knew it wasn't him.

The gruff voice said something else and a hint of a memory flickered, revealing Tobias, glaring at her—

Except he wasn't glaring down at her, like he usually did. They were eye to eye.

Behind him, more fire melted away, exposing smooth stone walls. Tobias stood across the room from her, with the Handmaiden's chair and table centered between them, in the middle of the outer room in her chambers at Court. He opened a door — was that the door to the hall? — and tensed.

Ivy — a remembered Ivy — stood framed in the doorway. Small, still — gloriously still — her eyes large, and her green aura a pale thin glow radiating around her body, indicating she was a young drake. Everything snapped into crystalline focus, the lock of her hair that curled along her jaw and accentuated her neck and her pulse fluttering too fast.

Beyond all that was an overwhelming stillness— *her* stillness. It filled her— no, it filled Grey. This was *his* memory. He'd never experienced anything like that stillness before. It called to him, his soul, every fiber of his being. It righted a darkened and tipsy world she— *he* knew was broken but had no idea how to fix. Not even the Handmaiden had created such clarity, such peace, with her magic.

"The Handmaiden's man was just leaving," Tobias growled to the Ivy standing in the doorway.

"Yeah," she— Grey said, unable to take his eyes from her.

A phone rang. And still Grey's gaze remained locked on her as if she were a lifeline he'd known he'd needed but hadn't expected to ever get.

"I've got to go," Tobias said.

"Is it this?" Grey managed to ask. Mother, it was so hard to concentrate and yet nothing had been so clear before.

"No."

"It that good or bad?"

"Is anything good right now?" Tobias glared at the Ivy in the doorway. "Do your job. Grey isn't staying." Except Mother, he wanted to stay—

No, he *had* to stay.

The Ivy in the doorway watched Tobias leave, but Grey continued to stare at her. In that moment nothing mattered, not even the ransacked chamber behind him. He had to step closer, feel her aura sliding against his, never leave her radius of clarity.

Except she was Tobias's agent. No matter what every cell in his body screamed, being near her was dangerous for both of them.

He should go. Leave… move… Just. Start. Walking.

But he couldn't make himself step away from her stillness and he'd be damned if he let himself move closer — something he'd have to do if she wasn't going to step out of the door, the only way out.

Maybe if he said something she'd come closer—

No, damn it. Maybe if he said something she'd get out of the way so he could leave.

His throat tightened at the idea.

Come on. He was a stronger drake than this.

He cleared his throat, and she turned and stared at him with her sharp, still — oh, so still — dark gaze.

His heart stuttered. His whole soul stuttered. He yearned to fall into her mesmerizing calm and remain there forever. In a delicate human body with gentle feminine curves and an open, innocent, heart-shaped face, she appeared fragile. But only if he ignored her eyes and her aura. Those spoke of a hidden strength, one not yet realized. Her soul held a certainty, a center, that was missing from his, and all he wanted was to stand within her aura and make her see the ferocity he saw coiled deep within her stillness.

Grey's shock flooded her. She— *he* couldn't move, couldn't think past her.

The remembered Ivy drew closer, step by agonizingly slow step, her wide-eyed gaze staying locked on him. Her aura inched closer to his. His breath hitched. Another step. Just one more.

She bumped the Handmaiden's chair and her attention dropped to it as if she hadn't expected it to be there.

Look up. Please, Mother, look up again.

But she clenched her hands and stared at her feet, the submission twisting in Ivy's— no, Grey's chest. He ached seeing her trying to make herself smaller and not reveal the power within her.

His pulse pounded fast. So did hers, along with the remembered her. It throbbed at the remembered Ivy's throat, revealed by the clarity she gave Grey just by standing in the same room. The muscles in the remembered Ivy's jaw clenched and she squared her shoulders.

E verything within Grey froze. Ivy was purring. Mother of All, she was purring.

And God help him, he was doing everything to ignore the purr curling in the back of his throat.

This was bad. Very, very bad.

Dragons only purred for their inamorata or inamorato.

Ivy wrenched her hands free of Grey's and the connection of his memory through her magic snapped off. Cold swept over him, filled with an aching emptiness, and he grabbed at her hands, the only thing he could think of to stop the chill. But she scrambled back, out of reach, until she hit the tiled tub wall behind her.

"I'm sorry. I didn't realize I was manipulating your memory."

"Ivy—" God, she'd purred. *He'd* purred!

This couldn't be happening.

He couldn't be inamorated. Not with a member of the Royal Coterie and one of Tobias's agents. Certainly not with a drake Nero and Diablo were going to murder if Grey couldn't convince them she wasn't a threat to their coterie. And if she was in danger, his soul would do whatever it took to protect her, even if that meant alienating everyone who cared for him or dying.

"I've never done that before," she said, her words barely audible over the rushing in his ears.

Inamorated. Souls bound to each other for life. Forever. Whether this was what they wanted or not. Whether it was safe or not. And with Grey a fugitive, wanted by the dragon prince who was also Ivy's doyen, he couldn't have a relationship with her. He couldn't bring someone into his life and endanger her like that.

"Ivy—" Except he had no idea what to say. He'd only just figured out Nero and Diablo didn't need to worry about her. With her condition, she'd wake the next morning and not remember them or their unsanctioned coterie. She could go back to being Tobias's agent. Yes, they still had the issue of her working with Grey and shooting the prince's new assassin, but Nero had already come up with an explanation. She'd needed to use Grey and Bolo was endangering the mission.

But inamorated? That was a permanent bond between souls that only happened once in a dragon's lifetime, and very few dragons found it.

She stared at him, but not with horror or realization, as if she hadn't heard herself purr or — and this was more likely the case — she was too young to know what purring meant?

"I'm sorry. I thought showing me that… *moment* meant we were… but I was wrong."

His chest ached and his throat tightened. She thought he was rejecting her and didn't realize the horrible truth. She was stuck with him, broken, haunted him.

"You weren't wrong," he said, unable to stop himself. He shouldn't tell her he cared. He should force her away, make her angry with him, and pray she never recognized the truth. This was his fault. He'd been drawn to her from the beginning—

Because he was freak'n inamorated with her!

How could he have missed something so big?

How the hell was he going to fix this?

Except he couldn't fix this. His soul had made its choice. So had hers. Logic, plans, political danger had nothing to do with it. Hell, the two inamorated drakes Grey knew were in love with humans. That was worse than this. Except while Anaea was on Regis's radar, she was a full sorcerer and that was enough to give anyone pause before trying to kill her or Hunter. And Regis didn't know about Ryan, making it safe for Capri to pretend nothing had changed and so avoid the prince's rage.

Ivy hugged herself tight, as if trying to hold herself together. Her wide-eyed gaze locked on his, and the ache in his chest grew, making it hard to breathe.

"The memory— *Your* memory was so—" She swallowed, her body so tense the action looked painful. "I've never experienced anything like that before."

The memory fluttered through him, and her aura swelled and brushed against his. Her eyes rolled back and another soft purr escaped her lips.

His own purr strained in his throat, stronger than before, and he fought to swallow it back.

Maybe she'd forget. Maybe she'd wake in the morning and not remember.

If her amnesia was like the effects of the rebirth spell — and it sounded like it was — her bond to him would be stripped from her soul with her memories. She wouldn't know the heartache of having found and lost her inamorato. She could carry on. Safe. Above all, she had to be safe. He had to protect her. Even if that meant protecting her from himself.

"When you're near, it's so hard to keep my magic under control." Her aura pulled back tighter against her body, a green glow that thrummed in time with her too-fast pulse, and she jerked to her feet.

He grabbed her wrist before she could flee. He couldn't let her leave thinking he was mad at her or that she'd done something wrong.

"You just surprised me." Mother, this was a mess.

Keep her away from you.

Keep her close.

Make up your mind!

But the battle within him to protect his inamorata and to keep her near raged within him. And keeping her near was winning.

Except he couldn't keep her near forever.

His throat tightened, and his chest ached. Letting her forget was the right thing to do. Mother, he wished *he* could forget. Just this one thing. But he never would. He'd remember finding and leaving his inamorata forever, and time would never ease this heartache.

Her expression softened, still edged with fear but now also with sadness. It tore into him and all he wanted was to tell her that every-thing was going to be all right.

And for her, it would be. Tomorrow she wouldn't remember. Tomorrow he would have to let her go.

But maybe the Mother would grace him with this one gift and give them tonight.

He forced warmth into his expression. "Did it work?"

Delight blossomed in her eyes, and all grief over what he needed to do vanished. He'd given her something more than just protection, something better than things that sparkled in the sunlight. Her plea-sure made her aura billow and caress his, sending heated desire swelling through him.

"I'll take that as a yes." Mother, he shouldn't sleep with her. That would just turn a bad situation worse, but now all he could think about was stripping away her clothes and driving her to the heights of pleasure for the rest of the night.

Because that was all they had.

"Oh, yes." Her gaze dipped to his lips.

God, he needed to taste her, needed to feel the slide of her body against his, around him. Hear her moan and purr and scream—

He needed to not let himself get any more attached than he already was.

She bit her bottom lip, a slight action whispering of desire and uncertainty, capturing him completely.

Who was he kidding? They were inamorated. It didn't get any more attached even if all they'd done was share memories. Kissing her wouldn't make it hurt any less, and while his soul ached at the thought of tomorrow, his body throbbed with the thought of right now.

Her gaze jumped back up to his, and the fierce dragon spirit he'd first seen curled tight in her delicate human form stared back, her eyes filled with the same searing desire coursing through him.

He had to stop this. He couldn't let her take them where they both wanted to go. But man, it was getting harder and harder to think straight.

"I'm not sure this is a good idea," he forced out.

"You're afraid I won't forget you in the morning?"

I'm praying you will. I'm begging you won't. "No. Associating with me is dangerous."

There. He'd said it. The whole reason *they* were a bad idea. Maybe if she added her willpower to his, they could choose common sense over desire.

Her lips quirked and she dipped in and kissed him, a sudden quick brush of her lips against his. Just like in the memory.

An electric shock snapped through him, stealing all breath and thought, and he grew hard in an instant. Mother, just a kiss. That was all it took.

No. Common sense. Remember? He needed to stay focused... for both of them.

"I've been afraid from the moment I woke up. With you, I'm not afraid. I can't explain it." She skimmed her cheek along his, just like in the memory. "I'm already associated with you."

"But this— This—" Except he couldn't think of a good argument.

She straddled his legs. "This is between you and me."

If he had any coherent thought left, it vanished. His soul had chosen, and his human body was more than ready to satisfy her. His erection throbbed, straining against his briefs, and the heat from her core radiating through her pants only made him harder.

"If all I get is tonight, then I want it all." She nipped his ear. "Tell me you're not interested."

Holy Mother! "You know it would be a lie if I did."

"Yeah, I would." She shifted closer, rubbing herself against him with glorious pressure.

He fought to turn his purr into a moan. "You're not playing fair."

"Oh, and you are?" She nipped his bottom lip. "I'm pretty sure you started playing dirty the moment you kissed me in the Handmaiden's chambers."

"You just saw that I couldn't control myself." And he wasn't going to be able to control himself for much longer here, either.

"Do I need to be worried about that?" she asked, her voice low, seductive.

"Is that a challenge?"

"Maybe." Another nip that sent more electric attraction snapping straight to his groin.

"You know you shouldn't challenge a dragon," he growled.

She shivered, her body trembling against his, and a purr escaped her lips. "Is that so?"

"Yes." He captured her head, tangling his fingers in her hair, and kissed her. Full and strong. No tentative brush, no whisper of skin against skin. It was demanding, and barely controlled.

She moaned into his mouth and he seized the opening, sliding his tongue against hers, fueling another moan, and a glorious shiver that pressed her body harder against his. A small part of his mind said he should go slow, savor the moment, be gentle. He didn't know if she'd had a lover before — or if she remembered having one. But the thrill of their connection, of their auras crackling against each other and the surety in his soul, made it difficult to think beyond anything else.

In that moment, there was only her. Her radiating calm, her spirit, and her pleasure.

She rubbed her palms along his jaw and a purr escaped. He tried to change it, hold it back, anything to withhold this heartbreaking truth, but she purred back. The vibration rumbled into his mouth and resonated in the core of his being. This was his truth. This was *their* truth. And the only thing he could do tonight was hang on for the ride.

He deepened the kiss, unable to control his hunger for her, for the feel of her lips and tongue against his, and slid a hand down her back, drawing her tighter against his body. She shifted, and her knee brushed his thigh, sending a bite of pain.

Ah, crap. He was still covered in blood and could still be expelling pieces of shrapnel. That wasn't sexy at all.

"I think I should get cleaned up first," he said into her mouth.

She drew back and frowned. A hint of uncertainty flashed through her eyes, and his heart stuttered.

"I still might have shrapnel in me. In the very least, my back is caked in blood." He skimmed his hands around her waist, brushing the bottom of her breasts with his thumbs and drawing a shiver. "It won't take long."

"It'll be faster if I help." She leaned close, her breath feathering across his jaw, then stood, sliding her body up his, her breasts a whisper from his lips in the most erotic, languid move he'd seen in his life. His breath hitched as if in one simple action, she'd stolen all the air from the room. Then she turned her back on him and stepped to the mouth of the glassed-in shower stall.

He jerked to his feet, unwilling to let her get even a few steps away, seized her waist, and drew her back tight against his chest. Her silky hair tickled her lips and her scent, fresh and green and warm, flooded his nose.

"That wasn't fair," he murmured against her neck, drawing in more of her delicious scent.

"Getting me all worked up then taking a shower without me isn't fair," she said, her voice trembling with another purr.

"You're right." He nuzzled her neck and teased his fingers under her shirt. Gooseflesh pebbled her skin and she melted into him, tipping her head back to give him better access.

"This isn't getting *us* into the shower," she groaned.

"No, it's not." He turned her, his lips finding hers again, and backed her into the glassed-in stall.

With a purr, she hit the tiled wall. "I can't really remember if I've done this before, but I'm pretty sure we're still doing this wrong." Her hands skimmed down his chest to the waistband of his pants.

"You mean you don't know if you've showered before?" he asked, unable to resist teasing her.

"Yeah, sure," she said, her gaze simmering with desire, turning the tease back on him and making it sexual, "the shower."

His libido surged into overdrive, and he tugged her coat off and let it drop to the stall floor.

She grabbed the bottom of her shirt and pulled it off, revealing firm, plump breasts barely contained in a white lacy bra. Her dusty pink nipples, erect with desire, peeked through the lace in a tantalizing tease he couldn't resist. He slid his thumb inside her bra and dipped in, stroking his tongue over her.

A tremor swept through her, and he drew her into his mouth and brushed his thumb over her other nipple. Another tremor shook her. She gripped his shoulders and threw her head back, exposing the length of her body. He trailed his mouth from her breasts, his hands following, to the waistband of her jeans, and unhooked the button.

She groaned, her hands, unable to reach his shoulders, pressed against the tile behind her as if she needed the wall to keep standing. He undid the zipper and slid the heavy fabric from her hips and thighs, then seated her on the bench, pulled off her boots and socks, and finished removing her jeans, leaving her in her white lace bra and panties with a small gold locket hanging around her neck.

Desire flushed her cheeks and her breath came fast, making her breasts rise and fall, taunting him to return. Her aura pulsed in time with her breath, strong, sure, and radiating calm. Always calm. The center to his writhing universe, the foundation stone to his soul. He couldn't fight this. Tomorrow he could pray she'd forget him. But right now, she was everything he needed and everything he craved, and she was alight with a dragon's ferocious desire. He'd never imagined he'd meet anyone so incredible and in his two thousand years of life, he'd never seen anyone so spectacular. "God, you're gorgeous."

"Even as a human?"

"It would be hard for me to do this if we were dragons." He captured her mouth again, kissing her with the ferocity consuming him.

She matched him, her own dragon spirit meeting his, exceeding his as she stood and urged him deeper into the stall.

This time his back hit the tiled wall. Her hand snaked out, and she flipped on the shower. Cold water slammed into his skin, but he didn't care. There was only her. There would only ever be her.

"If you keep this up, I'm going to go insane," she growled against his lips. "If I have to wait for you to clean up before you satisfy me, you're cleaning up. Now."

He purred back at her, turned her, and pinned her against the wall. "You're looking for satisfaction?"

"I thought we'd agreed on that." She hooked a leg around his waist and drew him tight against her, only flimsy pieces of wet lacy fabric covering her.

God, he was wearing too much. Another purr rumbled through him.

"Didn't we agree on that?" She fumbled with the button on his slacks.

"We did." He undid the button for her and she eased the zipper down. So God damned slowly.

His erection bulged against the front of his boxer briefs, and her pupils dilated, making the pressure within him, the desire to drive into her, even stronger. Her tongue darted over her lips, and her fingers danced along the edge of his waistband, a hint of uncertainty creeping into her eyes, then her thumb brushed his sensitive tip and that electric snap, that explosion of libido, surged through him, making him groan.

Her eyes widened and she brushed him again, a little stronger, snapping more electricity and drawing another groan. Sensual realization narrowed her eyes, and she dipped her hand inside his briefs and wrapped her fingers around him. Just that and his legs were shaking. His whole body was shaking.

He had to lean in, drawing closer to her, and pressed a hand against the wall beside her head to keep standing. With his free hand, he teased his fingers inside her panties and skimmed her folds.

She gasped and her grip on him tightened. *Holy Mother!* He bit back a purr and concentrated on satisfying her. Her first. Always her first. If this was all they had, he wanted to know she'd been well and truly satiated — and a part of him, a small part, wanted it to be so satisfying that she'd be unable to forget.

He brushed her again, this time rubbing his thumb against her clit and drawing a full-body tremble from her that tightened her grip again. A purr rumbled from her throat. He matched it and teased a finger inside her, circling her clit with his thumb.

Her head tipped back and her eyes fluttered shut.

"Oh, my," she breathed, her trembling growing as he worked in another finger and increased speed and pressure with his thumb.

Her breath came faster, making her gorgeous breasts rise and fall, the lacy fabric scraping against his chest. Her grip on him tightened as if holding him was all that kept her together, and he stroked her until she was writhing against the wall and moaning.

"Please, Grey," she gasped, and she drew him to her entrance.

He eased inside her, her muscles clenching around him, drawing him in, and straining his control. He needed to go slow— *wanted* to go slow. But she tightened her leg around his waist and drove him further inside her.

"Oh, yes," she purred, her muscles quivering around him.

He eased out until just his tip was inside her and plunged back in. She moaned again and locked gazes with him, her eyes filled with searing desire. He thrust again and again, faster and harder, driving her pleasure higher and higher until her orgasm tore through her.

She roared his name and dug her nails into his shoulders. Her body shuddered as waves of pleasure crashed through her, and his orgasm ripped into him. Bliss seared every nerve in his body, leaving him breathless and his knees weak.

"Holy Mother!" he gasped.

"Holy Mother, indeed." Her eyes opened and her gaze locked onto his, capturing his soul.

Her stillness burst through him on another wave of pleasure, giving him glorious clarity, and he let his magic sear this moment of her into his memory forever.

She was mesmerizing. Gold flecks caught the light in her dark eyes. Strands of wet hair teased curving lines along her neck and sent rivulets of water over her breasts. Pleasure parted her lips, and her body, hot and wet, clamped around him.

His soul purred. He purred. This was the way it was supposed to be. He was hers. Forever. And he would hold this memory close, with the perfect clarity she'd gifted him, forever.

26

Nero, his head pounding, stepped into his freezing living room with its broken, tarp-covered windows, and headed to the bar. He didn't bother with the light. His night sight was strong enough for him to see clearly in the dark and he knew where his thirty-year-old fine oak scotch was hidden.

His bottle of ten-year-old fine amber sitting on the shelf with the other bottles of liquor — the ones he used for those infrequent guests who visited this house — was half full. It had been three-quarters empty last time he'd looked at it. None of the kids had expressed an interest in it — he had no doubt they'd experimented with everything they could find in the house and with their enhanced abilities and magic, it was futile to lock the liquor up. Which was why he'd been forced to move the fine oak's hiding place from his office to under the sink. It also meant Diablo must have finished off the amber and replaced it.

Nero bit back a growl. They were going to have to have a talk. And not about the scotch. Challenging him in front of Grey and Ryan was behavior that couldn't stand. Any other doyen would have grounds for rebirth. And while Grey and Ryan weren't going to see Diablo's challenge as a weakness in Nero, if Diablo did it at Court, he endangered Nero's position as Regis's favorite and a doyen to be feared by other doyens.

It was such a God damned shame, too. If Diablo wasn't so headstrong, he would have been given the position of Third in Command of both of Nero's coteries. But Diablo had challenged his word as if he'd wanted Nero to put him in his place. Which wasn't as ridiculous a thought as it would have been a month ago. The Diablo who'd been in his office a few hours ago was more like the young, wild dragon who'd changed allegiance 203 years ago from the Minor Black Coterie to Nero's to protect his sister, Raven, after she'd been reborn and the doyen of the Minor Black Coterie had wanted nothing to do with another hatchling in bad standing with the prince.

That Diablo had been angry, and Nero wasn't sure if he'd even known over what. Together with Raven, Nero had been making slow progress with Diablo's rage, but the breakthrough hadn't come until they'd welcomed Pete Matthews — who became Andy Reynolds — an awkward seventeen-year-old human mage with an out-of-control empathic power that was mentally and emotionally crushing him. Somehow that human and Diablo had forged a connection, and if either of them had inclinations toward the same sex — which neither had that Nero could tell — he would have been certain the connection had been of the soul variety.

But Andy's murder had shattered that and while Diablo hadn't completely returned to the beast of his youth, there were moments that made Nero wary. He couldn't afford to lose his best hunter. Not with even one of those unnatural human mages Zenobia had created for her coup still running around, or the leak in the Asar Nergal still unidentified, and certainly not with Regis growing more mentally unstable by the minute.

The door to the living room opened and the tarps covering the windows snapped. Raven stood in the doorway, the light from the hall creating a hint of warm halo around her and throwing her face into shadow.

"I thought we were supposed to meet in your office."

"I was just grabbing my scotch first." Nero opened the cabinet under the sink and grabbed the box hidden at the back.

"The good stuff?"

"I think all dragon souls hanging in the balance demands the good stuff." That, and his head just wouldn't stop pounding.

"You don't think it's that bad," she said, but she didn't sound certain.

"I think I don't know enough about Grey and I know nothing about Tobias's agent to properly assess the situation." He tucked the box under his arm, grabbed two glasses, and headed to the door. "And my head still hurts."

"With your healing, that alcohol isn't going to do much to take the edge off."

"It'll do enough." Even if all it did was take the edge off his Hand-maiden-given magic that made him dugga. He'd managed to keep the power to sense human magic under control while Zenobia had built her army and the evidence against her was the most damning, but it was as if holding back, ignoring the spikes of awareness as those mages were created had broken his control and warped the magic. He could sense there were mages out there… sometimes — he hadn't been warned about Ryan — but it felt as if there were more than there should be, certainly more than what he'd sensed after he subtracted the bodies from those he'd felt Zenobia making. And unless the mages used their magic in a big way, he was having a hard time pinpointing any of them, which wasn't usual, either.

"I don't think Grey should be a worry. He has too much at stake with us to endanger our *puzur*." Raven fell into step beside Nero as he headed back to his office.

"I had assumed Grey was loyal to Hunter and the Handmaiden, but bringing Ivy here gives me pause."

"I'm pretty sure he didn't have any choice. He couldn't even stand when they came through the gate. From what Diablo says about free gating, I'm surprised he didn't gate them to the main anchor at Court."

"That would have been better for us and the kids." Nero set the box and glasses on his desk, opened the bottle, and poured two quar-ter-full glasses. He eased into one of the low-backed leather tub chairs facing the desk and offered the second glass to Raven. "I think she thinks I'm Grey's doyen. One word of that at Court and we're all in Regis's prison and the kids—" Mother, he didn't want to think about how Regis would kill his kids.

The original Asar Nergal — and he'd been a part of it from the beginning — had been ruthless. *He'd* been ruthless. He and all the other drakes had been more dragon than human in those early days, and filled with fear. They'd slaughtered man, woman, and child, anyone who held a hint of earth magic aura, all in the name of self-preservation.

Raven took the offered glass and eased into the chair beside him. "You brought me on as your Third because I can offer a different perspective."

"Don't sell yourself short. I made you my Third because you have a special gift with the kids. You can connect with them in ways I can't and they trust you." It had been a pure accident that Raven had stumbled across his *puzur*, his secret second coterie. She'd been newly reborn and her coterie had disavowed her. The Handmaiden—

Nero snorted. Okay, so maybe it hadn't been an accident. The Handmaiden had opened a gate and told Raven to petition Nero for acceptance into his coterie. Raven had gated into the middle of an awkward dinner where Nero had been trying to calm the tears of a crying teen whose family had tried to kill her because they'd thought she was possessed by the devil.

Raven had known right away what the kids were and hadn't cared. The sting of her *family's* betrayal had been too raw, and she'd embraced these misfit humans with an affection Nero hadn't known was possible for a dragon. Her instincts with hatchlings — human and dragon — far exceeded his and he didn't doubt, even though she denied it, that she had at least a hint of empathic earth magic.

"I didn't spend much time with Ivy, but I've spent a lot of time with Grey in the last two weeks. After helping Hunter and Anaea and Capri and Ryan, I have no doubt he'll do anything to protect his friends."

Nero took a sip of his scotch. The liquid, rich with hints of orange and spice, slid over his tongue, but he couldn't bring himself to focus past the immediate problem and enjoy it. "But are we his friends?"

"I think so and so do you. You would have killed him if you thought he was going to endanger the *puzur*."

Which was the real truth. Somehow, in just a few weeks, his coterie had changed, and Anaea and Grey and now Ryan and Capri had become part of it. And it all felt right. It felt like family.

It still didn't ease the two-thousand-year-old ache in his soul, but then, nothing would. His inamorata hadn't survived the Great Scourge. And there wasn't a damned thing he could do about it.

That was the hard truth about being so unlucky as to be cursed with being inamorated, and two thousand years had done little to alleviate the hurt. Time did not heal all wounds. He couldn't help but feel sorry for Hunter and Anaea and now Capri and Ryan.

The only thing that seemed to fill the void was gathering and helping these dragon and human misfits. It didn't fix that missing piece in his heart, but it helped distract him enough that he'd managed to survive and protect his *puzur* for centuries.

Except now his *puzur*, his kids who couldn't protect themselves against the full wrath of the dragon prince, were in danger... maybe. "This still doesn't help me figure out what to do with Tobias's agent." Light flickered across his sight and pain snapped through his skull. Yes. There were mages out there. He knew that already.

"Anaea said the moment you demonstrated your dominance over Diablo, Ivy became submissive." Raven stared into her glass. "It can't be easy being a young drake in the royal coterie as well as being in Tobias's employ. Most of the dragons working for Tobias are at least four or five hundred years old or older."

"You think she's eager for a change?" Maybe he could work with that.

"I think she's scared. And given how she was ready to shoot all of us to protect Grey, she trusts Grey."

"So if Grey trusts us, she'll trust us?" Okay, he *could* work with that.

"Anaea and Ryan think it goes beyond that," Raven said. "Anaea threatened her to see what would happen and she's pretty sure the two are inamorated."

"That's annoying." Being inamorated made rational drakes irrational. That got drakes killed. And he had no idea if that negated everything else he thought he could work with.

Another flash of light and snap of pain. For the love of the Mother, stop trying to warn him of a threat and show him something useful.

"If it's true and Ivy thinks we're Grey's coterie, she won't do anything to endanger us."

"That's a big if." He downed his drink in one swig and poured himself another half-glass.

"The other option is to dispose of her and risk having Tobias go after Grey." Raven cocked an eyebrow.

"And with Tobias's resources, as soon as he turns his attention to Grey, he'll find our *puzur*." Nero blew out a heavy breath, but it did little to ease the tension tightening his neck and shoulders. "Fine. You've got until Grey and Ivy get the coin piece from the museum to figure out how to deal with Tobias."

Raven finished her drink and stood. "And what will you be doing?"

"Trying to figure out how to deal with Tobias as well." Another snap of pain, this one stronger, seared through his head. It consumed his vision with white light, radiated down his neck, and filled his chest. For a second he was on fire, every nerve alight with agony, then his vision cleared.

Except he no longer stood in his office.

A freezing wind cut through his suit. He stood on a riverbank, in a deserted gravel parking lot for a warehouse. To his right, through the naked tree branches, towered a bridge with a tall sweeping metal arch, its light glimmering in the half-frozen water on the other side of a chain-link fence. That bowstring-like arch had to be the West End Bridge, which meant the water was the Ohio River.

A few feet away, a crumpled form groaned. The form's aura strobed with great pulses of yellow light, both powerful and human. Any drake without the ability to tell the difference between a human mage's aura and a drake's wouldn't see the strobing. All they'd see was a clear, radiant strength that shimmered tight to his body. They'd see a baby drake, barely a hatchling, and they'd see the potential for ferocious, dangerous magic.

The question was, had this human come into his power naturally, or was he a by-product of Zenobia's coup? Nero had realized too late that some of the humans forced to body-share with Zenobia's dragons, those who hadn't developed earth magic fast enough, had been tossed — most likely insane — back into the human world. Except earth magic didn't develop at a consistent rate and some of those humans were now coming into their magic.

And from the strength of this human's aura, his magic was something powerful and dangerous.

His aura flared and he screamed, tipping on his side and curling into a ball. Agony tightened his face and made the muscles in his neck taut. He gasped for breath, his cheek pressed against a frozen puddle, and screamed again.

Diablo, Nero called, focusing his mental connection with all the members of the Asar Nergal to just Diablo.

What? Diablo growled.

What? the growl came again, an echo whispered across the mental connection.

Nero fought to concentrate past the pain in his head to create a clear connection. *I've got a new one.*

New one, the echo hissed. *New one?*

Nero ground his teeth. White lightning burst through him. His mental connection with Diablo wavered, the angry black drake's essence flickering.

Gone, then back.

Gone, then a shadow of what it had been.

Gone, then—

Crack.

Sharp pain sliced across his cheek. He jerked forward. Something popped and another *crack* bit his cheek. Raven snapped into sight before him, her hand raised to hit him again, her eyes wide. The parking lot vanished, but the agony screaming through his head remained.

"I'm back."

"You were convulsing again," she said, her voice trembling. Her gaze dipped to his feet. He let his follow. His crystal glass lay in pieces on the floor in a puddle of expensive scotch.

A gust of wind whooshed behind him. "What the hell?" Diablo growled.

Nero straightened as best he could in the chair, his head throbbing. He couldn't let Diablo see him like this. It was bad enough Raven had. Thank the Mother none of the kids had seen it.

"Sorry. We got cut off," Nero said.

Diablo's gaze dipped to the floor and his eyes narrowed. "Is that the good stuff?"

"There's a mage in a parking lot. The West End Bridge is in sight."

"Which side of the river?" Diablo asked.

Nero had no idea. "I don't want to make it too easy for you."

"Yeah. Would hate to do that. You know I need to deliver clothes to Grey and the you'll-take-care-of-her drake."

Nero jerked to his feet and twisted his pain into what he hoped looked like rage. "And I *will* take care of it. You find this mage before you need to finish with Grey."

"Or what?"

A rope of wind snapped past Nero and slammed Diablo face-first to the floor. "I've had just about enough," Raven growled.

Diablo bared his teeth and wrenched against the wind, but Raven's power surged and kept him locked in place.

"It's been a difficult day. Stop behaving like a hatchling and start acting like a member of this coterie." Her wind yanked him to his feet and shoved him against the already broken bookshelf near the window. "Please."

The rage in his eyes softened. For a moment, it looked more like soul-rending agony than rage, then he blinked and, while the rage returned, it simmered behind a sense of tenuous control. "The West End Bridge?"

"Yes. Listen for the screaming."

"Wonderful. A painful birth of earth magic usually means something dangerous," Diablo said.

"And I don't know if it's one of Zenobia's rejects or not."

"Even better." Diablo rolled his eyes. "The human might be insane."

"So be careful." Raven poured a half-glass of scotch into her empty glass and handed it to Nero. "I'm sure Ryan has a bag packed for Grey and Ivy by now. I'll get it and meet you at the safe house."

Nero downed the scotch in one quick gulp, letting the liquid burn down his throat. "I'll work on getting you more information."

"Don't bother." With a whoosh, Diablo vanished.

"He's angry about Andy," Raven said, pouring more scotch into the glass.

"He's going to be the threat he's worrying about if he's not careful." A reckless drake was a dead drake. But maybe that was what Diablo wanted. Maybe his connection with Andy *had* been of the soul kind. Before Hunter and Anaea, Nero wouldn't have thought it possible for a dragon to be inamorated with a human, and now there were two of the dragon-human pairs living under his roof.

White light flashed across his sight but didn't manifest into a vision. The newly birthed human mage in the parking lot screamed again, and the echo in Nero's head screamed, too. A drake without control of his magic was also a dead drake.

27

Diablo gated to the West End Bridge, the beast within him screaming to break something. Nero's agony had slammed into him through the psychic connection the moment the doyen had reached out. It had stolen all thought, leaving only his beast's instinct to fight anything, everything. Just fight.

Mother, he didn't know how Nero did it, and from Nero's behavior, Diablo was pretty sure the doyen didn't know his pain sliced through the psychic connection. If Diablo had been thinking straight, he would have warned Nero. Most members of the Asar Nergal were loyal to Nero, but that didn't mean some of them weren't also opportunistic. A weakness like that could open the door to challenges, and while Diablo didn't doubt Nero could handle any upstart drake — he'd handled Diablo's beast just fine — constant challenges would make the public coterie unstable and put the hidden one, the *puzur*, in danger.

This was a mess. Grey bringing that green drake into the middle of his kids, endangering them and his sister—

Now Nero had his dugga magic striking him with crippling pain. It was bad enough Regis was likely going crazy, but the word whispered through Court was that the Handmaiden had disappeared and so had King Constantine. Actually, word was that Regis had finally murdered his father, sending his soul into the universal ether and not bothering to have him reborn, since a reborn gold drake could be a contender to Regis's throne.

A frozen wind gusted in his face, pulling him from his fury to pay attention to his surroundings.

Stupid, stupid drake. That'll get you killed, too. And then who'd be around to protect Raven?

Except it had been Raven who'd slammed him to the floor with her wind magic and reminded him of who he was... or at least was trying to be.

When had she become the responsible one? She was still so young, barely over two hundred years old, and yet she was the one with a steady head, able to sort through the mess of emotions flooding her from her empathic ability, when all he could do was try to block as much of his as possible.

Except even when she was tossing him across Nero's office and looking fierce and in control, he had sensed her fear. Fear for him — more like heartbreak for him over his best friend's death, which only made his beast furious — and fear for Nero.

The wind gusted again, carrying a ghostly hint of a scream and an emotional whisper of fear, heart-rending, desperate fear.

It seized tight in Diablo's chest and his empathic power flared, connecting against his will to this human. More pain, more fear, more desperation.

It crushed him, stealing his breath in a way he'd never experienced before. Whatever this kid was experiencing, it was overwhelming.

He scanned the area, straining to hear another scream and figure out where the kid was. He had a fifty-fifty chance of having randomly picked the correct side of the river, but without another scream or burst of pain, he wouldn't know if he'd guessed right. He'd arrived just off a walking path in the leafless bushes on the wrong side of a chain-link fence. To his left stood a construction trailer with the company's logo painted on the side in dark red and blue, a dinged and dirt-covered backhoe, and a pile of dirt and cement dividers. Over his shoulder towered the West End Bridge, recognizable from its great sweeping steel arch.

Another flare of agony hit his empathy, followed by another scream. The kid wasn't far away. This side of the river, down the path on the other side of the bridge. He gated to the fence's other side and bolted toward the pain, his footsteps crunching in the ice and salt slicking the asphalt. A quick glance over his shoulder confirmed the path was clear even though it was only early evening. He drew up his gate magic — so powerful he didn't need a power word, just a thought. A gate formed in front of him, catching his next step and tossing him out farther down the path without making him lose stride. Another check for witnesses and another gate mid-run.

He gated past the opening of the bridge, flashing from one shadow on the path to the next without missing a step. The scream came again, and the pain slammed into him. He lurched out of another gate, his knees buckled with the force of the agony, but caught his balance and slid across a frozen puddle into another gate that tossed him out near a flickering orange streetlight standing at the edge of the path and a parking lot.

Someone whimpered, and the pain enveloped him, now a giant wave he couldn't keep back no matter how hard he tried. His beast surged in response, needing to fight against it, kill the danger, not knowing it wasn't in danger. He gasped, trying to breathe past the pressure in his chest. A few feet away, a body writhed in the gravel, a brilliant yellow aura pulsing like a desperate heartbeat.

"Hey," Diablo said, fighting to keep his beast back. He drew a few steps closer, but not within reach. An aura this bright and with this much pain meant that whatever magic the kid had developed, it was powerful from the get-go and most likely deadly. For those rare humans whose earth magic awakened, empaths curled into balls and sobbed or went catatonic, wind and water magic came on slowly like a wave or a building storm, while enhanced physical abilities like speed and strength didn't get noticed until they accidentally ran into or broke something.

The kid whimpered and his chest heaved with rapid breaths. He shifted just enough to glare at Diablo with a brown eye lit by his aura, making it appear gold.

"Hey." Diablo plastered on his calmest expression, but his body — and the beast — remained tense, and he still didn't draw closer. Nero had said he didn't know if this mage was natural or not. Another reason not to step too close. Natural human mages were less likely to go insane, especially if Raven got to them soon enough, but the unlucky bastards Zenobia had abducted — and forced to share their bodies with a dragon soul long enough for their earth magic to awaken — were almost all without a doubt insane. Very few human souls were strong enough to survive that kind of shock and stay intact.

The not-really-gold eye blinked, and the kid's aura flickered, vanishing for a too-long heartbeat and dousing the parking lot into darkness. Even the streetlight behind Diablo went out, leaving only the pile of snow on the far side as the only pale spot around.

"I'm here to help," Diablo said.

Or kill you if you're a danger to my puzur.

He shoved that thought back.

The eye opened again, and his aura exploded into brilliant luminescence. Pain screamed through the empathic link and the kid gasped. "Help me?"

"Yeah." Although it would be easier if he just passed out. With this kind of pain, if they got into a taxi, the driver would likely demand they go to the hospital and not Raven's warehouse on the outskirts of town. But gating with a newly awakened — and conscious — mage was more problematic. Experiencing that without understanding how the world really worked usually broke their minds completely.

Another blast swept through Diablo. The kid convulsed, his aura blazing. He screamed then gasped, three quick breaths, before another explosion roared through him. His knees pulled tighter to his chest, and he sobbed.

The pressure in Diablo's chest tightened. His throat hurt, and he wasn't going to admit that it was more than just the kid's emotions affecting him. His beast howled at the pain and the fear and, Mother of All, how much Diablo wanted to help this kid. No one deserved this. Certainly not a human. Their lives were too short for so much torture.

"I'm going to get help," he said.

He ran out of the kid's sight then gated in behind him and punched him in the head, knocking him out. *Please let that have been so fast he didn't know what hit him.*

The kid sagged, his too-tight muscles suddenly limp, and his aura softened. Diablo had known it was powerful but hadn't realized how sharp it had been. The tightness in his chest eased — but not as much as he'd hoped, with the beast howling for the fight it hadn't gotten.

With his enhanced strength, he drew the kid into his arms and realized he probably wasn't a kid. While the young man could still be in his late teens, it was more likely he was in his twenties, although after living almost four hundred years it was sometimes difficult to actually determine a human's age. It was unusual for a human mage to come into his power so long after puberty — adding more evidence to the idea that this human had body-shared with a dragon and was most likely crazy — but hey, Ryan's magic hadn't fully developed until his thirties, so it wasn't impossible.

Diablo summoned a gate to the safe house and stepped through. Regardless of how old this kid— *man* was, with the power still radiating from his aura even while unconscious, this human had a challenging road ahead of him if was going to stay sane. But that was now a problem for Raven.

28

Ivy stared out the window at the glittering lights of the Vancouver skyline and rubbed the collar of her robe across her jaw, savoring the feel of the soft fabric against her still-sensitive skin. After making love in the shower, they'd stripped in full, cleaned off, and made love again in the bed. Then they'd cuddled, the ever-present ache in her soul gone, and her heart filled with such warmth she was certain she was glowing.

She'd stayed there until Grey had drifted off. She'd wanted to stay there forever, never leave his embrace, but she wouldn't be able to do that until she'd figured out how to escape from Regis and Tobias.

With a renewed heaviness in her heart, she'd slipped from the bed, careful not to wake Grey, wrapped herself in the robe, and explored the suite. She'd found a washer and dryer and tossed their underwear in to dry, but — save for collecting their phones, Grey's wallet, and her passport — she didn't bother cleaning up the rest of their clothes still scattered in the bathroom. Diablo was bringing them new outfits to help them blend in with the reception-goers at the museum in less than an hour, and, if she was being honest with herself, she really didn't know what to do with the clothing once gathered.

Now she stood at the floor-to-ceiling window at the back of the living room, listening to the hum of the dryer and stroking the robe against her jaw, wishing it was Grey's rough stubble instead, wishing they were back in the shower and nothing else mattered but him making her feel all those incredible things again.

A shudder swept through her, drawing a renewed ache between her thighs and making her crave him again. She pressed a finger against her locket, unable to stop herself. She'd promised she wouldn't save his memory, but she'd never said she wouldn't save *hers*. And Mother, what a memory! If she couldn't figure out how to escape Regis and Tobias, she wanted to have their lovemaking seared into her locket forever.

Except everything within her cried to be free. More now, since she'd realized the truth about her and Grey. He hadn't admitted it and she hadn't been willing to ruin the mood and press for information, but they had purred. And just like she knew what a refrigerator was, she knew what purring meant. Her soul had picked him. A drake of a different color and element, from different coteries and an enemy of her coterie. She'd gotten the impression it was dangerous for him to return to Court and if she returned, she doubted Tobias would ever let her leave again.

She couldn't put if off any longer. She had to cash in on her agreement with Grey. Surely he would help her. He'd purred, too. That meant his soul had chosen hers as well. They were inamorated, forever bound to each other, and would never find another love like this again.

But she didn't know if being inamorated meant she could trust him. It certainly didn't mean she could trust his friends or his doyen.

She bit back a growl.

None of that mattered. She would use what she knew to force them to help her.

Except that was only fooling herself. Even if she had the experience to know how to leverage her knowledge without it backfiring, she wasn't that kind of drake. Despite being desperate, the idea of hurting Grey like that made her insides squirm.

Mother! She'd just met the man. A connection between them had to be impossible. And if she didn't imprint as much of today as she could into her locket, she wouldn't remember him tomorrow.

That made the ice in her gut flare, hard and sharp. Maybe that was why he hadn't said anything about the purring. He knew she'd forget and had decided any kind of relationship with her was too difficult.

Her throat tightened. He was probably right. And really, all they had was this one evening. It had been a wonderful couple of hours or so at most. No more than a moment... one glorious, amazing moment. She couldn't understand how thinking about this drake who she didn't really know filled her with such desire and heartache and yearning and grief.

One of the three phones on the kitchenette counter chirped, and she rushed to answer it before it woke Grey. All of his wounds had been closed when they'd left the shower and moved to the bed, but that didn't mean he was fully healed, and if there was even the slightest chance they were going to run into Jet at the museum, she wanted him as healed as possible.

"Hello?" she asked into the phone. Her gaze jumped to the other two phones. It wasn't Grey's or Diablo's—

Which meant it was hers.

Her heart skipped a beat. She hadn't thought she'd missed her check-in time, but—

She had no idea what time it really was.

"What the hell have you gotten into?" Ophelia growled.

"Well, I—"

"The Handmaiden's man was spotted in Seville with someone who fit your description."

"Well, yes—"

"There were gunshots and an explosion. Regis's new assassin showed up looking like he'd lost a fight."

He had, and she'd been the one who'd shot him. "Yes—"

"You were supposed to go to the Handmaiden's residence and figure out what this black drake—"

"Her name is Jet."

Ophelia hissed. Ivy was certain the drake was baring her teeth with pure aggression. "Let me guess. Grey told you," she said, her tone darkening on his name.

Ivy fought the urge to growl back. "Yes."

"And he convinced you to go to Seville."

"He didn't have to convince me. The chamberlain wants to know what's going on and that's what I'm trying to find out." Except that hadn't really been her assignment. She'd only gone with Grey because she was terrified the drake after the coin was Regis and she couldn't let him get his hands on it and because she had to find a way to stay in the human world.

"You were told to read the memories in the Handmaiden's residence then go to the office tower in Newgate, not chase a dangerous drake — while in the company of an equally dangerous drake — to Spain."

"Ophelia—"

"No. Where the hell are you? You're getting to a gate, and you're meeting me in Newgate."

"I can't do that." Even if she wanted to return to Court, Grey needed her near to keep his memories at bay so he could break into the museum. She couldn't abandon him now.

"You can and you will," Ophelia said. "Somehow you've attracted the attention of the dugga of the Asar Nergal, and he's demanded Tobias permanently transfer you to his unit."

"The Asar Nergal?"

"The unit formed to hunt down and kill human mages. Ivy—" Ophelia's tone softened. "The dugga is a good man, but he won't understand your..."

"My condition?" Ivy asked, using the same term Grey had used to describe himself. It was no wonder their souls had picked each other. They were both broken.

"Yes, your condition," Ophelia said. "The Asar Nergal's job is dangerous. I don't even know how the dugga learned about you or your earth magic."

Neither did Ivy. The only drake she'd revealed her secret to had been Grey, and he hadn't made a phone call since she'd told him. Unless Tobias or Regis had told him.

"Meet me in Newgate. Tobias needs a report and I need to figure out what to do about the dugga."

"No." Dugga or not, Ivy had to see this through. But a new fear tightened within her. Even if she never returned to Court and figured out a way to hide from Regis and Tobias, could she hide from the dugga? His job was to hunt down humans trying to hide. She turned and stared out the dark windows at the lights of the city's high rises. He had to know the human world better than the chamberlain or the prince.

"What do you mean, no?"

"I mean I have to—"

A gate whooshed behind her, and Diablo, holding a small black suitcase, appeared in the window's reflection. His gaze locked on her and his eyes narrowed.

"Who are you talking to?" He dropped the suitcase, flashed out of existence and reappeared in front of her.

"I've got to go." She hung up on Ophelia.

"Who were you talking to?" Danger radiated from his aura in palpable waves, even more intense than when she'd first met him at his doyen's house. Was he the dugga? Ophelia had said the dugga was a good man, but Ivy wasn't certain that Diablo was.

"If I didn't report in, Tobias would send someone after me."

"And what did you report?"

"Nothing."

"Yeah, right." He flashed a hint of teeth.

She shifted back. Yes, it was a sign of weakness, but he was clearly the more powerful drake. "I don't know how loyal the chamberlain is to Regis, but there's no way in hell I'm letting the prince get the coin."

He sneered, exposing even more teeth. "Those are traitorous words."

"I mean—" Crap. She had to be more careful than that. The wrong word to the wrong drake, and she'd be arrested or killed. "The coin is too dangerous for anyone to have."

Diablo snorted. "I'm pretty sure you really meant the first one. Regis can't have it."

"I—" This was a trap, and she had no idea how to get out of it. Except she'd already said what she'd said and meant it.

Diablo's sneer deepened.

God damn it, she was already caught. "And if my prince wanted loyalty, he wouldn't trade me like a game piece to the dugga," she said under her breath. The fear in her gut snapped sharp.

Shit. She shouldn't have said that, either. Not even whispered it. But she was just so tired of being used. While in the shower with Grey, she'd finally done something for herself, and it had felt good. So good. She craved more and sure as hell wasn't going back to the way things were when she woke that morning. She wanted new thoughts imprinted in her locket when she woke tomorrow. She wanted to know she had drakes she could trust. She wanted to know she didn't have to be afraid any more.

Diablo barked a harsh laugh. "So that's how he's doing it."

"Doing what?"

"You honestly don't think after meeting me and Nero and the others that we'd let you return to Court."

"Not return?"

"Diablo," Grey said, his voice dark. He stood in the doorway to the bedroom, a towel wrapped around his waist hanging dangerously low on his hips.

"Did you know?" she asked.

The muscle in his jaw clenched, and the ice within her exploded, racing into her chest. "You knew when you shared that memory? When we—" Her throat tightened and heat flooded her face. "That's why you could trust me not to tell anyone, because you knew I wouldn't be able to."

"Oh, man, you two?" Diablo snorted. "I thought you had better sense than to sleep with a member of the royal coterie."

"Ivy—"

He'd lied to her. A lie by omission, but a lie nonetheless. "You owe me."

"I'm pretty sure he's already paid," Diablo said.

"We made a deal, and I'm cashing in, or God help me—" She grabbed her locket and glared at Grey. "God help me, I will tell Tobias everything."

Diablo seized her, grabbed her head, jerking it to a painful angle, and wrapped an arm around her neck. "I don't think so."

Grey's eyes flared wide then narrowed with fury. With a roar, he lunged toward them.

Diablo's gate whooshed around him and Ivy. The world twisted, then hardened, and they stood on the other side of the room.

Grey wrenched around to face them. He'd lost the towel and stood gloriously naked, his powerful muscles tense, his hair, only half dry, hanging wild around his head, making him look ferocious.

"Let her go," he growled, everything about him radiating danger.

"She threatened my coterie," Diablo said.

Ivy clawed at his arm, trying to break free, but his grip around her neck tightened, cutting off her air.

"You just heard her. Nero has already taken care of it," Grey said.

"Once he has her, he'll what? Lock her in the basement? If she has access to a phone, she's still a danger. Taking her head at least will limit her suffering."

"She's not going to tell Regis anything."

"She was just on the phone with Tobias."

Black specks danced across her eyes. Her pulse pounded faster and she grabbed her locket. If she passed out without imprinting anything there, when she awoke she'd forget everything. She'd forget Grey.

"I made her a promise."

God, that felt like a lifetime ago. She'd never left Court before today. She'd seen vast mountains and a frozen garden and an enormous library.

Diablo's grip relaxed a fraction. "Why the hell would you make her a promise?"

She'd seen a ferocious drake, now standing naked before her, risk everything to protect dragonkind. He'd protected her with his body when Jet had thrown that grenade, and he'd used that body to bring her pleasure she hadn't known was possible.

Mother, she didn't want to forget any of it. All she wanted was to be her own dragon, to make her own decisions, to trust someone.

She met Grey's gaze. It was filled with pain and love and that sizzling, sure connection she'd seen when they'd made love.

"It doesn't matter. I owe her. She doesn't need to use what she knows to get her favor."

"I don't trust her." But Diablo's grip didn't tighten again.

"I do."

"With your life?"

The pain turned to sadness. Yeah, she was probably going to forget parts of this in the morning, but she'd be damned if she forgot everything.

"With my soul."

Diablo tensed, his arm tightening, the muscles in his chest hard against her back. The pulse in his arm pounded against her neck. One thud of his heart. Two—

"Ah, fuck. Not you, too?"

Grey quirked an eyebrow. "You know me. If I can make it complicated..."

"This is just fucking awesome." He released her and jerked away. "It doesn't mean she's less of a danger."

"Working for the dugga will keep her out of Court," Grey said.

"I don't want to work for the dugga. That's what I want to use my favor for. I don't want to work for anyone, and I don't want to be trapped at Court not knowing who I can trust." Ivy tightened the tie on her robe. "If it didn't bring Regis's wrath, I'd beg your doyen for sanctuary. But if Regis knows where I am, he won't let me go."

"You've got an awfully high opinion of yourself."

Her throat tightened at the truth. "My earth magic is too good at finding traitors."

Diablo huffed. "Yeah, right."

"You have a secret conversation and my magic will show me the memory of it."

Diablo's expression darkened. "I can see how Regis would find that useful."

Grey grabbed his towel off the floor and wrapped it back around his waist. "Did you bring the clothes?"

"Yeah." Diablo jerked his chin toward the suitcase. "And I brought the blueprints for the museum. It looks like secure doors use a keypad lock. You'll need to connect your phone to mine to get my app to hack those, along with my video surveillance takeover app."

"Hey." They were talking as if everything was fine when nothing was. "We haven't finished our conversation."

Diablo snapped his attention back to her and glared. "Are you going to endanger my coterie?"

A shiver swept through her and the cold in her gut surged. He was dangerous. Without a doubt, he'd kill her and not think twice about it. She ground her teeth and matched his glare. "Are you going to help me escape Court and the dugga?"

"Not my debt," Diablo said, a wicked gleam lighting his eyes.

"Stop messing with her." Grey extended a hand, palm up, the same offer he'd made in the bathroom, one of trust and an invitation to join him.

She slid her hand into his, her fingers entwining between his and his memory fire caressing her skin. A hint of lightning-hot attraction zinged through her, and she fell into his gaze. He held her heart and soul. She would go with him to the ends of the earth, fight his battles with him — probably fight with him, too. They were dragons, after all — and love him for eternity, whether she wanted to or not.

"You two are disgusting," Diablo said. "For the love of God, just tell her Nero is the dugga and be done with it."

The words muddled in her head. "Your doyen, Nero, is the dugga?"

"Which is why we're not worried about you being transferred into the dugga's employ." Grey brought her hand up and brushed his lips against her skin, drawing another shiver.

"He's also not Grey's doyen," Diablo said. "I'm guessing that would be... Hunter?"

"Hunter will never be doyen of a coterie." Grey's gaze jumped past her to Diablo. "No matter what other drakes want, and he'll never challenge Regis for the throne."

"Well, someone should." Diablo grabbed the suitcase and opened it up on the chair across from them. "With Regis's traitor-finder no longer in his employ, it'll make everything easier."

The muscles in Grey's jaw tensed. "It'll also make everything more dangerous. More coups mean more souls in jeopardy."

"Not if someone has this coin." Diablo tossed a black dress shirt at Grey.

"The coin will only make a bad situation worse." With an apologetic glance, Grey brushed his lips across the back of Ivy's hand again then released her. He pulled a suit jacket out of the suitcase before Diablo could throw that at him, too.

"Which means we need to stay on mission." Ivy was certain she didn't know all of the political ramifications, but it was clear having the coin — even Regis just knowing about the coin — was bad. "We get the coin piece and then I swear my allegiance to a new doyen."

"Wonderful." Diablo shoved a black, silky dress into Ivy's hands. "Another misfit to add to the mansion. We're going to run out of rooms."

"You're not going to run out of rooms. You have a whole wing currently unoccupied." Grey shrugged into the dress shirt. "Besides, with all the earth magic in the house, I'm sure it won't take long to build an extension."

Diablo rolled his eyes at Grey. "Sure, let's just ask the sorcerer to add the windows instead of blowing them out next time."

"You know a sorcerer?" But the information in her locket said the Handmaiden was the dragons' only sorcerer. She caught Grey's gaze. "You could ask her to... you know."

"Hunter would kill him if they... you know," Diablo said, his tone filling the words *you know* with sexual innuendo.

Heat flooded Ivy's face and a hint of rage at Grey having sex with any other drake flared in her chest. "That's not what I meant."

Diablo flashed her a wicked grin. "I know, but it's so much fun to mess with the newly inamorated."

"Anaea is new to her sorcerer's ability," Grey said, "so it's—"

"Complicated." Diablo rolled his eyes. "And when you're situated in the mansion, Grey will have time to explain everything. If you two aren't too busy with... you know."

She glanced at Grey, shrugging into the dress shirt, the towel still slung seductively low on his hips. More sensual desire swelled within her. In a few hours, everything would be different. She'd be free, with her inamorato, and ready to explore a new world full of possibilities.

29

Servius squared his shoulders, his stomach churning and his pulse racing, and raised his hand to knock on the door to the Handmaiden's outer chamber.

Regis had summoned him and the only thing that had prevented him from fleeing was that the summons had come in the form of a page and not a handful of guards to haul him to prison.

I haven't been discovered. I have not been discovered. The words rushed through his head, over and over again. *Running now would give everything away.*

Mother, he hoped that was true.

Maybe Regis had summoned him to congratulate him on Grey's death.

But that didn't make sense. Regis didn't know that Grey had been a danger to Servius's plans. He shifted, his hand still poised to knock.

Stay focused on the plan. You have not been discovered.

Jet was on her way to the temple in Arrapha — she was probably already there. Soon she'd be on her way to Vancouver to get the other coin from the Chang'an temple, and then back to the Handmaiden's secret residence to finish the spell to join the pieces. After that, they'd meet in the arena and he could claim his rightful place as emperor of the dragons.

The words rolled through his panicked thoughts, bleeding through the fear of being discovered and filling him with certainty.

This was the way it was supposed to be. Anyone looking at Regis could guess he was soul sick and rumor at Court said that Constantine was missing, likely murdered. Someone sane had to be in control.

The muscle in Servius's arm quivered, reminding him he still had to knock and face Regis before he was ready to take the throne.

If Regis even suspected anything, Odyne's magic would be tearing into your soul already. Running would only give you away.

He made himself knock before he could change his mind.

Mother help me.

A guard opened it, revealing Regis sitting in the Handmaiden's chair at the bare room's center.

"Took you long enough," Regis said, his voice low, dangerous. "I thought you'd gotten lost."

He knows. He has to know and he's toying with me. "I was in prayer to the Mother when your page arrived."

Regis's eyes narrowed. "Didn't the messenger mention it was important?"

The young dragon had, but confessing that endangered Servius's plan, and taking the throne was everything. The page was just going to have to be sacrificed for the greater good. "I don't think so."

"Send the hatchling to Odyne. Maybe that will help her remember." Regis jerked his chin at a guard and the dragon rushed out of the room, leaving three others. Too many for Servius to fight if he was crazy enough to make a move on Regis right now, unless he wanted to reveal his sorcerer's power.

The prince's gaze jumped back to Servius and for a second the look in his eyes wasn't sane. Servius didn't know how to explain it. It wasn't that Regis's expression had changed any, more that the sense of the soul staring back at him was suddenly feral.

Regis blinked and the feralness vanished. "I need your connections."

"My connections?"

"Yes. Those connections that knew Grey had gone to Seville." Regis leaned back, making the wooden chair groan under his weight. "Who are they?"

"Your Highness—" Panic squeezed Servius's chest. He didn't have connections and couldn't give any names, but he couldn't refuse

Regis, not without risking his ire. Everything would fall apart if Servius was imprisoned. "We've been chatting recently— again— today. Perhaps I can help and you don't need to wait on their summons."

"Have they been talking about Grey again?"

"Grey?"

"Yes. Grey. He's after a rebirth coin."

Servius's heart skipped a beat. "A rebirth coin?"

"Bolo heard Grey and Ivy mention something about that before they gated away." The hint of feral beast returned to Regis's eyes. "Grey's been keeping secrets. I didn't know he could rapid free gate, but according to Bolo, he gated away before the hatchling could apprehend him in Seville."

"In Seville?" Servius asked, then realized all he was doing was repeating everything Regis said in the form of a question. "Was this near the *ekas?*" *Shit, another question.* "Like my contacts said?"

"You mean the *ekas* that burst into flames? The royal property they destroyed?" Regis asked, his tone dark. "Bolo caught them running out of the building after they'd lit it up."

That meant Jet was wrong and Grey and Tobias's agent were still alive.

The panic in Servius's chest squeezed tighter. Grey had known to go to the *ekas.* Servius had to assume, even if the chances were slim, Grey knew about the coins and was going to go after the pieces. Servius had to call Jet, get her to hurry up in Arrapha, and get to Vancouver in case that was where Grey went first.

But that wasn't the worst of it. Regis knew about the coin.

"What do your contacts know about this coin?" Regis asked.

"I'll have to ask them. What does this rebirth coin do?"

Regis glared at him. "My guess would be it casts a rebirth spell."

"Right, yes—" Crap. He needed to buy time, figure out what to do. "I meant, how does it work?"

"I don't know. And the drake who would know, Ivy, just received a permanent transfer request from the dugga himself." Regis slammed his meaty fists against the chair's arms. "I want to know how the hell the dugga learned that Ivy can read the memories from objects and rooms."

Maybe because you mentioned it? Servius bit the inside of his cheek before the words spilled out. Tobias's agent was a dragon whose earth magic was reading the memories stored within objects and rooms. That explained how she'd known where Jet was in the Handmaiden's residence. She'd used her magic and watched Jet hide. It wasn't a surprise Regis wanted to keep her, and it was less of a surprise the dugga wanted her, too.

"I'll go talk to my contacts right now." Servius dropped into a deep bow but stopped himself before getting up and leaving. He had to protect against the chance that Grey would get to the coin piece in Vancouver first. He couldn't count on Grey going to Arrapha. "My contacts did mention they'd heard Grey was in Vancouver, Canada. At the museum that's restoring the dragon statue from Chang'an."

"Vancouver, huh?" Regis flashed his teeth, all aggression with the feral monster flickering again in his gaze. He glanced at a guard. "Tell Bolo he gets one more chance."

GREY CHECKED THE WIDE FRONT STEPS OF THE MUSEUM, SEARCHING for Jet, as he and Ivy approached. Lights glittered on damp, empty concrete planter boxes and turned the large windows of the modern addition to the historical building into luminous eyes, allowing them to see all the people inside the front foyer, dressed in their finest for the early evening reception.

"I don't see Jet inside, but there are a lot of people here," Ivy said, her voice low.

He didn't see Jet hanging around outside, either, but that didn't mean she wasn't there — the drake could camouflage herself and they wouldn't know she was there until it was too late.

"If our math is correct, she should still be hiking out of the gate-locked perimeter of the Arrapha temple," Grey said, praying he was right as he shifted his knife's shoulder holster, hidden by his suit jacket and tucked under his left arm. He'd liked the knife even less than the short sword he'd been forced to take to the Handmaiden's secret residence, but any sword would be even harder to hide under his suit jacket than a knife, so a hunting knife it was. Thank the Mother, the museum was small and the security specks indicated it didn't have metal detectors at the doors.

A part of him squirmed with unease that they'd taken so long to rest and grab a quick meal. Even just a few hours could make the difference between getting this coin and not. But those few hours of rest could also make the difference between winning or losing a fight with Jet.

Not to mention sharing his memory with Ivy, or maybe sealing their soul bond... or whatever had happened that had settled the writhing gloom within him. He'd felt the difference the moment he'd woken. At first, a flash of panic had raced through him. She wasn't in bed or the room and that meant her aura had been out of range, but his memories hadn't flooded around him. They were still there, pushing at the edge of his senses, but his magic had seemed content to just be, as if the Handmaiden had eased her soothing power into his mind.

The panic had exploded into fear when he'd seen Diablo attack Ivy and she'd confronted him about knowing Nero's plans for her. And he was drake enough to admit he was still confused about how lucky he'd gotten. Ivy didn't want to return to Court, Nero had figured out how to get her away from Regis, and—

And Mother of All, things might actually work out.

He was afraid to let in too much hope, but it was hard to keep it back.

He'd found his inamorata. Diablo wasn't going to kill her, and Regis no longer had his talons in her. She'd even confirmed that the constant ache within her where her memories should have been was gone. The experiment had been a success. Neither of them knew how long the effect would last, but that was okay. They'd get the coin piece, return to the hotel, and have the rest of eternity to figure everything out.

"If we want a good cushion of time, we still need to be in and out of the restoration room in half an hour." Ivy flashed her teeth at him, looking sexy as hell. He knew it was supposed to be a look of determination — there wasn't any indication she meant the look otherwise — but he couldn't help seeing a dragon's challenge and sexual invitation.

He flashed his teeth back at her, unable to keep the heat from his expression. "And we want a good cushion."

Her grip on his arm tightened and she shuddered, making his

desire harden even more. "If we're going to get through this, you need to stop looking at me like that."

He was tempted to ask, "Like what?" But she was right. It was hard enough for him to think past finding a nook and making her purr again, like she had in the shower and then again in the bed. Teasing her really only teased him, and they had a job to do. "In half an hour, we'll be back at the hotel."

"And then I really hope you don't like that suit because I'm ripping it off."

He fought back a groan. "Now who's teasing?"

"Sorry."

"Don't apologize." He squared his shoulders and they headed up the museum's wide steps. "But I expect you to keep your promises."

"Don't you worry about that." A hint of a purr escaped her lips.

He wrenched his attention away from her and scanned the foyer again, hoping it would drag his mind back to the job at hand.

Still no sign of Jet. Also, thankfully, no sign of any other dragons. It would be a complete disaster if they came across someone who recognized Grey and knew Regis wanted to arrest him. Even worse was the weight and tingle of the gatelock spell embedded in the Chang'an dragon statue. The spell had shivered over Grey's skin the moment the taxi had drawn within two blocks of the museum, and the feeling had continued to grow as they got closer. This was a powerful spell and fully in effect, not like the diminishing one on the *ekas* in Seville. If they got into any kind of trouble, there was no way he'd be able to summon a gate for them to escape. No matter how desperate he was.

Of course, that meant no other dragon could surprise them or escape, either. Grey just didn't know how much of an advantage that really was.

He pulled open one of the heavy glass doors and let Ivy enter first. Inside, heat and the roar of many voices engulfed him. Somewhere, barely on the edge of his hearing, someone played classical music. The musicians, a string quartet, sat on a small stage on the far left, while waiters in their black and white uniforms wove with dancer-like precision between guests, their trays laden with hors d'oeuvres and champagne flutes, flashes of light among the black suits and gowns.

To their right stood a makeshift coat check, and beyond that, behind free-standing white panels, was the caterer's staging grounds.

"You started the app on my phone?" he asked as they headed to the coat check. They'd decided he'd keep an eye on their surroundings while she kept an eye on the cameras, and had given her his phone along with a quick lesson on how to use it. She'd slid it into her purse — a medium sized black bag with a thin strap long enough to cross her chest — along with the gun she'd taken from Jet in the Handmaiden's secret residence that had been reloaded thanks to Diablo and his delivery of clothes and supplies.

"Yep, and I'm already running the program to hack the security feed."

"Good." Diablo had said the program was created by Capri's computer whiz Clean Team member, Gig, which meant it was fifty-fifty computer code and magic. It hacked a building's security system and gained control, so they could put the video on a loop. Diablo claimed the best way to work the program was to change each camera to a loop as they approached it, but Grey and Ivy had agreed — after Diablo had left, of course — that they'd set all the cameras in the secure areas on loop and not worry about getting fancy.

Ivy shrugged out of her borrowed coat and handed it to Grey. It was a rich wool with sleek lines that accentuated Ivy's curves. It had been Raven's — like the low-cut dress that showed off Ivy's precious gold locket, with all her memories, and the heels — and unfortunately, the plan meant they were abandoning it here.

A twinge of guilt tightened Grey's throat. Raven had known what would happen to it, and she'd offered it anyway. All of Nero's *puzur* had been like that. Sure, Grey had come with Anaea, who'd desperately needed training in her sorcerer abilities so she didn't kill everyone around her, but they'd been just as welcoming to Grey, assuming he'd be around for meals, giving him a room so he could stay close to Anaea, sharing conversations and jokes and all the warmth he hadn't had in almost two thousand years. His own coterie had never been that warm, even before he'd forged his friendship—no, his *brotherhood* with Hunter.

Now here they were, sacrificing their clothes and possibly their safety for him and Ivy. Yes, Nero asking for Ivy to be transferred to the Asar Nergal was a brilliant move to get her out of Court, but too many moves like that and Regis would grow suspicious — if he wasn't becoming suspicious already.

When this was done, Grey was going to owe Nero and Raven and even Diablo more than he could repay. And he would happily try to pay the debt if it meant he could live worry-free with his inamorata.

A ding from Ivy's phone cut through his thoughts.

"I should take this." She stepped to the side and looked at the screen.

Grey handed over their coats to the young man minding the coat check, took the offered ticket stubs, and drew up beside Ivy.

"The app has control," she said, her voice low.

"Good." He glanced at the white partitions where the caterers were working. At least half a dozen people stood at long tables, preparing food and opening champagne bottles, while a dozen more came and went, dropping off empty trays and dirty glasses and picking up new ones. No sign of Jet and, thankfully, no sign of any other dragon. "The first door to the secure areas is back there."

"But the other door is past that." Ivy jerked her chin toward the other side of the room, past all the people where the closed main doors to the museum stood.

They'd studied the blueprints of the museum and agreed the security door off the foyer was their first choice, while their second choice was the security door inside the museum proper. There was also another good access point at the back, where large museum pieces were loaded in and out, but that door didn't have a keypad and required lockpicking skills.

"How much do you want to bet the museum's front doors are locked?" Ivy asked.

"Not a bet I'm willing to take." He'd never learned to pick a lock. Hunter had always been by his side in those infrequent moments when he'd needed to break and enter, and after that, his job with the Handmaiden hadn't required much of anything—

Although now that he thought about it, working for the Handmaiden had apparently required his God-damned inability to forget, since he was certain he was the only drake who'd have been able to figure out the Handmaiden's clues to stopping Jet.

"I guess it's still plan A." Meaning the first security door with its keypad lock. "And I hope your magic is fast enough that no one notices us standing by the security door."

Ivy frowned and chewed her bottom lip. "If we get a little closer— Maybe right beside those partitions there, I might be able to get the door to tell me its code."

"You can read an object's memories from that far away?" The partition was easily a good seventy-five feet from the door.

"The door is connected to the wall. I'm hoping I can send my magic through the wall to the door." She met his gaze, her eyes filled with worry and hope and determination.

Warmth swelled in his chest and lower. The urge to hold her, tell her she was amazing, convince her she would be— no, *was* a powerful drake filled him. He wanted to worship her body and soul and, Mother of All, he *had* to keep her safe. Except nothing about this situation was safe. Even if Jet wasn't there, there was still a chance she already had this coin piece, and with the coin joined with a medallion, no dragon soul was safe.

He wrapped an arm around her back and drew her close, savoring her scent and the feel of her body pressed against his. "Give it a try."

Her breath feathered across his cheeks and the pulse at her throat sped up. "I need to touch the wall."

"Yeah." He stepped them back, pressed her to the wall, and brushed his lips across hers. Just a whisper of a kiss, nothing more, or he'd lose what little control he had.

Her eyes fluttered shut and she melted against him, a tension he hadn't realized had been there seeping from her body. Then her aura pulsed, she opened her eyes, capturing his soul again, but her gaze focused inward. A line formed between her delicate brows and her lips pursed.

Mother, to kiss those lips in full, feel her flesh slide against his and their auras crackling against each other, heightened with passion.

A purr curled in his throat.

He wrenched his attention from her and scanned the foyer. There'd be plenty of time to indulge later.

Jeez, how had Hunter or Capri managed to keep themselves together once they'd realized they were inamorated? Being this close to Ivy— Heck, being anywhere near Ivy made it hard to think straight.

Ivy gasped and tensed in his grip. With a growl, her aura pulsed again then pulled tighter to her body and dimmed. "I can't believe I've got it, and with you standing right here."

"I can. You're amazing."

"Yeah, well." She kissed his cheek and slipped from his grip. "You're biased."

"Guilty." He entwined his fingers with hers and headed toward the partition, determined to look confident. "Hunter says if you look like you know what you're doing, no one will stop you." God, he hoped that was true.

"Hunter has a lot of experience going places he's not supposed to?"

"About two thousand years." Hell, Grey and Hunter had been going to places they weren't supposed to even before the Great Scourge, when they'd been little more than hatchlings.

They passed the first white partition and the closest cook glanced up. Grey ignored him and led Ivy past a waitress shifting a tray of full champagne flutes on her palm. No one said anything, although Grey was sure if questioned, they'd all be able to describe them to the authorities.

The security door stood at the back of the foyer, a plain gray door partially hidden by a pillar and beyond the last of the caterer's tables. Ivy glanced at the phone as they approached and tapped on the screen.

"The security cameras are now on a loop and the code for the door is 5-5-7-3-6."

Grey typed in the code. The red light on the security panel turned to green and the lock on the door clicked. He resisted the urge to glance back. Looking around would give them away. No museum employee would check behind him as he entered a secure area he was supposed to be able to access.

Inside lay an empty, institutionally gray hall with white fluorescent light panels in the ceiling.

"The coast is clear and also in the adjoining hall," Ivy said, and they headed to the end where the new construction entered the original building. Here the hall continued to the left or exited into a stairwell on the right.

Ivy glanced at the phone. "All clear in the stairwell, too."

Grey eased the door open, straining to hear any indication Jet was lying in wait. Which didn't make sense. Why would she be waiting to ambush them when she could get the coin and be gone, all without risking a confrontation?

Still, he couldn't help the nagging feeling that things were going too smoothly. There hadn't been any drakes at the reception, no one had stopped them from entering the museum's secure areas, and so far they hadn't run into any guards.

"The hall at the bottom of the stairs is empty and so is the restoration room." Ivy pursed her lips. "Does this feel too easy to you?"

"I was thinking the same thing." He cracked open the security door at the bottom of the stairs and glanced into the hall. No one. "When we get into the restoration room, can you—"

"—use a little magic to see if Jet has already been there?" Ivy flashed her teeth. "Priority number one."

They rushed into the hall, stopped at the second door — the restoration room — and Ivy used her magic to get the key code.

"The keypad says Jet hasn't been here." Her aura flared as they entered the restoration room.

Grey glanced into the darkness, looking for any hint of an aura, his night sight not strong enough to see clearly to the back, but good enough to make out a massive statue in front of him and at least a dozen workstations on either side. Still no sign of Jet or anyone else.

"The room has no memory of Jet, either."

"I wonder if something is actually going our way for a change." He turned on the overhead lights — for Ivy, because she didn't have any night sight — and they flickered to life, revealing an enormous room with a high ceiling.

In the center stood the Chang'an dragon statue, a larger-than-life representation one and a half times bigger than what Grey had been before the Scourge.

Ivy gasped. "It's beautiful."

Sculpted with magic, the granite drake stood on its haunches, its wings unfurled, one front leg stretched up as if it were about to leap into the air. Every inch of the statue had carved scales, large ones covering the back and tail and smaller ones on its belly, chest, and neck. Each scale had an intricate swirling pattern that, even with magic, would have taken years of concentration to engrave.

Grey hadn't been a pious drake before the Scourge and the fall had given him conflicting emotions about the dragons' goddess. The first time Grey had seen this statue, it was just after he'd almost died in the humans' ninth crusade, because his memories had overwhelmed him. He'd hiked his way into the temple in Chang'an, dropped to his knees, and prayed to the goddess to take his soul. Instead, the Handmaiden had answered his call, whispering in his mind that she'd help him if he met her in her chambers at Court. "*Sag sed ed sedu,*" she'd said, a promise to soothe his heart and raise his soul. He'd become her servant in exchange for magic to stop his memories, and he hadn't returned to Chang'an since.

And all the Handmaiden had asked in return was to read and reread her journals, searing every minuscule detail into his mind with the magic he had begged her to help control.

Funny how that had turned out.

Ivy gasped and flicked off the overhead light. "There's a security guard coming down the hall."

The glow from the phone's screen illuminated her face, casting it in a ghostly complexion as her wide eyes remained locked on it.

Grey rushed to the statue. If their luck was at an end, he wasn't waiting to get the coin piece. The tapestry had portrayed a glow emanating around the dragon statue's heart, but even with the fluorescents off, no light emanated from the statue.

The heavy thud of steady footsteps sounded outside in the hall.

Grey ran his hands over the scales, pressing on the statue's chest. There had to be a latch or something. But nothing shifted under his touch, and no shimmer of magic tingled over his skin, recognizing him as a dragon and releasing a magical lock.

The footsteps drew closer and slowed.

Ivy's eyes widened even more.

Maybe there'd been something in the journal the Handmaiden had made him read. He tried to remember the book's details, but his mind had gone blank. His aura wasn't anywhere near Ivy's and yet there was nothing, no swirling fog, not even a hint of anything that had happened before the last month.

Son of a—

Now was not the time to finally get his wish.

"He's at the door," Ivy hissed, her hand dipping into her purse. "I don't want to shoot him. What do we do?"

G rey fought to bring even a tickle of his magic forward to find the coin before the security guard entered. Nothing. Not even a flicker of memory.

"Grey?" Ivy hissed, drawing a step closer — and making it harder for him to use his unwanted magic.

God, there had to be a way to get this coin. Jet wouldn't have his memories, but she also had the page she'd torn out of the book that Grey hadn't read.

"He's at the keypad."

Shit.

Shit shit shit.

"Hide." Please, Mother, he just needed more time. And space from Ivy. Something that went against everything his soul was saying.

Ivy glanced left and right and a vise gripped his chest. She didn't have night sight and had no idea where to go.

He rushed to her, grabbed her arm, and pulled her around the statue. She pressed the phone to her chest, cutting off the light, and they hunched low. Heat swelled through Grey. He wrapped his arms around her, drawing her close, even though what he needed was to put distance between them.

The lock on the door clicked and light bled into the darkness from the hallway.

Grey's pulse pounded. He didn't know what he'd do if they were caught by the human. He couldn't kill the man, but he couldn't leave the museum without getting the coin piece.

A beam of light from the guard's flashlight swept over the room with the speed of a cursory glance, then the door clicked shut, engulfing them in darkness again.

"Thank the Mother," Ivy said.

Thank the Mother, indeed. Now he needed to get away from Ivy long enough to search his memories for anything to do with the statue.

He drew close to her, unable to stop himself from sliding his lips across her cheek as he whispered to her, "Stay here. I need to use my magic."

She turned into him. Her lips found his and she kissed him with a quick, heated passion. "Not going anywhere."

He bit back a groan. "You make it so hard to leave."

"I'm sure I make other things hard, too."

"You have no idea." He dipped in for another kiss and the image of the dragon sitting in the Chang'an temple flickered across his sight.

"Did you hear something?" Ivy asked.

"I—" Another flicker of the dragon. It had been a cloudy day, but somehow, at the moment he'd sagged to the flagstones in front of the dragon, a beam of sunlight had cut through the clouds, in through a temple window, and hit the statue's back, giving it a luminous halo as if it were alive with a dragon's spirit.

"Grey?" Ivy asked, her breath warm against his cheek. Her grip on his arms tightened. "Your aura is pulsing. Like you're using magic."

Which was impossible. Her aura crackled against his. There wasn't even a hint of memory fog and not a whisper of that alley.

Water rattled against a window and the reek of garbage filled his nose.

Wonderful. Just when he'd thought he'd found a way to get rid of his magic. He wished the memory had stayed with the temple.

The reek and rattle vanished and luminous light filled his vision again. Soft chanting wafted on sun-warmed air, and little specks of dust danced in the sunbeam like earthly manifestations of soul magic.

Way better than the alley.

The light vanished and the alley returned.

Damn—

Except he'd just thought about the alley again.

His throat burned and his blood oozed between his fingers. The drake who'd attacked him chuckled, the sound dark and grating. His face materialized out of the darkness and his lips curled back, revealing broken teeth.

God damn it. Grey was sick and tired of seeing this all the time. What he really needed was to get away from Ivy so he could remember the damned journal.

The journal snapped into focus. He was in his suite at Court, lounging in his oversized cushioned chair — the only chair he'd found that comfortably fit his large frame. The embossed leather book cover pressed against his hand as he brushed his fingers over the thick, yellowed paper. Everything was crystal clear, in better focus than his memories had ever been, as if he wasn't just there but was also hyper aware of every little detail—

Just like when Ivy was near and she brought the present into sharp focus.

"You really can remember every little detail," she said, her voice soft. "That crease in the page, the weight of the book—"

"Sorry. Didn't mean to share." He pushed the memory to the back of his mind, not releasing it but trying not to focus on it, either. He hadn't even thought to share his memory with Ivy, but it had happened. He was going to need to pay attention to what he was thinking when she was around. No point sharing any of his other horrible memories. The one from the alley was more than enough. "You need to keep an eye on the security cameras. I'll go to the back of the room."

"No, don't." Her grip on his forearm tightened. "I don't know if the room is big enough for me not to affect you. Might as well stay, share it with me, and do it as fast as possible."

"This is a terrible idea."

"Do you have a better one?"

He wished he did. But she was right. While he hadn't been able to sense her aura from the hotel bedroom to the living room, he'd still felt her effects on him. He hadn't had a memory blackout since. Not even a whisper of memory fog. It was foolish of him to think the effects only went one way.

"Fast as possible." He drew in a breath and concentrated on the memory of the book, but there wasn't anything else written that referenced the statues or the temples. The Handmaiden could have put something in code, but so far the clues had been obvious. At least obvious to him with his experiences.

He glanced at the statue, the scroll work in the scales barely visible with his night sight. A hint of remembered sunlight illuminated the dragon and the Handmaiden whispered in Grey's head again. *Soothe the heart and raise the soul.* At the time, that had been more than he'd wanted. He'd just wanted the memories to stop. And after almost two thousand years, he'd wanted those memories to stop forever. He yearned for what she'd promised, a soothed heart and a raised soul.

He'd thought she'd meant rebirth, his soul stripped from this human body and the constant ache of his memories gone. Except he had a nagging feeling what she'd really meant was finding his perfect match, a soul that soothed the ache within him and made him a better, stronger drake.

He pressed his palm to the statue's back. "*Sag sed ed sedu.*"

Magic, like a bolt of lightning, snapped up his arm. Ivy yelped and jerked back as if it had zapped her, too. Stone ground against stone and light flared from the statue's front, blinding him.

He blinked, fighting to clear his sight, and stood, centuries of fighting experience refusing to let him get caught unprepared by rushing around to the front of the dragon to face whatever was happening.

The scrollwork on the four scales over the statue's heart was lit with magic, and they were sliding apart. Inside, in the middle of more glowing scrollwork, lay half of a disc the size of Grey's thumbnail, square instead of round to fit within the square hole cut in the center of the medallion. For a second it shimmered with luminescent white magic, the color of the Handmaiden's sorcery, then the light faded, leaving a plain brass chip.

"That's it?" Ivy asked. "It's hard to believe something so small and simple could control the fate of all dragonkind."

"The Handmaiden has always been funny like that." Her most important moment, her biggest plans, were done in secret. In this case, without the participant, Grey, even knowing. She'd been preparing for the eventuality that Grey would need to find this coin piece from before he'd entered her service. He wasn't sure how he felt about that. There'd always been something different about the Handmaiden. For the most part, he'd always thought it was because she was the only dragon sorcerer. When he was struggling the most with his memories, he couldn't help but wonder if there was more to her than just a sorcerer.

He shoved those thoughts away. She'd manipulated him for the good of dragonkind, and in the process, he'd found his inamorata. He'd just have to consider that a win and move on.

He brushed the tip of his finger past the open scales to test for traps. When nothing happened, he grabbed the coin piece. The metal was warm as if even though he couldn't see anything unusual about the coin, its power couldn't be fully contained and he could feel it. The scales slid shut and the light dimmed, throwing them back into darkness.

"Let's get out of here." He shoved the coin into his pocket — not having a better place to put it. There'd be time to give it the proper reverence it deserved once they were back at the hotel.

Ivy glanced at the phone, swiped on the screen to change cameras, and frowned. "I think we have a problem."

"A Jet kind of problem?"

"A Bolo kind." She pointed to the screen. Somehow, Bolo had gotten past the locked door in the lobby behind the caterer's station. "He must have gated here, used his magic, and discovered us."

"What are the odds of that?" They could have been anywhere in the world just as easily as they could have been in Vancouver. "Someone must have pointed him here."

"But who?" she asked.

"My guess is whoever Jet is working for." Grey grabbed her hand and a shiver of desire slid up his arm. "The only person who'd know we might be here would be Jet and Jet's employer. They have to be sending Bolo our way to keep us distracted." But that still didn't help Grey narrow down the already slim list of suspects to the one dragon responsible.

"Well, it isn't working." She flashed him her teeth and jerked her chin to the back of the room. "If we go out the back, we can avoid him."

"Sounds good to me." Grey led her past the dragon statue, and they wove their way through the workstations to a large freight elevator.

"The loading dock is clear," she said, and Grey hit the button to make both sets of doors in the elevator open without changing floors.

Cold air swept over them and the musty smell of damp concrete flooded Grey's nose. Beyond lay a wide-open space with four metal loading bay doors. Against the far right wall stood a few crates and boxes, lit with the red glow of an EXIT sign over a human-sized security door.

Ivy glanced at the phone. "The cameras outside say the driveway is clear."

Grey squeezed Ivy's hand and they rushed out of the museum into the cool early evening air. Orange streetlights shimmered in the puddles on the driveway and on the brick wall of the museum's modern addition that stretched along the left-hand side. Above, clouds raced across the sliver of the moon, indicating a storm was coming. And one was. Even if they prevented Jet and her employer from joining the coin pieces, other drakes would rise against Regis. The storm was inevitable.

But for now, all they had to do was get back to the hotel and complete their part in preventing this one disaster.

Something crunched. A footstep against the asphalt.

Everything within Grey froze.

Ivy's aura flared, and she jerked to face the back of the building. "Jet."

"God damn, I hate that power of yours," Jet growled as she stepped out of the shadows at the building's edge, her camouflage magic flickering and vanishing from around her. She lunged and grabbed Ivy's purse. "Give me the coin piece."

Ivy heaved back, but Jet yanked on the purse and the strap — strung across Ivy's chest — jerked her forward and out of Grey's grip.

He drew his hunting knife and swung at Jet's arm. She twisted closer to Ivy, knocking the phone from Ivy's hand and sending it skidding across the driveway, while keeping her grip on the purse strap. Grey's knife nicked Jet's jacket but didn't catch flesh, and she drew her saber and sliced the purse strap in one quick move.

Ivy grabbed at her purse, but Jet wrenched it from her grip and leapt back. She tore the zipper open and tossed Ivy's passport and credit card on the ground.

"Where is it?" she growled and pulled out the gun — the only other thing in Ivy's purse.

"We didn't find it," Ivy said.

"Yeah, that's why you're sneaking out the back." Jet rolled her eyes and pointed the gun at Grey. "Hand it over."

The security door behind her flew open, revealing Bolo in the doorway, and Jet's attention jumped to him. Grey leapt at Jet, batting the gun out of her hand, and driving his knife toward her gut.

She twisted out of the way. The knife sliced her jacket and came away red with blood. She rammed her elbow toward his head, flipped grips on her saber, and stabbed at him as he wrenched to the side.

Bolo growled and rushed toward Grey, but Ivy rammed her shoulder into him, knocking him off balance.

"Bitch." He grabbed for her arm to catch his balance but caught the shoulder of her dress, his fingers curling into the fabric.

She wrenched back and the strap tore. Metal reflected light, and Ivy's chain broke, caught in Bolo's grip. Her locket flew free and her eyes flashed wide.

Time slowed, everything caught in too-crisp detail thanks to Ivy's presence. Grey's heart pounded, a hard thud, as every muscle bunched. She couldn't lose the locket. She needed it for when she woke tomorrow morning.

He shoved Jet aside. Her saber dipped and nicked his thigh, but he didn't feel it. All he could feel was hot fury and frozen fear. He lunged for the locket. It shot past his hand and bounced across the asphalt toward a sewer grate. He slammed into the ground, stretching to grab it, but it brushed his fingertips and dropped through the grate.

The pressure in his chest snapped and stole his breath.

It was gone.

Her locket was gone.

No. No, he could fix this. He'd go into the sewer and get it back. He'd—

Ivy screamed and wrenched his attention back to her. Bolo had drawn his katana and wakizashi and was sneering at her.

Shit. Deal with this mess then get the locket.

With a growl, Bolo lunged at Ivy, who scrambled back. Her foot hit a patch of slippery asphalt and she toppled backward.

Panic clenched Grey's chest as Bolo slashed at her. She dove to the side. Another slash. Another dive.

Grey scrambled to his feet, grabbed Bolo's arm, and yanked him around. The young orange drake stabbed at his gut with the wakizashi. Grey blocked the strike with his knife, but searing pain bit his back and chest.

"Gotchya," Jet hissed, so close her breath dampened the back of his neck. She leapt back, more agony screaming through him as she withdrew her saber from his torso, and drove it toward his back again.

He heaved to the side. The blade sliced his ribs and pierced Bolo's chest. The orange drake howled and slashed at Grey with his wakizashi.

Grey shoved his shoulder into Bolo's chest and wrenched the katana from his grip. The sword skittered across the driveway. The orange drake plunged his wakizashi into Grey's shoulder. Another bite of pain, but it didn't matter. The only thing that mattered was protecting his inamorata.

He slammed his knife into Bolo's chest and used that as his grip to toss him across the driveway. The orange drake couldn't catch his balance and skidded away.

Ivy scrambled to her knees and her eyes flashed wide. She screamed, but a roaring bang cut her off and agony exploded in Grey's head.

31

E verything within Ivy howled. Blood misted out the side of Grey's head, his eyes rolled back, and he dropped to the ground. No twitch, no gasp, not even a hint that he was breathing. Blood rushed around his skull in a sickening dark halo, soaking his blond hair and oozing across the asphalt.

He was dead. Mother of All, he was dead—

But he couldn't be dead. The only way to kill a dragon was to take his head. He'd breathe again. He'd wake up.

He *had* to wake up.

Jet knelt beside him. Ivy growled and jerked forward, but Jet shot her in the chest. Pain screamed through Ivy's body and all thought flew from her mind. She fell backward onto her butt and for an agonizingly long heartbeat, she couldn't think, couldn't move. All she could feel was excruciating pain.

Jet rifled through Grey's pockets and pulled out the coin piece.

"He's my kill." Bolo staggered to his feet and tightened his grip on his long dagger. "They both are."

"I thought there was a moratorium on killing dragons," Jet growled. "No soul lost and all that crap."

"My prince wants the silver drake's head and that's what I intend to bring him." A dark excitement flared in Bolo's gaze and for a second he didn't look sane. He was a beast trapped in a human vessel and he was going to kill Grey.

"Well, I shouldn't get in the way of the prince's business." Jet flashed her teeth at Ivy and glanced at Ivy's gun, lying beside Jet's feet. "I'd also hate for you not to feel challenged."

"What?" Bolo glanced at the gun then back to Jet.

"Who do you think will get to the gun first?" She shrugged and marched down the driveway. "Too bad I can't stick around to watch."

Bolo's eyes widened and his attention jumped back to the gun.

Ivy's heart skipped a beat. She had to slow him down long enough for Grey to wake up.

She dove for the gun.

So did Bolo.

He tossed Grey's knife at her. She jerked to the side, lost her balance, and crashed to the ground. He rushed past her, but she grabbed his ankle and yanked. She couldn't let him get the gun. Jet's first gunshot still screamed through her body. If Ivy was shot again, she wouldn't be able to protect Grey, and everything within her said she had to protect him.

Bolo kicked at her. She shoved his foot to the side, toppled him over, and heaved him toward her. He twisted and jabbed his long dagger at her. The blade sliced her shoulder, and she wrenched him even closer.

"You can't win," he hissed. "I'm the stronger drake."

"Strength has nothing to do with it." She seized the front of his jacket and, with a force she hadn't realized she possessed, tossed him behind her. She scrambled for the gun. Her fingers brushed the grip as Bolo grabbed her foot and wrenched her back.

She kicked him in the head and dove for the weapon.

His grip on her ankle tightened. She seized the gun, jerked around, and fired two shots. The first shot skimmed his cheek and the second slammed into his shoulder.

He howled and yanked her close.

She fired again. Dead center in the chest. His eyes widened, a wild light burning there. He tore the gun from her hands and tossed it to the far end of the driveway, then smashed a fist into her face.

Pain exploded across her cheek, and flecks of light swarmed her sight.

Another crack of pain, and another, as his fist connected again and again. He seized the front of her dress, wrenched her up, and slammed her back into the ground. The back of her head cracked against the asphalt and the light specks grew brighter.

"I'm the prince's assassin," he growled. "That's for shooting me."

Another punch. White lightning roared through her cheek, and she had no doubt he'd broken bone. She fought to stay conscious and clear her sight.

He towered above her and sneered. "I'm taking the silver drake's head and when I'm done, I'm taking yours, too."

Behind Bolo, Grey still lay unmoving. Not even a hint of his chest rising or falling. Ice filled her gut and swarmed into her chest. Her throat tightened. He was not dead. He couldn't be dead.

Bolo's sneer deepened. He strode to his sword, picked it up, and stalked over to Grey. "Not so fucking tough now, are you?"

Fire roared through her ice. No way in hell was this drake taking her inamorato's head.

Bolo raised his sword, and she seized Grey's knife and rushed at him. He jerked toward her, his blade swiping at her. She leapt to the side. His sword sliced her shoulder, drawing more screaming pain, and she wrenched the knife up the inside of his sword arm, cutting deep into muscle and tendon. His weapon dropped from limp fingers and she slammed Grey's knife into his eye.

Bolo screamed and dropped to one knee, but didn't collapse. He ripped the knife from his face, blood gushed down his cheek, and he roared.

The fire in Ivy's chest flared in response. He wasn't going to stop. She had no way to incapacitate him.

It was her and Grey or him, and she would do anything to protect Grey.

Bolo lunged at her. She dropped to her knees, ducking inside his swipe with the knife, and seized his sword. He swung at her again and she slashed the blade across his chest.

He gasped, blood rushing across the front of his shirt, and his good eye widened. Screaming, she swung again at his neck. He swept the knife up to block the strike but wasn't fast enough. The sword bit into his neck and caught on his spine.

Blood sprayed her in the face and chest and she jerked as hard as she could and severed his neck. His head and body crumpled to the ground with a wet *thunk*. She stared at him, her breath heaving, spiking pain from the gunshot wound and the gashes in her body and white agony screamed through her face.

He was dead. It was over. His soul was lost to the universal ether and there was one less dragon in the world.

Trembling shook her, making the sword in her bloody hand quiver.

She'd killed him.

Killed. Him.

And protected her inamorato.

She dropped the blade and rushed to Grey's side. He still wasn't breathing. She grabbed the front of his suit jacket and shook him, but he didn't start breathing. Mother, he had to start breathing. He still had his head. He couldn't die. Not when she'd just found him.

The trembling increased. Her teeth were chattering and that made her broken cheek hurt even more.

Someone had to help her. She could drag him away from the museum, out of range of the gatelock, but she couldn't free gate and there was no way she could carry him back to the hotel.

Mother, help.

Her throat tightened and the trembling turned into full shakes. She couldn't lose him. Not like this.

A growl rumbled within her.

God damn it, she wasn't going to lose him. She was a drake and drakes were powerful predators.

The shaking didn't ease, and she forced herself to look away from him and find his phone. It lay face down on the ground by the museum's back door. She staggered to it and swiped a finger across the black screen.

It lit up. Thank the Mother. She dialed the only number in the contact section and scrambled back to Grey.

Wake up. Please, just wake up.

"What?" an angry voice said over the phone.

"He won't wake up," she said, blurting out the only thing running through her head.

"Who won't—? Ivy?"

Her throat tightened and tears blurred her vision. "He won't wake, and he's not breathing." She pressed her hand to his chest, praying she'd be able to feel his pulse, a breath, anything to tell her he was still alive. Blood covered her hands and had splashed up her forearms. Her pulse sped up. "And I killed him. Oh, Mother, I—"

"Ivy, where are you?"

"Outside the museum. At the back." Her shaking grew stronger. "He won't wake and I— I—"

A black gate whooshed into existence against the closest loading bay doors.

"I'm coming," Diablo said.

"I can see you." She pressed harder on Grey's chest. Still no movement.

A figure materialized in the black vortex, edged with a hint of aura distinguishing his shadowy form from the darkness of the gate.

"Right here. Help." She jerked to her feet.

A man about her height, with short dark hair and swarthy skin, leapt out of the gate. His aura crackled against her, dark and powerful, indicating he was an ancient black drake, and wild blue memory fire blazed from something around his neck and over his arms with centuries worth of powerful memories. Definitely not Diablo.

The black drake's gaze jumped from Bolo's decapitated body to Grey then up to her, and he tightened his grip on a sword as long and as wide as his bulky forearms.

"Looks like Jet has already been here," he said.

He knew who Jet was and that she would be there. This had to be her employer. "She has the coin piece so you can leave." Please. All she cared about was Grey.

"But I hear you're awfully useful, too."

Her pulse stuttered. No. She wrenched her gaze down, searching for the closest weapon. Bolo's sword lay a few feet away. She lunged for it, but the man seized her arm. He yanked her toward him, driving the sword through her back and out her gut. Agony screamed through her.

He wrapped his free hand over her throat, jerked her tight to his body — the sword still spearing her — and squeezed.

At the far end of the driveway, someone rushed into sight.

The ancient black drake hissed something, and a vortex whooshed to life behind him. "You belong to me now."

The figure bolted toward her but was still too far away to recognize as her assailant jerked her back and the darkness of his gate swept around her and wrenched her away from Grey.

32

Diablo skidded to a halt halfway down the driveway, his mind whirling, trying to figure out what the hell he'd just seen. Ivy, her eyes wide with panic and pain, covered in blood, one shoulder of her dress ripped, a sword tip protruding from her chest, and Servius clamping a hand around her throat, had just jumped through a gate.

An impossible gate. With the power of the gatelock embedded in the Chang'an statue, it had taken all Diablo's concentration to make a gate at the end of the block. He had no idea how the hell Servius had made a gate right there. He didn't know much about the black drake, but surely gossip would have spread about him if he was powerful enough to gate through a gatelock. Diablo didn't know of anyone who could gate through a lock, and he'd made it his mission to learn which drakes had stronger gating magic than him.

Mother, this was a mess. Not to mention the only reason Servius would be here was that he was somehow connected to the coin. And from the two bodies lying on the asphalt, it was a big mess.

A few feet away lay the first body and its decapitated head. It looked like Bolo, the young upstart trying to be the prince's new assassin. On the other side of the driveway lay Grey, his blond hair dark with blood.

"Ah, fuck." He leapt over Bolo's body and dropped at Grey's side. No wonder Ivy had sounded desperate on the phone. Blood oozed from a wound at the side of Grey's head that looked a lot like a bullet wound, and he wasn't breathing. Which didn't mean he was dead, but it didn't mean he was alive, either.

Diablo felt for a pulse, but couldn't detect one. The beast within him growled. This wasn't good. Hunter would go on a rampage if he learned Grey was dead. Diablo didn't doubt Anaea would, too. And Ivy—

Mother, he didn't want to see what would happen to Ivy. He'd only heard stories about how drakes reacted when their inamorato was killed and it was never pretty. Payne, the only drake he'd met who'd been inamorated — before he'd met Hunter and Capri, of course — had gone insane when he'd heard his inamorata had been killed, and the Handmaiden had rebirthed him. Diablo couldn't imagine what would happen with Ivy actually seeing Grey go down. He wouldn't wish that on anyone.

Something trembled against his fingers, still pressed to Grey's neck.

The beast froze, but Diablo couldn't tell if it was Grey's pulse or just his imagination.

"Come on, asshole. Don't you dare force me to clean up your mess." It had been hard enough taking care of Andy's estate, and now he was stuck with the most frustrating, adorable kitten that reminded him of his dead friend every time it meowed. He was not going to do that again. Never fucking again.

Off in the distance, a siren chirped, jerking his attention from Grey to his surroundings. He was at the back of a museum packed with people. He had no idea if Grey and Ivy had gotten the coin piece or still had control of the museum's security cameras, and he had — for all intents and purposes — a corpse on either side of him. He couldn't stay there.

He heaved Grey onto his shoulders — thank the Mother for enhanced strength or he'd have had to drag the silver drake — hauled him out of the gatelock's radius, and summoned a gate. It dropped them into the middle of the hotel room, where he laid Grey on the floor. In the light of the single lamp that had been left on, Grey didn't look any better. Blood still oozed from his head onto the beige carpet and his complexion was clearly ashen.

Shit. God damned fucking shit.

He had no idea how to fix this. He didn't know if this could be fixed.

He growled and resisted the urge to kick Grey's body.

He didn't know enough about anything in this situation to make any kind of a decision.

What he needed was information. He pulled out his phone and dialed Anaea.

"Hello?" she asked, her voice soft and unsteady. A hint of fear and desperate determination seeped around Diablo's beast. Even just calling her on the phone made his empathy connect with her. It amazed him she hadn't collapsed into a catatonic ball by now, what with new powers explosively developing on a daily basis and her inamorato refusing to see her while he searched for the Hand-maiden. It was enough to make any drake go mad, let alone a human.

Seeing Grey like this might throw her over the edge, but Diablo didn't have a choice. She was the only one with any kind of magic that might help him.

"I need you at the hotel. Bring the medallion." Worst case, they shoved Grey's soul into a new, less damaged body—

No, the worst case was Grey's soul had already left and disintegrated into the universal ether. A thought he wasn't going to think about. No way in hell was an ancient drake like Grey being taken out with a bullet to the head.

"The medallion? Oh, my God—" The line went dead and a white vortex appeared against the bank of windows. Anaea rushed out, the medallion hanging around her neck on a thick gold chain.

"Can you tell me if he's dead?" Diablo asked. *Mother, don't let him be dead. Please don't let him be dead.* They weren't close, but that was just a matter of time. Between one blink and the next, Grey had become a member of his coterie, his real coterie, Nero's *puzur.* They were a family with ties stronger than blood.

Anaea's magic wind gusted around her and dropped her to her knees by Grey's side, her eyes wide, her face ghostly. She pressed her fingers to his neck, her wind knocking a vase off a table on the other side of the living room.

"Anaea. Is his soul still in there?" It had to be there. Grey had been struggling. Diablo had known that the moment he'd met the silver drake. Something haunted him and tore into his soul, and an hour ago, when Diablo had last gated into this hotel room, that ghost had been weakened, overwhelmed with such joy and uncertainty and—

Diablo bit back a growl. Now was not Grey's time. A drake didn't just find his inamorata and then die. Things like that didn't happen.

"I don't know," Anaea said, her body trembling and her breath coming too fast. Her wind picked up strength, ripping the large painting off the far wall and tossing it into the kitchenette. Dishes rattled in the cupboard over the sink and stove and a half-filled glass of water on the kitchenette counter tumbled to the floor and shattered. "He's not breathing. I can't feel a pulse. What do we do?"

"Use your magic." She had to do something, had to have a way of knowing he was still alive.

His beast growled and he hugged himself, fighting the need to join Anaea's wind and trash the hotel room. Unconscious, Grey wasn't giving off any emotions, so Diablo's empathy couldn't detect anything, but there had to be a spell, an instinct, something that would tell Anaea Grey was still alive.

"I don't know what to do." Anaea's wind shoved Diablo to the side, knocking him over the arm of the couch, and the cupboard doors crashed open and half the glasses flew across the room and smashed against the wall.

Her gaze turned inward and a tight line formed between her brows. "I don't—"

The medallion suddenly flickered with light, a sign that the magic within it was activating to absorb a soul.

With a gasp, she jerked back. Her wide-eyed stare jumped to his and her fear, sliced through with heartache, slammed into him.

"He's got to still be in there," she said. "The medallion wouldn't start to activate if his soul was gone."

"Thank the Mother." A pressure in Diablo's chest eased and his legs buckled. He sagged into the chair beside him and dropped his head between his knees. He couldn't catch his breath, couldn't breathe past the lump in his throat. "Thank the Mother he's not dead."

Not like Andy. He couldn't get his mind to move past that.

Of course, with the medallion activating, that meant the medallion's magic sensed his body was too damaged and it was better to move his soul... maybe. Diablo didn't know enough about the medallion to know how its magic worked, and he was sure Anaea knew less about it than he did.

"We should get him in a bed. Diablo—" Anaea's tone turned sharp and he jerked his head up and met her gaze. "Where's Ivy?"

"Servius took her. She was covered in blood and impaled on his blade and—" *Fucking stupid drake.* There was still a decapitated body lying in the driveway at the museum, and pools of blood. He pulled Capri's number from his contacts and dialed.

"What?" Capri growled, her emotions snapping into him when their phones connected. From the growl and frustration, it felt like he'd interrupted something. Well, too fucking bad. He'd gotten her out of Regis's prison and she owed him. She also owed Grey for protecting her inamorato during the mess with her arrest, and Diablo had no problems cashing in those debts right now.

"I need a rush clean-up at the Royal Vancouver Museum. Loading bay around back."

"Isn't that where Grey was going?"

"Yeah. Where are you?" Neither Capri nor the two other members of her team could free gate, and there wasn't time to wait for them to get to a gate then gate to Vancouver then get to the museum.

"I'm in Nero's house."

"The solarium?" Her usual hang-out with Ryan.

"Yeah, but I'm not decent."

"I don't care. Call your team. You're all flying Air Diablo tonight." He hung up, grabbed Grey, and gated them into the bedroom — if he didn't move Grey, he'd never hear the end of it from Anaea, since he doubted she was strong enough to move the drake, especially from the floor onto the bed.

Anaea rushed through the bedroom doorway, along with her wind. Her fear had deepened, but she'd wrapped a suffocating grip of determination around it and her magic no longer gusted to the degree that things flew around the room.

"Call Nero. We need a plan. We have to assume Servius is Jet's boss and he has both pieces of the coin and Ivy." Diablo climbed off the bed and his gaze dipped to Grey, still as death, his face ashen. Blood still oozed from the wound at the side of his head — and, from the blood on the pillow, a second injury hidden in his hair. Diablo had never heard of a dragon surviving a bullet to the head. Of course, usually after the drake was incapacitated with the gunshot, the next move was decapitation. With Grey's slow healing, he had no idea how long it would take him to recover from something like that. Could a drake fully recover from that? Was any drake's soul magic strong enough to fix something as complicated as a brain?

"We also have to assume he's not going to wake up anytime soon," Anaea said, her hold on her magic trembling and the painting above the bed rattling.

He pulled the painting from the wall and shoved it under the bed. "Let's get his inamorata back before then." Because Grey wouldn't recover at all if something happened to Ivy.

33

Ivy staggered as pain shot through her chest and cheek. The ancient black drake who'd dragged her into his gate had taken her back to the anchor on the cliff's edge near the Handmaiden's secret residence. He'd pushed her through the tunnel and across the ice garden and now shoved her against the stone wall beside the Handmaiden's gray door.

"Move, and I impale you again," he growled, his breath misting against her cheek and drawing a shiver of cold and fear.

He pulled his phone from his coat pocket, texted something, then returned it to his pocket. A few seconds later, the door opened with Jet standing in the entrance.

Her eyes narrowed. "What the hell are you doing with her?"

"I'll need her magic once I've taken the throne." The black drake pushed Ivy past Jet into the antechamber with the settee in the center of the room, the coat rack, and the glass and wrought iron door at the back.

Heat swept around Ivy, and the pain in her chest from both the sword and the gunshot wounds burned hotter, as if the few minutes in the freezing mountain air had numbed her. Everything but the ice in her gut turned into an inferno, and agony squeezed around her heart and tightened her throat.

"She can find traitors. That's invaluable," the black drake said.

"And what will you do if she refuses to work for you?" Jet

slammed the outside door shut and stalked past Ivy to the inner door. "What then, oh King Servius?"

"That's Emperor Servius. Earth magic comes from the human body. Not the dragon's soul." He jerked his chin to the inside door and cocked an eyebrow.

Jet rolled her eyes and opened the door for him.

He pushed Ivy onto the second-story balcony, sending her staggering across the dried pool of Grey's blood. She caught her balance on the wrought iron railing.

"With the coin pieces joined, I can rip out her spirit and replace it with someone who's loyal."

A shiver rushed over Ivy, spiking more pain through her. She was dead if she didn't help him. She doubted this drake — Jet had called him Servius — would rebirth her into another body. And even if she was reborn, she wouldn't remember Grey, she wouldn't have the power he needed to keep his magic at bay, and she didn't know if they'd still be inamorated.

Her throat grew tighter and she fought to breathe past the knot. *He couldn't be dead. Mother of All, please. Just let him be alive.* But he hadn't been breathing. He'd been shot in the head. Even if Diablo got to him, there might have been nothing he could do to help Grey.

A tremor swept through her, forcing her to grip the railing to keep standing. Her gaze dropped to her hands and forearms, covered with blood, and the memory of Bolo collapsing to the ground, his severed head rolling into a puddle, flashed into her mind's eye.

Jet snorted, strode past Ivy, and headed down the stairs. "Don't look at me. I like the magic I got just fine. Besides, it's only been a few years since I've figured out how to extend my camouflage to cover my tracks. I can't wait to see what I can do in a couple hundred more."

Ivy's pulse roared. She'd killed Bolo. Taken his head. Something she'd never done before. She was sure something like that would have been imprinted in her locket with a force of emotion that would have brought it to the forefront of all the memories imprinted there.

Her hand jumped to her throat, the instinct to touch her locket making her move before cold realization added to the churning in her gut.

The locket was gone. Fallen down the sewer grate. When she fell asleep — and at some point sleep was inevitable — and woke, she'd forget everything, being shot and stabbed, killing Bolo, getting caught in Servius's horrible plans to take the throne. But she'd also forget Grey. She'd gladly remember all those horrible things just to keep her memories of Grey, his smile, the hard strength of his body pressed against her... how he made her feel.

Even if she imprinted her memories into her clothes and was still wearing them when she woke, she still wouldn't be able to get to them, not without her power word that had been engraved on her locket.

"Come on." Servius grabbed her arm and shoved her toward the stairs. "You're going to watch history being made."

She staggered to the main floor and followed Jet through the maze of bookshelves, back to the nook where she and Grey had discovered the truth about why the Handmaiden's chambers in Court had been ransacked.

It was hard to believe it hadn't even been a full day since Tobias had told her to read those memories then sent her here, out of Court for the first time.

The podium, where they'd read the book Jet had torn the page from, glowed with magical power. It swirled in a complicated glyph that hadn't been there before. The coin pieces sat on the podium's ledge, joined together to look like one coin save for the band of light splitting it in half.

Magic tingled over Ivy's skin, making the hair at the back of her neck stand up, and she had a sense that she couldn't explain, that the spell to join the coins was powerful.

Which was what it all came down to. Power. Power over other drakes, but more importantly, power over one's life. Regis had too much power over everyone. That much had been clear from the moment she'd woken and read the memories on her locket. Other drakes had defied him and she'd unwillingly been a part of the regime that had captured and punished them.

She'd known even then that she hadn't had a choice except to obey. She worked for Tobias and they belonged to the prince. But Servius wasn't acting much different from Regis. If she didn't use her magic to help him, he'd kill her.

She was a pawn, had always been a pawn for stronger drakes. How could she grow beyond a hatchling if she never remembered anything? Even with the help of her locket, she'd been at a disadvantage, and without the locket, she was helpless. She should have never left Court, should have figured out how to escape Tobias before ending up at the museum, and should have never agreed to help Grey figure out what was going on.

Except she couldn't have stopped herself from doing any of that. Ophelia had practically tossed her out of Court, she hadn't known nearly enough about anything to develop any kind of escape plan, and Grey... Grey held her heart. She'd have gone anywhere with him.

Her vision blurred with tears. *Please don't let him be dead.*

A single tear leaked down her cheek.

Jet glanced up from the glowing podium and sneered. "Jeez. Are you crying for yourself or because you couldn't stop Bolo from taking Grey's head?"

Because Grey wasn't breathing and she was helpless—

Mother of All, she was pathetic. Real drakes didn't cry.

"You mean you didn't kill Bolo?" Servius asked.

Jet raised an eyebrow. "Bolo is dead?"

And Ivy had killed him. She had. With a ferociousness she hadn't known lay within her.

"Head severed from his neck." Servius's dark gaze turned on Ivy.

Jet followed his gaze, and Ivy pressed back against the bookshelf, unable to fight the urge to make herself as small as possible. Ferocious or not, these drakes scared her.

"Wow." Jet barked a harsh laugh, making Ivy jump. "Looks like you've got more bite than expected. Might make a dragon out of you yet, hatchling."

If she survived this. Except she wanted more than just survival. Before she'd met Grey, she'd wanted her freedom. Now she wanted it more than ever.

She blinked back more tears. Grey would want her to have her freedom, and she knew a doyen who'd arranged for her to be free of Regis, Tobias, and the Dragon Court. Mother of All, she might not be able to stop Servius, but she sure as hell could get away from him. Nero's coterie might not be Grey's, but there was a friendship there.

Grey trusted them. He'd brought her to them when he was injured and they'd needed a safe haven. Without a doubt, they'd want to get revenge for Grey.

Light flickered from the coin and Servius shifted closer to the podium. "How long is this supposed to take?"

"The book said a quarter of a day," Jet said.

"Six hours."

"That's going to be a long wait."

Servius pursed his lips, his attention locked on the coin. "This is complicated magic. If the Handmaiden wasn't so skilled as a sorcerer, knitting the coin — and, more importantly, the spell in the coin — back together could take days, even years." He glanced at Jet. "You should go back to the museum and kill Grey."

"Grey won't be getting up any time soon. He's such a slow healer. That bullet to the head will have him down for hours if it didn't outright kill him," Jet said.

Ivy's throat tightened and more tears blurred her vision. Grey hadn't been breathing.

Jet leaned against the doorframe and crossed her arms. "I say I've completed the job you hired me to do."

Servius roared and slapped his wrists together. The ground under Jet wrenched up. It tossed her onto her back, then curled around her forearm and locked her in place. "The job isn't done until I'm emperor."

Jet's eyes grew wide, fear racing across her expression, then she flashed her teeth and growled. "So what? You can control stone."

"I can do more than control stone." He shoved back his sleeves, revealing four thick bands of tattoos, one set wrapped around his wrists, the other around his forearms, which he pressed together. Light flared from them, and wind snapped from his hands and sliced into Jet's shoulder.

Jet's complexion paled. "Holy Mother, you're a sorcerer."

"I'm the rightful dragon emperor, and the goddess has given me the sorcerer's power as proof. You'll swear your allegiance to me, or I'll hunt you down and ensure your soul doesn't even make it into the universal ether." He bared his teeth at her and hissed. "Are we clear?"

Jet glared at him and another blast of wind sliced into her.

"Are we clear?" The earth around her shook and a tornado roared around Servius, yanking books and knickknacks from the shelves and flinging them around the nook. "Are. We. Clear?"

"Yes." Jet's gaze dropped. "We're clear."

"I can't hear you," Servius growled.

"We're clear, Emperor Servius."

"Good." He flashed his teeth, his expression half aggression and half satisfaction, and tapped his wrists together. The stone capturing Jet melted away. "If Grey isn't dead, he needs to be an unfortunate casualty of war. He knows how to get here. He can't live to tell anyone else what's happening."

Mother, No. She couldn't stop Jet from going back to the museum and killing Grey, if, God, he wasn't dead already. She could only pray Diablo had gotten to him in time. *Please, oh, please.* But she also couldn't let Nero or anyone go up against Servius without knowing how powerful he was. She had to figure out a way to escape. They had to be warned.

34

An inferno consumed Grey. He couldn't breathe, couldn't see past the darkness, and couldn't hear or sense anything. There was only pain. An unending agony howling through him, squeezing his head and chest in a vise. Crackling, searing... flickering?

No, the *darkness* was flickering. Hints of white...? Not quite white? Something soft at his back.

A woman screamed.

Ivy.

Ivy was in trouble. Jet and Bolo were attacking. He had to get to her. Protect her. Mother, he had to see past the pain and get up.

Except he had no idea what had happened. They'd been fighting. It didn't sound now as if anyone nearby was fighting... but that could be the agony making it impossible to hear anything... except he'd heard that scream.

Ivy's scream...

Ivy *had* screamed. There'd been a bang, then pain and darkness.

Another scream cut through the haze, and instinct jerked his head toward the sound and fire exploded behind his eyes.

His consciousness wavered, the darkness flooding over the not-quite-white, but he managed to hold on and focus. An open doorway materialized out of the haze with a hint of light beyond. A woman— *Ivy? Please let it be Ivy* — rushed into the room.

One minute she stood framed with the light behind her. The next she was at his side as if she'd rapid free gated the few feet, even though he hadn't felt a whoosh of wind.

His brain stuttered and when he could focus again, bright blue eyes wavered into sight. Sharp cheeks, delicate chin, and a short pixie haircut. Anaea.

Not Ivy.

His throat tightened, sending more agony racing through his head. Ivy wasn't safe. Bolo and Jet were still—

Except he couldn't figure out how to finish the thought. They were still something. A danger? Out there? But if they were out somewhere, where was he? He had to be somewhere, too, but he had no idea how he'd gotten where he was or what was happening.

God, it was so hard to think. The pain kept making his thoughts jump, little jerks that shot white lightning through his skull and threatened to steal his consciousness.

Anaea leaned closer, her cheeks wet with tears, her white aura so bright it hurt his eyes.

He said her name. Anaea's name? No. Ivy's? He was sure he'd said something but, Mother, he didn't know any more.

Anaea frowned, her expression confused as if she knew he was trying to say something but hadn't understood what. More tears trickled down her cheeks and her aura faded for a heartbeat, revealing a pale complexion — paler than the first time he'd seen her, and she'd been dying from cancer back then.

Another figure rushed into the room. Bigger, darker, and radiating danger.

Grey tensed and more pain screamed through him. The room blackened, his consciousness teetering on the edge. He dug mental claws into his awareness and wrenched himself back to consciousness. He couldn't pass out again. He needed to find Ivy. The only thing that mattered was Ivy.

Anaea moaned and grabbed her head. She turned to the figure, her body shaking, her breaths desperate gasps.

"I got this," a raspy tenor growled. The figure nudged Anaea out of the way and Diablo's face jumped into focus. "Drink this. It'll make you stronger."

Diablo slid a hand under Grey's head and pressed a glass to his lips. Cool liquid slid over his tongue. He swallowed and Diablo eased his head back.

"What did you give him?" Anaea asked.

"Carfentanyl."

The weight around his chest increased, but not painfully, softly. It enveloped him, like a heavy cocoon, and the jagged edges of agony dulled, just a fraction, just enough that he could almost concentrate on Anaea's expression.

"What the heck is that?" Her voice had grown soft, suddenly far away.

"Elephant tranquilizer."

She gasped and grabbed Diablo's arm. "That'll kill him."

Diablo's face blurred and darkness swelled around the edges of Grey's vision.

"How is it that you keep forgetting we're not human?" Diablo snorted, the sound slicing through the darkness. "I'm just hoping with his slow healing, it'll knock him out long enough for his soul magic to do its thing. I'm not sure with your newly developed empathy you can handle him being awake right now."

Something soft brushed his cheek and a tingle of an aura slid against his. Ivy. Warmth flooded his chest and he fought to open his eyes and look at her. But he couldn't make his lids open, couldn't concentrate past the pain and the darkness and—

IVY SAT AT THE BACK OF THE NOOK, HER KNEES HUGGED TIGHT TO HER chest and her chin on her knees. Servius had shoved her there after Jet had left, and while she had no way of telling time, she was pretty sure not much had passed. An hour at most. Certainly not the six hours needed to complete the spell to join the coins. And while he hadn't used his magic to imprison her, he still stood between her and escape — and with his ability to control wind and stone, running wasn't an option.

Sure, he might appear to be mesmerized by the magic in the podium knitting the coin back together, but she didn't doubt his magic would capture her before she made it out of the nook. It was the only explanation as to why he hadn't bound her with stone or

rope. If she was going to be of any use to Nero and his coterie —
even if they just wanted to hide from Servius — she needed as much
information as possible.

She opened her mouth to speak, but her words caught in the
knot in her throat, and the ice in her gut churned to arctic
proportions.

Servius glanced at her and cocked his eyebrow. Blue memory fire
danced near his neck over a heavy silver amulet on a silver chain and
along his arms over his shirt, where his tattoos were. She could only
imagine the emotion imprinted in the tattoos' ink. They had to have
been drawn there by magic, since his soul healing would have
dissolved them — unless, of course, the human he'd taken the body
from had already had the tattoos. It was surprising with an aura as
powerful as his, clearly indicating he was an ancient drake, that he'd
have so few things on him alight with memory fire. This was not a
sentimental man—

Or he knew about her powers.

The urge to say her power word tickled the back of her throat,
but not because of the overwhelming ache in her soul. That had
disappeared the moment Grey had shared his memories with her
and it was still gone. No, it was the need to learn something,
anything, that might help Nero defend himself against Servius that
compelled her. Knowing he was a sorcerer was good information,
but if she could learn something more, it could be the difference
between life and death — and having your soul reborn counted as
death, since it stripped everything away from a dragon that made
them who they were.

"What?" Servius barked, his voice low and filled with danger.

"I, ah— I've never met a sorcerer before." It was a lie, she'd met
Anaea, who both Grey and Diablo claimed was a sorcerer and who
terrified Ivy, but it was the first thing she could think of.

"Don't be an idiot. Of course you've met a sorcerer before."

Ivy's pulse stuttered. "I have?" Did he know about Anaea? If he
did, then did he know about Grey's association with Nero?

"The Handmaiden. When she rebirthed you, I'd say—" His eyes
narrowed. "I'd say less than fifty years ago." He cocked his head to the
side. "Certainly less than a hundred."

"Right. Of course. The Handmaiden." Except she couldn't

remember the Handmaiden, only that she'd been told things about her. "I only met her the once and so briefly."

"And let me guess, you think she's wonderful." Servius rolled his eyes at her.

"I—" This felt like a trap. If she agreed with Servius that she thought the Handmaiden wasn't so great, would he turn on her for denouncing the dragons' only sorcerer? Except she wasn't the only sorcerer. There was Anaea and now Servius, who had more than enough magic to be dangerous. "I don't really know her. I don't—"

"Don't tell me you don't know anything." Servius's gaze slid back to the coin as if he couldn't bring himself to look away from all that power for too long. "Even a hatchling with only a year in this so-called existence knows something."

"Tobias doesn't let me out much." Her power word flooded her thoughts. Just say it. Find out what the most recent memory on his clothes was. But he knew about her magic and would know what she was doing. She couldn't just take a peek without risking everything. He might value her magic, but that didn't mean he wouldn't outright kill her if she endangered his plans.

"Because the chamberlain has no magic. Power over you is his power." The muscles in Servius's jaw clenched. "The only real power Tobias holds is what Regis gives him. Do the prince's bidding and you can have anything you want."

"And when you're king?" Her pulse pounded. She didn't expect him to tell her his plans, but maybe he'd let something slip, a little detail that could give Nero the upper hand and meant she wouldn't have to risk using her magic.

"Drakes would no longer need to live in fear. I'll protect all drakes alike."

Except her and those he suspected of betraying him. He'd keep her to root out traitors, and if she didn't, he'd rip her soul out and give her body to someone else.

Her pulse roared. She didn't know what to do or how to learn anything about him. Worst of all, she had no idea how to escape when or if she learned anything.

"The reign of the Sumerian dragon king is over. This is the birth of a new age of the Zhongguo dragon emperor." Servius bared his teeth at her and his aura flared. His forearms bumped together and a gust of wind swept through the room, shaking the books in the shelves. "Obey me, and you have nothing to worry about."

That sounded an awful lot like Regis, but she was smart enough not to ask how Servius would be different.

"I'll bring dragonkind together, join the coteries like Constantine did before the Great Scourge." He glared at her as if he expected a response.

But she didn't know what to say to that. "I know all the doyens will follow you."

"There will be a few who won't, but I have a fix for that." His gaze leapt back to the coin. "The trick, little hatchling, is to strike before anyone knows you're attacking."

A hint of memory flickered through her. Just a flash. The ground hurtling toward her, and a sense that his body was too small and too crowded.

Her heart skipped a beat. She hadn't even said her power word and she was seeing things. He was going to realize what she was doing and kill her.

"Human sorcerers taught me that." His gaze drew inward.

Her pulse jumped into a wild tattoo. He wasn't acting as if he'd noticed. Maybe she could use her magic.

She whispered her power word and the earth snapped back into focus, rushing toward her as she dropped to her knees, while someone else screamed inside her head.

No. Not her head. Servius's. It felt like a memory of his first body. The fall had just happened, and his soul had been forced into a living human vessel already containing a human soul. The human soul howled, captured in a mental box created by Servius's soul magic, while Servius pressed his hands to his chest, trying to regain his mental balance. His fingers touched something heavy around his neck. The medallion he was currently wearing. That was where she was getting the memory.

But this wasn't a memory she wanted. She needed to see his plans or something about him. Anything other than his first moments as a human.

The image jumped to Servius in his current human body, his aura small and weak, indicating he was still young. He grabbed the medallion from a tabletop, but hints of magic crackled over his fingers, heating the silver and burning his hand. With a yelp, he dropped it onto the floor and stared at his hands. Magical energy crackled over his skin, but somehow she knew it wasn't lightning or fire, but raw sorcerer's power. Power he feared and couldn't control. Yet.

Which wasn't useful information, either. She already knew he had the sorcerer's ability, the power to draw on the primal energy of the universe and bend it to his will with concentration, chants, and glyphs.

Except *that*, the thing about chanting and glyphs, she hadn't known. She must have learned what the sorcerer's ability was from the memory in Servius's amulet. But that still didn't help.

Her magic jumped to Servius trying to weave a spell. She wasn't sure what was supposed to happen, but light exploded around him and drew a scream.

Darkness enveloped her. Servius growled and his face — his present-time face — appeared out of the darkness. Behind him, magic radiated from the podium, growing stronger as if it was still building in power.

The ice within swept into her chest. He'd discovered her using her magic and she hadn't learned anything. Her throat tightened. Why couldn't she have just learned something useful? But that wasn't who she was. She was a hatchling and broken. Even if she could learn anything new, she had no way of telling anyone. Not even to avenge Grey or protect his friends.

A hint of fire curled tight around her heart. Grey hadn't thought she was helpless. She might be young, but she'd still protected him by killing Bolo. She was a dragon, with magic, and if Servius knew she was using her magic on him, she was damned well going to get something useful.

She concentrated on her power word, filling her mind with it and focusing on how her magic felt swelling into the recesses of her soul. Darkness swept around her again, a breath of wind hissed past her, and her vision jumped back into a memory.

The medallion sat on a table again while Servius sliced a small thin line into his forearm, connecting it with another blackened line, then trickled ink into the wound. The muscles in his jaw clenched, and his expression was tight. His aura flared and crackling white magic danced over his skin as he prevented his soul magic from fully healing the wound and expelling the ink.

The memory flickered but stayed with Servius, his attention focused on the minuscule piece of tattoo he'd created... except Ivy was sure time had passed. At least a few days where he'd spent the entire time pouring his sorcerer's magic into the wound, preventing his soul magic from properly healing it and adding strength to the spell he was building.

With a sneer, he sat back. It was finally done. He pressed his forearms together, but nothing happened. Emotions from the medallion indicated this was supposed to work. He'd spent years drawing the glyphs into his arms and imbuing them with the magical power to summon wind.

He flipped open a book and stared at the page. All the glyphs were correct. He hadn't made a mistake. Each line had been drawn with agonizing concentration. So much time had been wasted on a theory that etching the glyphs with blood and ink into his human vessel would give him earth magic.

With a huff, he sagged onto a hard wooden chair and stared at the mark on his arm, his fingers absently tracing the whorls in the medallion.

This had to work. He couldn't have been wrong. His eyes narrowed, and he leaned forward.

The image wavered and a second ghostly image overlaid the first as if she was seeing his arm from two different memories at the same time.

He frowned and his gaze locked on a small sliver of clean skin, shimmering with soul magic in the middle of the line he'd just carved. The glyph wasn't complete. Just that small break, no wider than a thread severing one line, and the whole spell wouldn't work.

Ivy gasped. That was it. Damage the glyphs on his arms and he'd lose control of the earth magics they mimicked.

Pain sliced through her chest, wrenching her hold on her magic.

"What do you think you're doing?" Servius growled.

She jerked forward, snapping free of the vision but driving Servius's sword deeper into her before she realized he'd impaled her again.

He bared his teeth and hissed, looking feral, more dragon than human. "Using your magic on me won't help you."

"I—" Blood bubbled into her mouth.

His sneer deepened. "Learn anything useful?"

"No, I—" She fought to breathe past the agony. She couldn't let him know that she knew how to stop his earth magic. "My magic is sometimes hard to control."

His eyes narrowed, but she knew from his memories that newly awakened magic was sometimes difficult to restrain — at least it had been for him — and he thought she was a hatchling. Meaning her powers could still be very new, too.

"This place. It has so much memory attached to it." *Please let him believe that.*

"And what did the Handmaiden's residence tell you?"

"That it—" Mother, she hadn't seen anything about the residence, but she had to tell him something. "That she—" The magical light around the coin flared. "That it took her a long time to make that pedestal."

Servius huffed. "Doesn't surprise me." He yanked his sword from her chest. Blood gushed from the wound, and her head spun at the pain and growing weakness from blood loss. Instinct pressed her hands to the injury, even though in a few minutes it would be sealed shut and her soul magic would be working to fix any damage done to her organs.

The soft thud of footsteps sounded, and Jet strode into the nook's entranceway. Her gaze slid from Servius and his bloody sword to Ivy.

"What?" Servius barked.

"Seems Grey is more resilient than first expected."

Servius turned to face Jet, his grip on the hilt of his sword tightening. "He's still alive?"

"I don't know." Jet squared her shoulders and raised her chin. "But someone called for help."

Servius glanced back at Ivy. "Who did you call?"

"Whoever was the first number on Grey's speed dial." Ivy forced herself to shrug, lancing pain through her chest, and praying Servius wouldn't see past the lie. "I don't know who that was. You knocked the phone out of my hand before I could talk."

"Probably the blue drake leading the North American Clean Team," Jet said. "I'd heard they were friends, and the location was spotless. No Grey, no Bolo, and no blood."

Servius swore. "Spotless location does suggest the Clean Team, but how close of friends are they?"

"You mean did Capri take Grey back to Court to face Regis's justice?" Jet crossed her arms, appearing more relaxed, but a tense wariness never left her eyes. "I can go to Court and find out."

"No. If Grey is imprisoned in Court, good, but we can't risk her protecting him." Servius's gaze leapt back to the pedestal and the coin pieces. "We also can't risk him having told her where we are. Even if a bullet to the head did stop him, we have to anticipate an attack. Any drake who learns about the rebirth coin will want it."

"Yeah." Jet's gaze followed Servius's to the coin. "But you're a sorcerer."

Servius flashed his teeth at her. "And a descendant of the Zhongguo dragon empress."

"The throne rightfully belongs to you," Jet said.

"Guard the entrance, and kill anyone who approaches."

Jet raised an eyebrow. "Kill?"

"The situation has changed." The light from the pedestal flickered, casting trembling illumination across Servius's face, making him appear wild and dangerous. "Some souls will have to be lost to the universal ether before this is done."

"Killing I can manage." Jet flashed her teeth and strode from the nook.

Servius glanced at Ivy. "Once I have the coin and the medallion from the arena, all dragon souls can be saved, but right now, if Grey told his friends about me, those souls will have to be sacrificed."

A shiver slid down Ivy's spine. Even if she could figure out a way to escape and warn Diablo and Nero about Servius, it might be too late.

35

G rey jerked awake. Agony snapped through his head then eased — although not nearly enough — to a throbbing pain. He forced his thoughts to think past it, to Ivy—

Ivy was in trouble. He needed to find her. Get up from wherever he was—

He blinked his vision clear and struggled to get his mind to work. It felt like he was thinking through water, with everything sluggish and strained.

Well, first order of business: find out where the hell he was.

He shifted his head, sending another burst through his skull and wave of darkness across his vision. When his sight cleared, he could see the few feet across a dimly lit room to an open doorway, with weak illumination spilling in from a hall. It looked like the hall in the hotel room in Vancouver.

He pulled his head to the other side. The painting that used to hang on the wall was gone, leaving a large square of paint a fraction darker than the rest of the wall, and the alarm clock on the night-stand was the one he'd seen the last time he'd woken in the Vancouver hotel. Now the time read 12:45. Given the lack of light spilling around the closed blinds, he had to assume it was night.

Definitely the hotel bedroom. Which meant he lay on the hotel's bed, covered with its heavy comforter, and, given the slide of the fabric against his skin, he had to be—

He shoved the comforter back.

Naked. Someone had stripped him down to his briefs, and white gauze had been taped over the injuries he'd sustained during his fight with Jet and Bolo: the hole through his chest where Jet had impaled him, the gash in his shoulder, the slice across his ribs, and the nick in his thigh.

Except if he thought about the injuries, none of them hurt. Only his head.

He peeled back the gauze on his chest and revealed a puckered pink scar. For most drakes that was less than half an hour worth of healing, but for him, it had to have been hours since the fight at the back of the museum.

Ivy had been alone with Jet and Bolo for hours.

He wrenched out of the bed. The room twisted, and his knees gave out, dropping him to the floor. Darkness swarmed over his vision and pain sliced through his skull.

Mother, why did his head hurt?

He pressed his palms to his forehead, but they didn't hit flesh. They hit… bandage?

What the hell happened?

He ground his teeth and fought to clear his vision. Anaea rushed into the doorway with Diablo close behind.

"Oh, my God," she said.

He tried to stand, but the room kept tilting and he couldn't catch his balance.

Anaea grabbed his arm and steadied him. "Tell me you recognize me."

"What?" That didn't make sense.

"You should still be in bed," Diablo growled. "I'm hitting him with another dose."

"Another what?" Why couldn't he get his mind to work?

Anaea tugged him up to sit on the edge of the bed. "Who am I?" she asked, her words slow and over-enunciated.

"If we knock him out again, the chances of any brain damage will be less." Diablo gated out of the doorway with a whoosh of wind.

"Brain damage? What the hell is going on?" Nothing was making any sense, and all he really knew was that Ivy wasn't in the room and he had to find her.

Grey tried to pull his arm out of Anaea's grip, but she held tight with a strength he hadn't realized she had — or he was just that weak.

Except he couldn't afford to be weak. He shifted to try again, and her clothes brushed against his skin, reminding him he was nearly naked beside his best friend's inamorata.

"Do you know your name?" she asked.

A shiver swept through him. He had an inamorata, too, and he had to find her. "Where are my clothes?"

Diablo gated back into the room. "Drink this."

"I'm not drinking anything until you tell me what the hell is going on and where's Ivy?"

Diablo's gaze jumped to Anaea and her grip on Grey's arm tightened.

That wasn't a good sign. "What?"

"Grey—" Her voice trembled.

Oh, Mother. No. Grey jerked out of her grip and stood, fury fueling his strength and roaring hot through him. He'd failed her. He went down during a fight and now— "Where is she? Is she—?" He couldn't say the word, couldn't bring himself to ask if she was dead.

"We don't know." Anaea stood and reached to take his arm again, but he wrenched out of the way. "Just take the drink and we'll talk about it."

"No. Tell me where Ivy is or I swear to God I'll— I'll—"

"You'll what?" Diablo growled.

The rage faltered, the edges sliced off with a spike of pain. He didn't know what had happened or where Ivy was or anything. God, he couldn't just go after her. He didn't know where to go.

"I have to find her. I couldn't protect her." His throat tightened and the pain in his head flared again. The muscles in his legs trembled and he pressed a hand to the wall to steady himself. "Bolo was attacking her and Jet—" A shudder swept through him. Jet had rammed her sword through his chest—

Everything within him froze, and he glanced around the room, looking for his shirt and pants. "Where are my clothes?" He couldn't help her naked. He needed clothes and weapons and information.

"You're not getting your clothes back until we've determined there's no brain damage," Diablo said.

Grey glared at him. "Why would I have brain damage? Can a drake even get brain damage?"

"Someone shot you in the head. And no drake has kept his head long enough for anyone to know if you can get brain damage or not," Anaea said.

His pulse leapt faster. Ivy's scream. Her too-wide eyes. The bang. The pain. That was how Jet had taken him out. "Jet shot me in the head?"

"Someone did," Anaea said.

"Did they get the coin piece? Was the coin piece in my pants pocket?" Maybe Ivy had it. But if he went down with both Jet and Bolo still alive...

He strained to keep breathing. *Just breathe. Just breathe. She's not dead. She can't be dead.* "Please. Tell me about Ivy."

Diablo's expression darkened. "Alive last time I saw."

The rage and panic churned into dread. "What's that supposed to mean?"

Diablo raised the glass in his hand. "Are you going to drink this?"

"Something to knock me out again?"

Diablo glared at Anaea.

"I heard you the first time. No, I'm not letting you knock me out again. If you don't know where Ivy is, then I need to find her."

"Well, you can't go off half-cocked," Anaea said. "Nero's been trying to get information on what happened so we can figure out how bad this is. I say we call him and figure this out."

Except there wasn't anything to figure out. He had to find Ivy. If Jet or Bolo had her—

A new thought jumped into his head. "How am I still alive?"

"If you don't know how soul magic works, I'm pretty sure that means there's brain damage," Diablo said.

"I know how my soul magic works." Grey rolled his eyes at him, spiking more pain through his head.

"You never know." Diablo shrugged. "No drake knows if getting shot in the head is damage that a soul's magic can heal."

"I'm perfectly fine." And even if he wasn't, Ivy was the priority. "No. Both Jet and Bolo were still alive when I went down, and I doubt Bolo would have just run off without taking my head back to Regis."

"Bolo was dead when Ivy called." Diablo's frown deepened. "From the amount of blood on her, I'd say she decapitated him."

"Jeez." Anaea sagged onto the edge of the bed. "I know it's a dragon thing, but that couldn't have been easy if this was her first time."

Anaea's first decapitation had been in the arena, when everyone had still thought she was Hunter. In a way, she had been Hunter. They'd shared a body at that time, and she would have had him to help her through that. Right now, Ivy had no one, and even if she had killed another drake before, she might not remember. Sure, she was still a dragon, but she hadn't had the feral dragon infancy from before the scourge or even the memories of a few decades to understand the truth about her dragon nature.

The memory of the locket, flying through the air and falling into the sewer, flashed across his mind's eye. If he didn't get her locket back, she wouldn't remember anything.

God, would she remember him?

Funny, how just a few hours ago in the bathroom adjacent to this bedroom, he'd believed forgetting him had been her best option. Now it made his chest ache. He wanted her to remember everything, wanted her to wake every morning knowing how deeply he loved her.

And none of that could happen if he didn't find her. He tried to glare at Diablo, but that only made his head hurt more.

"You need to stop that," Diablo said. "Anaea's empathy can't take all that pain."

"It's not as bad as before," she said.

"No, you're right." Grey drew in a steadying breath, but it did little to ease anything, pain or fear. *Ivy. Find Ivy.* The words roared around and around in his head and in his soul. *Or revenge her death.* "You said Ivy was alive."

"Servius took her. He gated her out while in the gatelock's radius. Don't ask me how the hell he managed that." Diablo pulled his phone from his pocket. "I'm calling Nero. You can tell us what happened and we can figure out what we're going to do."

That would just take up too much time. Time he didn't want to waste while Ivy could still be alive and in danger. *Please, she had to still be alive.*

His pulse pounded, radiating more pain through his skull, as he glanced at the clock. 12:55. He'd already lost ten minutes. He couldn't afford to lose any more time with this argument. There were only two reason for Servius to have been at the museum: he was checking up on Bolo or he was Jet's employer. Given that Servius had never been a member of Regis's entourage, Grey was willing to bet he was involved with getting the rebirth coin. "Tell me it's only been six hours since the museum."

Anaea nodded. "Yes, but—"

"Good." That meant Servius would be in one of two places, and once Grey got his hands on Servius, he'd find Ivy... or kill the drake who'd murdered her. He hissed his power word and summoned a gate against the bedroom wall.

"What the hell are you doing?" Diablo growled.

"Finishing what I started." The vortex formed faster than he expected, fueled by the panic and rage racing through him. He leapt into the gate, but Diablo grabbed his arm at the last minute and they lurched through together.

36

Grey's gate tossed him into Hunter and Anaea's dark living room, with Diablo close at his heels. The black drake's foot had barely hit the floor before he opened another gate with his rapid free gating ability, vanished, and materialized a split-second later in front of Grey.

"Get out of my way." Grey moved to shove Diablo aside.

The black drake sidestepped the shove, stepping close, and pressed a palm against Grey's chest, stopping him. "You can't go after him naked."

"That's why I'm raiding Hunter's closet." Grey seized the front of Diablo's shirt and tossed him onto the floor. "I'm not an idiot." He wrenched away and strode through the open-concept kitchen and living room. The cold air — since Anaea wasn't staying at her northern residence and had the furnace turned down — drew goose bumps and made him shiver, while his head still pounded, but none of that mattered. Only Ivy. Always Ivy.

"You can't face this... whatever this is without help." Diablo flashed to his side, seized his arm, and shoved him against the hall wall. "Jet's almost taken you out twice now—"

"That's because I wasn't trying to kill her and wasn't properly armed." Grey snapped an uppercut into Diablo's jaw, stunned the drake, and pushed him out of the way.

Diablo hissed and bared his teeth. "She has camouflage magic."

"If she's been somewhere where I've been before, that's not a problem." Grey marched into the spare bedroom. Hunter's new body was narrower in the shoulders and waist than Grey, but his old body had been a pretty decent match in size. Grey had been sneaking boxes of Hunter's hoard from his old suite at Court — before that had become too dangerous — and there'd been at least one box of ancient carvings wrapped in some of Hunter's old clothes that Grey had snuck out.

"How do you even know where she is?" Diablo tapped his temple. "You're not thinking this through. This has to be brain damage. It can't just be an inamorated thing."

Grey opened a box. Not the carvings. "If Servius was there because of Bolo, I'd be dead. Which means Servius is the one after the coin. The coin pieces can only be joined with a spell in the Handmaiden's secret residence. Since no one is supposed to know he's at the residence or where it is, I'm assuming he's at the residence right now, waiting for the spell to finish and hoping I won't show up again. Knowing what I know about the Handmaiden and the spell, it can't be stopped and started again once it's been activated."

The next box had the carvings. He pulled out the top piece, protected in a black T-shirt, and carefully unwrapped it. Hunter would understand Grey borrowing his things, but he'd be heartbroken if he lost another piece of his hoard. It had been hard enough for the red drake to abandon it all when he'd fled Court.

"Okay, so you know where Servius is going to be." Diablo leaned against the doorframe and crossed his arms. "That still doesn't deal with Jet or the fact that she's probably waiting for you."

"Her magic isn't perfect. There are telltale signs." He pulled the T-shirt on. It strained against his broad chest and muscular biceps but thankfully didn't impede his range of motion. "If I have a moment to concentrate, I can use my magic to determine what's different and pick her out."

"Nero is not going to like this."

"I don't care what Nero likes. I *have* to find Ivy. And yes, it's all an inamorated thing."

"Sounds more like an insanity than love," Diablo hissed.

"Yeah, well, fuck you. And fuck Nero if he doesn't understand." Grey shifted the next two carvings aside and pulled out the one wrapped in a pair of Hunter's jeans. "I know you can't help because of Nero—"

"Oh, I didn't say I wasn't going to help."

Grey's thoughts stuttered. "You can't endanger your *puzur*." If Grey had figured anything out about Diablo in the last couple of weeks, the tough-guy routine wasn't a routine and the kids in the *puzur* were everything to him. Grey didn't doubt Diablo had hidden more than one body that no one would ever find in order to protect his family.

"And I can't fucking let you do this by yourself. You're going to get yourself killed and then I'll never hear the end of it from Anaea." Diablo flashed his teeth, the expression cocky, but it didn't reach his eyes. "And she's powerful. I really do not want to piss her off."

"I can't let you do this."

"I'm not sure you have a choice." Diablo grabbed Grey's forearm, stopping him before he pulled the jeans on. "But know if the fight goes to Court, I'm not sure I'll be able to help without endangering everything. Right now if Servius and Jet tell Regis they saw us fighting together, Nero can probably convince the prince those two are crazy, but if we're seen together in Court—"

"Then let's finish this before it goes there." Grey pulled on the jeans and turned to the closet where Hunter hid his arsenal.

"We still need to be smart about this. Let's bring Nero in, get a plan." Diablo snorted. "Maybe get an arsenal."

"I'm not waiting on Nero. I'm not waiting on anything any more." As smart as waiting was, there just wasn't time. If Servius was watching the Handmaiden's magic join the coin pieces, he wouldn't be at her residence for long. "It's been almost six hours. The spell to join the coin pieces is nearing completion, then Servius is most likely going to Court to get the medallion from the arena. If you're going to help, it's now or never." Going to Court would be a disaster. He'd do it, but his chances of getting out again were slim once Regis and the Court guards were added to the mess with Servius and Jet. Better to stop it all before it got there. Better to get to Ivy as soon as possible. Now.

"There's always time for a good plan."

"I know," Grey growled. Logic said plan. Everything else howled get to her now... or avenge her.

Now. Now.

He felt the memory of her in the shower, the water sluicing over her naked skin, her body wrapped tight and hot around him, her head tipped back as pleasure roared through her, her aura crackling against his.

Diablo jerked back, surprise flashing across his expression for a second, then it darkened back to a wary danger. "In the shower? I thought that was a water drake thing."

Everything within Grey froze. "You saw that?"

"Oh, yeah," Diablo said. "If you were trying to shock me, you should have tried something else."

"You saw that?"

"Yeah, and I really didn't need to." Diablo frowned. "You didn't do that on purpose?"

"I didn't know I could." Before today, he hadn't shared a memory with anyone, and he'd thought he'd only been able to share with Ivy because of her earth magic and her soul's condition.

"Another reason to hate being inamorated," Diablo said. "It fucks up your earth magic."

Both Capri and Ryan had mentioned something about their magic changing when they'd met, how their powers had become — and still were — difficult to control.

"Wonderful. So now I'm going to accidentally show everyone everything." With his inability to forget anything, he had a lot of secrets, not to mention a lot of other people's secrets.

A shiver swept cold down his spine. If he was in the wrong company, he could accidentally reveal Nero's *puzur* to the wrong drake.

This was bad. So very bad, and it didn't matter, not until he got Ivy back.

Something rustled out in the hall and a hint of wind whispered across Grey's cheeks. Brilliant white light shimmered at the hall's end, growing brighter until Anaea stormed around the corner. Her magical wind whipped around her, tugging at her shirt and rattling the single small sky painting on the wall.

Her gaze landed on him, freezing him in place, and she bared her teeth in a dragon's show of aggression. "Stop being an idiot."

"Holy Mother," Diablo hissed.

Grey squared his shoulders and met Anaea's glare. "You're an empath now. You tell me if I can stop."

Her wind snapped with a sharp slice against his cheek, making his headache pound. The heat of blood welled against his skin, then oozed down to his jaw.

"Tell me I can stop," he growled.

"Hunter can't lose you." Her wind faltered and her aura flickered. "I can't lose you."

"And I can't lose Ivy. You can feel how I feel. I know you can." Mother, he didn't want to hurt Hunter and Anaea or anyone. But the need to find Ivy, to know she was safe, protect her, avenge her, die with her if it came to that, clawed through his chest, made his insides squirm, and snapped through every cell in his body. He couldn't stop if he tried, and they were running out of time. "Catching Servius and Jet at the Handmaiden's secret residence is the best plan, but I have to go now."

"It's no plan." Her aura flared and her wind snapped around him, a howling tornado that wrenched him to his knees.

"It's the only plan," he roared into her storm, willing her to sense his need and desperation. "And you know it."

The wind slammed him back against the wall then vanished. "I won't let you go alone."

Grey snorted, unable to stop himself. What he wouldn't give to have Anaea at his side. "Hunter will kill me if I put you in danger. And your powers are still unreliable. What happens if something sets off your empathy or you suddenly develop another kind of earth magic during the fight?"

"Hunter can meet you there," she said.

The pressure in Grey's chest twisted. "Is he answering your telepathic calls?" He knew the answer. It explained Anaea's unpredictable magic.

"He's not. He's still afraid if he answers, he'll put his search for the Handmaiden on hold for too long."

"Because being inamorated is a fucking mental illness," Diablo growled.

Anaea glared at him.

"Tell me it isn't," Diablo said. "Hunter refuses to even spend his nights with you because he's afraid he won't be able to leave in the morning. You can barely get Capri to do her job, and you—" He glared at Grey. "You're going to commit suicide."

"I'm not going to commit suicide, but I am going to take two dragon souls and send them into the universal ether."

Diablo flashed his teeth and growled. "They deserve it."

"But how many drakes think that? We were predators. Killing is in our nature, but every soul we kill now takes us one step closer to extinction. How long before there aren't any of us left?"

"So you're not saying they deserve it?" Diablo cocked an eyebrow.

"I didn't say that. Besides, you said you're coming with me." Grey stood and opened the closet door, revealing a gun safe that took up the entire closet with an electronic keypad on its face. He typed in the code and opened the heavy steel door. Inside were swords, knives, daggers, a crossbow, handguns, and two sniper rifles. "And I have an arsenal. I'd hardly say that's suicide."

"Fine." A hint of Anaea's wind whipped through the room. She growled and it vanished, proving Grey's point that she didn't have control of her magic. "If I can't go with you, take this." She unhooked the chain that held the brass rebirth medallion around her neck and held it out to Grey.

God, how he wanted to take it. Having it meant he could stop Jet and Servius *and* save their souls, but it was also a huge risk. "If Servius gets his hands on this, he'll have everything he needs. He won't have to go to Court to pull the medallion from the arena."

"I know you've been holding back in your fights. I've felt how much it frustrated you when you gated into Nero's house with your back full of shrapnel." Anaea strode into the room and pressed the amulet into Grey's hands. "Take the bitch's soul. Take this Servius's soul, too, and get Ivy back."

37

Grey hugged close to the inside of the tunnel at the edge of the shadows and peered along the sight of Hunter's M1903 Springfield rifle — a match to the one Grey had used in the humans' First and Second World Wars. Everything beyond the tunnel in the Handmaiden's frozen garden was still. Even the wind. Cold stung his skin, his breath misted around his face, leaving freezing damp trails along his cheeks, and bright sunlight sparkled in the ice sculptures.

A shiver swept over him, and he fought to keep still and not tense up. In only the T-shirt and jeans and with his slow healing, he felt the cold more than most drakes. And while the medallion was ever so slightly too warm for the brass to be heated by just his body, it wasn't enough to stave off the chill. But none of Hunter's old jackets had been snuck out of Court and even if they had, Grey was just that much broader across the shoulders that the thick fabric might have impeded his movements. Which meant he was just going to have to suck it up and concentrate past the cold, as well as past the still-present pounding in his skull.

"Do you see anything?" Diablo asked from behind Grey, his voice low, his hand on the hilt of the short sword he'd borrowed from Hunter's arsenal.

With the gatelock preventing anyone from gating outside the residence's radius, Diablo was at a disadvantage in a fight. His usual fighting style of keeping his opponent off balance by rapid free gating was out and while Grey knew the black drake was good in a fight, he didn't know how much losing that ability would throw him off.

With luck, it wouldn't come down to that. The goals were fast and aggressive. Get to Ivy... or avenge her. Stop Servius from joining the coin pieces.

Diablo had insisted that while having the medallion was great, if there wasn't an easy opportunity to use it, they were sacrificing any and all souls necessary to stay alive.

Grey couldn't have agreed more. He was tired of pussyfooting around his fights with Jet. She'd tried to kill him more than once and this whole mess had yet to take up a twenty-four hour period. Saving her soul or Servius's wasn't worth risking his or Diablo's souls, and it certainly wasn't worth risking Ivy's.

Grey drew in a steadying breath then slowly exhaled and concentrated along the rifle's sight into the ice garden while trying — and failing — to ignore the howl of his soul to find Ivy. Now. Now. *She had to be alive. She couldn't be dead. She just couldn't be.*

Soon. Soon. It was the best he was going to get. And the first step was to determine if Jet was outside guarding the Handmaiden's door and then shooting her.

He drew in another breath and fought to pull just a hint of his memories of the frozen garden forward and not let them overwhelm him.

Rain rattled against a windowpane and the reek of rotting food swept around him.

Shit.

He shoved that memory aside, but the flicker of memory fog flooded over his vision again and the *thwump* of cannon fire roared in the distance. Grey stared down the sight of his M1903. Somewhere a man screamed.

Shit shit shit.

He'd hoped sharing his memory with Ivy and sealing the bond between their souls would have fixed his problem, if not permanently then at least longer than a quarter of a day. He hadn't noticed anything back in the hotel room or Hunter's house. But adrenaline hadn't been pumping through him, and the howling need to find Ivy was only growing stronger in his head.

Now. Now. Still his thoughts. Calm his pulse. Use what he remembered. But the shadowy threat of his memories was stronger than ever.

"Grey?" Diablo asked. "What's going on?"

Grey gritted his teeth. He had to do this to save Ivy. The alternative, that she was dead, was not an option. *Mother, she had to be alive.* He didn't know what he'd do if she was dead. He could barely breathe just thinking about it. "Nothing," he said between gritted teeth.

"Are you going to be able to hold your shit together long enough for a fight?"

"My shit is fine." Besides, the only way to fix his problem was to get close enough to Ivy and her memory-soothing aura.

"Then find Jet and shoot her." Diablo shifted. "I really need to hit something and I'd rather it not be you."

"But you would if you had to?" Grey wasn't sure he wanted to hear the answer.

"Now that I know how slow you heal, I'd try to find an alternative."

"You'd try? Gee, how kind of you."

"For the love of— Find Jet. She's out there and bored out of her mind. I just can't pinpoint her."

Grey glanced at Diablo. Had he just confessed to having more earth magic than only rapid free gating? Admitting that wasn't like the black drake at all.

Diablo's eyes narrowed, and he huffed. "It's an Asar Nergal thing. Just—" He jerked his thumb toward the tunnel's mouth. "Hold your shit together and let's get this party started."

Party wasn't the word Grey would have picked, but the sentiment was right. If the spell to join the coin pieces wasn't complete by now, it would be soon. He just needed, as Diablo put it, to hold his shit together long enough to get to Ivy. He could do that. For her, he could do anything.

He focused along the rifle's sight again and concentrated on the wall beside the door. He hadn't been to the Handmaiden's secret residence often. But that didn't matter. The only thing that did was keeping control of his magic.

The reek of garbage wafted around him.

Focus on the wall.

Someone screamed and sunlight flickered on water.

The. Wall.

The memory of the wall flashed into sight with only a hint of shadow in the crevasses, indicating the sun was in a different location than what he had just been staring at. He drew up the wall in the present, underlying it beneath the memory.

No sign of Jet or her magic.

Grey shifted his attention over, still on the double walls but closer to the ice-bush Ivy had hidden behind.

The memory of her jumping out with her hands and fingers curved like claws rushed across his vision.

"Stay focus," Diablo hissed. He sounded far away, his voice tight with strain, but over what Grey didn't know.

For a second Grey fought to cling to the memory of Ivy. Panic tightened his chest, but the fog of his memory vanished.

Now. Now.

Find Jet and the problem would be solved.

He shoved the memory of Ivy aside and concentrated on the memory of the wall. He needed to just remember the wall. A quick comparison. A—

Light shimmered beside the ice-bush.

Grey squinted, a part of him worried it was a remembered flash of water on sunlight, not the tell-tale shimmer of Jet's camouflage magic.

The shimmer shuddered. Cannon fire thudded behind him. Sunlight did flash on water and a woman sobbed. A crowd roared then a voice hissed, "How fast can you heal?"

Not fast enough. It was never fast enough.

Fuck. No. Hold it together. For Ivy.

His thoughts jumped back to her, her soothing green aura, the feel of her body pressed against his, and how calm and crisp everything became when she was near.

A shimmering halo materialized around a figure crouching near the stone wall and half hidden by the ice shrub. The halo's lines were so sharp he could make out the figure's body and his memory filled in the rest, revealing Jet. She faced the tunnel's mouth, but he couldn't tell if she'd seen him or not.

"Got you," he hissed, and lined up a shot at her chest — he wasn't going to risk missing by being overly ambitious and going for a headshot. One quick inhalation, and on the exhale, he squeezed the trigger.

The bang cracked through the quiet garden, and the shimmering aura wrenched back. Jet's camouflage magic vanished. She screamed and clutched her chest, just above her heart.

As planned, Grey shoved the rifle into Diablo's hand and stormed out of the tunnel's mouth. Without rapid free gating, a blitz attack wasn't Diablo's strength, but he also couldn't have made the first shot on Jet.

Grey roared, keeping the memory of Ivy's soothing aura tight in his mind, and drew his broadsword. The need to find her, offer his teeth and claws for her defense, and bring her meat and shinies surged through him as he raced toward Jet.

She staggered to her feet, and another bang shattered the garden's quiet. Jet's shoulder jerked back and she dropped to one knee. Another bang. She dropped to her other knee and sagged forward.

Grey swept his blade toward her head. She leapt to the side, barely dodging the attack but managing to draw a sidearm from a hip holster with the movement. His sword sliced the air beside her head. She rolled out of the way.

Another crack roared through the garden and a bullet slammed into the rock beside Jet's head.

"Really? A sniper? That's hardly fair." She glanced toward the tunnel. "Guns aren't a sanctioned weapon."

He jerked his chin toward her gun. "You should talk. Oh, and yeah, you tried to blow me up with a grenade."

"How *did* you survive that?"

"Wouldn't you like to know." Grey swung again, and she dove under the strike, aiming her sidearm at his chest. He twisted and lunged in as she fired. The bullet skimmed his biceps with a whisper of pain but his adrenaline consumed any agony. He grabbed the top of the gun and rammed his pommel against her hand. With a yelp, she released the weapon, hopped back, and drew her saber.

Her eyes narrowed and a deadly chill settled across her expression. This was the dragon others feared, the cold-blooded bounty hunter who thrived on hunting down humans.

"You should have just minded your own business," she hissed, her breath misting around her face as if she were a fire drake and not a water drake trapped in a human vessel.

"And you should have left things alone." He tossed the sidearm behind him into the snow, unable to secure it on his person without risking that Jet would take it back. "The Handmaiden hid those coin pieces for a reason."

"If I hadn't taken the job, someone else would have." She shifted, widening her stance.

"But the coins are found, the job is done, and you're still here." He wanted to scream at her. *Just hand over Ivy.* But that would reveal what she meant to him, and that could put her in more danger.

"The job isn't done until Servius is emperor." She lunged forward and slashed at his sword arm.

He blocked the attack and bashed her lighter weapon to the side, but she hopped clear of his reach before he could swing again.

Another crack from the rifle. Jet screamed and a line of blood welled along her cheek.

"Too bad he missed," Grey growled.

"Are your ears still ringing from the headshot?" Jet flashed her teeth at Grey. "I shouldn't have assumed that hatchling Bolo could finish the job."

Grey lunged in. Jet sidestepped the attack, but Grey swept his sword up, slicing at her arm. She wrenched her saber up to block, and he bashed it aside. He swung again, pressing his advantage. No way was he going to let up. She wasn't as strong as him and didn't have the reach. She yanked her sword up with another block that barely kept his weapon from striking her before she sidestepped out of the way.

Another swing, this time for her neck. Another block. His sword ground against her blade before she jerked down, letting his weapon swipe the air above her head.

With a growl, she lunged in. He twisted and swept his blade down as the tip of her saber nicked his ribs. A kiss of fiery pain licked his skin, but he heaved forward and rammed into her, shoving her back. Her foot hit an icy patch and she fell backwards as another crack from the rifle roared around them. The bullet hit the Handmaiden's gray door where her head would have been.

Behind him, Grey could hear Diablo's fast footsteps as he raced toward them. The rifle only had five shots before needing to be reloaded, and while the black drake could reload or draw one of the sidearms they'd taken from Hunter's arsenal if he wanted to stay in the fight, he needed to close his distance.

Jet's gaze jumped behind him and her expression darkened. "I see you brought the devil with you." Her sneer deepened. "Didn't think you'd make that kind of a deal."

"Why don't you set your saber down and surrender." Grey slashed down. She rolled to the side and swiped at his ankles, forcing him to hop back, then with a roar, she lunged at him.

He leapt back and blocked her jab, but she shifted and sliced his forearm with a knife in her offhand. His fingers went numb — she'd severed the tendons — and the sword fell from his hand.

Fog swarmed across his vision and someone hissed, "How fast can you heal?"

Shit. He mentally clawed for the memory of Ivy's aura.

The garden snapped into sharp focus as Jet swept in with another slice from her saber. He heaved to the side and shoved her off balance before she could jab him in the ribs with the knife. She stumbled and her back hit against the door to the Handmaiden's residence. With a hiss, Jet threw her knife into the snow by the door, said the power words to unlock it, and wrenched it open.

Grey lunged at her. She sidestepped and rammed the door into his shoulder. His foot hit the icy patch she'd slipped on before, and she snapped her foot out with a sidekick that toppled him backwards. His butt hit the ice and he slid back into a solid ice shrub.

Diablo was still midway across the garden, the rifle in one hand, his borrowed short sword in the other. Jet's gaze jumped to the black drake as she tossed her saber into the Handmaiden's residence, pulled a grenade from an inside pocket of her jacket, and released the pin. She tossed it at Grey and bolted inside.

"Grenade!" Grey batted the grenade away from him, and Diablo and dove for the door after Jet. He caught it before it closed, wrenched it out of her grip, and opened it wide enough for him to slip inside.

The device erupted with a massive explosion, the force slamming the door shut behind him and locking Diablo out. Grey could only pray the black drake had gotten out of the way in time, but still couldn't count on Diablo being in any condition to keep fighting — even if Grey had made certain the black drake knew the words to open the magical lock on the Handmaiden's door. Regardless of how fast Diablo could heal, that kind of explosion could permanently disable a drake if a limb was severed and no one was around to help it reattach.

"Why won't you just die?" Jet growled. She grabbed her saber and dove at Grey, the blade aimed at his heart.

He leapt to the side, letting it slice his shoulder, and grabbed her sword arm. She rammed her foot into his chest. Bone cracked, and white lightning exploded through him. More hazy memories danced at the edge of his vision, and his grip on her arm weakened. He ground his teeth, forcing his mind back to Ivy.

Jet jerked free of his hold and slashed at his neck. He rolled to the side. Pain burned through him as he scrambled to his feet and awkwardly drew his borrowed Colt semi-automatic from his shoulder holster with his left hand. The .45 felt awkward in his offhand, but until the tendons in his right healed, he was going to have to hope his offhand aim was good enough to get the job done.

Jet lunged in, moving too fast for him to get a good aim, and slashed at his gun arm, while drawing another knife and jabbing at his gut. He heaved forward and caught half her knuckle guard and half her blade with his shoulder again. Pain flared where she sliced. He batted the knife down and to the side with his injured hand. The blade cut through his heavy jeans and nicked his thigh.

She flashed her teeth and twisted, drawing the knife back toward his gut. He jerked away, but she flicked the tip of her saber at his gun hand, forcing him to yank it back or risk losing it. He needed distance if he was going to have the second to aim and hit something vital — the only way he was going to incapacitate her enough to win this fight. But she pressed her attack, slashing at his gun again. He ducked under the swing, away from the knife, aimed the gun for her gut, and fired. She leapt to the side and screamed. He didn't know how solid the shot had been, but he'd gotten her.

He yanked his hand up to grab her jacket, but his fingers still wouldn't work. She wrenched a backhanded swipe of her saber at his neck, and he rammed his shoulder into her chest and slammed her back. She hit the settee and jammed her knife into his gut.

Pain exploded through him. His chest was on fire from the broken rib and now the gash in his gut, hazy memories billowed at the edge of his consciousness, barely held back by the memory of Ivy's aura, and the heat from the medallion grew. If the magic within it hadn't yet been awakened and glowing, it would be soon.

Jet rammed her knee up into the other side of his gut. Another crack, another broken rib, and more searing pain. With a roar, she shoved him to the side, using her knee and the knife in his gut for leverage, then scrambled over the side of the settee and bolted for the glass and wrought iron door leading into the residence proper.

His pulse pounded. He couldn't lose sight of her and let her use her magic to disappear in the maze beyond. He also didn't know how many other dragons Servius had in his employ and couldn't afford for Jet to get to help. Certainly not until Diablo managed to get inside — and Grey wasn't going to contemplate the possibility that the black drake was too injured to help.

Grey dove over the settee's arm after her, rolled to his feet, and fired before being certain about his aim. The bullet skimmed her shoulder and shattered the glass behind her.

She wrenched the door open, and Grey forced his legs to move faster.

He fired again.

Missed.

Shit.

He had to keep her in sight, had to get to her before she called for help — if help hadn't already heard the grenade go off outside or the gunshots.

He dove for her and she jerked to the side. He swung his arm out, slammed it across her chest, and rammed her back against the wrought iron railing of the landing. She drove her knife into his chest, clipping the edge of the medallion, sending heat radiating through it, and piercing his flesh above his heart with a hard, powerful thrust.

The reek of garbage filled his nose and rain rattled on a window. His throat burned. His whole body burned. They were going to kill him, take his head, and there wasn't a damned thing he could do about it.

"How fast can you heal?"

Not fast enough. Never fast enough.

But for Ivy, his healing had to be fast enough. She needed him, and he needed her.

He wrenched his attention back to a murky present with a hazy green tint. But it was enough. He stood on the balcony in the Hand-maiden's residence, Jet had her knife stuck in his chest, and the brass medallion under his T-shirt was ever-too-slightly warm to be natural.

"I know you're not a fast healer." She dropped her saber and reached to draw another knife from her belt for better close-combat fighting.

"How fast I heal doesn't matter if I take your soul," he growled.

Her gaze dipped to his chest and her eyes widened. The medallion might not be glowing, but this close, anyone could see the outline under his T-shirt.

"How did you get a medallion?"

He cocked an eyebrow. "Are you really asking that? The prince's former assassin owed me a favor."

"Servius will want that. He won't have to go to Court to get the one from the arena." She opened her mouth and drew breath — probably to yell to Servius.

Grey rammed his elbow into her face. Her head jerked to the side, but she still managed to jam her free knife into his gut and yank out the one in his chest. Pain lit up his torso, and a hint of darkness swarmed at the edge of his vision — consuming memories or blood loss, he wasn't sure which. He jammed the gun into her ribs, fired, and drew a howl of pain, then dropped the weapon. With a roar, he dipped low, grabbed the waistband of her pants with his good hand, and tossed her over the edge of the railing.

She screamed and hit the stone floor, her eyes wide, her expression shocked. Grey grabbed the gun and bolted down the stairs. He hit the floor as she rolled to her side, but Servius stormed out of the maze of bookshelves and Jet's attention jumped to the ancient black drake. He held something small that glowed with bright white light in one hand and had his other hand clamped around the back of Ivy's neck.

Grey's heart skipped a beat and his sight snapped into crystal clarity. She was splattered with blood, one strap of her dress had been ripped off, and the fabric had been torn in two blood-crusted gashes and a hole in her chest, as if she'd been impaled with swords and shot.

"Are you really still trying to stop me, silver drake?" Servius shoved Ivy to her knees and tapped his forearms together. A blast of wind slammed into Grey and tossed him into the bookshelves behind him. The air burst from Grey's lungs, a fiery agony exploded through his chest, and the shelf boards cracked, tumbling him and all the books to the floor.

"He—" Jet rolled to her hands and knees. "He has the—"

Grey jerked the Colt up and fired. The bullet hit her in the head, sending a spray of bloody mist across the floor, and she collapsed, her eyes wide and vacant.

Servius's eyes narrowed. "He has the what?"

"The temper of a fire drake," Grey growled as he stood. "Let Ivy go, give me the coin, and I won't send you to Tobias in little pieces."

"I didn't think you worked for Tobias."

"Maybe I'm trying to get into the prince's good graces." Grey met Ivy's gaze, unable to resist the draw of her soul on his, even though it risked revealing to Servius how much she meant to him. The fear of losing her that had clamped tight before he'd entered the Handmaiden's residence now ignited into a rage, and a growl bubbled in his throat.

Look away. Just God damned look away.

But he couldn't. He was lost in her eyes. She was his lifeline, his focus.

The rest of the room clicked into sharp clarity, every crack in the stone-tiled floor. Jet's blood oozed into the grooves between those tiles. Servius's gaze was wary, while Ivy's was tight but attentive. She was waiting on his lead. She'd gotten off her knees, but remained crouched, ready to bolt as soon as he gave the sign.

Except Servius could control wind — a surprising revelation since the black drake had managed to keep quiet even the suggestion that he possessed an earth magic ability. If Ivy made a run for it, Servius could just grab her with his wind. Of course, if Grey distracted him, she might be able to get away.

Servius glanced at Ivy then back to Grey. "You think rescuing Regis's favorite spy will help with that?"

Grey offered a half shrug. Better to not let Servius know what Ivy meant to him.

"Regis is soul sick."

"That's why the coin and the green drake are going to Tobias." Grey adjusted his grip on the Colt, keeping it half-hidden by his thigh. He had three shots left.

"Then leave them with me. I'll be emperor before the day is done."

"And how many drakes will be left?" He had to make it count, and the first shot would have to be from the hip, like how the gunslingers shot in the cowboy movies — something that had always looked impressive but he had no experience with.

"How many drakes will be left if Regis remains?" Servius asked. "Someone has to do something, and that someone is me."

"Let's wait for the Handmaiden to return and get her blessing."

"That bitch can go to hell." Servius flashed his teeth. "She's just as complicit as Regis is in his atrocities."

Grey jerked the gun up and fired. Ivy dove away from Servius. He tapped his arms and a blast of wind slammed Grey back into the wall. Blood welled in a thick line along Servius's cheek. If it hadn't been for the wind, Grey would have shot him in the head.

Ivy was still scrambling away — a few feet and growing — while Servius roared, his eyes wild with rage. Grey leapt up and raced toward him. All he needed was to buy Ivy time to get away. After that—

Well, he had no idea. Maybe Diablo would make a miraculous appearance and help, or Ivy would get her hands on a gun and shoot Servius.

Another blast of wind swept Grey into the air and threw him into the second story railing. His legs tipped up, and he toppled backward onto the landing and skidded through the broken glass into the Handmaiden's antechamber.

Grey scrambled to his feet, his back burning with glass cuts, and rushed back onto the balcony. Ivy screamed and grabbed at a wind-rope now lashed around her neck. With a twist of his hand, Servius jerked her back into his grasp. At his feet, Jet groaned and climbed onto her hands and knees, already starting to recover from the gunshot.

"Do your job," Servius growled. "Kill him." His gaze locked on Grey's, and he bared his teeth with full aggression. The black vortex of a gate formed against the bookshelf beside him and he dragged Ivy through.

Grey's thoughts stuttered. How the hell had he summoned a gate with the Handmaiden's gatelock in full effect?

His memories flickered at the edge of his vision and he mentally wrenched forward the memory of Ivy's aura.

Jet staggered to her feet and drew a sidearm from inside her jacket. "You're fucking dead."

She fired two quick shots, and Grey leapt back into the doorway to the antechamber.

The front door flew open, and Diablo rushed in, holding his borrowed short sword. Blood crusted along one side of his jeans and jacket, but it didn't drip onto the floor, indicating whatever injuries he'd sustained from the grenade had already healed.

"Took you long enough," Grey said, now more than ever wishing he could heal that fast.

Jet's footsteps rushed up the stairs and Diablo quirked an eyebrow. "You haven't killed her yet?"

"Don't think I haven't been trying."

"Jeez. Amateurs." He raced past Grey onto the second story landing. Two more quick shots erupted then Jet and Diablo raced into the doorway — Diablo missing his sword. Diablo yanked the gun from her hand and slammed his elbow into her jaw.

Grey shoved the Colt into the back of his jeans and drew the medallion's chain off over his head.

Jet yanked a knife from a hidden sheath in her jacket and sliced at Diablo's arms, her movement jerky and her expression tight. He leapt back, but kicked her in the chest and shoved her into Grey. He wrapped his forearm around her neck and pressed the medallion against her back. With three quick words, he activated its magic and heat roared from the medallion, over his hands, and enveloped Jet. Her body went rigid. She screamed and flames rushed over her.

Diablo wrenched back. "Holy Mother," he hissed, his eyes wide, as if he'd never seen the assassin's medallion in action — and if he hadn't spent any time with Hunter while he was working, he probably never had.

The fire flared with blinding brilliance, then whooshed back into the medallion, filling Grey with an unsettling chill. Jet's eyes rolled back and she collapsed to the floor, her soul in the medallion and no longer in her human vessel.

Grey slung the medallion back around his neck and dropped beside her, his chest burning with the agony of cracked ribs and more gashes than he wanted to acknowledge. Somehow he managed to keep his concentration on Ivy's aura as he ripped open Jet's jacket and did a quick search for weapons. She'd used all but two small throwing knives and a grenade. Not worth it, and there wasn't enough time to search for anything she'd really hidden on her person. Ivy was still in danger, and now Servius had the finished rebirth coin.

"Do you still have the rifle and the extra magazine?" He straightened and strode to the exit, his body screaming at the movement.

"I can't endanger my coterie by going to Court with you." Diablo didn't sound happy about that.

Grey opened the outside door and grabbed for his broadsword, but the tendons in his wrists hadn't knitted back together, and he couldn't get his fingers to work. "I know, but I can't let him get the medallion out of the arena."

"And you sure as hell can't face him alone. You're bleeding from— I have no idea how many wounds, and you can't even pick up your sword."

"The bleeding will stop." Eventually. It was his broken ribs that were going to keep hurting for longer than he liked. Grey grabbed the sword with his left hand. "And the tendons will work when I need them to."

"Yeah, and if I wish hard enough, my life would be normal." Diablo rolled his eyes. "Just because you want something doesn't mean it will happen."

"It doesn't matter." Grey glanced across the garden, searching for the rifle. If he couldn't find it in the next ten seconds, he had to move on. Servius already had a head start and Grey still had to get outside of the gatelock before he could summon a gate to Court.

A crater lay off to the side of the garden, and a whole section of ice shrubs and miniature trees had been shattered. A trail of blood, bright red against all the white, led halfway from the Handmaiden's door to a half-destroyed wall of ice shrubs, and there, mostly hidden by a chunk of ice, was the Springfield. "You're going to call Capri and tell her to tell Tobias what's going on. We were friends before I became royal enemy number one. That should keep your *puzur* safe. I just have to hold out long enough for that."

"He'll have to arrest you."

"Then he'll arrest me. Servius can't have the coin and neither can Regis. Tobias understands that."

"Really?"

"He wouldn't have called me in at the beginning of this mess if he didn't." And Grey prayed that was the case. He rushed toward the rifle, struggling to sheathe the broadsword at his hip while holding it in the wrong hand.

Diablo raced up beside him, grabbed the sword from Grey, seized his waistband to stop him, and slid the blade into the sheath. "You're going to get yourself killed."

"As long as Ivy is safe, I don't care." And that was the only thing that mattered. He had to save her, and with Servius controlling wind — and Grey's current state of injury — the odds weren't good that he'd be able to stop him. Slowing him down would have to be the goal.

"I'm pretty sure she'd disagree with that."

Grey shoved away from Diablo, bent — agony snapping through his chest at the movement — and retrieved the rifle. "The magazine?"

"You're a fucking moron." Diablo yanked the rifle from Grey and replaced the magazine.

"I just need to stall him and get Ivy to safety." Grey took the rifle back and rushed toward the tunnel.

Diablo raced after him. "She's a dragon, too. She more than proved that when she took Bolo's head."

"I know that. But she's still a hatchling. She has no fighting experience and no magic that's useful in combat." The shadows in the tunnel enveloped him, and the tingle of the gatelock weakened. "Servius can gate through a gatelock. I have no idea how powerful he is and I'm not stupid enough to think I can take him on my own. I don't have any combat magic, either." He caught Diablo's dark gaze. The black drake's expression was hard to read. He didn't look happy, but Grey wasn't sure about what. "I promise I won't endanger your *puzur* when I'm arrested."

"I've seen the results of the prince's torturer's magic. I'm not willing to take that bet." He glared at Grey. "And what about the medallion? What will you do if Regis gets his hands on that?"

"That's why you need Capri to explain *everything* to Tobias." The tingle of the gatelock vanished, and Grey pressed his hand to the side of the tunnel to summon a gate.

Diablo grabbed Grey's shoulder, spiking pain through the still unhealed gashes and drawing a grunt that Grey couldn't keep back. Diablo jerked his hand away and wiped Grey's blood off on his jeans. "The prince's chamberlain is obedient to the prince."

"He's made it clear he's the Handmaiden's man, not the prince's." And Grey was betting his life and the safety of the medallion on that.

Grey hissed his power word and a speck of black vortex, darker than the shadows in the tunnel, burst to life against the wall.

"You're risking the life of every dragon on that," Diablo said, his voice dark.

Grey pulled the medallion out from under his T-shirt. "Then take it and be around so when I'm arrested, you can take my soul."

"Don't be an idiot. I'm not going to kill you. The medallion is your best bet for ending him. If he has wind, getting close and hissing a few words is going to be easier than cutting off his head." Diablo flashed his teeth and growled. "But don't forget. Fuck up and we're all screwed."

And that included Ivy. "Gee, thanks."

The vortex whooshed to its full size and Grey slid the medallion back under his T-shirt.

Diablo grabbed his arm, stopping him from stepping through. "Don't die."

"Gonna try awfully hard not to." In the very least, he was going to save Ivy.

39

I vy staggered out of Servius's gate into shadows. She clutched the knife tight in her hand — she'd snatched it from the floor of the Handmaiden's residence during her failed attempt to flee — and held it close to her leg, hiding it in the folds of her dress, praying Servius wouldn't notice it.

Grey was alive.

Light flared to life around her from a source she couldn't pinpoint, which told her it had to be the magical lighting at Court. They stood at the edge of the center entrance to the massive arena, filled with the blue memory fire of thousands of years of memories. The walls and seats had been carved out of granite and swept into a massive domed ceiling high above, but she couldn't make her mind focus on where she was. Not even all the memory fire billowing around her could make her think past the single thought whirling over and over again in her head.

Grey *was* alive.

The pressure in her chest and gut had clenched tight the moment the Handmaiden's residence had shaken from some kind of explosion outside. Then the gunfire inside had tightened it even more. She'd prayed it was Grey, but knew it could have been Diablo or Nero or even the ferocious sorcerer Anaea, there to avenge Grey. She almost hadn't believed her eyes when Servius had snatched the completed coin from the podium, dragged her into the main chamber, and Grey had been standing at the bottom of the stairs. Blood had shimmered wet on most of his black T-shirt and stained his jeans, revealing the toll fighting Jet had taken on him. But he still had radiated ferocious strength, his body tense, ready to jump into battle. Then his gaze had locked with hers, and certainty had burned through the ice devouring her insides.

He was alive and he was coming for her.

She knew it in the core of her being.

Servius strode toward the arena's center, and his wind snapped around her neck and jerked her after him. She stumbled forward, fighting to breathe against the magical constriction.

Grey was coming. All she had to do was bide her time and make sure Servius didn't get the medallion and gain control of the complete rebirth spell. If he did, then everything she and Grey had gone through would have been for nothing. She knew how to stop his magic — break the line of one of his tattoos. Just a little nick. That was all it would take. But without some kind of a distraction, he'd see her attack and stop her before she could cut him.

She had to stay patient. Grey was alive. Everything else she could figure out. The words swirled, a mantra in her head.

Servius's wind jerked her a few more stumbling steps to the arena's center, then lashed around her forearm — thank the Mother not the one hiding the knife! — and yanked her to her knees. She tucked the knife deeper into the folds of her dress, her pulse racing. If he saw it, all chance of eliminating his magic and helping Grey was lost.

"I've been waiting for this for centuries." He tapped his tattoos together, and a band of stone snapped up from the arena floor and clamped around her wrist. "You, as you are now, haven't even existed for a fraction of the time I've been working toward this moment."

She tugged against the cuff, squeezing her hand as small as she could, but the stone clamped tight, and there was barely enough room to twist her wrist.

Servius sagged to his knees beside her, close, but — even if she hadn't been trapped with a stone handcuff — still out of reach. Not to mention he still had his sheathed sword at his hip and she didn't doubt he had spent many years learning how to use it. From his pocket, he drew out a copper disc the size of the joined coin and set it on the arena floor. White light shimmered off it, along with a hint of memory fire, and Servius glared at her.

"It took me fifty years to craft this spell." He pressed his index finger on top of the disc and hissed a few quick words that Ivy couldn't understand. The white light flared and veins of light slid out from the disc in a spider web radius, twice the size of her palm across the floor. "In a little more than five minutes the Handmaiden's spell locking the medallion in the heart of the arena will be gone."

Her pulse leapt into a rapid tattoo. Five minutes wasn't nearly enough time. Jet was injured, so Grey might be able to defeat her in that time, but to get to the gate anchor then gate to Court—

It was up to her, and she was only going to have one shot. She tightened her grip on the knife. If she attacked Servius, he'd defend himself with wind and stone, and that wouldn't stop the magic pulling the medallion out of the arena. But if she made it look like she was attacking him, she might have a chance of damaging the disc.

To do that, she had to get free. She curled her thumb tighter to her palm. Maybe the cuff wasn't evenly shaped. If it was slightly wider at one spot, there might be a way to slip through. "Controlling the rebirth spell won't make dragons follow you."

Servius sat back on his heels, his gaze rising to the ceiling. "Dragonkind is looking for an alternative to Regis's rule."

"And you're that alternative?" She shifted, trying to change the angle of her wrist.

"You're not going to get free," he said without even looking at her. "If you had a knife, you could cut off your hand, but then you'd be busy fighting the pain and holding the stumps together to get it to reattach. I'd just encase you in stone while your soul magic was trying to put you back together until I had the medallion, then I'd rip out your soul and give that body with its earth magic to someone loyal."

"You're going to give my body to another drake anyway."

"Not if you swear your allegiance to me."

"Will you release me if I swear?" She doubted he'd believe her, just like she couldn't believe anything he said.

His gaze slid from the ceiling to her. "Trust must be earned."

A bang cracked through the arena. Servius's eyes flashed wide, and he jerked to the side, tapping his arms together. A blast of wind exploded around him. Blood from a graze that cut under his eye and across his temple oozed down his cheek. His expression snapped to darkened rage and with a roar, he wrenched around. A whirlwind exploded from his hands and blasted across the arena into one of the side entrances.

The wind jerked Grey into the light and wrenched a rifle from his hands.

She yanked at the stone cuff. She had to get free, had to help Grey. He had no way of defending himself against Servius's magic, let alone defeating him.

"Just die," Servius howled. His wind tossed the rifle into the seats at the back of the arena.

"Why won't you?" Grey drew a gun from his shoulder holster and fired. The gunshots roared through the arena with three quick explosions.

The whirlwind around Servius swept stronger, ripping at Ivy's hair and clothes, and the bullets slammed into the floor behind the black drake, sending flecks of stone into the tornado that sliced at Ivy's face and bare arms.

"I'm the emperor, that's why," Servius yelled, his voice booming through the arena, caught up and somehow magnified by his wind. "And you can't stop me."

He tapped his wrists. A spike of stone surged out of the floor a few feet from Servius and the whirlwind wrenched Grey forward.

Ivy's heart froze. Her whole essence froze, as if time had somehow slowed down and she was sentenced with the inability to do anything but watch. She couldn't even find breath to yell.

The wind slammed Grey off his feet, across the arena, and onto the spike, driving it through his chest. He screamed. His eyes rolled back, his head dipped forward, and for a heartrending second she feared and prayed he'd pass out. But he jerked his head up, his eyes wild with agony, and bared his teeth in full at Servius.

Ivy yanked her hand against the stone cuff. She couldn't lose Grey. Blood slicked her wrist where she'd rubbed it raw, but her hand was still too wide.

"You should have minded your own business." Servius flicked his finger and the wind slammed against Grey's back, driving him further onto the spike.

Grey screamed again and wrenched the gun toward Servius.

A blast of wind ripped it from Grey's hand and tossed it into the seats with the rifle. The spike shuddered then reformed, as if concentrating on manipulating the wind made him lose a fraction of control over his stone magic.

Servius sneered and drew his sword. "I've never taken the head of a dragon before. But at least the arena medallion will save your soul."

Maybe if she broke the spell pulling the medallion from the arena, she'd distract Servius enough for Grey to get free. She kicked at the disc, but it was too far away.

Grey clawed at the spike, but the wind kept battering his back, driving the stone deeper into his chest. Blood leaked over the spike and down the front of his jeans and his breath came in sharp gasps.

Ivy dug the knife tip into the cuff and knocked off a chip, but that wasn't going to be fast enough.

Servius stepped closer. "In a few minutes, I'll have the arena's medallion and control of the full rebirth spell." His gaze jumped to the disc and the glowing spider web of magic on the arena floor. "You can be my first new servant."

"The hell I—" Grey coughed and blood bubbled over his lips, splattering the spike in front of him.

Ivy pressed the knife to her wrist. Lose the hand and save Grey. Except Servius was right. The shock of losing it might take up that split-second she'd need to cut Servius's tattoos.

Servius slid the tip of his sword up Grey's chest to his neck. "Is it hard? Taking a dragon's head?"

Grey's gaze leapt to Ivy's, capturing her soul. His love for her swelled warm and sure around her heart. He was her inamorato and would do anything to protect her. That was why he'd come here, even knowing Servius controlled wind. Grey had known he wouldn't be able to win this fight. She could see that in his eyes. He'd come here for the chance to save her. The need was imprinted on his soul with a magic he was unable to resist. She knew it because that magic flowed through her veins, too. She would do anything to save him, or she would die trying.

Losing a hand wasn't going to help. But breaking it—

She scrambled to a crouch, kicked off her shoes, and slammed her bare heel down onto the side of her hand as hard as she could before she could second-guess herself. White lightning shot through her thumb and palm and seared up her arm. She fought to swallow her scream, and black specks swept across her vision, threatening her consciousness, but she held on and yanked her ruined hand free of the stone cuff.

Servius drew his sword back and lined his swing with Grey's neck. He sneered and Ivy leapt at him. One strike, just a nick, that was all she needed.

He swept his sword toward her. She barreled forward, rising to catch the blade in her shoulder. It sliced deep, burning agony down her knife arm. Her fingers went numb. She was going to drop the blade and fail. Grey was going to die.

The ice in her gut and chest exploded, and a fierce fire roared within her. She forced her grip on the knife tight and wrenched the blade up the inside of Servius's arm.

He jerked back and sneered. "You'll need a better hit than that to disarm me."

The wind trapping Grey on the spike stuttered, and the spike trembled.

"Disarming you wasn't the goal."

A thin line of blood wept through both wind and stone tattoos on Servius's arm. His eyes widened. The wind gasped then vanished, and the spike started to crumble.

"That's not going to stop me." He slammed his fist into her face.

Something cracked in her cheek and pain flashed white-hot agony through her head. Her legs lost strength, her whole body jerked, suddenly weak, and darkness consumed her.

40

G rey roared as Ivy collapsed unconscious to the ground. The spike in his chest shattered and with a strength he hadn't known he possessed, he drew his sword with still-numb fingers and lunged at Servius. The only way to ensure Ivy's safety was to finish off Servius or hold out long enough for Tobias and the royal guards to arrive.

Except with two earth magic abilities and the power to gate through a gatelock, Servius had to be a sorcerer. It wasn't impossible for a dragon to have two earth magics, but the only way he could pass through a gatelock was if his gating ability wasn't natural, therefore bypassing the lock. Who knew what other magic abilities Servius possessed?

But none of that mattered. Only protecting Ivy.

Agony consumed Grey and blood gushed from the hole in his chest. His breath rattled and wheezed and his head spun from blood loss, but protecting Ivy spurred him forward. She was the only thing that mattered.

He swung his sword at Servius's neck, but the black drake blocked with his blade and wrenched down, jerking the sword from Grey's weakened grip.

"I'm glad Jet didn't kill you." Servius bashed his pommel into Grey's face, smashing his head back and sending stars dancing across his vision.

The arena tilted and Grey staggered back. The muscles in his legs gave out, dropping him to his knees.

Get up.

He fought to catch his breath. The metallic tang of blood filled his mouth and choked him.

Get up for Ivy.

But the strength he'd found moments ago had vanished with his breath and all his blood now pooling on the arena floor. If he died, she'd be helpless—

Except she wasn't helpless. She'd caught Servius's blade with her shoulder, sliced his arm, and somehow his earth magic had vanished. Even without any martial experience, she'd fought back and given Grey a chance. A chance he wasn't going to let go to waste. He still had the medallion. All he needed was to press it against Servius and say three words.

"I'm going to chop off your head and toss it onto Tobias's desk." Servius sneered, jerked his sword back, and swung for Grey's neck.

He lunged up, rammed his shoulder into Servius's chest, and barreled him over, landing on top of him. The black drake bashed his sword pommel into the side of Grey's head. Fog flooded his vision and a hint of reeking garbage wafted around him.

Son of—

He couldn't get lost in a memory. He—

He could use it. He'd made Diablo see a memory. Why not Servius?

Another crack to his skull, while Servius rammed his other fist into the gash in Grey's chest.

The fog snapped into a blinding light that roared through him. He gasped, fighting to breathe and concentrate.

The pain was like that night in the alley when he'd been jumped and had his throat slit — actually this pain was a hundred times worse, but he needed a memory, and this was the nastiest one he could think of on short notice.

He mentally clutched at it, at the pain burning his throat, and the feel of his blood oozing hot between his fingers.

"How fast can you heal?" the voice hissed.

"How fast can I what?" Servius asked, and his face materialized through the haze of Grey's memory, his gaze unfocused, as if he wasn't seeing Grey. "How fast can I—"

Servius's grip weakened, and his sword slipped to the floor. Grey yanked the medallion out from under his T-shirt and snapped the chain.

"Not fast enough," Servius said. "Never fast enough?" He frowned, then his gaze locked onto Grey, clearly seeing him.

Grey hissed the words to activate the medallion. Servius's eyes flashed wide. He screamed and jerked, but Grey held tight and slapped the medallion to the side of Servius's face.

Searing heat exploded around the black dragon. He bucked and threw his head back as if to scream, but brilliant white light roared out instead.

Something cracked, the sound sharp against the roar of the medallion's magic. White light shot from a fissure in the floor by Ivy's head, and the heat increased. Now both medallions were fighting to absorb Servius's soul.

The heat burned over Grey's hand and charred his flesh. He ground his teeth, clinging to his soul and wrapping his mind in the memory of Ivy and her soothing green aura. Just a little longer. For Ivy, and it would be done.

Light exploded around him and with a whoosh, the heat and brilliance vanished back into the medallion. Servius lay limp, his eyes vacant, his soul now in one of the medallions. The fissure over the arena's heart still glowed, and the medallion was now only half submerged in the stone floor. A copper disk — most likely the vessel containing the spell to unlock the medallion from the arena's floor — still pulsed, along with a spiderweb of magic lines on the floor encircling the medallion.

Grey heaved off Servius's corpse, grabbed the knife by Ivy's hand, and rammed the tip into the disk. Light sparked from it and the glowing magical spiderweb vanished. The stone around the medallion froze, locking it in place, now half revealed. Regular stone magic wouldn't be able to pull it out — it hadn't before — and as far as Grey knew, there weren't any other drakes with enough sorcerer's ability to finish the job. Not without many, many years of concentration.

Beside him, Ivy lay unconscious. Her brown locks veiled her face but didn't hide the torn shoulder strap of her dress. A tear in the fabric at the back of her dress and the blood crusted around it told him Servius or Jet had run her through with a sword.

A flicker of heat rage flared in his chest, but couldn't move past the agony pulsing through him. Ivy had suffered because the dragon Court was a mess. But for now, she was safe.

He shoved Hunter's medallion into his pocket, drew Ivy into his lap, and cradled her against his chest. Blood already splattered her face and arms, and even if holding her added his to the mix, he wouldn't have been able to stop himself if he'd wanted to. He had to touch her, had to ensure she was all right. He belonged to her and had no idea what he'd do without her.

Quick footsteps pounded on the floor behind him, but not the dozen or so he'd expect if Tobias was bringing a squadron. Grey dragged his attention from Ivy toward the steps.

Tobias and Ophelia rushed into the arena, swords drawn.

"Just the two of you? Didn't Capri stress the importance of the situation?"

Tobias's eyes narrowed, his gaze sliding over Ivy in Grey's lap. "I was hoping you'd take care of it and I wouldn't have to arrest you."

"How kind." Grey coughed, choked on the blood in his throat, and fought to breathe. More blood rushed down his chest with the sudden contraction of his muscles and pooled around him. "Yep, everything is taken care of."

Tobias sheathed his sword and strode to Grey's side. "Let me take Ivy."

Grey tightened his grip on her. He'd just gotten her back. No way was he handing her over.

Tobias crouched and reached for her.

"I've got her," Grey growled.

"She's my agent," Tobias said.

Ophelia stepped close, her sword still drawn. "Where's her locket?"

"I have to get it." Grey tightened his grip. If she didn't have her locket when she woke, she wasn't going to remember anything. It was in a sewer in Vancouver, but he had no idea if he could gate there and find it before she woke. And he had to be there when she woke.

"She won't remember you," Ophelia said, as if she could read his thoughts.

"I don't care." He couldn't do anything else but be there. "She can't stay here and continue being Regis's pawn. She's exposed to other drakes who could abduct her like Servius did." Grey staggered to his feet, agony burning through him. It didn't matter if she never remembered him or if she was no longer inamorated with him. She'd said she wanted to be free, to stop being used by Regis and Tobias, and he would God-damned do everything in his power to ensure that happened.

"That's not for you to decide," Tobias said, taking a step toward him, his eyes narrowed.

Grey jerked away from him, his legs trembling with the effort to stay standing. "It's not for you, either."

Tobias drew his sword. "She can't make that choice."

"Because she won't remember?" God, how long had Tobias been using that line on Ivy?

"Yes," Tobias growled.

"She remembers enough."

"Not without her locket," Ophelia said.

"And I'll find it." He glanced at Ophelia. Both she and Tobias had their swords drawn. He'd never be able to win a fight, not as injured as he was. He would have to make a deal and pray it was good enough for them to let him leave.

Grey dropped to one knee, balancing Ivy against his chest, and pulled Hunter's medallion from his pocket. "Take the royal coterie's medallion and take the rebirth coin probably in Servius's pocket." If this wasn't a good enough deal, he'd fight. Mother of All, he'd fight to his last breath to honor Ivy's wishes. Grey bared his teeth in full and growled. "You will *not* take Ivy."

Tobias growled back. "What the hell is wrong with you? She can't leave with you. Even if it's best to get her out of Court, you're a wanted drake. I've had to issue a warrant for your arrest. You're—"

Ophelia sighed. "Inamorated."

Tobias glared at her. "He's what?"

"Inamorated. The only way you'll get Ivy from him is to kill him. Or she renounces him and returns to you willingly." Ophelia slid her narrow sword into the sheath at her hip. "Tobias, this is good for her. This is what we wanted for her, a new coterie."

"I wouldn't say Grey has a coterie."

Ophelia quirked a half smile. "He does." She turned to Grey. "When the dugga starts demanding why he can't have Ivy in his employ, I'll have to send him your way."

Grey hissed. "You just do that."

Her smile deepened, as if she knew some inside joke.

"We're leaving." He dropped the medallion and stepped back.

"Oh, for the love of—" Tobias rolled his eyes at Grey. "Pick that up, and here—" He rifled through Servius's pockets and found the coin. "You need to take this, too, before I have to summon the guard."

His mind stuttered. *Take this, too?* That didn't make any sense.

Ophelia chuckled. "I think you've broken him."

"I thought we had an understanding," Tobias said, his voice low. "When I first called you to look into this, I thought you knew where I stood."

"I thought I did, too." Except Grey wasn't certain any more if he did or not. Very few drakes would risk their lives by disobeying their doyen and prince.

"I'm the Court's man, and stability and peace between coteries are my primary goals," Tobias said. He glanced at the dark entrance on the far side of the arena, then looked back at Grey. "We both know I can't let Regis have the medallion even if it does belong to him."

Ophelia took the coin from Tobias, grabbed the medallion from the floor, and held them out to Grey.

"As for the coin… Regis knows about it," Tobias said. "But I'll tell him the magic to join the pieces was destroyed and the spell on the coin doesn't work."

Grey stared at the medallion and coin in Ophelia's hand. "You're playing a dangerous game."

"I'm not playing anything." Tobias's expression darkened. "I just need to hold Court together long enough for the Handmaiden to get back and fix this."

"You think she will?" A hint of fog fluttered at the edge of Grey's vision. He couldn't keep standing here. He needed to sit and let his body heal.

"She has to." Tobias jerked his chin at Ophelia. "Gate him wherever he wants to go."

He wanted to go home, but he wasn't sure where that was. No, it was wherever Ivy was. Next best choice was Nero's mansion, but telling Ophelia that would endanger his *puzur*. "There's a hotel in Vancouver. The Sutton Court."

"I'm familiar with it." Ophelia drew close and slid the medallion and coin into his pocket. "Keep her safe."

"With my life."

She hissed her power word and a black vortex burst to life against the floor beside him. "Her power word is *si*."

"Thank you." He stepped into the gate. Darkness enveloped him, his sense of the world tilted, then his foot hit the floor and he stepped into the living room of the hotel room in Vancouver.

Grey's knees buckled and he fought to stay standing. He wasn't going to worry about how Ophelia knew exactly where to send her gate. All he could focus on now was getting Ivy to the bedroom where they'd made love and pray being there was enough for her to remember who she really was. It didn't matter if she remembered him or how he felt about her. All that mattered was that she didn't wake terrified and knew there was someone with her who she could trust.

41

Nero hung up on Tobias and shoved his phone back into his pocket, stared at the bottle of scotch at the edge of his desk, and contemplated pouring another drink. God, his head hurt, and light now constantly flashed across his vision.

But it had nothing to do with Tobias's news, which had been that Nero's cousin, Servius, was dead and had been the one behind ransacking the Handmaiden's chambers at Court. As well, the chamberlain's agent, Ivy, was no longer in the prince's employ and not available to be transferred to work for the Asar Nergal. Tobias implied she'd come to the same end as Servius, but didn't outright lie, while making it clear that mentioning Ivy to Regis would upset and enrage the prince.

Nero didn't doubt Ivy would be a sore topic but knew from Diablo that while the green drake was no longer a member of the royal coterie, she wasn't dead. Neither was Grey, and it seemed the Court's chamberlain was willing to disobey his prince to let the inamorated drakes be free — or as free as they could get with an arrest warrant hanging over Grey's head.

Light flickered across his sight and pain snapped in his skull, a warning from the magic that made him dugga of the Asar Nergal that there were active human mages in the world. Mages he hadn't added to his *puzur* and by doing so somehow changed how the dugga's magic perceived them.

According to Diablo, who'd called a few minutes earlier, Grey had barely survived the fight with Servius and had only managed to defeat the ancient black drake a matter of seconds before Diablo would have jumped in and helped.

Another flicker and snap, but Nero's vision didn't change. He remained in his office and the dugga's magic didn't reveal anything about this new threat.

He poured himself another two ounces of scotch and downed it in one gulp. A part of him was grateful Diablo had managed to stay hidden, but a bigger part raged that they'd been forced to let Grey face Servius alone. Whether it had been anyone's intention or not, Grey had become a member of his *puzur* just like Anaea and Ryan and even Capri. And now, he supposed, Ivy.

Crack. More lightning and pain, and still no change of location.

"For the love of—" He jerked to his feet, frustration and rage demanding he take action, even if the only thing he could do was stand. "Show it to me or shut the fuck up."

The world vanished with a lightning strike that blinded and burned him, searing every cell in his body. Everything was white... and cold... and at the edge of his vision came a faint, steady beep.

He fought to breathe past the agony. The seam between a white wall and a white ceiling materialized, and the acrid bite of an antiseptic filled his nostrils.

The beeping grew louder and faster. He tried to turn his head, get a better look at the room, but it was as if he were trapped inside the mage, not an outside observer like he usually was.

"It's not real," a raspy, broken alto whispered. "This is not happening. It's not real."

Something creaked and a soft slow thud — footsteps? — drew closer.

A woman leaned into view, wearing dark-rimmed glasses and a white coat. "Your pulse has spiked. What do you hear?"

"I don't hear anything," the alto said.

"I can't help you if you're not honest."

"I don't hear anything." *Nothing. Nothing. Please.*

Another blast of pain swept through Nero and he ground his teeth against it, embracing the sudden rage boiling through the agony and staying with this human mage. He'd missed someone and she'd fallen into the human's medical system. He had to find her. If he got to her soon enough, she might not go insane and he wouldn't have to issue the order to kill her.

He'd need more information before sending Diablo, but given how unpredictable his dugga's magic had become, it was best to get the conversation started.

Diablo. He focused on his mental connection with the black drake.

The beeping grew faster.

"Tell me what you hear," the doctor said.

"Nothing." *Please, nothing.*

Diablo, Nero called again, concentrating on the connection in case Diablo's lack of response was a fault in Nero's magic and not the black drake ignoring him.

The alto groaned. "I hear—"

"Tell me." The doctor's eyes narrowed, and panic shot through Nero.

Diablo!

"Oh, God. I hear—" The alto gasped as if she couldn't catch her breath. *I don't hear anything. It's not real. It's. Not. Real.*

What? Diablo barked.

Heads up. I've got another one, and we might have to move quickly on this. The pain flared, roaring through Nero's head. He had to hold on and figure out where this mage was.

Where is he? Diablo asked.

She. And I'm working on it. He needed a location and then more information before he sent Diablo into any human facility.

The doctor's hand flew into sight and grabbed the alto's face, forcing the woman to look at her. A strange aura flared about the doctor's face and Nero's pulse skipped a beat. He had no idea what he was looking at or if what he saw was his ability to see an aura or the alto's.

She's in a hospital, Nero said. The location was there, at the tip of his tongue, but he couldn't draw it forward like he used to be able to do with his dugga power.

That narrows it down. Got a continent?

"What do you hear?" the doctor hissed. "Who is he talking to?"

"No one."

He needed more information, but the beeping kept getting louder and faster and the pain now consumed his body. The alto's panic filled him... or was this his panic? He didn't know any more. The only thing that mattered was finding her.

Come on, Diablo growled. *I could use a fight.*

"Who?" The doctor jerked the alto's head forward.

"The devil." The beeping became wild. "The devil." *And God help me, he's sending the devil after me.*

Everything within Nero froze. *You can hear me?*

No. I can't hear anything. Nothing. This isn't real.

You can hear me?

No, I can't. "Get out of my head!"

The connection exploded into blinding, searing agony that consumed him, body, mind, and soul, and dropped him to his knees back in his office.

He had no idea what had just happened, but he had a horrible feeling he'd just discovered the leak in the Asar Nergal, and the leak was him.

———

PAIN SNAPPED THROUGH DIABLO'S HEAD. AGONY HAD BURST THROUGH the telepathic connection with Nero and they'd been cut off. The beast within him roared, screaming for the fight Nero had just promised, and Diablo summoned a gate before the thought was fully formed in his mind.

The black vortex swept around him and tossed him into Nero's office. The doyen was on his knees, clutching the edge of his desk as if hoping it would help him stand, but the pain in his expression and the fear radiating from him in giant consuming waves said he wasn't sure even the desk could help. That only made *the beast's* rage stronger — and it had nothing to do with Nero looking weak.

His doyen was in agony, and even if Nero wanted to denounce the dugga's power, the Handmaiden needed to be around to take it from him. But Nero would never give up the dugga's position, no matter how painful the magic. As dugga, he could control which human mages were killed in the name of protecting dragonkind. The kids he'd saved, those innocents, were as much a part of his life as his dragon coterie, and he would never endanger them or risk someone else discovering them.

Which only made the beast howl even more for a fight. To hurt something like Nero was hurting. Break something like Nero was breaking. *Feel* something other than Nero's pain and fear and determination.

Nero groaned and his grip on the desk slipped, dropping him back to the floor.

Diablo rushed to his side and helped him sit in his desk chair. "What the hell happened?"

"I don't know."

"Where is the mage? Is she a danger?" God, just one little brawl. The fight with Jet had been satisfying — grenade and all — but having to watch the fight with Servius, praying he wouldn't have to endanger his *puzur* by stepping in and helping at the last minute while clawing back the beast howling to participate, had worn his nerves thin.

"I don't know."

"You don't know or you won't tell me?" *Don't bench me. Not now.* He didn't care if he had to storm into a high-security prison. He needed to hit something.

"I don't know." Pain snapped through Nero, tightening his expression and slicing across Diablo's empathic link. "I said it was a heads-up. When I have actionable intelligence, you can pick her up or kill her."

"You think she's one of Zenobia's?" A crazy mage could make the situation dangerous... and more satisfying.

"I don't know what I think," Nero barked and another blast of pain slammed into Diablo.

His beast writhed against what little mental control he had over it. Fight. Hurt. Feel. "Whatever."

He couldn't stay there. If the beast broke free, he could hurt one of the kids. It was bad enough that after Andy's death they'd started keeping their distance from him as if they knew he was barely holding himself together. He'd tried to concentrate on one of the relaxing mental exercises Andy had taught him, but that only made him think of Andy and infuriated the beast.

Nero's pain surged, and it took Diablo everything he had not to reveal that he could feel it, too. *Get the hell out of there.* It was his only option. With a growl, he summoned a gate on the floor in front of him.

Nero's eyes narrowed, tightening, and Diablo could sense he was willing himself to concentrate past the pain. A calm shuddered around him, and his emotions hardened to a focused determination. There was business to take care of and his pain and everything else needed to be set aside. That was why Nero was doyen and dugga. Even with almost four hundred years of life, Diablo had never been able to control himself like that.

"Diablo—"

The beast would never allow that kind of restraint. "What?"

"If Grey doesn't say it, thank you."

Diablo flashed his teeth. "Oh, Grey will say it." But the truth was, Grey didn't have to. The silver drake had protected the *puzur*, not to mention he had it bad enough. He was inamorated.

"I'll call with more information."

"Call, huh?" That was new, but given Nero's headache, it wasn't surprising if the dugga was giving up on telepathic communication for a while.

"Yeah. I'll call." Nero bared his teeth and growled.

"Whatever." Diablo stepped through the gate and into a shadowy, damp passage. At the far end, blinding light blazed and a crowd roared. A few feet ahead of him stood two dragons, the first an orange drake Diablo didn't recognize, in a stout human male. From the drake's aura, he wasn't very old and likely didn't have any earth magic. He rolled his shoulders and cracked his neck, while a small, female yellow drake — the second dragon there — in a beige pantsuit with an aura indicating she was about the same age as Diablo turned to face him.

The yellow drake flashed her teeth, and Diablo didn't doubt it was half in aggression and half in sexual invitation. "I didn't think you were coming."

"I'm taking the last fight."

"It's my fight," the orange drake said.

Between one heartbeat and the next Diablo gated to his side and rammed his fist into the drake's throat. His head hit the wall behind him and he sagged to the floor. "You were saying."

The orange drake gasped, his mouth opening and closing but unable to say anything.

Diablo turned his glare on the yellow drake, who gestured toward the mouth of the passage and the underground fighting ring. "The fight is all yours."

His beast growled. He'd let whoever his opponent was get in a few good shots. Hopefully, the drake could hit. Then the fight would be all his.

42

She woke with a start, staring at a white ceiling, her pulse racing, and something soul-deep within her aching. There was something she needed to do. Something she needed to remember. Someone—?

An urgency filled her, but she couldn't figure out why. She'd been doing something? No, she'd been with someone?

Her gut clenched, filled with icy panic, and she sat up. She lay in a bed in a room she didn't recognize, with a man she didn't recognize sitting on the floor and sagging over the edge of the bed beside her. A strange blue fire blazed around him and licked over the blanket toward her.

She jerked back and he wrenched up with a gasp as if he, too, had just been asleep. He was enormous, with broad muscular shoulders straining the fabric of his T-shirt that was crusted with—

She had no idea what and didn't want to know. A towel had been wrapped tight around his chest, but a bright red stain — *oh, my God, that was blood!* — had seeped through, revealing what had to be a massive, untreated injury. His pale gray eyes locked on her were filled with pain and hope and something she couldn't quite place that made her insides squirm.

She scrambled to the far side of the bed before realizing she wore a crusted and torn dress. Blood coated her hands and splattered up her forearms. What the hell had happened to her? Had she injured him? Had she—?

Her mind stuttered. *She*. There wasn't anything else but *she*. No name, no sense of who she was, only what. A green drake. But she wasn't in a green drake's body.

Whoever *he* was, he was going to regret holding her and hurting her. But those thoughts didn't feel right. Somehow, deep in her soul, she knew — just like she knew she was a she and a green dragon — he wouldn't hurt her, he'd protect her, and she needed to protect him.

"You're all right. You're safe," he said, his voice a deep, exhausted rumble.

"Where am I?"

"The hotel room in Vancouver." His gaze searched hers, but she had no idea what he was looking for.

"*The* hotel room," she said. "This is a specific room?"

"Yes." He shifted and gasped, his expression tightening with pain and his arm pulling tight against the bloodstained towel.

She shifted toward him before realizing what she was doing and managed to stop before getting within reach. She didn't know who he was, why he was on fire but not on fire, or even who she was. And yet everything within her said he belonged to her and she to him. Except she couldn't figure out anything else beyond that. "Do I know you?"

"I think the first question I should answer is who *you* are." His hand shifted on top of the comforter, inching closer to hers but not making contact. Blue flames licked over his fingers and her throat tightened, the need to say something clogging it, but the words wouldn't form in her head.

"No, you need to tell me why you're on fire and not screaming in pain?"

He frowned, then realization swept across his expression. "That's how you see it."

"You're not answering my question."

"I'm not really on fire." He drew in a ragged, wet breath and the pain returned to his expression.

The ice in her gut squeezed tight and swept up her chest around her heart. "Answers later. You need help, you need—"

"I'll be all right."

"You're bleeding."

"It'll stop. Eventually."

Something flickered at the back of her mind. They'd had this conversation before. But not here. Someplace else.

"Why can't I remember?"

"You have a condition. Every time you fall asleep, you forget who you are."

She felt like they'd talked about this, too. "But I know I know you. I just don't know how."

A hint of a smile pulled at his lips. "You do know me. Your name is Ivy. You're a green drake and you have the magic ability to read memories from objects."

"Magic abilities?"

"Yes."

She snorted as she ran his words over again in her head. "You didn't answer my question. How do I know you?"

He raised his hand in an offer for her to take it. "Say *si* and find out for yourself."

"*Si?*" Blinding white light flashed across her sight and energy snapped through her body. The urge to wrap her essence in the blue fire flickering over him surged through her, and she grabbed his hand.

For a second there were two of him, the man sitting at her bedside battered and bloody, and the man standing before her in the Handmaiden's chamber in Court, his gaze locked on her as if she were a lifeline he hadn't realized he'd needed.

He. Grey. A dragon who couldn't forget, the opposite to her, because she couldn't remember.

The ache in her soul eased, as if just connecting with him filled her, completed her. His memory jumped to them in the hotel bathroom, sitting on the edge of the tub and him offering to share a memory with her to ease the ache in her soul. He knew her. He loved her. He'd fight for her — and with her — and he'd die for her.

Memories flashed through her. His memories. Their first meeting, both fights in the Handmaiden's residence, their battle in Seville, and how he'd clutched her unconscious body in the dragon Court's arena and defied Tobias's order to hand her over.

But there was also the sense that this wasn't everything. Along with his affection was a sadness that he'd lost her locket and she was missing essential memories about who she was. And beneath that a tight, painful thread of fear that their soul-bond wouldn't survive her memory loss, as well as the determination that he would respect her choice and not push if she didn't reciprocate his love.

"How could you think that?" A purr bubbled in her throat. She drew closer to him, cupped his cheek, and met his gaze. "Silly dragon, the inamorated bond is stronger than that. My soul picked you. It knows you like I know I'm a green drake."

He brushed his lips against hers and the purr rumbled in full, vibrating through her chest and throat, resonating through every fiber of her being.

A hint of sadness crept past her joy. "You're still going to have to tell me who I am every morning, though."

"Hey, that's not a problem. I get something out of you reading my memories." His breath feathered warm across her cheek and a flicker of memory, of him confessing to her that her magic calmed consuming memories he couldn't control, swept through her.

"Well, so long as you get a little something out of this, too."

He drew back and flashed her teeth at her, sending a shiver of desire sliding through her. A flash of them naked in the shower filled her mind's eye. "It'll be hard, but I'm sure I'll find a way to manage."

"Ha, I have no doubt it's hard." She hooked a finger into the collar of his T-shirt and tugged him forward, capturing his lips with hers and adding a new memory to his collection.

GREY GATED INTO THE SUITE HE AND IVY HAD BEEN GIVEN IN NERO'S mansion earlier that morning. Mid-afternoon sunlight shone through the windows, warming the comfortable and casually appointed living room, and the warmth spread around his heart. *Theirs.* This space was theirs. His and Ivy's. And the people in this house felt more like family than any coterie had in centuries. Raven hadn't even blinked an eye when Grey and Ivy returned to the mansion — Grey crusted with blood, but thankfully no longer bleeding, and Ivy in Raven's ruined dress. The black drake had been expecting them and — with Nero's agreement — got them set up in the suite and even added them to the household duty assignments with the kids and the other dragons.

Raven then took Ivy clothes shopping — since Ivy couldn't return to Court for any of her things, not even her hoard — leaving Grey to call Capri and beg her to beg Swipe to use his magic to erase all the blood from the hotel room in Vancouver. She'd agreed on the condition that he buy her an orchid to help replace the hoard she'd lost when her house had burned down a few days ago. He'd buy her a hundred orchids, as well as add to Raven's and Nero's and Diablo's hoards if he thought it could repay the debt he owed them. There wasn't any way he could thank them enough. He certainly wouldn't have survived the last forty-eight hours without them.

Once the call with Capri was done, Grey had taken a quick trip back to Vancouver, then returned to the mansion and changed into clean clothes. He'd then gated to Anaea and Hunter's house, where Anaea had two soulless bodies on her deck, waiting to receive Jet and Servius's souls. With Anaea standing by, in the event he needed a sorcerer's help, Grey drew the coin from his pocket, placed it in the medallion, and activated the magic to rebirth Jet and Servius's souls. Anaea gated the new hatchlings to a secure location to ensure that their souls' memories had actually been wiped clean in the rebirth process and neither remembered their previous lives. If that was the case, Nero would accept them in his Major Black Coterie and they'd be given residences in Rome.

Now Grey was back, ready to spend time with Ivy. His chest still hurt. Hell, most of him still hurt, and hints of memories flickered at the edge of his vision. But none of that mattered. Only Ivy and their future together.

He checked the bedroom and bathroom. Empty. She either hadn't returned from shopping with Raven or was somewhere else in the mansion. He opened the door to the hall as the door to the suite across from him also opened.

Ryan stepped out of his suite and flashed a hint of teeth. "Welcome to the family. Have you been assigned chores yet?"

"First thing Raven did. How many loads of laundry do you think there'll be?"

"Oh, I wouldn't want to ruin the surprise."

"Gee. Thanks." Grey pursed his lips. It felt wonderful and weird to have a coterie again… for the first time? He wasn't sure if he'd ever really belonged to the silver coterie. Still, this was going to take time to get used to. "Do you know if Raven and Ivy are back from shopping?"

A knowing warmth filled Ryan's gaze. "I'm told the need to be constantly near her will ease up eventually, but I'm still waiting on that."

"You've only been inamorated for less than a week."

"Yeah, and in dragon speak, *eventually* could mean a century or two." Ryan jerked his chin down the hall. "Come on. I could see your lady from my bedroom window. She's in one of the lawn chairs watching the guys replace the windows in the living room."

Grey headed to the end of the hall and down three flights of stairs with Ryan before the human turned to go deeper into the mansion, and Grey went out a side door and marched through the snow around the side of the house to find Ivy. It didn't matter he only wore slacks and a dress shirt, or that he was getting his shoes wet or that snow was slipping, freezing and damp, around his ankles into his shoes. There was only Ivy.

He rounded the corner and Ivy's gaze jumped from the men working on the windows to Grey, as if she'd sensed his arrival. Her face lit up with joy and desire, and she held out a hand, inviting him to join her.

He met her smile and crouched beside her. "Like what you see?"

She jerked her chin at the house. "Some of those guys are cute."

"Are you trying to make me jealous?" The warmth in his chest swelled. She held a new-found confidence since waking in the hotel room, and while a part of him hoped it was because of how he remembered her, he knew it was all her. This was the powerful green dragon spirit he'd first seen, coiled tight within her delicate and alluring human form. This was the woman he'd do anything for.

She turned her attention back to him, her dark eyes capturing his soul, and her magic turning everything crisp and clear and perfect. "You know I only have eyes for you." Her smile turned wicked and desire surged through him. "Of course, that could be because you shared that memory of the shower with me."

A purr bubbled in his throat. "I have every intention of breaking in the shower in our suite before the day is done."

"I have every intention of taking you up on that." She walked her fingers along the arm of the lawn chair closer to his hand, clearly an invitation for him to hold it. But there was something he needed to give her first.

He slid his hand into his pocket, his fingers brushing the small oval object, and drew out her locket.

She gasped and her joy radiated through her aura in a brilliant flash as she took it. "You found it. You went into a sewer and got it back for me."

"You know I'd do anything for you."

Her nose crinkled and mischief sparkled in her eyes. "Tell me you've cleaned up since crawling around in a sewer."

"Read my memories and find out." He flashed a hint of teeth in invitation.

She flashed hers back, the look pure desire. "Better yet, let's go make new memories."

Memories he could share with her tomorrow morning.

A purr slid through him, and he drew her to her feet and pulled her close. Memories that would tell her the moment she woke and said her power word that she was safe and loved.

That he was safe and loved, too.

Memories he was glad he'd never be able to forget.

Don't miss the next book in the series!

PURSUING FLIGHT
A Dragon Spirit Novel: Book Four

Their connection is as wild as their magic... and just as dangerous.

Nero survived the loss of his inamorata by the skin of his dragon-spirit's teeth. Since then he's focused every ounce of his power — magical and political — on hoarding the most unlikely of treasures: innocent human mages. Rescuing them instead of following orders to murder them.

Now his secret, forbidden coterie is under threat from Rebecca Scott. Victim. Soldier. Mage unaware. A woman trapped in a tortuous lab experiment, whose pain and terror echo down the unbreakable cords binding them together.

Unsure if her hell is real or a PTSD-induced nightmare, Becca jumps at one slim chance to escape the sadistic white-coats probing her broken psyche, following a strange, alluring voice throbbing from somewhere deep in her bones.

When Becca's desperation yanks Nero to her side, he makes a staggering discovery. This courageous, half-crazed woman is, impossibly, his second inamorata. But even if she gets her wish to carve their souls apart, it's too late for him. If her heart stops, so will his... and everyone under his protection, human and dragon, will be lost.

ABOUT C.I. BLACK

C.I. Black has always lived in a world of imagination. When she's not daydreaming, she puts her flights of fancy down on paper writing urban fantasy, paranormal romance, and romantic suspense books.

She's the author of the Dragon Spirit series and the Medusa Files series. You can find a complete list of C.I.'s books at www.ciblack.com.

www.ingramcontent.com/pod-product-compliance
Lightning Source LLC
Chambersburg PA
CBHW031157020726
47499CB00002B/401